First published in Great Britain 2016
by
Sphere
an imprint of Little, Brown Book Group

First Isis Edition
published 2016
by arrangement with
Little, Brown Book Group
An Hachette UK Company

A catalogue record for this book is available
from the British Library.

ISBN 978–1–78541–280–6 (hb)
ISBN 978–1–78541–286–8 (pb)

Published by
F. A. Thorpe (Publishing)
Anstey, Leicestershire

Set by Words & Graphics Ltd.
Anstey, Leicestershire
Printed and bound in Great Britain by
T. J. International Ltd., Padstow, Cornwall

This book is printed on acid-free paper

THE PRIMROSE PATH

REBECCA GRIFFITHS

LARGE
PRINT

THE PRIMROSE PATH

As a teenager, Sarah D'Villez famously escaped a man who abducted and held her hostage for eleven days. The case became notorious, with Sarah's face splashed across the front of every newspaper in the country. Now, seventeen years later, that man is about to be released from prison. Fearful of the media storm that is sure to follow, Sarah decides to flee to rural Wales under a new identity, telling nobody where she's gone. Settling into the small community, she soon realises that someone is watching her. Someone who seems to know everything about her . . .

For my husband, Steven.
Without you, there would be nothing.

Primrose Path: the pursuit of pleasure, especially when bringing disastrous consequences.

The Oxford English Dictionary

Fifty Years Before

An August moon pokes a white tongue of light through a gap in her bedroom curtains. Fear, hard as a pebble, fills her dry little mouth as she hears the clunk of a gate swinging wide on to Cwm Glas' yard. Her father and brothers, back from The Bear in Bryngwyn after last orders. Beth pulls the covers tight around her, fastens the top buttons of her nightdress and waits. Waits for their revelry to mutate into its usual blackness.

At any moment, heavy boots on the stairs, and Emyr will come. He is the first in line these days, not her father any more; he stopped when she started to bleed. She thinks of the barn and wishes she was there. Safe in there. Climbing the woodworm-riddled ladder with Dai who pedals over the fields to see her. The two of them squeezing down between mildewed bales of hay and sacks of feed to lie with her bruises, listening to the breath of Tiny, her little dog, as he watches for trouble through the timber slats in the floor.

Her body stiffens and slackens with each crash and thud from below. Fingers, raw from household chores, respond to the rise of aggressive shouting by pressing their nails into the flesh of her palms, leaving behind the little half-moons that she won't turn the light on to see. Sometimes she stares at her hands and is shocked just how like her dead mother's they are. Chapped and red and larger than they should be for her size, because she has always been told she is small, it is another thing they beat her for. As if being small for her age is somehow her fault. Like the turn in her eye is her fault.

The door to her bedroom is thrown wide. A drunken Emyr, silent and swaying, engulfs the threshold. His bulk silhouetted by the bald bulb on the landing. Terrifying, the vacant look she knows will be on his pig-pink face, and the orange down carpeting his over-developed forearms. Conscious of his weight balancing at the bottom of her bed, Beth pulls her bare feet under her and hears the sucking of heels as boots are pulled off, the rustling of clothes and unzipping of his fly as he pushes free of trousers that stink from years of dealing in sheep shit and afterbirth. She won't fight, any more than she will cry, as he rips away the flimsy bedcovers and yanks up her nightdress to expose her underdeveloped fourteen-year-old body. The days of crying and fighting are gone. Learning to detach herself from the shame of it long ago, she takes her mind elsewhere.

Emyr doesn't take long this time, and she prays, alone again in the dark, for Rhys, Wynn and Idris to be as quick. And turning her head to the side to wait for them, pushing her hot little face into the musty-smelling pillow for the comfort that isn't there, she blinks on to the dark, feeling how strangely dry her eyes are.

2

CHAPTER
ONE

Present Day

She will try it out. This place that has taken her the best part of a day to travel to. See how things lie in the spring. It is the only way to tackle her past, the root of her trouble. At least this is the idea. And on this, her first night, she has her back curved low over the side of the bath trying not to splash the indelible Nice'n Easy dark-brown hair colourant on the pristine white-tiled surround. Feeling a great deal safer now she is going by a different name, she hopes dyeing her hair will keep her safer still. The collar of the top she should have taken off before she started feels wet and cold against her skin, but still she keeps at it: rinsing and rinsing; the shower hose held high above her head as soft Welsh water, which doesn't seem to want to clear, cascades through what was, until twenty-five minutes ago, beautiful golden hair. She watches it swirl away down the plug hole, hoping it will take her past life with it.

To stop her mind loitering on things she would rather forget, she chants her new name over and over, wanting to familiarise herself with its sound: "Rachel Wright . . . Rachel Wright." Envisaging the hoops and swirls of the signature she has been practising. Her voice quivers with the pressure she puts it under and it would be embarrassing if anyone could hear, but who's listening? There is no one for miles, so what does it matter? All that matters is not thinking. Not about that. Her natural colouring has worked as a device to define her, scheming away behind the scenes, trouble's harbinger. Even her mother, someone supposed to be on her side, said that if you had the good fortune to be born blonde and honeyed-skinned with deep-blue eyes as she had been, then you deserved all you got. If you stood out from the crowd and made people look at you without trying, then it served you right and you couldn't complain when it made bad things happen.

She stops chanting the name. It isn't working. The vivid pictures she keeps of her past are too strong and, attached to a lengthy ribbon, they threaten to tug her back to the place from which she is trying to disentangle herself. Downstairs, something rattles. She turns the taps off to listen. A cow maybe, rubbing against the gate, except the nearest cows are at least two fields away at Cwm Glas farm. The wind then, she decides. The wind bumping up against the thick velvety blackness outside. A blackness she never knew in London. When it dropped down over her recently converted barn it was the biggest shock of all. For there are no street lights here. There is nothing here.

She shuts her eyes and reaches blindly for the little bottle of conditioner. Clumsy in its complimentary plastic sheath, her hand catches a corner of the box and the contents slip down inside the bath. Forced to look, she reads the word Clairol in letters spaced out along the top of the packet.

Claire.

The benign face of her ex-husband's new wife, the stepmother of her now thirteen-year-old daughter, floats into view.

Splashing it away, she untwists the lid of the bottle that tempted her into being "a shade braver" as she scanned the shelves at the Boots outlet in Paddington station. She squeezes some conditioner on to her palms, massages it through and waits, eager for the glassy shine the six-quid's worth promised.

Finished at last, she strips off the polythene gloves and kneads the flesh of her lower back. This wasn't the best thing to do. Not after all the lugging and lifting she had done once RiteMove had gone. She picks at the image of the brace of big-bellied fifty-somethings, sees again their synchronised sweating and matching baby-blue Aertex shirts as they shifted from foot to foot in her kitchen. Complaining about leaving the removal van unattended in a virtually traffic-free lane, they had left her with most of the heavy stuff to shift on her own. "It's all right," she'd said, refusing to engage with their disgruntled expressions. She flapped them away. "Off you go. I can manage."

Nothing new there. Managing is something she has always done, there being few people in her thirty-six years, aside from her father, that she could rely on. But it is such a mediocre word, *managing* — as if in the achievement of it you are only half doing a job. She had mulled this over while assembling the bed. A bed she had been assured by the person taking her booking and credit card payment over the phone was going to be put together for her on delivery. She should try clawing some of her precious inheritance back; it isn't as if she has it to waste. But she won't, this move to Wales is supposed to be a fresh start, one free from negativity and, smiling, she consoles herself with how she at least made them carry the double mattress up the stairs.

CHAPTER
TWO

Idris Tudor could have sworn the girl had long blonde hair when he first saw her. But watching her now, on her walk up the steep sheep track on the opposite hill, he sees it is dark and cut shorter.

He shifts his bulk from his position behind an upstairs window and lets his breath steam the already smeary glass. Careful, he doesn't want his binoculars touching the curtains, not because they are fly-encrusted things no one has bothered to change since his da was alive, but because he fears any movement, even from this distance, could alert the girl to him. But he needn't worry, for Idris to be seen is near-on impossible. The girl is too far away for a start, and no one but Evans the Post thinks to come along this stretch of tapering lane. It doesn't lead anywhere.

He picks at a boil on the side of his neck but can't get a purchase. Inspecting his chewed-down fingernails he decides they aren't equipped for the job. Shame, he thinks, his gaze refocusing on her nice round arse as she makes her climb in tight-fitting jeans. He preferred her blonde. Blondes are more his thing. A good-looking bit of stuff though, nevertheless. Dead classy for around here, and he wonders, not for the first time, where she's come from and why she's living on her own. Whatever her reasons, she's certainly an improvement on the types he meets on overnight trips to Somerset with his haulage business.

Idris has never had any luck with women. He didn't once have a girlfriend at school, not that he attended school for long; hating the discipline of the classroom, the hierarchy that was the playground, he steered well clear of girls. He had hoped things would improve when he got older, that was why he and his brother Wynn signed up with that dating agency in Llandafen. But to his crashing disappointment, it was still only the ugly old trouts he got to mingle with there. It's about time he had something better.

Repositioning his binoculars on the girl who is pacing it out over the hill, the strawberry mark on the side of his face growing hot with excitement, he shivers with delight. Safe enough within his hidey-hole to drink her in at leisure. *Brrrr.* He shakes himself, vigorous as a big wet dog, setting his jowls wagging. Even in her wellingtons and anorak this one looks the business. And he wonders, not for the first time over the past couple of days, what he can do to get close to her.

CHAPTER
THREE

The doorbell goes at the exact same time Jennifer D'Villez lifts the telephone to her ear.

"Oh, *Lynette* — hello." Slightly breathy, she presses the palm of her other hand to her forehead in a gesture suggestive of a headache. "Sorry, d'you mind waiting? I've got someone at the door." She sets the receiver down with a neat little click on the lacquered mahogany telephone-table seat once belonging to her mother.

It is Mr Antonelli. The gardener. His pink-ringed eyes giving Jennifer the once over before looking past her and into number seventy-seven's exquisitely furnished hall.

"I told Mister D'Villez I come by this week — tidy before frost." His Neapolitan accent is strong, despite living twenty years in the London Borough of Haringey with views of Canary Wharf.

"Go ahead," she offers, not filling him in on what has happened to Mr D'Villez in the meantime. "You know where everything is, I'm sure." And dropping a bunch of keys into his fat little hand, she hopes one of them will unlock her late husband's shed. "I'll bring you out a cup of tea."

"Very nice, missus."

He shuffles off round the side of the house and she waits for the customary squeak of the bolt on the gate before going back inside to her telephone.

"Lynette — you still there? Sorry about that, something Donald fixed up." Jennifer sits. Comfy on the velvet upholstery, she crosses one leg over the other to silently appraise the flattering cut of her new Armani jeans.

"I'm ringing to see how you are?" Lynette Brown — a woman who tries her best to look like that Mariella Frostrup from the BBC, has taken to grinning through her words in the same way too.

Jennifer relaxes a little inside her merino roll-neck. She likes Lynette Brown and with her handicap of under-five, she is the perfect golfing buddy. "Oh, you are sweet to think of me. I'm doing all right, you know . . . keeping busy." Jennifer doesn't elaborate on how she's made a start on clearing out her late husband's things, waking as she did with ideas of how to claim back what has always been known as Donald's Room: a masculine space that, although part of her house, she has never felt comfortable in. "As I said at Don's funeral, it was a blessing really — him suffering for all those years, poor thing."

"You heard from Sarah yet?" Lynette asks.

"Not a dicky bird," she tells the vaguely playful voice. "To be honest, I didn't think she'd stay, not once probate came through."

"How d'you feel about that? Donald leaving everything to Sarah, I mean."

"Well, it was his money," Jennifer replies stiffly, slightly taken aback by her friend's bluntness; she has never liked discussing money. "We agreed years ago." It sums up their closeness, the father and daughter bond I had no chance of penetrating, she thinks, but doesn't say. "It's great," she continues, infusing her voice with a brightness she doesn't feel. "It's given her choices; she's an independent woman now."

"So you've no idea where she's gone?"

"Not the foggiest," Jennifer sighs. "It's an absolute mystery to me."

"Has she gone to friends, d'you think? Friends you and Donald didn't know about?"

"What friends? Cooped up with us like she's been for the last ten years. Since her split with Spencer and coming back here, it's been a job to get her to leave the house." Jennifer coughs up a tight little laugh. "No, sad as it is to say, any friends she had dropped by the wayside long ago."

"Why don't you try finding her?" Lynette suggests.

"Where would I start?"

"Well, you remember Audrey — Audrey Reardon?"

"Audrey?" Jennifer's mind cartwheels.

"Yes, you know her — red hair, big jewellery, used to play bridge with us?"

"Vaguely, think I might have met her once."

"Yes, well, she stopped coming, didn't she, when her husband left, and that's what I'm getting at. Big CEO he was, can't remember who for, but anyway, he ran off with his PA. Half his age — shocking business." Jennifer hears the woman exhale. "The shit planned it all. One day he was there, the next he'd vanished. Audrey said she came home from shopping and all his stuff had gone. Left her right up the swanny with bills, mortgage, kids' school fees — but this bloke she hired, this private investigator, don't ask me how, but he tracked them down. I could get his number for you?"

"Ooo, I don't know," Jennifer, unsure. "Sounds a bit over dramatic; like something off the telly."

"Have a think about it, it's worth a try."

"Maybe," Jennifer remains unconvinced. "I'll let you know; hopefully I won't have to go that far. There's someone closer to home I want to try first."

"Oh — who's that then?" Lynette, greedy to know.

"Probably a long shot, I'll tell you if it comes to anything."

"A shame she couldn't have told you what her plans were, saved you this worry," the friend coos. "You and she always seemed so close."

Did we? Jennifer thinks. Did we really? Her coffee, now cold, has formed a skin not unlike her own: creased, thin, puckering at the edges, but she won't let the fears of her own mortality suck her down. Too much talk of death these past few years. Donald certainly strung his out for long enough. She is free now, free to play her eighteen rounds with the girls without needing to feel guilty about leaving him alone with Sarah. Although hadn't he always preferred to be with Sarah? Wasn't this the problem? Made to feel the cuckoo in the nest the moment she brought their longed for daughter home from the maternity hospital. His golden child. With her beautiful yellow hair, her

12

willowy figure and arresting blue eyes. Jennifer would often look at her and wonder where it was she came from. She has nothing of her — a woman who has to try hard to look this good. If she hadn't given birth to her those thirty-six years ago, she would never believe she was hers.

Lynette is still talking when Jennifer re-joins her and, pulling herself back from wherever she's been, she looks down at her well-manicured hands.

". . . so I said, I'd do the flowers this week, but if she's going to keep letting us down . . ."

A tapping on the window of the patio doors. Jennifer leans forward in her telephone seat to check it isn't that blackbird throwing itself at the glass again. It isn't. It is Mr Antonelli. Grinning at what he can see past his own reflection and making a T sign with his stubby mud-caked fingers.

Cheeky sod, she thinks, thanking Lynette for calling and ending their conversation with, "I'll see you next week at the club."

"*Promise?*" The word, delivered like a slow smile, is squeezed along the cable, down the handset.

"I promise."

"Try not to worry; I'm sure Sarah'll be in touch when she's settled, and if not, let me know, I'll get the number of that chap for you."

CHAPTER
FOUR

It's gone nine before Rachel wakes and it takes her a moment to realise where she is. Disorientated and slick with sweat, she presses her fingers to her forehead and chest, dipping them into the pool of moisture that has collected between the cleft of her breasts. Her nightshirt is clammy and its frilly detail around the collar, along with the sheet she lies on, is equally sodden. Heaving herself out of bed, her mind thick with images from yet another nightmare-troubled sleep, she tugs on a dressing gown and a pair of her father's old fishing socks and heads downstairs, stifling a yawn with a clenched fist. Her dreams seem worse since leaving London, the visions of blood and trauma more vivid, more real; it is making her fearful of sleep.

Absent-mindedly massaging the starfish-shaped scar on the inside of her wrist, another leftover from her traumatic past, her stomach growls from beneath her layers. Hungry, although, thinking about the meagre contents in her fridge, nothing stirs her into actually fixing something to eat. She needs to find a decent supermarket, doubting the shop at the local Esso garage will stock much. But the idea of travelling to Llandafen still feels too daunting, even though Tracy

Morgan, her neighbour from nearby Cwm Glas farm, offered to take her and show her around.

What is she afraid of — that people will recognise her? They haven't done so far, and with her new dark hair, she looks completely different. But habit breeds habit, and since that day, dumped at the bottom of her parents' road after eleven days of capture and sexual degradation, Rachel struggles to go anywhere or do anything considered normal. Everyone, because of what she experienced, is a potential danger and she will never stop looking over her shoulder.

Scarcely days after her father's funeral, WPC Ruth Blackwood, her kind face splintered into all colours of the rainbow by the stained glass panel in her mother's front door, had been a nasty blast from the past. "Promise me you're not going to panic," the woman, now promoted to Detective Sergeant and dressed in plain clothes, told her calmly. "I'm just here to warn you that now Blundell's high-risk status has been downgraded, he's applying for parole and will probably be out by Christmas. Not that you need concern yourself with him, there'll be so many conditions to his release he might as well still be inside — no, the worry is what the press'll do when the story breaks, and remembering how it was for you the first time around . . ." DS Blackwood had pulled a face. "It might be better to go somewhere and lie low for a while."

It was DS Blackwood who gave Rachel the idea to come to Wales. The plan to change her name and appearance and start again in a place no one knew her took shape one damp afternoon in late spring over a plate of home-baked scones and pot of tea made by the hovering Mrs Pepper, her mother's cleaning lady — round as a Marmite jar with flat brown brogues and home-permed hair smelling of beeswax — who peered out nervously from behind the rust-coloured rims of her spectacles.

"Where were you happiest?" Ruth Blackwood asked in a sombre voice as Mrs Pepper tidied the vacuum cleaner away under the stairs. Her sobriety spared her the need to spell out how the tabloids would rehash everything, remind readers of Rachel's whereabouts and make her an easy target if Blundell tried to find her again. Perhaps the recently promoted Ruth Blackwood — who sat clasping her hands, their short-nailed fingers in a bundle on the table top — thought that by not giving it oxygen, by not fanning the flames of fear she sensed leaping around Rachel's heart, it would fizzle out.

Rachel took her time to reply. Not because she didn't have her answer ready, but because she wanted to wallow for a moment in what the hook of the question brought to the surface of her mind.

"Fishing," she said eventually, thinking of those long summer days with the sun warm on her back, the air thick with insects. "Sitting on the banks of the Towy with my dad."

A bittersweet memory she's held on to since childhood, and one that cut through the strawberry-sweet jam and fruit-stuffed scone dissolving on her tongue. For fishing had other connotations. DS Blackwood knew it the moment Rachel said the word;

it jolted her back to her own memories of that day. The day of the funeral. When one million people lined the route to Westminster Abbey and more than eighty per cent of the Met were on duty, melting inside their dress uniforms, the sky a spooky cartoon blue in the unexpected heat of that early September Saturday. They weren't there because they predicted trouble, but to pay their own private respects to the dead Princess. And it was while the rest of the country, perhaps the world, had its attention firmly focused on the gun carriage carrying the Royal Standard-draped coffin that the nineteen-year-old version of the woman she had sitting opposite her now was snatched at knifepoint from a remote Northamptonshire riding stables.

So instead of successfully steering the conversation away from Blundell, DS Blackwood had inadvertently brought it right back. Fishing was what Sarah — as she was known then — talked to him about after being shoved, disorientated and terrified, blindfolded and gagged, into the back of his van and driven out to God knows where. It was her knowledge of angling that kept her alive. Roped down in a chair when he wasn't defiling her body in that remote hovel of a cottage. The tying of flies. The merits of fly fishing. The various methods of casting. Naming the best rivers for salmon and trout. What fly went with what. The thrill of catching her first fish. Useful, the anecdotes she could ply him with from beyond her brutalised body, before being left alone in the cold and dark, with nothing but the sound of birdsong. No traffic, no people. She told the police officers in the interviews that were to follow, a younger Ruth Blackwood among them, how this shared hobby made her abductor soften towards her. That these treasured childhood memories saved her life.

CHAPTER
FIVE

We stay like this until dawn. The dead girl and me. Sitting side by side behind the rain-peppered windscreen like old friends. Now she is quiet I don't want to break the spell. It's nice to have the company; I get so lonely on my own. Funny thing is, I don't think I really meant to do it, something went wrong. I snapped.

It was when she started screaming, really screaming. And I'm not good with that kind of noise. Reminded me too much of when I was a kid with my parents at each other's throats all the time and me, powerless to do anything. But the girl wouldn't stop, would she? And I tried asking nicely. It was why I had to drive all the way along here, away from the suck and sigh of the sea, terrified someone would hear.

All I did was put the flat of my hand over her shrieking mouth. Sick of the sound of her, I couldn't think straight. Then she bit down. Hard. I felt her teeth, sharp as knives, score deep into the spongy flesh of my palm. Then there was blood. My blood.

Now that wasn't right, was it? I couldn't have that.

CHAPTER
SIX

Dai Jones, edging open his kitchen window and letting in the blustery wet-moss smells of autumn, is rattling a box of Go-Cat in an effort to tempt Gabriel in from the garden. His mind curves around again to the woman who's just moved into the Tudors' old barn. Sensing something vulnerable about her, he was reminded of Beth in an instant. Not that Dai should be thinking about Beth, with his wife of forty or so years not three-months buried. His thoughts should only be of Elsie and because they are not, he feels guilty.

Giving up on the cat, he returns to his breakfast, but before long is distracted by something moving on his periphery. He looks up from the precise buttering of two slices of toasted granary to find Miss Roberts' face, milky and round as the moon, floating above the chrome taps on the other side of his kitchen window.

"Just passing," she sings, sharp as the wind, which after blowing like the devil all night, has hardly let up come morning. "Shall I come in?" she calls, already standing on the arabesque-churn of his living room carpet, letting in the cat and a swirl of russet-coloured leaves. "On my way to clean the village hall, I was . . .

brought you Welsh cakes." She must have been up with the lark, the doily-covered plate is still warm, making it difficult to protest at the extravagance.

"You're not doing anything to help my waistline," Dai does his best to smile. "Without my Elsie here to keep check," he taps his midriff, liking the opportunity it gives him to drop his late wife's name into the conversation. He doesn't want the woman getting ideas. Although he fears, looking at Dilys' new silk scarf and matching lipstick, it may be too late for that.

Dilys Roberts. Local gossip. As flat-chested as she is footed, and as barrel-girthed as she is barrel-curled. She means well. It is why Dai is careful to be kind. His wife was the one who wouldn't tolerate busybodies, but she isn't around to act as buffer any more. Elsie is deep under the cold, terracotta-coloured earth of Bryngwyn's Chapel cemetery, leaving him as exposed as a stretch of beach and susceptible to whatever the tide brings in. Dai holds out his hand, takes the plate of sugared offerings and makes room for them on the cluttered sideboard. He must push aside the silver-framed family snaps and glazed Royal Doulton shepherdesses, coyly smiling amid souvenirs from Tenby and Conwy. Things his wife left behind.

"Got time for a cuppa?" Dai asks to be polite as Gabriel, purring and circling, presses his princely jet-black shape against his calves.

"Oh, I shouldn't," Dilys says, wriggling out of her coat and plopping down on his sofa, suffocating a freshly plumped cushion. From her sitting position, her palms collide noisily with her generous thighs; it is a sound that seems to satisfy her. Dai thinks of Elsie as he heads back into his tiny, pristine kitchen — another leftover from their ruby-red years together — and listens to his dead wife tutting at him above the rising rush of boiling water.

"You met that new woman yet?" Dilys calls through. Dai doesn't answer, he is busy smiling at Gabriel who, head in his shallow plastic bowl, is delighting in his breakfast after a night on the tiles. He hears Dilys again; impatient, thinking he needs clarification: "The one who's moved into Tudor's old byre?"

Dai loads the tray with mugs of steaming tea. Perturbed at knowing how the two of them take it — dropping in a sugar lump for him and two for her, a splash of milk — he has tried to make it up to himself by not using Elsie's prized tea set.

"Only to wave to," he says, stepping into his living room. "She walks past the house now and again." He puts the tray down with the poise of a professional waiter, careful not to touch Dilys' nylon-clad knees. Before sitting, he reaches behind him for the plate of Welsh cakes, thinking how his evenly browned toast will be cold now.

"They say she's from London."

"Do they?" he says, not asking for clarification.

"Not married neither, by all accounts."

"No?"

"Very pretty. You'd have thought a pretty girl like that would have a man in tow, wouldn't you?"

"Suppose you would."

"Bit odd, don't you think?"

22

"If you say so."

Dilys seems to forget he is there and plumps for a second Welsh cake, slurping from her mug. Dai averts his eyes, watches a bubble form and break on the surface of his tea.

"You're hopeless, you are." Dilys pokes him with her words.

"Am I?" He doesn't look interested.

"Someone new moves in around here and you've nothing to say?" She fetches up a squeaky little-girl laugh.

Conscious of the protests from his empty stomach, Dai takes one of Dilys' cakes and puts it to his lips, wanting to test it. Sugary and comforting, it is small enough to put inside his mouth without biting it in two. Nice, he thinks, letting it dissolve on his tongue. Lots of currants. Dai likes currants. Admittedly he prefers them fresh, not dried ones like these. He has a freezer-full of red and black ones harvested from the garden last July. Ideally he would like to be in his garden now, pruning and tidying for when winter well and truly sets in. He wants to gather the last of the roses for Elsie's grave before the wind lays claim to them.

"Heard from your Anthony?" Dilys is good at keeping the conversation going. And watching the ribbons of steam clouding her blue-rimmed glasses, he can see how hungry she is for news of the boy she watched grow up and still asks to be remembered to.

"Rang last night." Dai, recalling the awkwardness of the conversation, rubs the tip of his nose between finger and thumb. "Merrill and baby are doing fine, I'm pleased to report. He said they were coming home from hospital today."

"Oh, that's wonderful news — they decided on a name for the little one yet?"

"Seren," he says, knowing how this will please.

"A good Welsh name. Good boy, Anthony."

Dai smiles, for real this time. Proud of the grandchild he probably isn't going to meet.

"You decided yet, if you're going out there?" Dilys is biting down on Welsh cake number three. A tongue, pink as his cat's, hunting the corners of her mouth for crumbs she might have missed.

"I'm thinking about it." He says looking at her sugared moustache.

"You should — it would mean the absolute world to them."

Dai isn't convinced. He remembers when he went with Elsie, months before her diagnosis. The only time in all the years Anthony's been living there. Merrill, his daughter-in-law, nice as she is, had nothing much to say to him.

"Brisbane's such a long way — I don't know." Dai sips his tea, thinks of the upheaval, the hours trapped in a metal tube going halfway around the globe. Pictures their faces at the airport. How quickly they would tire of him. Of course it would have been different with Elsie. Elsie would have known what to do with a newborn baby, he doesn't have a clue. "Besides," he sighs, "think I'm getting a bit long in the tooth to be gadding about."

24

"Rubbish, David Jones." Dilys snaps back her neck. "Do you good. The weather for one." And she looks out at the rain mottling the glass, then, leaning forward, finds a wet leaf on her shoe she missed earlier.

"I'll think about it," he says again, knowing he won't.

"Anthony must be missing his mother."

Dai would love to remind Dilys how mother and son hardly saw one another during the last fifteen years of her life, but doesn't, seeing her drifting off with that pearly glaze misting her eyes whenever Anthony is mentioned.

"That boy," — he watches her drag her mouth down at the corners, amplifying her sadness — "he was your Elsie's two eyes."

Dai, who has never fully understood this strange expression, looks at Dilys' vigorously moving mouth, at the way she's rubbing her swollen legs and complaining of bad circulation. He has the scent of the Oil of Wintergreen she puts on them in his nostrils. The cloying woody odour spinning him back to the smarting, vaporous stench of his school changing rooms, over fifty years ago. His shoulders chafed from the stiffened seams of his mud-wet rugby shirt, the dread of what was to come thumping in his mouth. A glass-slippery floor slides under the studs of his boots making him bang against the fat brass pegs where Thomas P.E. hangs the mildewed towels for showers. Thank God for time. Without its steady passing he'd still be there, his expression fixed in terror. *What sort of tackle d'you call that, you spotty bastard? — You lost us the fucking game.* He hears the dreaded chorus.

Reckon the Dai Spot needs a good kicking, teach him a lesson, eh boys? The row of beefier lads, their fists curled at the ready.

If only he hadn't cared whether these boys wanted him in their gang. Been indifferent like Beth, who, teased and bullied, never let it bother her, levelling people with her stare. She was special, set apart and not quite of this world. Not because she had spots and played the trumpet like him, but because of the bright light shining from inside her. Something that in spite of her brutal home life, refused to be snuffed out.

"I'd better get going," Dilys breaks his reverie. The dark of her eye finding him from behind her spectacles. "I'll drop by later in the week, see how you are."

Don't bother, he wants to tell her. Hating the disruption she brings like a mushrooming cumulonimbus on the horizon of his day. Elsie's voice elbows its way into his head: *Tell her, go on — honesty's best. Tact with the likes of Dilys Roberts is hopeless — she's got the hide of Welsh Black bullock.* And he forgets himself. Giggles.

"What's the matter with you?" Dilys, sharp as a snake, flicks out a forked look that pins him down for a second or two.

"That'll be nice; I'll look forward to it," he lies, his mind working out ways to nip this woman's fixation with him in the bud. Showing Dilys to the door, he sees the girl they've been talking about walking in the direction of the village.

"Hello." He says, raising a hand in greeting, before stepping back inside his cottage. He notices how pretty she is and thinks regretfully that she is going to attract some unwanted attention in a place like this.

CHAPTER
SEVEN

In storage since her divorce, it comes as a shock, digging down inside a crate, to find a photograph of her and Spencer on their wedding day. Laughing and clasping hands, acting happy for the camera, they played a convincing part that June day fourteen years ago. But Rachel remembers the cracks. The ones they'd been trying to plaster over since her abduction three years earlier.

With the remembered weight of satin against her suntanned skin, she sees herself as she was, basking in the attention from her guests. Not that her groom bothered. Impervious to whether his bride was enchanting or not. And why, later in the evening, the Chinese lanterns lit and the blues band in full swing, Rachel conducted an experiment of her own. She disappeared. Wandering around for well over an hour, a ghostly figure amidst the vast spread of gardens at Ayot Hall. Her satin shoes slicing into her heels, her ribcage crushed beneath the bone and cross-lace of her bodice, making it difficult to breathe. Grievances that would become paltry in comparison to the burgeoning realisation of what she had done by agreeing to become Mrs Spencer Moran. Because on returning to the marquee with everyone curious to know where she had been, Spencer, who was shaking his stuff on the fish-slippery dance floor, was no more conscious of his absent bride than he was of having his hands, newly furnished with a gleaming gold band, wrapped around a buxom-bottomed bridesmaid.

Looking back, it must have been sheer determination keeping her with Spencer. Clinging to dreams of being a bride and her father walking her down the aisle accompanied by favourite hymns; silly teenage fantasies she refused to let go of. Letting go would have meant her abductor had won. Her refusal to feel any sexual stigma was what pushed her back into Spencer's bed, fiercely resolute that the last man to touch her wasn't going to be that bastard Blundell. She often wonders where she would be today if the events all those years ago never happened. This isn't what she'd have chosen, she is sure of that. Watching life go on over her shoulder, a frightened thirty-something divorcee. Haunted by what was done to her and plagued by the images of a brutal killing, with a daughter halfway across the world she will never see grow up.

The humping of boxes has given Rachel backache. Too long in one position, she shifts a little, extending an index finger to press on her Roberts radio, wanting the company. Radio 4's PM programme cuts to the news and the measured tone of the announcer: *The body of a young woman found by a local dog walker under the Grand Pier at Westburn-on-Sea this morning, has been identified as Issy Lake . . . the twenty-three-year-old primary school teacher reported missing after a night out with friends four days ago . . . initial reports suggest . . .* She doesn't want it, doesn't want the distressing images the report is so keen to ply her with, and she hits the off button.

She knows Westburn. Her father used to take her to this Somerset seaside resort as a child. Booking them into a B&B with a potted palm and a lilac-walled dining room reeking of cabbage. Her father's job as regional sales manager for Rowntree's was something her mother loved to ridicule. She was the one with the money and never tired of telling him so. Belittling his achievements by implying he did little more than peddle sweets from the boot of his car. These nights away with her dad, free from orders of *elbows off the table* and *no shoes on the bed*, are the most treasured moments of her childhood. "Why d'you want to go?" her mother would quiz through sips of strong, dark coffee and the single menthol cigarette she allowed herself each morning, citing how so and so from school was doing this, that and the other with their summer holidays and why couldn't she be like them. Rachel wasn't interested in the things her mother thought a nice middle-class girl should be. No matter how much she was nagged, she could never muster the enthusiasm to practise on the highly strung Grotrian-Steinweg piano hogging the morning room and she hated the after-school tennis lessons. All she did there with any real conviction was ogle the athletically tanned legs of older boys through the mesh surround. What she really loved was growing things. Working alongside her father in his vegetable plot. Him encouraging, nurturing, in

30

ways her mother never did. She loved long car journeys with him too, sitting up front in his company BMW, the monotonous, grey motorway snaking west.

It wasn't that she had any particular predilection for Westburn. She certainly hadn't liked the used syringes she found by the swings or the flock of matted-haired crazies wandering aimlessly about the town who, out of their skulls on cider or smack, would unceremoniously urinate against the knee-high wall of the B&B. She definitely hadn't liked the dog turds, and her memory tells her the place was festooned with it, the same way it was in spent chip wrappers and polystyrene burger cartons. What she did have a fondness for was its overriding sense of neglect. Even during the height of the season, bustling and sunny, it felt like somewhere time forgot. The flaky-faced amusements throwing vulgar motorised chimes into the street, the dated record shops where you could stand all day with headphones clamped to your ears, listening to Chesney Hawkes and Bryan Adams for free. The seedy, wet-sand feel of the bucket-and-spade shops that sold everything from inflatable lilos to netted-together flip-flops.

She had a special affinity with the cafés along the esplanade too. Greasy Spoons, her father called them, and mulling this over she would press her nose flat against the windows and peer into their condensation-streaked worlds. The fatty smells of the All Day Breakfasts mixed with cigarettes and sweat off the red banquettes finding her through the air vents as she watched waitresses moving about in flower-patterned housecoats left over from the war. Fascinating, the startling white of their peroxided hair, the wedges of bingo-wings flapping under arms adept at passing and clearing, wiping and serving. Working women; nothing like her mother.

Her father hit his sales targets in Westburn and called her his lucky mascot. Not that Rachel put his success down to luck, she put it down to him being away from her mother. On his own he was free to shine. With his film-star looks, his exotic-sounding surname, erect with clipboard, catalogue and order book, he was unrecognisable as the emasculated man he was at home. They would celebrate his triumphs with a bumper bag of chips. Eaten straight from the paper, on a salt-bleached bench, their spines pressed to a plaque commemorating the life of someone who loved the view they were having. Strange, the power of smell. She only has to whiff hot vinegar and she's back there. Back on Westburn's beach with the great corroding skeleton of its Grand Pier in view, her father whipping off his socks to splash in the shallows.

All this happened before his illness. Brought on — Rachel always thought she could read this in her mother's face, although she never said as much — by her abduction and subsequent release. His heart couldn't stand it: his precious daughter, held by some maniac. Not knowing if she was alive or dead. And his shock when he opened the front door to find her dishevelled and covered in blood. Rachel swore she heard the sickening snap when he let the pressure go. He never recovered. Suffering his first attack within two months, it was followed by a stroke a few years later and then more recently the severest attack of all. It was why, after her marriage to Spencer broke down, she stayed on at Muswell Hill for as long as she did, caring for him until he died.

In many ways her father's death has set her free. The inheritance has allowed her to buy a modest home, and investing the remainder like she has will give a decent income off the interest. Safe as long as no one finds out who she is, she thinks, unpacking the last few knick-knacks from the crate and choosing where to put them. She shouldn't feel threatened, not now she's tucked away in Wales and has changed her name and appearance. Surely she can believe in the security she is building around herself and ease up on her anxieties. Even when Blundell gets out, DS Blackwood assured her the conditions of his release will restrict his movements.

Rachel jumps. Someone is knocking her door. A quick glance out of her front windows: there's nothing parked in the lane, they must have come on foot. It will be all right, she thinks, deciding to answer it. What harm can come to her here?

CHAPTER
EIGHT

Idris Tudor stubs a big bald toe against the leg of his mam's old dining table and swears. He is always doing that. *Put some slippers on then*, her voice finds him. He would if he could remember where the hell he put them. Hobbling, he picks his way around the poky kitchen stuffed high with junk he hasn't bothered to clear out since his father died, wearing a jumper not changed for weeks. Aiming for the solid-fuel Rayburn, he runs the gauntlet between rusted paint tins and rubbish bags.

Reaching the stove, saliva gathering in his mouth for the six fatty lamb chops he has cooked, Idris fishes the blackened tray out of the oven with the cuff of his jumper. Smells of singed wool sting the air and he drops it on the cup-scorched surface. His attention is momentarily distracted by a bluebottle. Left behind by summer, trapped within the confines of his home. It bashes itself repeatedly against the window, desperate to be let out. Surprisingly swift for his size, Idris swats it with a heavy fist, enjoying the tiny crunching sound it makes. Unclenching his hand, he takes a second to pick at the substantial scab forming on his palm. A sizeable gash a week ago, he had worried he might need to have it seen to. Always suspicious of those in the medical profession, with their questions in exchange for potions, Idris tells himself he'd been right not to visit the doctors, the wound has healed well enough on its own and there shouldn't be much of a scar. It reminded him of when he was a boy and got a splinter off the ladder in the barn that girl has moved into. Wanting to climb to the top level to see what his sister Beth and that runt Dai Jones were up to, his hand swelled up like an overripe plum and became so hot and infected he had to have the splinter surgically removed in the end. Septic was the word Doctor Peeves used. A man from England with woman's hands and ideas about health and hygiene that no one with any backbone in the farming community would listen to.

With thoughts returning to his supper, Idris licks his lips and fetches the bottle of ketchup from the kitchen cupboard. Sauce-encrusted, he untwists the lid and sucks the remnants off his fingers. Without bothering with a plate, he smacks the bottom of the bottle in the same way he's seen exasperated mothers smack their offspring in the Co-op, and lets the redness shoot out over the row of near-cremated offerings.

Cooler now, he carries the tray without need of his makeshift oven cloth into the adjacent room that smells of stale water and mould and heads to the sagging sofa, with its covers as flimsy as the material of his late mother's dresses hanging in the wardrobe above. He nestles down like one of his Black Rock hens in a hollow made by his body over the years to share his evening meal with the condensation-dripping plaster and whatever shit is on the telly. Idris eats ferociously, eyes focused on the flickering screen. A man blunted by loneliness.

CHAPTER
NINE

"Hey, they've done a great job of this place."

Rachel steps aside to let Tracy pass. She likes Tracy, likes her kind, freckled face and ready smile. Stopping to chat as they've been doing in the lane, Rachel thought it was about time she asked her in for a coffee.

"D'you think?" She grins, trailing behind to watch Tracy's reaction as she steps into the beam-clad sitting room.

"I do," Tracy tilts her head in appreciation. "You wouldn't believe the state of it before those contractors got to work. I'll tell Hywel." She giggles, "he thought it was a joke when he heard what was going on here. Reckoned it would never make a home. But look at it — it's gorgeous." Tracy gives Rachel's arm a little squeeze before reaching out to stroke the smart enamelled surround of the woodburner. "Wow, love this," she says. "It'll heat the place lovely. You'll need wood though — I'll get Hywel to sort you some."

"Really?" Rachel presses her palms together. "You're so kind."

"It's no bother." Tracy smiles. "Honestly, I'd never have thought it could look this good. Best bloody thing that idiot did, selling it on — the place was just rotting away."

Rachel doesn't need to ask who that idiot is. She knows it's the last surviving son of the family who used to own her barn along with the land and farm that Tracy and Hywel now own. Tudor. The family name was on the deeds.

"I've boiled the kettle, fancy a coffee?" Rachel heads back into the open-plan living space.

"Go on then." Tracy darts a look at her watch. "Another ten minutes won't hurt."

"Have a seat." Rachel offers up one of the two wooden chairs. "Sorry it's a bit sparse. I've ordered stuff from Furniture Land in Swansea, but it'll be weeks before they deliver."

"If you're struggling, we could help out — you've got a bed and things have you?" Tracy, eyebrows expectant, sips from her mug.

"Oh, yes, I've got a bed — I had some stuff in storage. Not much, but enough to see me through. Thanks though."

"Well, you only have to ask." Tracy blinks, her eyes moistened by the steam rising off her coffee. "Oh, one thing — and I hope you don't mind me saying — but me and Hywel were talking." She looks awkward, unsure whether she should share what's on her mind. "You here on your own, a woman on her own — we thought . . ."

"Spit it out, Tracy." Rachel forces a laugh. "You're worrying me."

"That you should have a dog."

"A dog?"

"Be good company."

"Yes. Yes." Rachel says, taking her time. "A dog. I'd like that. Not that I've had much experience with dogs."

"Thing is, see, we kept back two from Meg's litter last May, but one of them's no good. Well, not that he's no good — Cadno — he's beautiful, just no good for working. He'd rather stay for a *cwtch* by the fire than be out on the hill in the rain with Hywel. A real one for the *maldod*, as my gran'd say."

"Are you saying I could have him?" Rachel sounds excited.

"If you like him, aye."

Yes, she thinks. A dog would push her to go out walking — force her out of the house, whatever the weather. She eyes the rain through the window; it doesn't seem to have let up since she arrived.

"Hopeless with the sheep, Cadno, but he's got bags of energy. Make a great pet."

"Are there good walks round here then?" Rachel asks this in spite of the isolated setting of her new home. She is someone who's been restricted to footpaths and bridleways, even in the years she was living with Spencer in Northamptonshire. "I've been out on the hill and down to the village a few times — but haven't seen any signs."

"Oh, *cariad*," Tracy laughs. "You don't need signs, you can walk where you like round here. You've got all our land for starters, look —" and scraping back the wooden chair, she stands up to point at the seemingly endless space beyond Rachel's big glass French doors.

After saying goodbye to Tracy, Rachel pulls on her anorak and goes outside under a break in the cloud. Delighted by her neighbour's enthusiasm about the interior she thinks — now she's definitely decided to stay — she should try to make something of the wasteland out here. But what a Herculean task. She isn't sure where to start. It was October when she came to Wales. The swifts and house martens long gone and any berries still gripping the brambles had begun to cultivate their furry mildewed coats. Bird-pecked and maggot-holed, the pear and apple windfalls left to rot in the long grass that has continued to grow after the dark sunless days set in. She longs for spring and the drier weather, it will give her the chance to start building for her future, and with the idea of laying down roots she wonders whether she should try turning the garden into a vegetable plot, in homage to her father. She is realistic, she knows the weather in this part of the world might not allow her to grow the same produce as he did, but she could make a start by planting fruit bushes come April. Perhaps she should ask the old boy in the long white house at the end of the lane who waves at her when she walks past. He seems to know what he's doing; always outside, his back bent over his immaculate garden, giving thanks under the lowering sky.

Poor Dad, she thinks — his remembered face never far away — had he ever been happy? Rachel likes to think he had snatches of happiness, the way she has. Blinking back tears, she tilts her face to the band of blue showing through high shreds of cloud and follows a tusk of sunlight as it illuminates a wide, smooth field, before throwing it back into shade. She has fallen in love with this place, the smell of moss and spongy earth, the plump thermals pulsing across the rain-beaten land. The air that echoes the rise and swell of the velvet-skinned hills, which, dotted with sheep, seem to breathe like living organisms. She could be happy here, if she can only convince herself there is nothing to fear.

CHAPTER
TEN

One morning, before heading off to help out at a charity jumble at Our Lady of Muswell, Jennifer D'Villez stands at the bay window of her sitting room looking out on to the street.

It has been sleeting in Muswell Hill — the first real day of winter — but now a bright spangle of light floods the room. Voices from outside ring out in the fresh cold air and she can see the leafless sycamores through the iron railings of Grand Avenue Park. Not that it does anything to lift her mood. She turns her attention to the rococo-style mantelpiece, to the one framed photograph she has of her daughter in adulthood. Self-doubt crowds her mind while her fingertips trace its silver filigreed edge. But the answer doesn't lie there; it comes from her reflection in the mirror hanging above. And moving her fingernails into the space between her perfectly plucked eyebrows, a frown buckles the thickening skin as she looks at what she believes is impossible to love.

Her heart falls at the sound of the doorbell and, rushing to it, she's alerted to the post on the mat. She stoops without bending her knees and shovels up the collection of flyers, bills and cards offering seasonal good wishes before opening the door.

"Haven't you got your key?" She snaps at the bespectacled, smooth-cheeked woman on the shiny wet doorstep. Then, immediately forgetting her, she drops her head to sift through the post.

"Don't like using it if you're in, Mrs D'Villez." Unperturbed as always by Jennifer's incivility, Mrs Pepper, number seventy-seven's charwoman, steps inside. Her liquid brown eyes, magnified by their thick-lensed glasses, shadow her employer's figure, clad in a Dolce & Gabbana skirt and cropped tweed jacket, as it recedes down the buttermilk passageway.

"Does it never occur to you I could be in the middle of something? Of course not," Jennifer answers for her. "I forgot — you don't mind disturbing me, do you?" Her sarcasm plugs the cleaner's ears like cotton wool. "And you said — I remember when I interviewed you — *I'd never know you were here* . . ." imitating Mrs Pepper, her voice tapers off and, chin in chest, she stares down at a blue and red rimmed airmail envelope. Dumping the rest of the post on top of the bread bin, she tears into it, tugging free photographs of a young girl and a sheet of Rizla-thin writing paper. Her eager eyes gobble up the handwritten sentences like a digital scanner.

"You staying at home today?" Mrs Pepper asks, pushing her spectacles up her nose as she follows Jennifer into the spacious kitchen with its warm smell of toast. It wasn't that she minded Mrs D'Villez being around, it was just that she liked to put the radio on, have a nice little sit down halfway through with a mug of something and one of those posh foil-covered biscuits Mrs D buys from M&S but never eats.

"No, I'm not." Impatient, Jennifer peels her eyes away from the handwriting and looks sideways at her. "Why are you so dolled up anyway? We off somewhere?"

We? Mrs Pepper panics, Jennifer's language confusing her. "I am. Yes . . . later . . . on my own . . ." she stammers, feeling her neck reddening and thinking she needs to explain, when really she doesn't. How she must leave on time this afternoon, make a quick dash home, before catching a train from Kings Cross. That she is to travel up to Pocklington, a small market town at the foot of the Yorkshire Wolds.

"Well, get your coat off then, there's lots to do. Look —" Jennifer, not listening, shoves a strip of paper into Mrs Pepper's hand. "I've done you one of my lists."

"Right," she says, relieved at her employer's disinterest and recovering herself a little. "I'll go and make a start."

"Er, no, hang on a minute — there's something I've been meaning to ask you," Jennifer says, turning back to her.

"Oh yes, Mrs D'Villez — what's that?" Mrs Pepper blinks from behind her spectacles, her colour returning to normal.

"It's about Sarah."

"Sarah?"

"That's right." Jennifer extends her slender neck, swan-like. "You know where she is, don't you?"

"Where she is?" Mrs Pepper looks puzzled. "Why would I know where she is?"

"Because the two of you were friends, because she talked to you."

Mrs Pepper takes a moment, eyes working from ceiling to floor, measuring the day's work she has ahead of her. "We were friends, yes, Mrs D'Villez, but she didn't tell me where she was going. I was as surprised as you when you told me she'd gone."

"And you're quite sure about that, are you?" Jennifer's tone communicates her doubt. "Because forgive me if I'm mistaken, but from where I've been standing, the two of you were as thick as thieves."

"I'm sorry, Mrs D'Villez, really I am . . . for your losses . . . you must be hurting terribly, but —"

"Do not," Jennifer, raising her voice a notch, "presume to know how *I must be feeling*, Mrs Pepper — I asked you a straightforward question, please have the courtesy to give me an honest answer in return."

"Are you accusing me of lying, Mrs D'Villez?" Her cleaning lady removes her glasses, proceeds to clean them on the hem of her housecoat. Without her spectacles, Jennifer hasn't noticed before, the woman has a look of vulnerability that is quite unexpected and at once softens her aggression towards her.

"No, no . . . of course not." Jennifer flaps a hand through the air. "I just need to find her that's all; to know she's safe."

"Of course you do, I understand — you must be at your wits' end. But please, what d'you take me for?" Mrs Pepper repositions her spectacles. "If I knew where Sarah was, if she'd told me her plans, d'you think I wouldn't have told you?"

Jennifer shifts from one foot to the other, digesting what her loyal cleaning lady is saying. "Well, I just thought, you know — you and her . . . but if you say you don't know, then you don't know. I'm sorry if you thought I was —"

"Please don't worry on my account, Mrs D'Villez. You've been under a lot of strain, I understand." She rattles the can of furniture polish she now holds in her hand.

"Good, yes." Jennifer says, placated for now. "You get on." And with Mrs Pepper dismissed, she returns to the sitting room and the peachy embrace of the Georgette couch to reread her letter.

CHAPTER
ELEVEN

It is love at first sight between Cadno and Rachel. The sheepdog's moist leathery nose seeking out her hand the moment they meet at Cwm Glas farm. A handsome animal, big in spite of his five months, with bright eyes and a generous black and white coat that feels soft under her fingers.

"*See*," Tracy says, obviously delighted, "he adores you already."

"Aye." Hywel, nodding from beneath the rim of his chequered cap, smiles in agreement.

"He's not going to let you go now, look at him."

"He's gorgeous, aren't you boy?" Rachel squats down to give the dog the serious attention his wagging eagerness deserves. "You and me — we're gonna be the best of pals, aren't we?"

"Mind you don't go spoiling him to death," Hywel jokes, calling after them as they head out of the yard and on to the lane. "He's a right one for the comfort, him. Just give us a shout if you have any problems — although," he says, turning to Tracy who has tears in her eyes. "I doubt the two of you will."

★ ★ ★

Heading towards the hills, wanting a good long walk, Rachel strides out alongside the dog. Breathing in the clean Welsh air, her mind clears on the way ahead. "You're a country girl at heart," her father said to her once. "Believe me, don't fight it — you'll never sleep well in city streets." And she did believe him. In the same way she believed that the swing he put up near his apple boughs would support her. That the Cox's Orange Pippin, come autumn, wouldn't give her tummy ache if the pips rattled when she shook them. She sees her younger self swinging on the moulded plastic seat, gripping tight the blue nylon rope and lifting herself up above neighbours' gardens, watching her father hoe between his rows of carrot tops and perpetual spinach. And how, at night in bed, in a room adjacent to her parents, she would push her chafed hands deep under the covers and press their soreness — warm as Bath buns — to the coolness of her sides.

Bath buns remind her of Mrs Pepper. Not that her bespectacled kindness was around when Rachel was small, her mother employed others then — faceless beings, nameless as clowns, with their painted smiles and resentful eyes. Mrs Pepper responded to an advert her mother had no recollection of placing and Rachel had sniggered at her name to start with.

"Come on, no one's called that for real," she said within earshot of the stout little woman in the funny pink beret. "It has to be made up."

Made up or not, what a godsend she turned out to be, arriving in the nick of time, a balm to the chaos and upset, giving Rachel something to cling to when everything else had capsized. During those bleak, stunted days, she talked to Mrs Pepper about what that farrier Blundell did to her in that out-of-the-way cottage of his and what he did to his wife when she turned up without warning. Friends were kind to start with, of course they were, but they soon tired of her emotional state and, running out of things to say, stopped telephoning and calling round. She might have been able to talk to her father if she hadn't been fearful of adding to the awful pictures she imagined were already playing out behind his eyes, but she could never talk to her mother, and certainly not to Spencer.

"He looked so normal," a tearful Rachel confided to Mrs Pepper, who looked calmly at her through her spectacles. "Yes, all right, I could tell he was a bit rough, with his tattoos and stuff, but he was a farrier, wasn't he? It's what they're like." Explaining how depressed she was, how she struggled to sleep because every time she closed her eyes all she could see was that monster pummelling his wife to death. Why she couldn't stick it out at her florists and had to sell the business, then her horse. Why, when she finally left her parents' house to go back to Spencer's on the outskirts of Northampton, she felt like a prisoner. The doctors and counsellors called it survivor's guilt, said her problem was she couldn't forgive herself for making friends with him, for making him see she was a human being. It made her wish the bastard had killed her too. At least then her mother, the press, and the great British public would have felt sorry for her. Sorry in the way they were for his poor, dead wife. Linda Blundell's murder elevated her to the heights of angel, saint and victim; Rachel's brush with death and the horror she witnessed should have earned her sympathy too. Instead all she got, because she had the audacity to survive, was drowned in police suspicion and pilloried by the press.

"But he must have liked you, sweetie," her mother's cleaner did her best to soothe. "He can't have been all bad, not really — not to have let you go like that."

Rachel smiles into the memory of Mrs Pepper as she negotiates her way through thick mud and loose stones. Hot, she takes off her hat, unzips her anorak, happy to let the wind blow through her. It was Mrs Pepper who found the place she is now living in. Thoughtfully cutting it out of her husband's Sunday supplement and bringing it along with her to work.

"I wasn't snooping," ever careful, ever meek, digging the advert out from within the cracked plastic innards of her spectacles' case. "But I couldn't help overhearing you talking to that nice police lady, saying how much you liked Wales." Her face, crumpled as a tissue, was soaked in empathy for all Rachel had lived through. "I know you like to stay away from the papers, and who can blame you, you poor dear," she said, squeezing Rachel's hand. "Every time they print something, it must bring it all back. It's why I've been keeping an eye out — I hope you like it — I think it'd be perfect."

Mrs Pepper's concern made Rachel cuddle her in a way she could never do with her mother. "Well, if you think I've been helpful my dear, I'm glad." Rachel saw how her thanks brought tears to Mrs Pepper's eyes.

"You have, you're so clever," Rachel said as she scanned the condensed details on the scrap of paper. "It looks perfect — right price too. I can easily afford it with the money Dad left."

Finding the property online was easy. She read through the sales particulars, telling herself to go slow, that nothing could be this straightforward. Except it was — the land, the potential for a sizable garden, the quality of the conversion itself — it fitted with what she'd been envisaging all along. It interested her how the place once belonged to a bigger farm and was now three separate dwellings so, although remote, neighbours wouldn't be too far away. A video on the website allowed her to walk through its interior, saving the need to travel to Wales, and after talking with a friendly, lilting-voiced woman at the agency, she made an offer that was accepted within the hour.

High on the hill, the wind tugging her hair, she stops in ankle-deep mud as the dog bounds after a rabbit. It makes her laugh, its white-bobbed tail disappearing, lightning fast, into the bank of colourless gorse. Pushing herself on, she wants the last view she will have of her house, which will disappear altogether the further she climbs. She thinks of Tŷ Haf; this dwelling she now shares with past lives. She senses them hanging in the air like electricity, making strands of her hair quiver and fly about her face and giving her the impression she is never quite alone. Living in this remote spot, she is realising, means a daily struggle to keep the outside out. Spiders spin their webs in the nooks and crannies she will clean with the nozzle of her vacuum. Field mice, leaving their trails of hard, black, seed-like droppings along her kitchen surfaces, make their nests in drawers of tea towels and tissues. Cadno might be more useful than originally thought, she thinks, registering the speed with which he darts around the undergrowth. He might help to keep the outside out better than anything. Even if he's no good with vermin, his presence alone will work as a deterrent to other unwanted visitors. Once again the question of her safety presses a cold finger of fear against her heart.

CHAPTER
TWELVE

Feeling lonely, I thought I'd have a drive around the town tonight, see what's doing. Nice now the rain's eased off, I park up, wind the window down to listen to the sea. I like the sea, I always have. The rhythm of the waves: steady, dependable; it's a sound that soothes me. Reminds me there are good things about this world, and it isn't all shit.

I check the clock on the dashboard. Not quite eleven. Good, I haven't missed it. Always good for a laugh — chucking-out time at the Lamb and Flag. If I'm quick I can park down Kingston Close, switch my engine off and not be seen. I turn the key in the ignition and without moving out of second gear, inch along the seafront before turning right at the next available lights. Quiet along here tonight, the wet pavements, oiled by the orange of streetlamps, are deserted. You could be fooled into thinking: seaside town, out of season; dead as a doornail. But give it a minute and trust me, all hell will break loose.

Here they come. The painted dollies. It's what I call them. With their gloss-pink lips, synthetic nails and all that flesh on show. You can hear them before you see them; they make one hell of a racket. A tidal wave of make-up and perfume, careering along on outrageous heels, hurling their arms about and singing at the tops of their voices. They couldn't give a shit.

I like looking at them. Out of bloody control, a groundswell of hedonistic abandon — something frightening and exhilarating rolled into one, and like nothing I've ever been part of.

CHAPTER
THIRTEEN

A panic. A flap. The leafless red-stalked dogwood and the slumbering honeysuckle come alive with a sudden surge of sparrows as Dai steps into his garden. Secateurs at the ready now the rain has stopped, he leans in to press his nose to the last of the roses. Breathing in their subtle bouquet, the delicacy of their vermilion red petals makes his eyes prick with tears. Why the tender things in life are so much harder to deal with than injury, he doesn't know. Clipping the best three, he snags a finger on a thorn and watches a bubble of blood bloom like the ruby ring he gave Elsie on their fortieth wedding anniversary.

On his walk to the cemetery, Dai follows the high-banked river. Fast and brown from excessive rainfall, when he crosses the stone-backed bridge the echoing water rushing beneath is near to deafening. The landscape has a striking clarity in this cleaner light. The verdant spread of pastures, the smatterings of outbuildings and low-thrown dwellings are cut sharp against the bite of cold. Tugging his zip to his chin, tying his perky red scarf tighter, he sees three horses, their dark bay coats already winter shaggy. On hearing his footfalls they charge to the fence to press suede-smooth muzzles into his hands, adamant he has apples up his sleeves. Dai slips on a fringe of wet leaves and reaching for anything to steady himself, grips a gate. The shock of the icy galvanised steel under his palms rolls him back to his courting days.

Elsie's mother took an instant dislike to him and, with no father around to win over with talk of rugby and trout fishing — Mr Herbert Watkins, chief stonewall builder, had died years before — there was only the flint-faced mother to chip away at. He hasn't thought of Nora Watkins for ages. She died in the second spring of their marriage, years before Anthony was born to show what a success they'd made of things. Nicotine-stained and ration-thin, her coffin weighed less than a child's and it still upsets him to think of it. He understands Nora better now. As a mere boy of twenty-one, eager for life and all he could take from it, he had no idea what it was like for a woman, widowed in her prime, who wanted the best for her precious daughter. Scrimping and sacrificing, investing all she had with little regard for her own needs, Nora worked herself into an early grave to bring up Elsie. Understandable then, her reluctance to hand her over to the first jug-eared youth to come sniffing around. And Dai was nothing then. Not halfway through law school, he had little to offer a girl who, according to her mother, was destined for great things.

Despite the opposition, Elsie and Dai were married within weeks of their twenty-second birthdays under an ominous mackerel sky. He used to wonder — in the tougher middle years — if they stayed together to spite those who said it would never last. "Chalk and cheese" was a favourite snipe of Nora's, and perhaps they were, but they lasted where others failed. They did love each other, regardless of him keeping part of himself back for Beth — or the memory of her, at least.

Sheep dozing in a pile, soaking up the last of the year's sun, scatter as he passes by a gap in the hedge. He turns with the bend in the lane and sees the chapel roof, its slabs of Welsh slate competing with a freaky cyanic dome of sky. He stops to shake a stone from his shoe and, alerted to the spread of chestnut wings, looks up. A red kite. Floating in a placid arc above his head. So close he sees the shiny black bead of its eye, the understated roll of its cleft tail.

The humble timber gate of the chapel cemetery squeaks when he opens it. Rust from its hinges comes off in his hands. He sees the graveyard is empty, apart from a woman in a dark blue anorak with a sheepdog, picking around the thatch of nettles and brambles that grow against the east-facing wall. He recognises her. She's the one who bought Idris' barn; the one Dilys says comes from London. Dai moves on, taking care not to tread where he shouldn't, finds his wife's grave and kneels. The bones of his knees scrape the marble surround as he leans in to stroke the chippings tidy at the base of Elsie's headstone. His lips moving, silently reading the inscription he chose. He empties the commonplace pudding bowl he keeps meaning to swap for something more fitting, replaces old roses with fresh. These should last if it doesn't rain too hard. But what to bring then? One more visit and the garden will be empty until spring. Maybe he'll cut a sprig of holly, she always liked the bush opposite the house, especially when laden, as it is this year, with fierce red berries.

Cardiff didn't suit Elsie, with its traffic and noise. She enjoyed her job well enough and was highly thought of; her ex-pupils returning with tales of their success would remember her at Christmas, sending cards written out to their favourite teacher. But in the years after Anthony was born, her requests to come home intensified.

"I miss the hills, Dai — can't we go back?" Her voice, soft through the darkness after lights out. Snuggling into his back, wrapping her arms around him as they drifted off to the distant wail of police sirens and indistinct shouts from the street below. And he would pat the hand that was resting in his, offering words he hoped would mollify, praying she would come round to his way of thinking. But she never did, tirelessly beetling away behind the scenes, calling into estate agents on her way home from work to see what might be affordable in rural Dyfed. Bringing home sales particulars of run-down smallholdings, crumbling farms, retirement bungalows; all claiming to be within budget, and strategically placed in his eye-line.

They survived twenty-seven years of urban living, Dai's dread of returning to what he fought so hard to break away from, dwindling year on year. He too began to long for space, a slice of the pastoral idyll retained from childhood. Tired of the daily grind, the repetitive thanklessness of his civil litigation work. He barely took a holiday in all the years he practised, family time was frowned upon and after he was made a partner one decade in, the responsibilities grew hundredfold. So when the opportunity to return to Bryngwyn came, he was happy to let Elsie steer things. Because aside from the awfulness of his own father's unexpected death, his mother's failing health and his boyhood home in disrepair, he saw it held a brighter future. One free of mortgage repayments and a living to be made, if they were sensible, from savings and the lump sum made when he sold his stake in the practice.

Leaning back on his heels, Dai thinks how good his wife was at reading nature's caveats and he listens to what she would have said in response to the abundant berries crowding the hedgerows: "Sign of a hard winter, love — you'd better fetch plenty of wood in." Elsie's voice finding him at the same time as another, differently accented one . . .

"Hello," it says apologetically, and he turns to find the woman he is coming to recognise. Her dark hair caught in a tight mare's tail at the nape of her neck, her pretty cheeks whorled through with the fingers of cold. She rustles awkwardly in new-looking waterproofs and tugs at the cuffs of her gloves, nervous, as though she needs to keep her hands busy. "Beautiful day."

Dai looks into her face and smiles. "It is indeed," he says, rising to his feet. "Hello, I'm Dai. Dai Jones from Bwthyn Dewen." He gives the name of his cottage like a question, pointing in the direction he has walked.

"Yes, we've waved to each other. I'm Rachel." And she extends a hand, giving him a soft little frown. "Sorry if I disturbed you." She indicates Elsie's grave.

"Not at all — how are you liking Tŷ Haf?" Dai asks, thinking there's little point pretending he doesn't know where she lives. He brushes the knees of his trousers and stoops to stroke her dog's head, which feels unexpectedly bony beneath his fingers.

"Very much," she tells him as they wander towards the gate. "Did you know it before it was converted?"

Dai takes a moment to grip the tip of his nose between forefinger and thumb before answering. "Yes . . . yes, as a child. But I've not been back for years."

He knows she interprets his reply as one weighted down with more than he lets on. That her home stores unfinished business for him. But the history he has with the place isn't something he wants to share.

Following the track that encloses the cemetery, they pass a little wooden sign that reads: *Y Llwybr Briallu*.

Rachel tries to pronounce it then gives up. "What does it mean?" she asks.

"What does it mean?" Dai smiles at her attempt. "It means 'The Primrose Path'."

"That's pretty," she says.

"I suppose it is," Dai, his mind turning. "Except, of course, in folklore its meaning's a bit more sinister."

"Why, what d'you mean?"

"Well now, how to put it into words . . . it sort of implies that if you take an easy or too pleasurable a route in life, it will lead to disaster or tragedy. Something like that. You know, old wives' tales."

"Makes sense." Rachel nods. "It does lead to the graveyard."

"Ah." Dai fetches up a laugh. "But in the other direction it leads to your barn."

Without warning comes a rush of wind that whips their faces and severs their conversation. Turbulent as a tube train along the tunnel of lane, a huge lorry, clattering-loud, hurtles at speed towards them. Thunderous and frightening, they need to dive on to the bank to avoid being mown down. Gripping on for his life, Dai loses count of the fat, black wheels that, spinning high as his shoulders, hog the mean strip of tarmac.

"Bloody hell." Dai, hearing her scream through the racket, sees her clasp the collar of her dog. "Who is that?"

"That," he tells her, extricating himself from the hedgerow, "is Idris Tudor."

"Tudor — the family who used to own my place? I didn't know they still lived round here."

"It's only him left now. He lives in the cottage just up the lane from you." Dai's face darkens. "He hasn't been bothering you, has he?"

"No." Rachel scrunches up her face, looks puzzled.

"You be careful —"

"I know. He's nearly had me before along the lane in that thing."

"No, I mean — the man is dangerous." Dai places a hand on her sleeve, holds it there for a second or two. Grave and earnest, the warning is enough to stop her in her tracks. "You're to watch yourself with him, d'you hear? I'm not saying he'd do anything, but . . . I know what he's capable of."

"What d'you mean?"

"Just that I've had trouble with him in the past so now I stay out of his way, and you . . ." he breathes through his words, ". . . you make sure you do too."

Falling into step, the trauma of the haulage truck forgotten, they reach Dai's cottage in no time. He likes the way Rachel compliments him on his garden path. Fringed with alternate violet and white heather, it does look particularly pretty for the time of year.

She accepts his offer of tea, which they drink from mugs — hers taken black, his the colour of old pennies — sitting together on the low stone wall his father built to divide lawn from vegetable garden. Seeing the way she turns her face for the last warmth from the autumn afternoon sun, he does the same.

"I love what you've done out here," she breathes lightly, keeping her eyelids closed. "My dad was one for the garden, taught me all sorts. I'll be making a start on mine soon."

At that moment, Dai's cat jumps into her lap and, opening her eyes, she gasps in appreciation. "Wow . . . now you're beautiful — who are you?"

"This is Gabriel," Dai announces, proud. "Mouse tickler and bird teaser — but no good with either, thank goodness."

"Well," Rachel coos, "when you look this gorgeous you don't have to be, do you boy? What beautiful fur." He watches her move her fingers through Gabriel's dense silky black coat. "I love his white paw," she laughs, touching it. "Is that the only bit of white on you?" And as if on cue Gabriel rolls over in her lap to allow her to inspect his tummy.

"He's lovely company." Dai says, wondering again why such an attractive young woman would want to tuck herself away in a place like this with only a dog for company.

"Like Cadno is for me — I don't know what I'd do without him now."

Dai sees her check on her dog who, having found a square of sunshine on the lawn, is resting, head on paws, unperturbed by the cat and the attention Rachel is bestowing on it.

"It's funny, I never saw myself as an animal person. Apart from my horse, which I didn't end up having for long, as a kid, there was only next door's cat to play with." She refocuses on Gabriel who is now licking her hand, purring loud. "And as lovely as he was, he wasn't a patch on you."

"This one's like a dog, mind — follows me everywhere."

She giggles. "Cadno wants to be in on everything too, even out in the garden."

"How much of a garden have you got?" Dai only remembers the pockmarked yard that was part of Cwm Glas when the Tudors owned it.

"A fair bit. Got an acre of field too — although I've no idea what to do with it."

"The garden or the field?" Dai lifts his mug to his lips, sips his tea.

"The field. I know what I want to do with the garden, especially now I've seen yours."

"Not looking it's best this time of year, but thanks." Dai swings an arm out in a curve across his years of hard graft.

"I'd really like to grow vegetables — nothing beats stuff you've grown yourself, does it?" And she gazes over, not for the first time, to the enviable tangle of slender onion shoots, the purple-veined beetroot leaves and tightly budded stalks of Brussels sprouts.

"D'you want me to fetch you some?" Dai asks, following her gaze. The way her head darts nervously from one thing to another, it puts him in mind of the rabbits he struggles to keep off his raised vegetable beds, the offspring of the bucks and does his father would shoot out on the hills and bring home for the pot.

"Oh, no, I didn't mean . . ." Rachel says, and Dai drops the image he has of his mother's bloodied hands, the iron-rich smell of rabbit guts decanted on to the wooden ridges of the draining board.

"Why not? Far too many for me — go on . . . how about leeks, I bet you like leeks?"

Refusing to listen to her protests Dai, up on his feet, is on his way to his father's old shed to retrieve the gardening fork. He senses Rachel's eyes and is conscious, suddenly, of the slight stoop of his shoulders, his thick grey head of hair. A kind girl, he thinks, seeing her pop Gabriel by her feet and tidy the tray. He won't ask the questions many around here would. Whatever or whomever she is so obviously hiding from, it isn't his business.

"There you go." Dai, his smart shoes swapped for wellingtons, holds a carrier bag out to her. "You enjoy."

"Oh, thanks, Dai. That's so kind." Rachel taps him quickly on the arm. The gesture is awkward, as if he is too hot to touch.

"Hey, I know what I meant to tell you," he says as they say goodbye. "Sunday week, the village square." He wags a finger, indicating Bryngwyn. "They've a really good market — Christmas market, you know the sort of thing. Live music. Local arts and crafts. People come from miles — it's the highlight of the year."

"Week Sunday? Yeah, I think I will, thanks Dai."

"Great," he says, smiling. "See you there."

CHAPTER
FOURTEEN

Slouching down the lane under the cover of darkness, Idris, back from a recent haulage trip to Somerset, makes a grim silhouette in his oversized boots and torn donkey jacket. Hard to imagine there being anyone bigger than him, but his father was. Ronald Tudor, in his prime, was a man with the strength of two and his reputed potential to harm spread its tendrils far into the community.

He remembers his father taking him for his first pint down The Bear in Bryngwyn. A Saturday night, the saloon heaving with rowdy drinkers and when Ronald Tudor crossed the threshold, a reverential hush descended. Everyone stopped talking, holding beer they were about to swallow in their mouths and parting like the Red Sea to give the man a wide berth. Quite an experience for the pubescent Idris, because up to then, he'd only seen his father throw his weight around at home, or down the mart if he suspected he was being diddled out of a decent price for a heifer, and in both places, there was never anyone big or brave enough to challenge him. Witnessing this strange spectacle didn't put him in awe of the man as others might have expected, it made him hate his father all the more.

Making a show. It was the last thing the self-conscious teenager wanted. Idris hated fuss, he just wanted to blend with the crowd. In his short time at secondary school he hadn't found it easy to make friends and at barely fourteen, forcibly stopped from catching the bus by his father's fist, he dropped out of the social loop altogether. Only now, on the rarest occasion, the mood snatching him out of the blue, will he rinse his face under the cold tap and venture down The Bear. Socially inept, he will stand up at the bar — which still has its fill of regulars — see faces he recognises, some he even remembers the names of. But they don't make eye contact, they don't make him welcome. They exclude him in much the same way they did in the playground.

Idris looks as if he might be on his way over to The Bear now. But he isn't. Tonight he has other plans. Deciding, once his meal was over and establishing there was bugger all on the telly, he would take a stroll down to Tŷ Haf, see if anything was worth viewing there. The whoop of a barn owl flying low between the hooded branches of trees makes him jerk his head up. White, the angel-spread of wings engulf the otherwise blackened tunnel of lane. He isn't spooked by it and doesn't notice the paring of moon swinging like a hammock between stars he has never bothered to identify. A cold, clear night. Rare, falling as it does between the mild winds and heavy rain that have plagued the country for weeks. Not that he is one who feels the cold, his unbuttoned jacket, flapping open like the wings of a big dark bird of prey himself. Idris is a man oblivious to the weather he was born under; there is little the year's turning can dole out that affects him.

It is the third time he's done this. The idea finding him as he drove past in his Scania lorry one night. Seeing her lighted windows, the stiletto of chimney smoke. He found a sizeable gap in the hedge, somewhere he could hide with his back tucked into the snag of hawthorn and bramble. And lucky for him, there are those large windows on her back door that give an eagle's view of her ochre-lit life. Tonight the girl is in red. A cable-knit, man-size pullover. The kind of thing his mother would have knitted him as a boy and made him wear when she took him into town to carry her shopping. It does nothing for her. So chunky it falls way down over her bottom and he can't distinguish where her breasts begin and end. He feels thwarted, having made, what is for him, the most gargantuan effort to come out. She is standing at the stove, sipping wine from a long-stemmed glass and pushing something around a bowl-bottomed pan. Lifting bits out, blowing on them and passing them to the dog. She seems to know what she's doing, expertly twisting a serving of spaghetti into another pan, her face over the steam of boiling water. Then her hand pulls at the neck of the jumper and bending her head, she blows down inside her clothes.

Go on, go on. Idris, willing her with his stare. *Take it off, you know you want to.* Then, *hey up.* Idris, shifting closer, sees her yank the jumper over her head. To his delight, she is wearing next to nothing underneath. Only a low-cut, flimsy black T-shirt thing. He shivers, not from the cold, as she leans forward to give him a generous eyeful, down into the smooth cleft of flesh going on between her small yet beautifully firm breasts. No bra, he guesses, massaging his crotch and growing in confidence, feeling he is safely hidden from the lights of any passing vehicle, he delves beyond his trousers, his underwear and right down to the clammy depths of his arousal. Then, with the sensation peaking to something almost too much to bear, he risks everything and steps through the hole in the hedge and into her garden, to press right up against her window.

CHAPTER
FIFTEEN

Jennifer, sitting at her late mother's Edwardian writing desk, lets her thoughts travel its chamfered edges and rosewood marquetry. This is where she stores Spencer's lightweight letters and opening a drawer brings back smells of her childhood: tobacco, humbugs, pencil shavings; only faint now, barely traceable. Her childhood ending with her mother's death half a century ago. Reaching blindly, her hand bypasses leaflets en route to their destination; souvenirs from family holidays in Wales. Her fingers rest briefly, unaware, on the majestic ruins of castles, wide yellow sands. A poet's boathouse with views of a broad, blue estuary. Steam railways and national parks. Honey pots visited as a family. Places her daughter could be living amidst now. The most recent tissue-thin letter from her ex-son-in-law implying what she already guessed.

"She was on about your holidays in Wales all the time, always nagging me to take her back," he confides in his inky octopus scrawl, careful to avoid using Sarah's name. Then, in his next sentence, he asks if Jennifer has sorted an email address yet? "It would make things easier — could keep in touch more often, send up-to-date photos of Laura online?"

Jennifer can, if she tries, still hear Spencer's voice. His habit of tapering demands into gentle suggestions. Kneading and warming his sentences so as to manipulate them into question marks. A trick of the charming, she always thought, eyeing the computer Sarah left behind. Jennifer is as reluctant to scrap it as she is to switch it on. She knows where she is with her Montblanc, Basildon Bond and stiff Manila envelopes she prettifies with good old-fashioned stamps.

Downstairs in the kitchen, water splashes into the kettle, the bolt slides. Mrs Pepper is stepping into the garden to give the sparrows the crumbs. Jennifer hears the clatter of dishes as she washes up the lunch things. Then the sound of her moving to the window to squeeze out the little mop against the side of the bucket that she will drag back and forth over the floor. She usually sings. A shrill bird-like voice that if Jennifer takes the time to listen, she finds she rather likes. It reminds her somehow of her childhood, but she can't place why. Mrs Pepper always wears the same dark blue housecoat and chequered scarf tied over her hair. Who does she live with? In all the years she has worked here, Jennifer has never bothered to ask. She lives with her husband, she decides. An invalid. Once an industrial worker but there had been some accident and now he relied on his wife for everything. He was very pale and sat all day with a blanket over his knees. Mrs Pepper took in sewing, ironing, anything to make ends meet. She had to; Jennifer couldn't imagine her earning enough from the hours she gave her. Their children had left home, each going to some far-flung place and they never saw them. The Peppercorns — one of each — would have grown up robust and ready for the world, but it had been too soon for their mother who had replaced them with cats that sit on her husband's lap in their dim little kitchen, instead of the grandchildren they'd been promised.

The truth is that Jennifer has no idea who Mrs Pepper is. Has no idea how resigned she is to the fact that Jennifer needed her, even though she has never expressed as much. Asking, in that motherly way, whether there were enough blankets on her bed, how much milk she had in her fridge, sighing whenever Jennifer spoke of her daughter and agreeing how sad it was she doesn't see her grandchild.

Mrs Pepper's husband, Stan, has his own theory. He might not have met Jennifer but he's heard enough and read the stories in the papers to be of the opinion his wife is wasting her time. The D'Villez tribe are a hopeless cause. Stan puts his wife's tenderness towards her employer down to not being able to have children. They wanted babies and tried for years, it's the only thing about Mrs Pepper's life that makes her sad.

The sizeable diamond on Jennifer's left hand snags on the ribbon she uses to tie Spencer's airmailed envelopes together. Quite a stack, her hand-span needing to stretch wide to accommodate them. The ribbon, a strip of blue left over from Spencer and Sarah's wedding, is the colour of the sea and matched the topaz in her daughter's engagement ring. A ring that incidentally hasn't been seen for years and Jennifer makes a mental note to ask Mrs Pepper to keep an eye out when she clears Sarah's old room ready for the decorators. The way she stores Spencer's correspondence makes them look like love letters — tenderly bound and squirrelled out of sight. But something is different. They look untidy, the bow tied badly — she didn't leave them like this. Have foreign fingers been rooting through her precious things, reading messages meant only for her? Her heart thumps in her mouth. Had Sarah found them, does she know her guilty secret, is this why she left without a word?

The discovery would have seemed the ultimate betrayal and the thought makes Jennifer queasy. Not that Sarah was honest with her. What about those secret telephone conversations with talk of deposits and completion dates? She knew where she was going, it's why Jennifer didn't notify the police — Sarah isn't a missing person; she just doesn't want to be found. But it's not about what Sarah wants; Jennifer needs to find her, to know she's safe. She can understand her desire to leave London, afraid of what the press will do when Blundell gets out, but to disappear without a word? It's hurt her more than she could ever have imagined. If she has gone to Wales as Spencer suggests, she could ask Lynette for the number of that private investigator, give him a list of places they used to holiday and ask him to search there.

Refocusing on the letters, Jennifer slips them free of the ribbon and thinks of Spencer's new wife. A woman who, no doubt deliberately on Spencer's part, features in more than her fair share of the pictures he sends of

Laura. The woman's lightly feathered fringe, benevolent smile and benign pale eyes seeking out her approval from beyond the camera lens. She has nothing of the dramatic effect of Sarah, but perhaps this had been the draw. The calmness of her, this mild, milky-fleshed Claire. With her freckly nose, sensible sandals and varnish-free toes. What trouble could she be, what waves would she cause to break on the clinically scented world of Spencer Moran?

The telephone on her desk rings. She picks it up.

"Hello," she says; her voice sharp.

Nothing — yet she knows someone's there, she can hear them breathing.

"*Hello*?" she tries again. "Who is this please?"

Silence.

"*Sarah*?" she tests the line. "Sarah — is that you darling?"

Whoever it is hangs up; the sound of its dismissal stings her ear. She presses 1471 eagerly into the handset and is told the caller withheld their number.

"Damn and blast," she shouts into the silence, dropping the receiver back into its cradle. "I need to speak to you, you stupid girl — I need to find you."

CHAPTER
SIXTEEN

Rachel rushes for the phone, its ring, loud and shrill in the otherwise emptiness. "No. You've got the wrong number," she tells the unsuspecting caller.

She's had a couple of these. It would be all right if it didn't make her stomach cartwheel. She knows she's probably overreacting but, with the publicised talk of her abductor's impending parole inveigling its way into her dreams, she's jittery enough. She's gone ex-directory, terrified the press will find out where she is. She could understand this terror if there'd been a phone line here before, but Tŷ Haf, as it's recently been christened, was only a dilapidated shell before she moved in.

The telecoms engineer came yesterday. Over two hours late, she made him leave his boots in the porch, but compensated by making him endless mugs of milky tea and allowing him unfettered access to the biscuit barrel.

"Course you're too out in the sticks for terrestrial telly here," he informed her, leaning nonchalantly against her stove. His fingers black from the wiring, his mouth busy crunching through her chocolate digestives. "There's no transmitter for miles."

His words worried her. Fearing this news would mean she wouldn't have access to the internet, knowing how much she needed it to keep tabs on Blundell's release date. Broadband was the only thing the engineer was positive about and told her even remote spots like this could receive it nowadays.

She hadn't liked the way the engineer looked at her when he talked of her remoteness. Sizing her up in a way he would have been taught to price beasts for market. She could tell he'd been raised on a farm. He had the smell of a farmer and knew things; commenting on her dog carrying too much weight, and when she explained he wasn't for rounding up sheep, made a sound like the injured bullock she helped Tracy free from barbed wire when Hywel was away up the hill.

"You new 'ere then?" The engineer fired his question and she nodded confirmation. "Funny that — cos I could have sworn I recognised you." He continued to stare as he slurped from one of her pretty mugs, his wet mouth squashed against the rosebud pattern. "TV then, is that it?" She can feel it now, the way panic flared behind her ribcage, making her want to run, but she stood her ground, fobbing him off by saying she must have one of those faces.

"Know much about rural living, do you?" he said later; putting her on the spot again and she told him about holidaying in the area as a child. "Not much then," he concluded, eyes glinting, draining his mug and leaving it by the sink for her to wash. "It'll be one hell of a learning curve, stuck all the way out here."

76

He dominated her kitchen, his bulk claiming it as his and, uncomfortable being in a confined space with any man, she stayed out in the garden. But with time dragging and wanting him gone, she forced herself inside to chivvy him up. Watching him gather his equipment together, irritated by the leisurely way he twisted — between hand and elbow — the snake of cable, followed by the slow dislocation of electric drill, laying their ever-decreasing components into the foam-cut spaces like beloved children he was tucking up in bed.

"I knew the family who used to own this farm — before it was all carved up," he said, carrying his stuff outside. "You met Idris yet?" Spiking his words with menace as he slammed shut the doors of his company van. "Nice looking lass like you; you want to watch it." He laughed an unpleasant laugh and, without waiting for her reply, positioned himself behind the wheel. "Never one to take no for an answer was Idris Tudor. Assuming of course, you would say no?"

It was his parting gift. This and the licentious grin he gave as he reversed out of the drive and accelerated away.

Rachel switches on the newly connected television to rid herself of the image of the engineer. BBC *Breakfast News*. The feeling is instantaneous, she hates it. Hates the smug Mr-and-Mrs attitude of the designer-clad presenters sitting cosy-close in their comfy studio. Rape and violent crime against women is to be this morning's topic, and with it come further references to the recent killing of Issy Lake, the pretty primary school teacher from Westburn-on-Sea. The camera swings to a Mary Whitehouse figure, invited in to give her opinion. Rachel can hardly believe what she's hearing and shouts at the others on the sofa to intervene. The woman is suggesting those who suffer this kind of treatment only have themselves to blame. "They need to take responsibility —" the sour-faced fifty-something, flicks back a fringe of lacklustre hair, "if you parade around in next to nothing, so inebriated you don't know what you're doing, then you're going to invite the wrong kind of attention . . ."

Rachel can't stand it. Switches it off. But not before the voice of the sanctimonious old bag has tricked its way inside her head. "What would the likes of you know?" she says, crunching through bran flakes. "Don't worry love; you're safe — no matter how crazed or desperate, no bloke'd go for you."

Remembering to take her Seven Seas tablet, determined not to slip back into her usual habit of dissecting the past, she looks at the dog who wriggles his response from his cushion by the door.

"Fancy a walk?" She claps her hands. Cadno doesn't need asking twice, and pushing her feet into the boots she keeps in the porch, they step out into a rare, cold, blue-white day. But despite the glorious sunshine, it takes her most of the walk to rid herself of the shadow of possibility that the telecoms engineer might work out who she is and come back to bother her.

CHAPTER
SEVENTEEN

A knock at the door.

No way.

Idris stops what he is doing with the floral sheen of his dead mammy's dress and peers out of an upstairs window. Horribly flustered, he slides the dress he had been stroking only seconds before, back on its hanger and slams the wardrobe shut.

"I'm coming," he hollers from behind the window pane, his nose grazing the coldness of glass. "Hang on, hang on." He panics, anxious she might go before he has the chance to reach her.

He races down the stairs two at a time and is still tugging down his jumper when he wrenches open his rain-swollen door. The girl, he notices in an instant, is far lovelier close up and, spitting on his palms, he uses his hands to smooth his hair flat as a form of greeting.

"Sorry to bother you." Her face is rosy in the sudden drop in temperature. "But you haven't seen a dog around here, have you? Cadno, a border collie — he's run off and I've been calling and calling."

Taller than he thought, Idris stares at her, not blinking. He isn't really listening to what she says; too busy feasting on her, his gaze dropping down over the padding of waterproofs, imagining the body beneath.

"Probably gone after a fox," he says, watching her. "There's plenty of 'em about this time o' year, see. Bugger all to eat out on them hills, with all the lambs gone." Idris shifts a little in the draught of the doorway, wipes his dripping nose with a heavy fist. "Want me to come and look with you?" He makes a point of tilting his head to the heavens. "Be dark soon, you won't want him out in that — they're talking storms again later."

"*Come with me?*" The girl flinches and, putting distance between him and her, steps back to stand in the lane. Her gesture obvious, her meaning plain. "Erm, very kind," she says by way of compensation, watching him gather his eyebrows together and twist his meaty hands in anticipation. "I'm sure he'll turn up. I'm just being silly, he knows where home is."

"One of the Morgan's dogs, is it?" Idris tunes his question into the force of the wind.

"That's right. Had him a week or so now. He's great company."

"Bloody useless for sheep. I'd have put the runt down."

Rachel jerks her head to the sound of howling and clanking chains and swings round to face the door of a corrugated lean-to at the side of Idris' house.

"You got dogs?" She asks, her face telling him she already knows the answer. That some busybody has been filling her in on how he keeps his rangy mutts tied up when he's away in his juggernaut. But he won't be made to answer. Not to this incomer. Ones that move to the country think because they buy a pair of wellingtons and a cagoule, they know what it takes to make a living out of these hills, in weather that never lets up.

"I'll fetch my gun." He offers, enjoying the fear that is congesting her face.

"*Your g-g-gun?*" she stammers, then implores; "No . . . no gun. No gun — *please.*"

Idris doesn't answer immediately, silently pushing his feet into a pair of clay-clogged boots. "It's the only way to deal with them," he says eventually, reaching behind him into the darkened chaos of his living space to retrieve his Beretta Silver Pigeon and pulling on his jacket, he pats the pockets to check for cartridges.

"My dog?" the girl shrieks, not understanding his meaning at all. "You're not going to shoot my dog?"

"Your dog?" He stops moving to look at her. Eyes bloodshot and quizzical through the folds of flesh. "Foxes, girl. Foxes." And snapping his spine upright, he points the muzzle of his firearm at the tumbling gunmetal sky. Pleased this won't reassure, not if she knows *cadno* means fox in Welsh.

CHAPTER
EIGHTEEN

Rachel shudders under the sound of bickering crows and the high, sharp whistle of a buzzard, their spinning shapes thrown against the clouds. She can't get away quick enough. That is one odious bloke. With his hobbling sheep, his ham-flesh fists and strawberry mark. She checks Idris' bulk is safe inside his hovel and satisfied, breaks into a steady run. Past the redundant farm machinery. Tractor tyres, vast as planets. Rusty dinosaur-like diggers dumped in fields, their great steel necks stretched to the sky. Such things, if taken in another context and deposited in the Saatchi Gallery, could demand six-figure price tags.

Up this end of the lane the hedgerows seem overgrown and prematurely bare. Skin-ripping briars and brambles claw like the hoary nails of witches at the sleeves of her anorak, startling her. Intermittently checking over her shoulder, she is nervous under the darkening sky, as huge branches of sycamore and ash loom black and leafless over her like mythical beasts. The only richness comes from the splay of bright holly berries. A vivid red set against the evergreen is a sight so beautiful it makes her gasp.

Eyes back on the lane. On the greying grass running central to the tyre tracks. She sees Idris all over again. Sizing her up, pricing her for market. An experience not unlike the telecoms engineer and she wonders if this isn't how it's going to be living here and that she'd just better harden herself to it. Yet her gut is telling her there is something odd about this man. That face, with its heavy creases resembling the corrugated iron sides of his outbuildings. And such grubby hands. The image of them makes her run faster, keen to get home so she can wash. Something he obviously doesn't do; she thinks of his rotary line of dirty clothes, waiting for the rain to launder them.

Idris Tudor.

Dai did warn her, she knows she shouldn't have gone knocking at his door; if she hadn't been so panicked about her missing dog she wouldn't have dared. Her mind carves up the syllables of his name, envisaging it as a turnip. Unfamiliar as she is with country living, she knows that man's no farmer. How can anyone live like that? And unable to pronounce the Welsh name given in a scratched-out sign tacked to his gate, she christens it with an alternative: *Shit Farm* and laughs. A mirthless laugh, out of relief to be escaping, she vows never to repeat the experience.

From nowhere, Cadno bounds towards her — fur plastered with mud. His soft white muzzle pushed forward in his usual eagerness, oblivious to her worry.

"Where've you been, boy?" She isn't angry; how can she be, look at him. He thumps his big, fox brush of a tail against her thigh, pausing for the cuddles he thinks he has a right to. They fall into step, dodging puddles and the frost-split grooves in the ancient tarmac. She stoops to grab for the scruff of the dog's neck when a single white van whizzes past. Diesel fumes burn the air and the back of her throat until they reach the fork in the road, the left of which leads down to Cwm Glas farm.

It occurs to her again how strange Bryngwyn is. Flanked by the jagged sandstone spires of the Brecon Beacons, it lies hidden amongst small round hills. Like a Welsh Tuscany, Rachel thinks, remembering long-ago summer holidays with Spencer. Handsome and tanned, the sleeves of his cotton shirts rolled up to his elbows, he had seemed more relaxed in the years before Laura was born. She remembers the Beacons from childhood holidays and coming to live in a place within sight of them is to be back amidst old friends. The crown of peaks, forming a horseshoe ridge of mountains, were what her father loved to paint, capturing with considerable skill their asymmetrical edges puncturing the strap of sky.

Her dad loved this part of Wales, felt the magic as she does and often talked of making this place of majestic castles, waterfalls and caves, grassy moorland and remote pewter-skinned reservoirs his home. To clear right out of London, rid himself of the soulless suburbia, which he said — after too much wine, on the rare occasions he was allowed too much wine — always stifled him. Much of Rachel thinks her decision to move to a place he felt at peace in is so the ghost of him can live the dream vicariously through her. Taking him with her on her walks, because he loved to walk — not golf courses or council parks, where municipal flower beds are manufactured into gaps filched from the urban concrete sprawl — he was someone who yearned for the wild. The wild he was allowed to taste once a year in the rented two-bed, pink-eyed cottage, with its overgrown garden that sloped down to the banks of the Towy. Whereas her mother, never equipped with the right kind of footwear and cajoled into leaving the smoke, needed to be shoved into this sumptuous space, with its softer winds and sudden showers. Often left sitting inside, looking out through the rotting gabled windows of their holiday-let at her daughter and husband laughing in a way he and she had never done. *No wonder she hates you.* The wind rushes at Rachel with its message. *It must have pushed her to the brink of insanity, watching you with him, taking her place.*

Rachel knows all about that kind of insanity. What it can drive you to. Hospitalised for long enough, and not in the immediate aftermath of those frightening days following her abduction, but later. Triggered, they said, by a bout of postnatal depression. A rush of hormones. Or were people just being kind? Making allowances on account of what she had suffered years before. After all, Laura was almost four by then. They gave her drugs to help her deal with it, the paranoia — because the consultants gave it a name before setting her on the conveyor belt to recovery. The course of treatment may have dulled her sensitivities but the problem never went away. The belief that Laura and Spencer where plotting against her. Making three become two. Perhaps she has more of her mother in her than she cares to admit.

A red car interrupts her thoughts; spraying sounds of thick wide tyres on the wet road. It slows to a stop. Tracy, obviously coming back from somewhere, is looking remarkably spruced up. It takes Rachel a moment to recognise her, unfamiliar as she still is with all the Morgan's vehicles.

"Hey, you all right — you look dreadful?"

Rachel fills her in about losing the dog and her bizarre exchange with Idris.

"Silly sod, him — he don't mean no harm." Tracy laughs, dismissing Rachel's concerns. "Wanted to impress you, I 'xpect. Don't get many pretty women around here and him living alone, poor dab. Should feel sorry for him really. Anyway," she says, changing the subject, "I'm glad I bumped into you — fancy coming riding next week? Up Brianne way." Tracy points at somewhere off in the distance. "Get great views up there."

"*Riding?*" Rachel, shoving her hands into pockets, sounds uneasy.

"Aye. Do us the world of good." Tracy, seeing Rachel's mouth open ready to deliver the negative, quickly adds, "Don't worry if you don't have the gear, they lend hard hats and those boots you got on'll be fine."

"Crikey. I dunno, Tracy. I haven't ridden for years, not since my daughter —" Rachel stops, realises her mistake.

86

"I didn't know you had a daughter." Tracy doesn't miss a trick.

"Lives in America . . ." she hesitates, then adds, "With my ex and his new missus. I don't see her."

"Oh." Tracy, awkward, stares at her hands gripping the steering wheel. "That's a shame. Whereabouts? I've got relatives in Connecticut."

"Maine," Rachel tells her, matter-of-fact. "Spencer, my ex, he's a research fellow at the university there."

"Ooo, wow." Tracy nods, her blow-dried hair sliding into her well-made-up eyes. "A research fellow, eh. What does he research?"

"He's a teuthologist." Rachel gives the word as if it's one she uses every day.

"*Tooth* . . . what?" Tracy tries and fails. "What's that when it's at home — dentistry?"

"No, nothing like that, to give you its true definition — as I was constantly told," she dispenses a sharp little laugh, "he studies locomotion and muscle physiology in cephalopods . . . well, octopus, to be precise."

Tracy nods. Bites her bottom lip. "Miss your ex, do you?"

Rachel giggles. "Not much."

Tracy's mobile bleeps from somewhere in the pleats of her cassis-coloured coat. "Hywel," she says, plucking it free and holding it aloft. She opens the text message. "Better get back, been gone ages — new calf's not sucking. Pick you up next Tuesday, about ten."

"*Tuesday?*" Rachel is miles away.

"Yeah — I'll drive us."

"Oh, yes . . . *riding.*" Rachel pulls the toggles on her hood tighter over her hair and screws up her face.

"Go on, it'll be fun," Tracy urges, her forehead creased in expectation.

"Yeah, all right then — why not?"

And watching a happy Tracy drive away, back to her bustling family, her purposeful life on the farm, Rachel feels more than a stab of envy.

"Come on boy," she calls to the dog, wanting his company to cancel out the resentment she feels about Tracy and the anxieties that always come when reminded of stables, farriers and horses. "Let's get you cleaned up — no way you're coming in dressed like that."

CHAPTER
NINETEEN

Monday morning and Our Lady of Muswell is empty. Jennifer, her name on the flower-arranging rota, has come via the flower stall with the fancy awning at the west side of Grand Avenue Park. Walked through the autumn drizzle, the three bundles of blooms swaddled in newspaper and cradled in her arms drip water on the toes of her knee-length boots, down the front of her cashmere-mix pencil skirt. Decanting the stinking water from last week's arrangements into a bucket, she wrinkles her nose and refills the containers with the fresh blocks of oasis she bought. The person whose turn this was last hadn't bothered with such sundries. *Cheapskates*. She will check afterwards, find out who it was. So sloppy, Jennifer tuts, knowing how far superior her displays will be; how her arrangements, because of her attention to detail, will survive the full week. She works quickly. The snip-snip of her scissors resonating through the hallowed hush of candlelight and what remains of yesterday's incense.

Sensing eyes, she looks up at the spot-lit serenity of the Virgin Mary. Her thoughts spinning again to the things she found when clearing out Donald's room earlier. Things she assumes he must have known about but as he's no longer around to ask, she can't be sure. Maybe they are why he barred her from his room, why he never left her, or asked for a divorce — it was obvious he was unhappy, had been for years. Jennifer knows how close he and Sarah were, maybe this secret, once confided, bound them tighter than ever. *Did you keep secrets?* Her silent question is directed at the life-size plaster figure with its disproportionately large pink hands, permanently pressed in prayer. *Is it such a terrible sin to want to protect your child?* After the initial shock of discovery, protective is how Jennifer is feeling, wishing she could make it up to Sarah, tell her that whatever it is she's done, she doesn't care.

No time for answers. Not from there. A swish of cassock from the shadows. The pious, echoing slap of leather soles on cold flagstone. Enough to make her look away from her working hands. Snip. *Too short.* She holds the ruined stem, a soft-headed chrysanthemum, tender as an infant's ear, out in her hand. An offering to Father O'Brady who, sliding into view, chooses to stand in an arrow-shaft of sun, wanting a heavenly light to illuminate his personage. Clever Father O'Brady.

"Mrs D'Villez," he chirrups in a voice as high as a girl's. "A fine job ye're doing there, if I may say." A Donegal accent, one she swears he hones for effect. The man can't have set foot on Irish soil since he started at the seminary. But she likes him and, without answering, smiles into the underdeveloped, sun-starved flesh of his face. "Quite a splendid job, indeed it is."

90

She sees his soft priest's hands press together, eternally in prayer like the Virgin Mary herself, looming ominous above their heads.

"A quiet mornin' for ye, indeed." He speaks again. Unrushed, pausing to breathe. "Although, any minute . . . there'll be the girls from St Thomas More . . . and you won't be able to hear yourself think." And he chuckles, that tuneful, untouched-by-life chuckle, before gliding away to see everything is in order for the Sacrifice of the Mass he will be administering later.

Jennifer thinks of the little children. The crocodile line they walk in from their primary school around the corner. Identical in blue gingham dresses, navy blazers and shiny shoes. Their socks pulled up to knees scabby from bumps and playground scrapes. Shame they need to grow up. She eyes the Virgin Mary again, her thoughts spinning to Sarah. St Thomas' was the Catholic school Jennifer and her sisters attended, and one she later enrolled her own daughter in. The uniform hasn't changed any more than their weekly visits here have done. Steered along the pavement by featureless teachers or a forgotten nun, clad in varying degrees of brown. She remembers an especially pretty child that she saw when she was working here, much like she is today. She has never seen the child since, although she takes special care to look out for her. A solemn-eyed thing. Fair hair, grown long and flowing down her back. The little mermaid — she gave her the name she once gave to her own child, in the years she had wanted to hear it. It had been like seeing Sarah all over again. Sarah, before she grew her spiky spine and started pushing her away.

Jennifer unwraps the second bundle of flowers from their newspaper. Unfurls Sarah's nineteen-year-old face and news of her abductor's imminent release. Gasps. Loud enough for Father O'Brady to turn, his voice slicing through the gloom, the polished wood smell and guttering candlelight. "You all right there, Mrs D'Villez?"

"Yes, yes. Everything's fine Father, thank you." She gathers herself and makes a show of resuming her floral displays.

"If y're sure?" His close-cropped head, haloed in the sputtering gloom is close to hers again. "I'm here — if ever ye need to talk." Too slow. He sees the photograph of the monster convicted for killing his wife and torturing and raping Jennifer's daughter. She braces herself for the spongy palm of the righteous, the feather-light touch on her upper arm. "Really, Mrs D'Villez, I am here, if ever ye need to talk."

She nods. It is all she can manage. The uncontrollable crumpling of her lips, the quivering of her mouth, she fears she is about to cry, so turns her head away. *I can't come to you for absolution. Not this time. Not with this. What burns a hole in my heart isn't my sin.* The images of what she found hidden in Donald's room burst like blisters against the thirty-three buttons meandering down the priest's stiff black soutane. Images that in their unearthing have inadvertently become hers.

92

"I know, Father," she says, churning the only conclusion she can make in her mind: how what she found must be handed over to those in the corporeal world; the wrongdoings they communicate will not wait for justice in the next. If only she could bring herself to do it.

CHAPTER
TWENTY

Rachel wakes from another nightmare-choked sleep to the sounds of high-pitched crying curling along the valley. She gets up to open her window and listen, her feet instantly cold against bare floorboards. Cadno hears it too. She wonders if it could be a fox as they wait for the cry to sound again, which it does — unsettling, ghostly, it bounces back to her through the dark. With no moon, all is a funereal-black her eyes can't penetrate and Rachel is glad to have the dog for company. Other nights, waking to noises, she can drift back to sleep telling herself they come from him. But not tonight. This is a different sound altogether and she squats to cuddle him, burying her neck into his bear-like coat.

The smell of him reminds her of Laura. Of the boiled-over oatmeal smell when she was first born. Of her mewling cries in the night, a sound not unlike the one she hears now. Always anxious for her child, and after Spencer banished the cot from their bedroom, she had to tiptoe along the dark of the landing to her baby's room. Sometimes staying for whatever remained of the night, sitting up in a rocking chair bought by her father to nurse his precious grandchild. Watching the dawn pick out the outlines of the furniture, the cuddly toys, the clutter of baby things. Then there were nights Rachel woke for no reason. The baby silent, the house quiet, Spencer sleeping by her side — his breath pummelling the hard skin of night, a sound that once identified, she couldn't think past. Lying on her back, heart racing, staring on to semi-blackness, her baby feeling too far away; she would slip out from beneath the duvet, forsaking her husband's sleepy smells and feet, to check their infant daughter was still breathing. Gripping the side of her cot and listening hard, a hand to the child's mouth, wanting her puff against her fingers, she watched her breathing beneath the baby blanket. Only then feeling calm.

This is how she kept Laura safe. This bundle handed over to her in the maternity ward with no instruction manual. Spencer, cross at waking alone, would stumble into the nursery come morning, find his wife slumped in the rocking chair and wake her up by telling her off. Shouting how it wasn't normal, that she was an obsessive. Telling her the baby was safe, they had the monitor tuned in beside the bed — what could possibly go wrong? Plenty, as things turned out.

CHAPTER
TWENTY-ONE

There is nothing in life more precious to Idris than his Beretta Silver Pigeon 687. The game-scene engraving, once clearly visible on its stock, has been caressed to a smooth plate of silver, and the heavily grained walnut has been buffed to a high shine by his over-attentive fingers. Finishing a rushed meal of charred sausages, he belches and tips himself out of the dip in his sagging sofa to retrieve his shotgun from its place of safety, propped up under a flap of mildewed curtain by the door. They sit together. The over-under and him. Side by side like an old married couple.

The Beretta once belonged to his father. His father's father before him. Decades old and worth a bob or two. Old in this case denoting something of quality, unlike the rest of the trash he inherited. But he had to wait for Wynn to die before the gun could properly be his. Being the youngest, his brothers had a slug at everything before him. Emyr. Rhys. Wynn. Nothing new there, his life has always been patched together from hand-me-downs; it's what makes him resentful. Like that record his da, who had a surprising penchant for musicals, would set to play under the wobbly stylus. The black plastic disc, tipped out of its monochrome sleeve, showing a funny-looking bird with a massive hooter who warbled on about some "Second-Hand Rose". That's me, he'd think, identifying immediately with the lyrics.

Barely twenty then, he had years of waiting to do. Only when Wynn died, a decade ago and years before his time like his other brothers, did Idris finally have a crack of the whip. There was never the need to include Beth. Younger by two years, she was only a girl, and girls didn't count — and besides, the stupid bitch had been missing for years. Shame of it was, by the time his turn came, his father's money had all been spent. His bank account sucked dry. The only thing liquid about Cwm Glas was the contents of the slurry tank, and Idris was forced to sell the farm. Breaking it down into top, middle and lower acres. Auctioning off outbuildings, farm house, tractor, mini-digger and baler. The best of the livestock. Not that this was enough, still up to his neck in debt, threatening letters flooded in from the bank and receivers. All he could keep, aside from the barn and a few boggy acres, was his father's crumbling cottage. Rundown, draughty and damp. No one wanted it. The poky hovel where his brothers dumped The Bastard when he could no longer work the farm. Like a broken-down carthorse put out to pasture, except there were no animals at Cwm Glas given such idyllic retirement packages. Animals that couldn't pay their way either by lambing, calving, or producing a decent crop of eggs, were unceremoniously shot. Left out on the hill for the buzzard and crow, their skeletons plucked clean, the bones scattered.

Shame they couldn't have done this to The Bastard. Instead they had to ply him with drink and hope that, with the little resistance he had for the stuff, it wouldn't take long. Taking it in turns to visit each afternoon, laden with discounted booze and standing on the threshold wringing their cattle-calloused hands in anticipation the devil had dropped by and taken him. Revenge for pulling them out of school before they had the chance to learn anything, do anything which might have opened up a different future from the one he had planned. For yoking them into positions which ensured they spent their lives as he had done, hock-deep in cow dung, their nostrils filled with the sweet-sour rot of silage, waging war with the weather. Lives scored into years, cut through with chores: sheds to clean, barbed-wire fences to fix, hay to gather, bullocks to test, lime to spread. The liver-fluke and maggot. No wonder there wasn't time for girls.

And anyway, what would they have done with them? Girls. They knew nothing about relationships. Who'd want what his mam and da had anyway, with their separate rooms? She, condescending to give him sex on his birthdays. It never took long, and was noiseless, but Idris knew. And when the tradition stopped, it was Beth who was sent to him, shivering under her nightdress along the draughty landing. Until she started to bleed. Idris snarls into the memory and wonders again how it was that The Bastard lasted so many years. Pickled, he used to think, like the jars of eggs and baby onions his mam preserved and stacked in the larder come Christmas. Cold, dead eyes, like his father's, floating in a substance the colour of the un-flushed toilet bowl come morning.

So the fate of Cwm Glas was sealed years before his brothers dumped their father in the cottage where Idris now lives. It was why, when Idris finally had his turn, there was no farm, and he was required to set himself up in the haulage business. The money from the sale of the main house and the two hundred or so acres of grazing bought him his dark blue streamline Scania V8 and compelled him into chalking out his delivery route. Printing a run of business cards. Advertising his name in the Yellow Pages and taking out small ads in local rags. Not that Idris ever had much of a name. His shoddy timekeeping quickly saw to that. Word that he wasn't to be relied upon travelled fast around here, forcing him further and further west. Still, he's nothing better to do with his time with the cattle gone and only the last remaining ewes and a handful of chickens to keep, his two border collies are no bother. Chained down in the wet-nosed yard, what's it to him if they never taste the freedom of the soft Welsh hillsides they were bred for?

A lone wolf these days, Idris is able to set off on a delivery at the drop of a hat. No need for B&Bs or motels either. Sleeping overnight in the cabin. It isn't a bad life. He even gets his hands on the odd woman. Idris, concentrating again on the shotgun, pulls it into his lap. Heavy as a three-month-old infant, he coddles it with a tenderness shown to no living thing. Stroking it from muzzle to back-strap, he eyes the head-and-shoulders photograph of his father that slipped to the floor from its nail in the wall years ago. Cockeyed in his plastic frame, it shows the bull of his neck buttoned down into a starched white collar, his chest puffed up in proud-blue blazer. An item of clothing Idris remembers being brushed down and put on for the Annual Llandafen Show. Cattle judger. Rosette dispenser. Ale swigger. Calf slayer. Sheep doctor. Crude obstetrics with flocks and herds. There wasn't much The Bastard hadn't seen. There wasn't much he wouldn't do. Years spent working the slaughterhouse in Wernadawen equipping him with the necessary, after his own father died, to take up the helm and run the farm.

Idris extends a leg and points with a toe. Alarmingly agile for his immense girth. He kicks out at his father's head, making the photograph slump further into the years of dust and debris down behind the TV. His thoughts swivel to the picture he keeps of his mam by his bed. The only photograph of her to survive. She is very young in it, far younger than when she had him, and because she was dead before he'd properly grown, he felt he never really knew her. His mother's death was even less of an event to his father than if one of his prized Jacob Four Horns had keeled over in the cankered sheepfold. Now all that remains of Nerys Tudor is her youngest son and a wardrobe full of dresses. Dresses he likes to bury his head amidst, wanting what remains of her smell. A smell he thinks he might find sometimes, even if it is only a remembered one. Rekindled by the slappers he invites into the leather-seated compartment of his Scania truck when the sun goes down. He might not be able to picture his mother's face independently of the photograph but he has the scent of her at his fingertips. The material of her clothes, as soft as the skin on the undersides of her arms, on the insides of her thighs. Not that he recalls ever being invited to touch her there. This is his imagination telling him. Based on the limited experience he's had with the opposite sex, the boundaries of mother and woman merging as they do, Idris is often confused. So confused, he needs to immerse himself in the silkiness of her clothes to release her spirit. Often going upstairs when the urge comes, to lie on the slippery eiderdown draped in one of her frocks, breathing back his kipper breath.

Idris shifts about in the crater his body has carved out of the settee. He might have to go and finish the job he started earlier and, rising to his feet, tugs the picture he keeps in his head of the tasty piece living in his old barn up the stairs behind him. Perhaps — the treads groan in protest at his lopsided weight — he should take her something soon. Something to thank her for the pleasure she is about to give him.

CHAPTER
TWENTY-TWO

Don't ask me how all this started. I suppose I'm just getting to that age and I always did have a weakness for pretty girls. About the only thing me and my father had in common, as it happens. And the way they go around — pissed out of their heads and dressed in next to nothing — well, they make it easy for me, don't they?

Take tonight for instance. Yes, I was out, driving around and singing along to whatever was on the radio, so you could say I was on the lookout for something. Breathing back the smell of my recent supper. A diversion from my usual and a knee-jerk decision, stopping at the drive-thru McDonald's for a double cheeseburger and extra-large fries that I wolfed down behind the wheel on my approach into town.

Then I saw her, on her own she was, stumbling drunk along the promenade in high-wedge heels, the sea air knotting up her long blonde hair.

"You all right there, love? Where's your mates?" I asked, turning the radio down and pulling up alongside. "Can I give you a lift anywhere?"

And she gets in, doesn't she, can you believe it? Giving me a great big smile, she opens up the passenger side and climbs into the seat. I was almost too stunned to say anything, I couldn't believe my luck. I don't think even my father found it that easy to pick them up, which pleases me no end. From what I remember, he had to spend a load of money on them first, promise them all sorts to get them to go with him. But with me it's different, they seem to trust me; I don't need to give them anything. All I do is offer them somewhere out of the cold.

"Put yer seatbelt on, love," I told her, not letting on how surprised I was. "To be safe."

CHAPTER
TWENTY-THREE

A discussion on *Woman's Hour* throws Jennifer back to the first time Sarah brought Spencer home. Her A Levels finished, she turned her nose up at university, insisting she enrol on a horticultural course at Watling Tech instead. Donald's influence, Jennifer sniffs; she wanted Sarah to get a degree, she had brains as well as looks, the girl could have done anything.

She supposes the good-looking Spencer, already in his mid-twenties with a string of letters after his name, had been a consolation prize. Of course Donald took an instant dislike to him, Jennifer knew he would, no man would have been good enough for his precious daughter. He was suspicious of Spencer's motives from the off, saying he was far too stiff for his fun-loving Sarah. Encouraging her, in what was left of the evening once Spencer had gone, to: "Drop him and meet a lad her own age. Have some fun." He kept saying it, as if fun was something that had been in short supply in Sarah's young life.

Jennifer remembers the row, it rattled on for hours. The two of them, sitting side-by-side in bed not touching, the subject of their quarrel lying in an adjacent room. It had been during this row that

Donald, no doubt imagining all sorts from the descriptions Spencer gave of his sterile, white-coated world, announced his desire to buy Sarah the florist shop in Northampton.

"I'm doing it," he said when Jennifer made noises to the contrary. "To make sure she has something of her own."

Jennifer tried dissuading him, saying it was all very well Sarah helping grow vegetables and flowers in the garden, but this was his retirement fund he was thinking of gambling.

"I'm not *thinking*, Jennifer, I'm *doing* — I've made my mind up." Donald was adamant. "It's my money — you said I could do whatever I wanted with it."

Of course this was before Sarah's highly publicised abduction made her famous. Before her face was sent into orbit by every two-bit rag. Not the fame she would have wanted — suddenly claimed as public property and put under the spotlight. She tried going back to the florist shop, wanting to make a go of the business. She lasted five days. Donald admired her integrity, said anyone else would have milked the media interest and revelled in the free publicity that fattened out her order book, even if sales were only from rubberneckers. Unlike Spencer, who seemed to very much enjoy his snatch at the limelight. Not the one plagued by nightmares and panic attacks, Donald said it was easy for him; normality restored the moment Sarah moved back into his house on Heron Way. Jennifer has to agree, from what Sarah told them, he barely skipped a day's research and had no problem motivating himself to make the drive to the Hatfield Campus, leaving their daughter to stare at his newly decorated walls and not daring to step outside. It was what Spencer and Sarah rowed about when they came for lunch one Sunday. Sarah, citing the octopus he scrutinised all day long in his lab. "They've more heart than you," she had cried, her own breaking. "You're right," his voice callous. "They've got three."

Jennifer stands to look at what she can see of the garden in the fading afternoon light: the earth-filled dormant beds bordering the lawn, the spaces choked with deadened stalks and weather-blown stems that, stark and starved of colour, make it hard to imagine summer again. The only glory remaining is the red from the Virginia creeper that scales the walls of the house. November's gift, fading now. She stares at Donald's shed, its warped wooden door — that the idiot Mr Antonelli didn't close properly — banging in the wind. The swing Donald put up for Sarah on her seventh birthday. Jennifer sees her as the little girl she was, her white-socked legs kicking higher and higher.

Turning from the window, the faraway lights of Canary Wharf jerking into life on the tangerine-tinged horizon, Jennifer sits back at her desk with a jolt. Checking that the things she found in Donald's room are still safely hidden in the back of the drawer, she toys again with the idea of destroying them. She doesn't understand what is stopping her, but something is. The feeling it is all her fault, perhaps, that she is a bad mother and her flaws brought this about? Wanting the distraction, she takes out the bundle of Spencer's letters, choosing one containing photographs of Laura sitting astride a pony. A beautiful picture, Laura giggling and happy, sharing her milk-toothed smile with the camera. So like your mummy, Jennifer thinks, her lips puckering with emotion at the granddaughter she doesn't see.

Deadly places, stable yards, Jennifer always thought it, and as things turned out for Sarah, she was proved right. She hated Pinkton Grange. The stench of the yellowing muck heap and vagrant flocks of chickens pecking about her ankles when she accompanied Donald up the M1 to meet the big bay mare Sarah had sweet-talked him into dipping further into his savings for. She could have understood her daughter's infatuation with riding if like her father she'd grown up on a thousand-acre farm in Quebec, because on the rare occasion Donald did speak of his upbringing, it was only to talk of the horses. To say how he and his brothers were set to work in the low-lying prairies of wheat and flax on their father's plantation, stories that clipped and curtailed, left Jennifer to build her own pictures of what it must have been like for him as a boy.

Jennifer tried to overcome her fear of horses, but she wasn't like Donald. The closest she had got to them was a time she was taken as a child to watch the Changing of the Guard and one slipped on wet cobbles, sending a Household Cavalryman plummeting to the ground. A sickening sight, which, in spite of it being nearly fifty years ago, she has never forgotten. In the same way she never forgot the trauma of her mother dying when she was barely ten. It is why nothing has ever been able to hurt her in the same way again. Why she became so cold inside, she excuses herself. The shock of her own mother's death was why she was inept as a wife, useless as a mother.

The image she keeps of her younger self isn't one she wants to see, but since Donald's death and the shocking discovery she made in his room, it comes to take her by the hand, as that long ago, darkly-dressed relative had done the day of her mother's funeral. Forcing her to stand on tiptoe to look again into her mother's coffin, at her closed-over lids held down by silver coins. Jennifer tilts forward in her chair. Rubs at the skin of her calves and feels again the tight new elastic of those frilly-edged socks that were bought especially for the occasion. What happened to them after the funeral, she has no idea, but she knows that she was never to wear them again. Same goes for the little black velvet coat with its heart-shaped buttons, that was as soft as the pelt of the poor dead mole she found flushed out on to the lawn in those freakish autumn storms, the day they dropped her mother into the earth in Our Lady's churchyard. When her sorrow was as raw and chafing as the wind had been against her baby-smooth, tear-streaked cheeks.

Looking down at the photograph she holds of her granddaughter, it's a mystery why Spencer was given custody of the child, and friendly as she is with her ex-son-in-law, he has never divulged what it was Sarah did. Jennifer is sure it had something to do with his decision to relocate to America and is in no doubt that Donald was privy to the details. The hours he and

Sarah spent together in that room of his; she's bound to have confided in him. Whatever it was, it must have been something pretty unforgivable, but with Donald dead and Sarah who knows where, Jennifer doesn't suppose she will find out now. Secrets, secrets, she sighs, her mind weighted by the ones she found lurking in her husband's old room that, since unearthing, she has been forced to drag around with her, engendering a feeling of vulnerability that disturbs her more than she dares admit.

Sweet smells from warm baking waft up the stairs. Competing with her memories, they make her stomach rumble. *What's that bloody woman doing now?* Jennifer, switching the radio off, steps on to the landing to call down: "Mrs Pepper? Mrs Pepper?"

A second or two later, the familiar scarf-clad head dips out of the kitchen. "Yes?"

"There's no need, really, whatever it is you're cooking —" Jennifer grips the balustrade, the undersides of her ringed fingers pushing hard into the wooden handrail.

"It's only a fruit cake, Mrs D'Villez. I used ground almonds, just as you like it." The woman's face, waxy and pale, is tilted upwards. Her eyes unreadable behind the thick lenses of her glasses.

"You have it," Jennifer snaps. "*Please.* Take it home with you. I'm sure you've a family you can feed it to. I haven't." *As you damn well know.*

She goes back inside her study, slams the door, shutting out the deliciousness. With her hollow insides a grumbling volcano, she sits back at her desk. The woman only does it to be kind, too stupid to deliberately set out to upset her. She feels a twinge, replays the conversation in her head and winces. It is almost enough to make her go downstairs and apologise. Almost.

CHAPTER
TWENTY-FOUR

Rachel waits until the tapered dagger of sunlight reaches the leg of her dressing table before getting up. She pulls on clean jeans and a snug-fitting polo neck, brushes her hair and tugs it back in a band. The dog shifts on the bed, poised for her say so. "Come on, boy." It's all he needs, springing up to follow her down the stairs.

After her daily habitual trawl through the internet for updates on Blundell's release and satisfying herself that there aren't any, she remembers there are bills to post and calls to Cadno who leaps up and bounds to the door. Head down, her fingers fiddling with the lock, Rachel looks up and into what has thrown a fat, black shadow over her.

"Brought you eggs." A big face engrained with dirt, close to hers. "They're layin' well for time o' year."

Startled, she scratches the scar on her wrist. "Are they? That's very kind." She takes the muck-encrusted box and steps away, anxious to put distance between her and Idris Tudor. Her foot slips on a thick wadding of wet geranium leaves, making her heart flip. Righting herself, she hears the steady thrum of an engine and sees his big, blue-fronted haulage lorry choking the lane.

"I'm off on a job," he says, as if this is supposed to impress. "Pick up in Swansea today and a drop in Somerset tomorrow."

"Long way to go." She bends to lay the eggs on top of a wooden barrel rigged up under the guttering to catch rain water.

"Aye. A fair stretch, but I'm used to it now."

"Business good then, is it?" It is only out of politeness, her instinct screaming at her not to encourage the creep.

"Keeps me well enough."

Keen to set out on her morning walk, her dog taking an embarrassing amount of interest in the weirdo's trousers, she knows she needs to remove herself.

"See you found your dog then?" he says.

"Yes. Yes, I did . . . well, safe trip and all that," she says with feigned cheeriness, and circumventing his unnerving bulk, heads out to the lane.

"Want a lift?" His piggy eyes find her from beneath a singular arch of shaggy orange eyebrow. "Village, is it?" He points at the mail she holds in her hand.

"Er . . . *a lift?* — No." She shakes her head, alarmed by his suggestion. "I like the walk."

"For your figure, is it?" His stare is unflinching. She feels its fingers on her skin: crawling, cold; foraging under her layers.

"*What?*" She doesn't think she heard him right.

"Not that you need worry there — you got a very tidy figure for a woman your age."

"*For a woman my age?*" She echoes, incredulous, and wants to cut wherever this is going off at the knees. "Thanks for the eggs, really, but I need to catch the post."

"So you don't want a lift?"

"No, I don't want a lift." As firm as she can be.

"Right you are then."

And he's gone, as suddenly as he appeared. Surprisingly nimble the way he swings himself up into his cab, pulls over the seatbelt and accelerates away. Rachel, relieved to be alone in the silence of occasional birdsong, is suddenly conscious of her heart, timpani-loud in her chest.

"Come on, fella," she calls to Cadno who, wagging keen, pushes his head like a little pony into the collar and extending lead she fishes from her anorak pocket.

After posting her letters, she heads for the hills and stopping to look how far she's climbed, she lifts her gaze from her shadow that, lengthening like the pointer on a sundial, marks out the bluntness of days in this headlong slide into winter. She sees the village of Bryngwyn, static under the perpetual motion of sky — which today is a purple cushion of cloud with bright fields belted below it. From up here, the houses resemble beads thrown haphazardly against a blanket of browns and greens and she can make out the raw blue curve of river as it bends, supple as a ribbon, in and out past the plain-faced chapel and redundant primary school with its wind-worked bell calling ghosts of children past from playground to classroom.

Breathing hard, she focuses on the way ahead. Going to make her fit doing this every day, she thinks, pulling a face into the slanting wind. Her goal is the highest dry-stone wall. Ancient in its skin of lichen, most of it nothing more than a snaking spine under the moss-rich grassland, the boulders themselves are only visible in parts. She will find a section of it she can lay claim to, a throne within the stones, carved out by centuries of rain. A spot with a crippled blackthorn tree, licked flat by the tongue of the wind, the view from up there will be her prize.

The dog alerts her. A dark wet shape, stretched out in the grass. She thinks it must be a deer, registering its matted fur and counting four split hooves. But something is wrong. It's a black cow. Her immense flank — a rising wall of muscle — stands only yards away. Her head pulled back, her neck taut, she is crying at the sky. A terrible scene unfolds and Rachel calls for Cadno who, sensing danger, is quick to her side. A stillborn calf. The fruitless labour of a chilly morning. The cow's inflated udder, pink as the rubber gloves that hang by her sink. This mother is in pain. Bellowing her haunting, almost human sound. Rachel feels her palpable distress as it is offered up to an indifferent cloth of milky cloud.

Her mother lost babies. Both before and after Rachel. Remembering the images cataloguing these losses is as easy as flicking back through the pages in one of her illustrated children's books. The triangle of blood left behind on the seat of a chair, seeping through the material of her mother's skirt. The blue flashing lights at midnight. The steaming mugs of sickly sweet tea. The gush of aunts — women in heeled boots and silk scarves — who took it in turns to leave their own families to come and hold their sister's hand. That once the directories of platitudes had been exhausted, would sit cross-legged on the floor drinking coffee, twirling their hair around ringed fingers and staring at the clock.

All except one — her favourite: Alice. With her ice-blue eyes reflecting the multi-coloured rainbow worlds of bluebirds fluttering from her ears. Whose dark red hair was as magically shiny as the photograph of a liver-chestnut in her *Children's Guide to Horses*. Alice took her out on trips. With the Archer's theme dwindling into the afternoon play, she would comb her fringe, apply fresh lipstick, and emerge from the downstairs cloakroom clapping her hands and making her armfuls of bangles jingle like the opening and closing of a cutlery drawer.

They would catch the bus up west, where Alice would buy her niece unsuitable clothes and later, her husband's credit card warm to the touch, say, "Come on kid, I'm gasping." Code for: let's go find a spicy-smelling barista bar and share handmade patisseries.

"When you're older, we'll ask Uncle Pete to drive us to the seaside," Alice promised above the sound of hissing doors, as they bumped along side-by-side on the upper deck, watching London skimming by. But she was happy to be alone with lovely Alice, whose warm vanilla scent and conker hair made men turn to look at her in the street. Drawn to her like a magnet, to her wide, silver-buckled belts and aubergine nail polish that made her finger-ends look like the iridescent beetles Rachel would find in the garden. An exotic creature, it was impossible to imagine her coming from the same place as Rachel's mother.

The frequency of the small hard bump under her mother's clothes that formed and fell away, lessened over the years, no matter how hard her mother pressed her hands to it and prayed. Until all talk of a brother or sister stopped, along with the visits from the aunts. She has a clear memory of herself as a child, squatting in the dark of the landing in her pyjamas, watching her parents moving around the lighted kitchen. Her father uncorking wine. The tinkling sound as he poured it into glasses. And tiring of it being two and not three, she learnt to feign nightmares. Yelling out in the dark so her father would rush upstairs to rescue his precious child from the monsters she told him were under the bed. Tenderly pushing her arms into her dressing gown, he would press her to his bristly cheek and carry her blinking into the over-bright kitchen and her mother's distress. To share night-time feasts of overdone toast. Black crumbs on teeth, on fingers, speckling the front of her dressing gown. Toast smothered with the barely-sweet marmalade one of her aunts had made, to try and mask the burnt taste of bitterness.

Rachel counts on her fingers and realises she hasn't seen Alice since her and Spencer's wedding. Uncle Pete's job took them to New York the following autumn and although they've spoken sporadically over the phone, Rachel never had plans to visit. Her aunt was kind in the months following the abduction, but because Rachel didn't feel able to share the true depravity of her eleven-day ordeal, she didn't gain Alice's sympathy. Alice eventually lost patience, saying Rachel couldn't hide away in Muswell Hill for ever. Perhaps she should write and tell her aunt how proactive she's been since her father died. Spurred into action by news of her abductor's release and the threat of unwanted press attention. But perhaps not. How would she explain her father's decision to leave her all his money? That she's used it to buy a place in the middle of nowhere and hasn't even told her mother where she is.

CHAPTER
TWENTY-FIVE

Working out in the fresh air has given Dai an appetite. Seeing he has little in his fridge, he decides to drive the forty minutes to Llandafen. Tesco will be open and it will give him the excuse to fetch fish and chips.

Friday night and Bowen's Chippy is heaving. Condensation runs like sweat down the huge windows that look out on to the wet pavement. It's cold tonight, the sky full of stars, but in here, amidst the steam and frying smells, he is way overdressed. After several minutes, waiting in line to place his order, Dai removes his coat. He asks, when his turn comes, for a large battered haddock and chips, his choice given to the crown of Tomos Bowen's daughter's greasy yellow head. To the smattering of whiteheads on the fine bone of her forehead and her pale, scribbling, pencil-holding hand.

It's nice in here, nice enough to sit inside and wait for his cooked-to-order supper that he will eat in the car before heading home. So he does, positioning himself on the cream padded seat that runs the length of the takeaway outlet, salivating under the weight of hot salt and vinegar smells and staring at the sea-blue tiles that cover the opposite wall. Fish and chips weren't really Elsie's thing. She would only agree to him having them on rare occasions. Fastidiously healthy, anything fried was always a no-no, especially takeaways. Although he does have a vivid memory of them buying chips and eating them out of brown paper bags in Tenby. Christmas time, just as it was getting dark, there were ropes of fairy lights, their colours reflected in the sheen of her long dark hair. They held hands as they sat watching the sun quiver and drop beyond the rim of the horizon, listening to the drag and draw of waves on the sand, long after the stars came out.

Elsie wouldn't have objected too fiercely to this place. Fresh and clean, Tomos Bowen certainly maintains a high standard. Conscious he is staring at a young couple being handed their packets of cod and chips over the counter, Dai lunges for a copy of the *Sun* for something to do.

A granular photograph of a pretty blonde-haired woman fills the page. Wendy Denny, the banner says, missing after a night out with friends in Westburn-on-Sea. Police fear her disappearance could be linked to Issy Lake, another woman from the town who was murdered earlier this month. She looks so young. Dai, sucking back his breath, reads on to clarify. Twenty. Barely more than a kid. Her poor family. He scans the editorial, is told Wendy is studying for a business degree at the local college and that she loves clubbing at weekends. It terrifies him to think of the wickedness out there, the wickedness he used to deal with. These girls — the ones who leave themselves wide open by gallivanting about in next to nothing, three sheets to the wind — they haven't a hope of defending themselves if they get into trouble. He's not saying all men are animals, but when you give them the wrong signals . . . he is thinking of the disturbing images given too often in televised news reports, showing debauched youngsters running amok in town centres up and down the country. And Dai, not for the first time, is grateful he didn't have a daughter, a son was enough to worry about; although if he had daughters, he can't help but think he'd have brought them up to have more self-respect. Young women of today don't appear to have any of the modesty of his generation. He doesn't mean to sound like a stuffed shirt, but they hardly help themselves, do they? No, types like these, he thinks, scanning the photographs in the paper again, he would almost go so far as to say it serves them right — that if you play with fire by cavorting around with everything on show, then you're going to get burnt.

His order is called and, replacing the newspaper back on the pile, he steps up to the counter. He looks into the dead-fish eyes of the Bowen girl as she counts out the money he hands over in exchange for his warm parcel. This is hardly the environment for a young woman either, he sniffs, thanking her. The question: boozing it up with your mates or selling fried food? He isn't sure which is the lesser of two evils.

CHAPTER
TWENTY-SIX

After more than a week of rain, Rachel wakes to a metal-blue frost and startling sunshine. Running a basin-full of tepid water, she washes and dresses quickly. Tracy rang the previous evening to remind her they were going riding and she needs to take the dog out before she leaves. It will be way too dark by the time she comes home. In these stunted days, with so much to cram in while the light lasts, she must remember to empty the woodburner too.

Rachel never sleeps or goes out long enough for the fire to die completely. The art of fire-making is something she mastered within weeks of arriving. Opening the vents to allow the flames to bite, closing them last thing to keep the embers hot, so it takes little to relight each morning. Kind of Hywel to bring her all that wood. Dry and hard, she stacked the brick-sized logs neatly into the nook of the low-roofed woodshed that squats adjacent to her house, and enjoyed the contented feeling it gave her when she stood back to admire her handiwork.

After making her usual check of the internet, flicking through the news on MSN for any updates on Blundell's release date — this checking and rechecking is something she does compulsively, several times a day — she closes the lid of her laptop and darts outside in her slippers. With her breath puncturing the cold, she unclips the field gate and feels the frosted grass crackle beneath her. She empties the tray of ash and the breeze blows it back in her eyes, blinding her. When she opens them again, it is on to Idris Tudor. His insidious bulk blocking out the sun. Equally shocking is the huge woolly, speckle-faced ewe he has tucked under his arm. Paralysed with fear, she gives Rachel her unreadable tiger-striped eye.

"To keep the grass down." Idris, the first to speak, strides past into Rachel's field as if he still owns it, and drops the sheep to the ground. The animal, realising its freedom, bolts away to bleat a protest into the bitter morning air. She watches it, bewildered, sees its fleece wobbling like a lanolin-laced jelly. Idris turns away, the crunch of gravel and he is back at his Toyota pickup and trailer which block the lane. Then a series of violent skittering sounds, hooves thrashing metal, as a second ewe fights to evade capture from within the tight confines of his trailer. Idris is stronger, proficient in the pinning and restraining, he has the creature under control in seconds.

"Come 'ere, you bugger. Come 'ere," he shouts, tugging it towards him and slipping its wriggling mass into the crook of his arm with mindboggling ease. And Rachel, like the sheep he brings as some strange present, doesn't have the means to challenge. All she can do is stare as he dumps the second ewe in the same way he did the first, reties her gate and disappears without another word.

What a freak, she thinks in the aftershock. Sinister, the way he keeps turning up under the pretext of something or other. When he's around it reminds her how alone she is. How remote her home is. There is something about him — the sheer facility suggested by his size that makes her feel more vulnerable than she might ordinarily do. Because no one would know. Tracy and Hywel aren't far away, but they wouldn't be able to hear her scream. This worries her. It isn't as if she encourages him, always careful to keep her responses curt. Not that he seems to get the hint.

Later, in her whitewashed outbuilding, Rachel is still unsure whether she should be going today. Having not set foot in a stable yard since Blundell, she isn't sure how she'll react being amidst horses again. She wishes Tracy hadn't put her on the spot, that she'd been given more time to think, but it's too late to back out now. Sipping her way through a large mug of instant, she rifles through bags of stuff she hasn't bothered to unpack. Stuff she hasn't room for inside but can't throw away, just in case. It stinks of cat piss in here, but she'll put up with it for the sake of finding her jodhpurs and hard hat.

She finds more than she bargains for, climbing the stepladder and stretching up to the top shelf that runs the length of her outbuilding. Along with her college horticulture books, her riding manuals — the unearthing of which she stores away in her mind for future reference — her hands land on something heavy and stiff. She hauls it towards her. Sees it is a huge, leather-bound *Atlas of the World*, so thick with bird droppings it can't have been touched for years. Leaning her weight against the uppermost bars of the stepladder to look at it more closely, the pages, sticky with dead flies and cobwebs, fall open like a natural hair-parting. Two rectangular photographs drop out and she climbs down to retrieve them. The first is black-and-white, its edges faded, the centre showing a sharp shadow definition. Mid nineteen-fifties, she guesses, looking at a picture of a little girl and boy peering out from beneath matching tartan sunhats. Bare legged in cotton shorts, they can be no more than seven and sit astride a pair of fairground carousel horses. So serious, she thinks, gazing into their faces, reading their expressions, wanting their story. Who are they? So endearing, yet so solemn. It bothers her. The second photograph bothers her more. In it, the same sweet little girl — slightly older, the image in colour — is clutching a tiny piebald dog, but again there is no smile. Wearing a white cotton dress, short socks and those old-fashioned brown leather T-bar sandals all post-war children had, her head is dipped to the camera and her soft, light-brown hair feathered by sunlight.

The atlas, propped against the top rung of the ladder, springs open again of its own accord. It shows a route the hardened adventurer might take through India, China, Mongolia, and on into what was then the USSR. The evidence of little fingerprints catches her eye. They scuttle like mad beetles up through the

Himalayas, the Plateau of Tibet, the Tarim Pendi. Over mountain ranges and vast floating lakes. The terrain, identified in colours turning from green to beige to impenetrable yellow, is set against the artificial blue of water. The huge pages are spliced through with strident red print. Scar-like scores showing where roads might be. Are these fingerprints made by the children in the photographs? Is this where they intended to go? Skimming through pages that aren't clumped together, she moves forward into Europe, to eventually unstick Great Britain. Here she finds a stapled facsimile of sheet music. Three pages of age-bleached shiny material. "The Trumpet Serenade", the music heralds in its weakened, grey print. The title set in amongst pencilled notes. Prompters put there by the teacher to jog the student player's memory of the single Bb, where and where not to breathe. Rachel can read a little music and so follows the notes travelling along the stave. Up and over the dotted crotchet, the detached quaver, taking the designated rests for scrambled breathing that are counted into the breaks in the bar. "Allegro ma non troppo," she says, deciding how this is unlikely to be Schubert's instruction; for the grouping of notes in simple duple time.

Tracy arrives bang on ten. Rachel hears her tyres on the gravel just as she is locking the door and shoving her feet down into a pair of stiffened jodhpur boots that crackle when she walks. The red Defender smells of wet dog and lanolin along with an underlying sweetness akin to rotting fruit. Not smells she likes. Things her urbanised nostrils are not accustomed to and ones she doubts Tracy notices any more.

The seat, beneath the anorak she can't bear to take off, is filthy. Countless chocolate and crisp wrappers clog the footwell and the dashboard is thick with animal hair. Tracy offers a half-hearted apology to Rachel who sits bolt upright, clutching her riding hat in her lap.

"Honestly, it's fine," she reassures. "You guys live on a farm, this is your business."

As passenger, it is her job to open gates. Tiptoeing through mud, using thickened clumps of reeds as stepping stones, she stands with the wind whipping her hair waiting for Tracy to drive through so she can secure the gate behind them. Unsure if the boots, not worn for years, are waterproof, Rachel daren't risk standing in water. She doesn't care what she must look like to Tracy, sitting up behind the wheel — the proverbial city girl, glaringly out of place in this rural backwater. She wonders why Tracy hasn't asked what it is she's doing here — she doesn't strike Rachel as someone who is backward in coming forward — although she's grateful she hasn't, forever fearful her true identity could be exposed.

"It's odd," Rachel says as the Land Rover bumps its way over potholes and rocks. The indicator still ticking, they have taken a left off the wriggly B-road and are following signs that read: Llyn-Y-Fan Trekking Centre.

"What is?" Tracy asks, eyes glued on the way ahead.

"I found some stuff in my outbuilding this morning — it isn't mine. An atlas, some sheet music and a couple of old photos."

"Not yours, you say?"

"No. And it's odd because I'm the first person to live there — aren't I?" Rachel has her nose pressed to the cold glass of the passenger window. Fascinated by the serrated spine of mountain that, usually way off in the distance, is looming so close, she feels she could reach out and touch it.

"Well yes, you are." Tracy hesitates, then slamming the brake, cleverly avoids a startlingly white goose and clutch of flapping hens that appear from nowhere. "But remember, the place was Idris' until quite recently. You knew Cwm Glas belonged to his family, didn't you?" She waits for Rachel's nod. "Well, when his brother died and Idris inherited, he was so up to his neck in debt, he had to sell up."

"How long you and Hywel had the farm then?"

"Crikey . . . must be going on nine years." Tracy takes a second, counts on her fingers. "Yeah, wow — nine years. Llew and Tom were five when we came here."

"So it was Idris who carved the place up?" Rachel, remembering the words of the surly telecoms engineer.

"That's right. He sold us Cwm Glas and the majority of the land straight off, I think. For some reason he kept hold of your place a while longer, selling it to developers last spring."

"Is it very different — Tŷ Haf?" Rachel asks.

"Not from the outside, but the inside, yes, of course. For a start they put an upper floor in. Before, I remember there was this hayloft, like a half-layer upstairs."

127

"A half-layer?" Rachel doesn't understand.

"I don't know how to describe it really — like your upstairs is now but only running half the length of it. It had a little wooden ladder taking you up."

"Sounds nice."

"Dangerous." Tracy snaps back her neck. "Our Llew had a fall, broke his collar bone playing in there."

"Ouch, that is nasty," Rachel says.

"*Kids*," Tracy gives the word as though it says it all. "You can't tell them anything."

"The photos I found were of children. Taken in the fifties — a boy and a girl. Could they be related to Idris, d'you think?"

"I don't know," Tracy shrugs. "You could try asking Dai. He's quite the fountain on local history."

"Dai? Dai Jones — yeah I know. Nice chap, lives in the long white house at the end of the lane?"

"That's him. Was great friends with Idris' sister apparently and yes, come to think of it, he did tell me they used to play in your barn when they were kids."

"Did they? That's interesting." Rachel, nodding, thinks of the funny little heart-shaped carvings she found in the upper beams of her house. "I'll ask him when I get the chance."

"Be a love, would you?" Tracy waves a hand over Rachel's knees. "Get us one of them chocolate éclairs — they're in the glove compartment."

Rachel flicks the casing open, slides her gloved hand into the open-mouthed bag. Oven-hot from the car heater, the toffee sinks under her fingers. "You know that Idris keeps coming round."

"Does he?" Tracy raises her eyebrows, interested.

"Yeah. Just turns up out of the blue. He brought me two sheep this morning." Rachel passes her the sweet.

"Ta. I love these — have to keep them in the car otherwise the boys get them." Tracy untwists the wrapper between teeth and hand. "Idris — two sheep? Get away."

"He said something about keeping the grass down."

"I suppose they will," Tracy says, chewing. "But if you were worried about that we could have put some of ours in, we could always do with the extra grazing."

"No — I didn't ask him for them. Like I said, he just turned up. He's always badgering me. The other day he came with eggs again — I don't even bloody well like eggs."

"He don't usually give nothing away," Tracy says half to herself, sucking her teeth. "What have you said to him?"

"*Nothing*. Crikey, I don't encourage him if that's what you're getting at." Rachel does her best to ignore the mildly accusatory tone of Tracy's question. "Honestly, Tracy, I don't want him bothering me — he gives me the creeps."

"Idris?" Tracy laughs. "He's all right. Probably just taken a bit of a shine to you . . ."

Rachel suspects Tracy is about to say she should be flattered, but changes her mind. "Well, I wish he'd just stay away."

"D'you want Hywel to have a word?"

"And say what?"

"That you don't want him calling round."

"I don't know — will it make a difference?"

"Could try?"

"Makes me look a bit soppy though, wouldn't it?"

"Get us another of those would you," Tracy says and Rachel giggles. "You can have one, it won't spoil your figure."

"I'm all right, really."

"You cold?" Tracy asks through more chewing, the sweetness of toffee on her breath. "Say, I can shove the heating up."

"Crikey, no," Rachel assures. "It's dead cosy in here."

"Well then, take your gloves off — you're making me feel hot just looking at you."

The Llyn-Y-Fan Trekking Centre is a sprawling jumble of tumbledown outbuildings. A squat farmhouse, once a pair of cottages knocked through, judging by the unevenness of roof tiles and stone, squints on to the rut-filled yard. Straw blows tumbleweed-style, catching her ankles before rolling away to gather in corners where piles of manure, once upon a time swept in an effort to tidy, have been left to grow into grassy hummocks.

Rachel puts on her riding hat and follows Tracy out of the car to stand, hands in pockets, listening to her conversing with the owner. A less than enthusiastic American woman, with a flat brown face and tall leather boots who, swishing a crop about her thighs, looks in need of spurring on. It's obvious from her tone that she is having difficulty believing the two unlikely

130

looking women who have just driven into her yard actually want to be taken on a hack into the mountains.

"Minky? Minky?" The American wails in a thick Jerry Hall drone. Eventually, a skinny teenage girl, decorated in body-piercings, lifts her moon-round face over a door in the darkened interior of the stable block. "Go fetch the diary, honey — lady here made a booking for . . ." she stops flicking her crop around, touches Tracy's arm, wanting to check, "a two hour trek?"

Tracy nods and steps aside to wait for news. She smiles at Rachel, who smiles back even though smiling is the last thing she feels like doing. Any enthusiasm she had mustered for today's excursion is fast evaporating. The riding centre is nothing more than a ramshackle of tilting byers pinned together by vast sheets of corrugated iron. How they survive the barrage of weather they must get all the way up here, she doesn't know. They seem to go in for corrugated iron a lot around here. Rachel, remembering Idris Tudor's fleapit of a smallholding, decides it isn't a million miles away from this dump. Heartbreaking, with its sagging barbed wire and weather-whittled stakes. Nothing like the neat post and rail of Pinkton Grange — a paradise of tree-shaded paddocks meandering through that obscure corner of golden-stoned Northamptonshire. Even the trees look stunted here. Buckled and stooped under the constant barrage of rain, they are poor cousins to the glamorous oaks along that majestic sweep of the Nene, where fine-bred horses sporting rugs the colours of seashells, graze beneath them.

Rachel feels the fingers of nostalgia pinch along her arms and with them a slight fluttering trepidation, like a trapped bird behind her ribs. She doesn't want to be here, what was she thinking? She hasn't ridden since she was nineteen. The horses look no better. The ones she can see are picking their way around boggy, weed-filled paddocks. Poor buggers don't look sound enough to trek to the water trough, never mind carry her and Tracy up a mountainside. She watches the American woman talking to a man who emerges from the same block as Minky. Wearing old-fashioned breeches and a torn Puffa jacket, he wheels a barrow piled high with dark yellow straw that steams its smells into the sharp air.

"My husband took your booking, apparently," the American informs Tracy. "Says you're to have Bilbo and Gerry."

Rachel sees the man lift his pitchfork and swing it in the direction of a muddy paddock that runs alongside the dilapidated ménage.

"They're in there," the American continues. "He says he hasn't had time to bring them in, so you'll have to do it."

Charming. Rachel turns in the direction of Minky, whose waxy countenance has surfaced from under the crumbling farmhouse porch. She runs, pleased with herself, into the yard. "Are you Tracy — Tracy Morgan?" she calls. The pages of the diary, caught by the wind, flap pathetic as the clipped wings of poultry. Tracy confirms she is, edging forward to claim her prize like a reluctant raffle winner.

132

"Yes, thank you, Minky — I'm dealing with the ladies." The man cuts the youngster off in an accent cultivated somewhere in England's home counties. "We don't pay you to bugger about, just crack on with the mucking out, will you?" Sarcastic and droll, Rachel wonders if he isn't showing off for their benefit. "And don't forget, you'll need to bring those horses in from the bottom fields."

The girl nods, meeker than ever under her dark flap of fringe. She snaps the diary shut and doesn't move, perhaps in need of further instruction.

"Put it back where you found it, then." The acerbic tone of the pitchfork wielder, and using it as indicator again, flicks it out at the farmhouse. "You know the drill — *never move the diary from the phone.* You are a silly girl. Why you had to bring it all the way out here, I don't know."

Rachel stares at him. While not quite believing his rudeness, she is familiar with his type — came across enough at Pinkton Grange. Probably fancies himself as some kind of horse whisperer. I'd tell you to sling your hook, mate, she thinks, catching Tracy's eye and shrugging her shoulders.

"Anything wrong, ladies?" The breeches-wearer tunes in to her.

Too far away, she pretends she hasn't heard and swings herself around on her heels to face the wind that bites into the tender flesh of her cheeks. She lifts her nose to it — a gesture of defiance — and smells snow. Only the truly weird would want to live out here, balancing on the apron of this gigantic sweep of mountainside. Suits these two down to the ground.

"Let Minky take them," the American tells her husband, her eyes undoing Rachel. "You've got enough going on."

"Nonsense, Bauble needs the exercise and it's only a couple of hours."

"Suit yourself," the woman hisses, before stomping off.

Within seconds Tracy is tapping Rachel on the elbow.

"Mr Cock's given me these." She holds out two mud-caked nylon head collars. "He's told me where the horses are."

Rachel grins. "*Mr Cock?*"

"Yeah, suits him, doesn't it?" Tracy lets go a high whinny of a laugh.

"Too right." And they giggle into their necks like naughty schoolgirls.

"Come on, let's go and catch our nags."

Rachel, following on behind, feels water seeping in through the cracked leather seams of her jodhpur boots. "D'you still want to go?" She asks, secretly hoping Tracy's gone off the idea.

"Are you kidding?" Tracy grabs Rachel's arm to steady herself on the slippery ground. "This is going to be a hoot. Apparently Mr Cock's taking us."

"I gathered." Rachel, grimacing.

"Hey, you wanna smile — reckon he's taken a shine to you."

"Oh, shut up." Rachel can't help but laugh.

"I'm serious, you wanna get in there."

"You are joking — I hope?"

The horses, a dark bay and a washed-out palomino, look up from their scanty grazing. They prick their ears as Tracy and Rachel walk towards them, pushing their muzzles into pockets, hunting for the treats Rachel didn't think to bring.

"Here you go, boy." Tracy bites off a chunk of carrot, feeds Bilbo or Gerry, as she slips a head collar over his nose and secures the cheek strap. She passes a carrot to Rachel, who in turn feeds the other one. The animals' thick woolly coats, unclipped for surviving night-time temperatures, are dusty when they pat their necks. It makes Tracy sneeze.

"I'm allergic to these babies," she says.

"You what?" Rachel tests her expression, looking for the joke. "You're a nutter, d'you know that?"

It feels strange to be up in the saddle. Stopping riding after Blundell, she was too scared to visit Pinkton Grange and didn't see Trinket again. Last she heard, her mare was sold and a cheque for much less than she was worth arrived in the post. The horses — hers is Bilbo and the colour of a muted daffodil — are placid and sturdy. Neither startle at the low-flying jet or the sudden flap of crows in overhead branches in the way Trinket would have done, and the hack, curving along the foothills of the mountainside, alive with hot autumn colours, is really enjoyable. Even Mr Cock isn't quite as awful as first thought. Checking over his shoulder, wanting to ensure they are having the good time they are paying for.

Rachel smells the sour scorch of iron on hoof before she even reaches the final gate leading back into the yard. Singed hair, she always thought of it as. Jumping down to unhook the gate, her legs buckle beneath her and, with no choice but to let go of Bilbo's reins, she grips the freezing metal gate to steady herself. The farrier, no more than a teenager, is wrapped in a scarred-leather apron. Busy filing down the rear hooves of a black Welsh cob, he's oblivious to the commotion he's caused. The sounds of metal on metal, the rasp of hoof wall and clouds of shavings, the colour and texture of Parmesan cheese — and like strobe images, she sees again those brawny tattooed arms, the sunburnt hands squeezing her throat, the flash of steel close to her face . . .

Tracy is by her side in a second. Holding Gerry's reins, she stretches out for Bilbo's before he has a chance to wander off. "You all right, *cariad*?" she asks, her head darting around, looking for Mr Cock who, behind her all the way up the lane, is now nowhere. "You look like you've seen a ghost."

"I've got to get out of here." Rachel, her cheeks bloodless, sinks down into the mud. "I've got to get out of here. I don't feel well, I feel sick. I need to go, I need to go now."

"Crikey, luvvie — all right. I thought we were having a great time — what's the matter, you ill or something?" Tracy trails the direction of Rachel's stare and sees the young farrier working away. "Is it him?" Tracy, not understanding. "D'you know him or something? Come on, Rachel, *please*." She tries lifting

136

her friend out of the filthy hole she seems insistent on squatting in. "You're frightening me."

With tawny-feathered hens pecking around her feet, the American woman strides to the rescue, snatching up Bilbo and Gerry's reins.

"What the hell's going on?" she shouts. Chickens scatter.

"My friend," Tracy: frantic, helpless. "I think she's having some kind of fit."

"Minky. Minky," the American yells for the same girl as earlier, but no one comes. "Where's Frank?" she asks Tracy, eyes wild. "What have you done with my husband?"

"I don't know — he disappeared." Tracy has unclipped Rachel's hard hat and is stroking her hair. "Come on, *cariad*, you can't stay there. You're covered in mud, its freezing."

"*Frank*," the woman shrieks. Her voice, a fluted descant, is lifted up by the fingers of wind. "Frank? Where the hell are you?"

"Here." Horseless, a saddle over one arm and a bridle swinging from his shoulder, Frank, pacing it out along the lane, looks flustered. "Whatever's the matter? Crikey, I only stopped for a second, un-tacked Bauble, let her into the field. Wanted to save time."

"Never mind all that." His wife is sharp, attacking the ferocity of the weather coming in off the mountain with her teeth. "This one's having a seizure." She points at Rachel. "Get her up, will you — she's upsetting the animals." And on cue, Bilbo and Gerry shake their heads, jingling their bits and making their matted forelocks swing.

Frank dumps the saddle and rushes to Rachel. With Tracy's help, the two of them lift her. Her body flaccid in their arms, they prop her between them and carry her into the stable block.

"Here," Frank says, pegging Bauble's bridle on a hook. "Give her some of this." And reaching into the pocket of his Puff a pulls out a curved silver hip-flask. "She's probably just overdone it."

Tracy presses the lip of the flask to Rachel's mouth. "Have a swig; it'll warm you up." And they watch as Rachel swallows, raising a hand for it to stop.

"I'm all right," she says weakly. "I just want to go home." She tilts her face to Tracy. "Can we go home?" So pitiful, so wretched.

"Come on," she says, giving Rachel a cuddle. "Can you stand?"

Rachel does and linking arms, taking unsteady steps, they head to the waiting Defender. Tracy settles her back into the passenger seat and starts the engine for the heaters to come on. "Need to get you warm, poor thing — look, will you be all right for a sec, I'd better go and settle up?"

On her own, Rachel uses the time to come up with a credible-sounding explanation. Something to account for the embarrassing scene she just made to plug Tracy's concern. She wishes things were different; she wishes she could tell her the truth about the farrier and what happened all those years ago — but then what?

CHAPTER
TWENTY-SEVEN

Honestly, you have to believe me — we were getting on great, me and the girl, sitting on my front seats looking at the moonlight shimmering on the water. It was almost romantic. I didn't have to coax her in or nothing. She did that all by herself. And it was nice, having someone to chat to for a change. She, telling me all about her family, what she was learning at college. Saying her name was Wendy, which made me tell her mine. She asked to put the stereo on, and in seconds the speakers — and they are brilliant speakers in here, better than anything I've got at home — sending out the voice of Elvis Presley singing, "Are you lonesome tonight?"

She joined in with me. Both of us singing along together, having a great time we were. Granted, she was a bit slurred, missing some of the words, but she had a sweet voice, harmonised nicely with mine as it drifted over to me through the dark.

But then she lost her nerve, started pulling at the door handle and demanding I let her out.

"Lemme go," she kept saying, over and over, like I was the one who had trapped her there, under the seatbelt she had willingly pulled over herself.

"Lemme go."

But of course I couldn't, she knew who I was — I'd given her my name by then, hadn't I?

CHAPTER
TWENTY-EIGHT

It's over six weeks since Sarah moved out. Jennifer, catching a bus, finds herself walking along Oxford Street packed with Christmas shoppers. With precious few to buy for, she is contemplating buying something for her cleaner, just for the excuse to wrap it and give it away. Not that she's given her presents before. A couple of extra fivers in her pay packet maybe, but nothing involving any thought. Giving to the cleaner was always Sarah's domain. Not that it was broadcast. It was their little secret. But Jennifer caught them once — Sarah stopping Mrs Pepper on her way out one Christmas Eve. The woman looking like a cousin of Paddington Bear, wearing her thick grey duffle coat and that awful raspberry beret she likes to pull down over her sticky-out ears. Sarah had planted a kiss on her cheek after handing over whatever it was. Such a spontaneous gesture of affection and something never shown to Jennifer. Watching from the shadows halfway up the stairs, the pain was almost physical.

She often found them together. Sarah, going off to find Mrs Pepper mid-morning, insisting she stop for a break and put her feet up. They would sit at the kitchen table and chat for the time it took to down a mug of coffee and guzzle the biscuits she was saving for an important church meeting. She suspects their closeness was forged in the days after Sarah's release, seeing the concerned glances Mrs Pepper would give, touching her arm to communicate: "You can talk to me — you can tell me anything." And had Sarah confided the terror of her captivity in the hired help? Shared how distressed it made her, the press insinuating she as good as seduced her captor with her sexual charm, made the monster fall in love with her — made him let her go? However distasteful a thought this is, Jennifer has to accept the poor girl needed someone sympathetic and whatever else she was — uneducated and from the lower classes — Mrs Pepper was certainly that.

Although it hurt that her daughter didn't come to her, she was grateful she didn't talk to Donald. Especially as she made sure to keep the lewd aspersions being made about Sarah in the papers well away from him, fearing the stories of Blundell's arrest and subsequent imprisonment might trigger another seizure. Details relating to the man's tempestuous marriage, his unconventional upbringing. A life spent in perpetual motion, those hunting for mitigating circumstances said, suggesting he was a classic product of a childhood lacking the stability of any permanent base, travelling the country with a funfair.

Jennifer passes alongside the vast glass frontage of Selfridges and stops to look at the window displays depicting silvery-scenes from well-loved fairy tales. She has a memory of bringing Sarah here as a child and wonders if they still have a Santa's grotto with twinkling lights and music. She feels her daughter's soft little hand in hers, tugging her inside; Sarah, when she was small enough to trust her mother to gather her up in her arms and bury herself in the peach-sweet scent of her Goldilocks hair. The involuntary crumpling of Jennifer's face as it prepares to cry is reflected in the window. Crikey, how old she looks.

Pull yourself together. She glares back unblinkingly hard at the woman she barely recognises. *You drove her away. You. You've only yourself to blame.* The sharp rebuke does nothing to stave the rush of tears, so she lets them come. Realising this is the first time she's cried. For Donald. For Sarah.

Conscious people are nudging each other and gawping, she moves on. Putting distance between herself and Hansel and Gretel, Little Red Riding Hood. Leaving Sarah behind, her nose pressed to the glass, just as she did aged five. A tot, shoe-horned into a scratchy tartan coat and patent-leather shoes. Clothes Jennifer kept, squirrelled deep inside a cavernous wardrobe, saving them for the other children she was going to have. She stumbles forward, releasing a wolf-like sound — a groan of the wilder, deeper places. *Where did it all go wrong?* she mouths, thinking again of the awful find in Donald's room, as she rushes into a forest of indifferent shoppers.

Up ahead, a man walks towards her. Sandy hair, good-looking, head and shoulders above the crowd. It stops Jennifer dead. She clamps a hand to her mouth, not trusting herself to scream. It's him. Blundell. He's out — *he's out.* Panic fizzes along her scalp — she's got to find her daughter; she's got to warn her. What's he doing, who's he's with? She sees the man more clearly now, smart dark wool coat, polished leather uppers, arm in arm with a pretty fair-haired woman.

As the pair move closer, Jennifer can see it isn't him. This is not John Blundell. A false alarm, she thinks, telling herself to breathe and dabbing with a tissue at the sudden perspiration that has blossomed on her forehead. Unsteady on her feet, she steps off the curb and raises a hand for a passing taxi, reminding herself that the shock of what she's just experienced could well become reality in a matter of weeks. She must find Sarah, the urgency of it clawing her heart . . . she'll ring Lynette directly when she gets home . . . get that private investigator's number . . . she's run out of ideas of where to try and the net is closing in.

CHAPTER
TWENTY-NINE

Idris leans forward to gob in the fire. Sees the look Beth used to give him. Beth, with her bantam-size frame, to which he, along with his three burly brothers, was permitted unfettered access. A family pastime, sanctioned by their mother.

A fighter jet. Ear-splittingly low over his bow-walled cottage. He rams his thick-set fingers in his ears and hunches his shoulders to it. *Bastards*. He blames them for the latest bout of miscarried lambs. Grey bloodless sacks of snot he finds in his reed-boggy pastures. He wouldn't know what they were unless he'd grown up seeing them from time to time. Idris sits tight. Waits for number two. Because the fuckers always come in pairs, like the bailiffs, and he's seen one too many of them in his life. And sure enough, within seconds, another is tearing open the skies above the sagging slates on his roof. The roar enough to rattle his fillings.

In the silent aftermath, his thoughts gather around him again like flies. Buzzing, annoying; finding their way into what remains of his hair. It isn't often he thinks of his sister. Her peculiar ways. So unsettlingly different from the rest of them, she wasn't even the same colouring. No trace of the orange lint that carpeted him and his brothers, she was lighter, cleaner somehow, unencumbered by her body. He used to wonder if she was human, the way she would float around the farm, impacting on nothing, colliding with no one, unless forced into it. Dishing out that taciturn look with the plates at mealtimes, she had a knack of riling them. It was rooted in the coolness of her gaze, speaking with a detached superiority that allowed her, whatever degradation was brought down on her physically, to rise above it.

Not that this made her special — there is no way Idris will entertain the idea of that. It might require him to think of her as something worthy. Something more worthy than him. She was just a stupid girl and no more significant than a blade of grass in a meadow full of the stuff. He watched his father pummel her to within an inch of her life once, not long before she disappeared for good. Idris feels a pang, remembering the shock it gave him when he thought The Bastard had gone too far and killed her. Her fault, so stubborn, she wouldn't back down. Insisting, in that firm way she had of jutting out her pathetic little chin, that his highly valuable and pregnant Welsh Black cow was in dire trouble. That she had a breech and if he didn't call Llewellyn-Jones-The-Vet double quick, hand over the necessaries, the beast would die. Idris has to admit, the soppy bitch always got it bang on. Only The Bastard never listened, did he? The cuss was more intractable than the weather. He remembers that night with the Welsh Black, out in the barn with Emyr. Watching more of the farm's profits sweating and thrashing away he had screamed into their father's absurd pig-headedness.

This barn — where Beth would meet that runt Dai Jones, the one he sold to contractors, where the new girl now lives — was where they put the new-born calves into crates for fattening. It was Idris' job to feed them extras round the clock, forcing them to gobble their body weight in crude protein, so their milky flesh was just right for when the meat wagon came. The wagon, in the good old days when Cwm Glas was functioning as a going concern, used to beetle its way up the lane once a month. Idris knew when Beth and Dai were in there. He could hear them breathing. They thought they were invisible, lying with the musty old feed sacks and last year's hay. But he knew. He knew of their secret trysts, when she should have had her hands in the sink or slopping out the kitchen. Misfits, he called them. Dai Jones, with his red spots. Fuck, he hated him, even if the only girl Dai could have was his wretched little sister, she was still a girl, and far more than Idris could make go with him — well, willingly anyway. It made him sick to think of them at it. Rustling around and giggling, it was obvious what they were up to.

He found their initials one day. Thinking they meant something to the world, they had curled their letters into the wooden beams that ran the length of the hayloft on the upper level. He remembers hiding in the shadows one time, the hot orange light of a late summer afternoon slicing in through the arrow slits, the air thick with dust and bluebottles. He has never felt so alone, listening to the fun they were having together. He's spent his whole life hunting for a special someone he could laugh with like that.

Idris decides it's about time he sorted himself out, seeing the hour on his DVD machine. He's got a 360 JCB tracked excavator to transport down to Westburn-on-Sea tomorrow; starting with an eight-thirty pick-up from Pontypool, it's a two-hundred and sixty mile round trip from here and will mean leaving at five in the morning. Not that sorting himself out amounts to all that much. He rarely shaves and doesn't wash unless he can help it. If he puts on a clean set of underwear then it will have to do until he's home again. Shifting himself, he slops to the bathroom in his dead father's boots.

Gathering together a dank-smelling flannel, toothbrush and toothpaste and hair-clotted comb, he shoves them inside his mam's old make-up bag. Its plastic innards, as cracked and flaking as the skin on the heels of his hands. Needing to pee, Idris unzips his fly and aims the product of three cups of tea at the greasy-looking toilet bowl. He doesn't flush. He has a thing about wasting water. So what if the holding tanks on the hill are full and it's been raining for weeks? The weather could change, and then where would he be? His habits don't bother anyone; it's only him living here. And in his refusal to notice the smell, Idris collects his makeshift wash bag and heads upstairs to pack the rest of his stuff, relishing the thought of what he's got planned for his night out in Westburn.

CHAPTER
THIRTY

I turn the headlamps off to see them tumble on to the street. Raucous and boisterous, gaudy as Christmas trees, they carry their riotous party out to the pavement. Shoving and pushing, shiny-mouthed and sharp-elbowed, they're a sight to behold. Reclining the driving seat so I can play with myself in the dark, what I'm hoping for is a glimpse of tit, a flash of arse.

Better than the pictures, this is. Better than those magazines that leave me feeling more cut-off than ever. This is free. And like a crow watching the lambs with its glassy eye, ready to swoop, I wait until these girls drift off and separate out, which they always do.

And then nothing can protect them.

I hear a noise but it's only a bin, empty and on its side, rolling in the wind. I'm okay. This lot are way too drunk and absorbed in themselves to notice me.

CHAPTER
THIRTY-ONE

Where's she off gallivanting to this time? Rachel thinks, turning to see Tracy — smart in dark velvet and a scarf the colour of watermelons — driving off in her Defender. Heading for the gate leading out over Cwm Glas' land, she stops to watch the poppy red roof of her neighbour's car as it twists along the lane. It surprises her, she imagined the lot of a farmer's wife to be way too demanding to afford such freedom; it certainly doesn't seem to give Hywel any.

Raining non-stop for days, it has kept her indoors, and it feels good to be outside again. She hates feeling trapped, even if it is only the weather doing it, too reminiscent of the tail end of 1997, back in Muswell Hill. The press camped under the walnut tree on her parents' front lawn, their cameras flashing every time the curtains twitched. On those first nights, unable to sleep, hearing the old pipes banging in the night, she would go to her window at the back of the house, throw it open to the north London sky. The lights of Canary Wharf quivering in the distance, traffic sounds, faraway sirens. Someone shouting in the street and the slamming of a car door. The smell of wet pavement and the intensified scent of box hedge.

She thinks it was because she felt so different she expected number seventy-seven to have changed too. But it had been just the same. The carpets, rugs, antique vases and telephone table-seat hogging the hall. The aquamarine tributaries running down beneath the taps in the bath. The garden. Her swing. Even her bedroom, surprisingly, had remained unchanged from when she moved out to live with Spencer earlier that year. Shell-pink and snug, with the creaky floorboard and the toy fox her father bought her from Brecon, curled and real-looking on the eiderdown. It could all be a terrible dream, she told herself, standing up at the window, shivering under her nightdress in the dark. Blundell could never have happened. Except there were bruises to prove it, the cuts that healed over into scars. She could, in those early days, still smell him on her skin, despite the baths her father would run for her, pouring in generous gloops of his wife's Eau Dynamisante. This was how she knew he existed. Hot, in chin-deep baths. Sliding below the lip of the water to listen to her heartbeat. If there were changes, they were in her and not in the house at all, and realising this made her think there could be two of her, living in two different worlds. The world before Blundell and the world she was to live in afterwards.

These days back home were strange and empty. A twilight time she wasn't sure how to fill. She read, mostly. Up in her room or, when her mother was out, with feet up on the kitchen table, listening to Mrs Pepper bumbling around in the background. Then, tired of licking the pad of a finger and turning pages on worlds better than hers, she would go into the garden, sit on the swing and smoke cigarettes liberated from her mother's desk. She went to the hospital once and the reporters even trailed her there. An appointment her GP wanted her to follow up. Important, he said, after the medical the police doctor gave her before she was allowed to wash. She fell asleep in a silent room, on a starched white bed, waking to a nurse moving around her. It was the only time she left the house in over two months. Until everyone considered it was time for her to go back to Spencer's and try to establish a semblance of normality. Spencer, who had redecorated the hall of his house on Heron Way. She could smell it the moment he opened the front door and saw the sign. Not a *Welcome Home, I've Missed You* sign, but one that read WET PAINT. Not that she believed him, touching its tacky membrane, leaving her fingerprints behind.

Deep in contemplation, Rachel continues with her climb and wonders if the greatest happiness isn't merely to watch the fluid folds of clouds as she is now. Living in such close proximity to nature — her eyes lifted by a ball of starlings, bunching then unravelling against the skyline — she is learning to read its messages, trusting it as something she can believe in.

Then she finds the smell.

Like walking into a wall, it slams into her. The bloated corpse of a vast-fleeced ewe. Capsized, her poker-stiff legs, outraged at death, stab the sky. *Christ*, the smell. She's experienced the likes of this before . . . blood . . . death . . . the memory of it never far away.

Up close, she covers her mouth and nose, preferring her gloves, sprayed sour-sweet by the cats who come to warm in her outhouse, to a rotting cadaver. Wanting to make sure, she steps up close. Curious, as the living are for news of death. She sees holes where eyes should be, accentuated in kohl-black clotted blood. A crow, centre stage, nods and dips in the long wet grass, waiting until the coast is clear. Rachel shoos it off. "Get away, get away." Her shouts frantic as she flaps her arms. But she knows this is futile, unless prepared to keep vigil, with the buzzard and fox waiting in the wings, the crow won't be alone for long. She blinks back tears, but still they come. For Laura, her father . . . for Linda Blundell. What she keeps of their faces imprinted for ever on her brain making the horizon between land and sky swim before her.

CHAPTER
THIRTY-TWO

The breakfast news gives Jennifer D'Villez unwanted images of Wendy Denny, the second woman murdered in Westburn. An incomprehensible number mutilated in a religious war in Africa. Thousands of innocent Syrian children dying from the unimaginable cold in refugee camps. But nothing of Blundell — the only reason she watches it. She knows his release is only days away, Tuesday's *Daily Mail* told her in a small article several pages in, the only relief was not seeing any photographs of her daughter.

"Terrible isn't it?" The cleaner, hovering nearby, the vacuum's nozzle ready in her hand.

"What is?"

"That's two of them now."

"Two . . ." Jennifer points the remote control at the screen, switches off the television. "Sorry, two what?" She turns her head in Mrs Pepper's direction but doesn't look at her.

"That's the second girl murdered in Westburn."

"Those *ladettes*, you mean?" Jennifer spits out the word.

"Yes, poor things —"

"If you say so." Jennifer, making her irritation plain, steps away to leave the room. Sometimes the unswerving gaze of her employee, through those thick glasses she wears, unnerves her.

"Mrs D'Villez." Mrs Pepper, about to lean down to flick the switch and activate the ever-grinning Henry vacuum cleaner, blocks her egress. "D'you want me to bring the tree down from the loft before I go?"

"To decorate, you mean?"

"Yes."

"Why — what's the point, no one's going to see it?"

"But it's Christmas, Mrs D'Villez. Everyone has a tree at Christmas."

"*Everyone*? Really? I doubt that very much Mrs Pepper, I doubt that very much." Thinking: stupid woman, Blundell certainly wouldn't have been permitted a tree in his six-by-eight foot brick-walled cell. He'll be free to celebrate it this year though, won't he? The thought, an uncomfortable one, makes her press a hand to her chest.

Against the hum of the vacuum, Jennifer, now sitting up at her writing desk, looks out through the window and marvels at her blue-frosted garden. She squints into the silvery light, sees a frost so hard, so intense, that rime has frozen on rime to give things a metallic and feathered look. She follows the flattened down lawn, from back door to bird table. A path made from slipper-sized plates where Mrs Pepper walks to scrape the bread board for the birds. She sees where Mr Antonelli has been too. His hardened footprints from three days ago. Beating a way from Donald's shed, the

154

latent flower beds, the dormant vegetable patch, around the swing and back again. The swing. It looks so cold. The plastic seat a block of hoarfrost. She imagines touching the metal frame. How it would bind her to it in an instant, sucking the moisture from her palms, claiming and freezing them there. Until, blackened and blistered from frostbite, her useless fingers would fall like dead leaves.

Jennifer straightens her back and opens her leather-bound desk diary, hoping there will be things to occupy her lurking within its heavy ivory-coloured pages. It falls open on December twenty-fifth. For some reason the snake of burgundy ribbon had been placed there. Christmas Day. She hasn't dared think about it. After the traditional eleven o'clock drinks party at Lynette's, what is there — an empty house? Well there's certainly nothing pencilled in here. She makes a note on a separate pad to ring Mrs Dobbs. There's bound to be something at Our Lady of Muswell's requiring volunteers. A lunch for the homeless drop-outs maybe, those who persist in sullying Grand Avenue Park with their makeshift camps and cardboard bedrooms. She doesn't relish the thought and can smell their characteristic sourness from here, but it's good to be seen helping those less fortunate, especially at this time of year. And who knows, scoring a good collection of Brownie points with those on the Church Committee, should the need for another favour on some parish issue arise in the New Year, might be useful; she will have them to cash in.

She makes a start at opening the cards that have piled up on her desk. Scanning handwriting on envelopes, wanting to find her daughter's. Then, alerted to a flash of red, she looks up, sees a robin on the window sill. Watching, herself barely breathing, as his plumped-up breast blows in-out, in-out: tiny frantic bellows. The bird takes off, flies to a filamented bough within the apple trees to make the perfect Christmas scene. She gives a stonewashed smile of appreciation that comes in spite of herself.

The telephone rings. Jennifer pounces on it.

"Mrs D'Villez?" A man's voice, assertive, self-assured, before she has the chance to say anything, surprising her how well he pronounces her name.

"Yes," she says, tentative, hopeful.

"Ah, hello, Derek Barnes here from Barnes and Lee Investigations — you left a message with my assistant?"

"Oh, erm, yes . . . yes, of course . . . a friend passed on your number, I'm erm . . . I'm trying to find my daughter."

"Right, okay — this is a straightforward missing persons then?"

"I suppose it is, yes — I just want to find out where she is. She upped and left you see, almost two months ago now, not long after her father's funeral."

"Okay, well obviously I'll need you to give me as much info as possible," the man says, cutting her off. "Could I suggest you come to my offices and we go through things then? And if you could bring a recent photograph . . . erm . . . let me check . . . let me check . . ." She hears a rustle of pages being turned. "Shall we say tomorrow — eleven o'clock? How does that suit?"

CHAPTER
THIRTY-THREE

A dazzling diamond of a day. Rachel, wearing a soft cashmere jumper as blue as the sky, has styled her hair for a change. She doesn't miss her blonde hair as much as she thought, although to keep her new colour looking fresh and shiny she must remember to buy some more dye when she next goes out. She finds a space to park alongside the redundant primary school and strides off in the direction of the multi-coloured strings of bunting.

The Christmas market is in full swing and live music, provided by an energetic eight-piece band, fills her ears and makes her grin as she walks jauntily into the hubbub and throng. Frying onions from a burger van make saliva gather in her mouth and there's a hog roast too, its tempting smells curling above the heads of the crowd. Maybe later, she tells herself, noticing how, along with the abundant open-fronted stalls with their striped awnings flapping in the breeze, there are larger marquees, food and beer tents, each boasting: the Best of Local Produce.

Eager to explore, she works her way through the riot of sounds and colours, nosing through knicknacks and homemade curios. Surprised at the high-quality goods at reasonable prices, the first thing she buys is a tiny plum pudding wrapped in muslin. Handing over her coins and pressing it to her nose to breathe in the currants and booze, she smiles her thanks to the vendor — a woman in her late sixties as round and jolly as the produce laid out on her tables. She then finds a stand selling everything from pretty Christmas decorations to generous bunches of holly and mistletoe and buys a beautiful berry-packed wreath and two wooden angels for her tree. In the mood for spending — there are so many things she needs to make her new place feel like home — when she lands on a stall piled high with sumptuous hand-sewn cushions and velvet bedthrows, she could buy the lot. But moving along to a tent filled with garden ornaments, it's a large stone gargoyle that really grabs her. An intruiging squatting presence with brawny arms and a glint in his eye, she imagines him looking good just outside her door, and within minutes has bought him. Asking the seller to hold on to him until she can bring the car round later.

"Ra-chel! Ra-chel!" Tracy, sitting with a couple of other woman, shouts to her. "*Rachel . . .*"

Still unaccustomed to her new name, she doesn't react, it's only when Tracy is by her side, squeezing her arm, she realises.

"Hey," Tracy's smile up close. "Great to see you."

"Hello — I was hoping I'd bump into you," Rachel beams. "Amazing isn't it? I'm having a great time. I've gone a bit mad." She pulls open the throat of her basket, shows Tracy the wreath and the other little packages. "*And* I've just gone and bought myself a gargoyle. It's supposed to ward off danger, I'm going to put him on my front step." Tracy makes a face, pretends to be baffled and they both laugh. "Seen some beautiful cushions too," Rachel giggles. "Naughty, but I can't resist."

"Nice for you — you said you needed things for the house. Local traders these — great quality, you won't find it in the shops."

Rachel reaches down to rearrange her purchases. "Hywel and the boys with you?" she says, looking up.

"Get away," Tracy laughs. "This is *me* time — I'm here with friends. Come and meet them. There was a beer tasting, and well, one thing leads to another." Laughing again, she points over to a marquee with tables set up outside.

"Girls," Tracy calls as they approach, "This is Rachel. My new neighbour. Rachel, this is Carole and Gaynor. Carole is the undisputed coffee-morning queen — she's got the most amazing house and her cakes are to die for."

"Aw, you are a love." Carole says. "Tracy, why not bring Rachel along on Wednesday?"

"*Wednesday?*" Tracy looks blank.

"Raising money for Macmillan?" Carole reminds her.

"Oh, yes." Tracy nods. "If she wants to?"

"More the merrier," Gaynor chips in.

"I'd love to, thanks." Rachel grins.

"What you drinking?" Tracy asks Rachel, then looks at the others. "We can have one more, can't we?"

"We shouldn't," they chorus. "But go on."

"I'll come and help you carry them." Rachel, springing to her feet, follows Tracy.

Then stops.

Jerks back her head.

A woman, standing a little way away, chatting to another couple. Late fifties, tall and elegant with short dark hair. Rachel forgets to breathe. It's her mother. She's tracked her down. She's here in Bryngwyn. It can't be her, it's impossible — there's no way she could have found out where she is.

Rachel, avoiding the guy ropes, ducks in behind a curtain of tarpaulin for a better look. Convinced with what her eyes tell her, panic turns over in her chest. Bloody woman, she can't help herself can she? Why can't she accept Rachel's come here to be alone — that she doesn't want to be found?

Then, watching the woman saying her goodbyes, Rachel sees to her relief that it isn't her mother. The woman is nothing like her. Exhaling, the dizziness ebbing from her body, her heart rate slows. Safe, she breathes, no one knows where she is, she can relax, for now. And withdrawing from the entrance, going deep into the shadowy recesses of the marquee, she raises a hand through the gloom, wanting to reassure Tracy who, having already ordered, is waiting for her at the bar.

CHAPTER
THIRTY-FOUR

Singing along to whatever's on the radio as usual; I'm parked up watching the girls living it up in sequinned boob tubes and salon-straightened hair. I love seeing them together, tottering along, bare legs blotchy from the cold, but so firm and slim, they get me going nevertheless.

It's been quite an eventful evening so far, if I take into account the fight I witnessed outside the Sandpiper Nightclub just after midnight. It was exhilarating, like being back in the playground. It got so heated, someone from one of the houses along the front must have called the police. Which spoilt it for me, because when they turned up I had to drive off.

Can't risk being seen; I know they've been out, clocking number plates, so I need to be careful. But they haven't got anything on me, so it's all right, and anyway, I know this place like the back of my hand — I know where's good to hide out.

Later, I was able to trail one of the girls. The taller of the two that had been fighting. So out of her skull on whatever she'd been taking, I got close enough to see she had blood all down her top and had split the skin under one eye. She didn't look round once, that's how trollied she was, and I was able to follow her all along Knightstone Road, up past the burnt-out shell of Grey's Hotel. In such a state, staggering about, I saw her get a heel trapped in the grill of a drain cover. Pulling it free made her fall over in her apology of a dress.

Shame I lost her, reeling off down one of the unlit passages that run along the back of Sainsbury's. It would have been perfect, but those lanes are just too narrow, there's no way I could drive down there.

CHAPTER
THIRTY-FIVE

Dai doesn't know why, but over a pint of Double Dragon and a game of dominoes with Denzil down The Bear Inn, their conversation swings to Muvvy Morris.

"That can't 'ave been her real name, surely?" Denzil gulps down half a glassful with the thirst of a steelworker.

"Course it wasn't." Dai takes a swig from his too. "At least, I don't think so."

They laugh. It sounds through the clattering, as their two pairs of hands, splayed over the table top, shuffle the tiles in preparation for their game.

"'ell of a formidable old bint though, weren't she?" Denzil, careful not to get too carried away with the shuffling — one false move and his pint will be over. "I can still see those lilac tents she used to wear. And those massive knees — big as me and me brother's heads."

"Can't say I got that close to her." Dai selects seven dominoes from the boneyard, taking care not to let his opponent see his choices.

"Lucky you," Denzil sneers. "Bloody 'ated havin' to go to her bungalow to pay rent for me da. She'd make us come inside, tell her about school. Can you believe that?"

"Well, she was a retired teacher; it was in her blood, wasn't it? Elsie was the same."

"Lord Almighty." Denzil swigs from his pint. "But Muvvy didn't half go on."

Dai says nothing, hands in lap, waiting for the go-ahead from Denzil to start their game.

"Blimey," Denzil says, eyes misty with memories, "you know there was bugger-all left after rent were paid. Youngsters these days," he gives an exaggerated sigh, "they don't know they're born."

Here we go, thinks Dai, draining his beer to fortify himself for the usual slog down memory lane. He holds his empty glass up to the light for something to do, wanting Denzil to choose his tiles so they can see who goes first.

"Go on then, I'll have another," Denzil deliberately misinterprets Dai's action. "Your round is it?" Pretending he's forgotten.

No, actually, it's yours. Denzil Reece. Four years his senior and tighter than a fish's arse. "And that's about as watertight as you can get," Dai says, not that his friend can hear over the scraping back of his chair, the clinking of gathered-together glasses.

He pays for the drinks and carries them, a packet of salt and vinegar held between his teeth, back to Denzil. Who, busy restacking the tiles in the order Dai left them, looks as if he might have been cheating.

"Talking of old Muvvy, d'you 'ear about Eglar John?"

"Eglar . . . Eglar." Dai sits, turns the name over in his mouth.

"Hundreds of mangy cats. Lived other side of Chapel."

"Yes, I know her — seventies, jet-black hair all down her back."

"Yeah, none on her 'ead," Denzil jokes. Dai ignores him.

"What about her?"

"She died. Two weeks she'd been lying there, telly on, electric fire. I'll leave the rest to you." Denzil tries his pint, smacks his lips together in delight.

"That's terrible, poor woman. Didn't she have family?" The full awfulness of it dawning on him, reminding him he has no family either. "Did no one in the village notice, what about her pension — surely someone at the Post Office?"

"Well, as it happens, it's her pension what's interesting. Been squirrelling it away for years she has, saved half a million quid. *Half a million squid.* Can you believe that?" Denzil thumps the table, making beer slop over their boneyard, some of Dai's lineup falling over.

"Yeah, all right. Bit of respect for the dead, eh?" Dai jumps on them, tipping them towards him before Denzil can see.

"Why, who's gonna hear?" Denzil snaps. "Look around you mate; the place is a bloody morgue."

Dai does look around, wanting to confirm what he already knows. The interior of The Bear, dark within its heavy beamed ceiling and high-backed faux-leather

166

booths, smells damp, unlived in. He thinks of Muvvy Morris, Eglar John, their remembered faces along with Elsie's, flit across his eyelids. *All dead now. All dead now.* He shakes his head, wanting to rid it of the all too frequent thoughts regarding his own mortality. Dai drinks some of his ale, savours it, then swallowing, opens the crisp packet down the middle and places it between them to share. "Some lucky bugger's in for a nice early Christmas present then," he says, munching.

"You what?" Denzil says, oblivious to the crisps, working out what to do with the tiles he's chosen.

"Eglar's half-million." Dai raises his eyes to the ceiling, sees baked-on nicotine, a reminder of the bad old days when you couldn't breathe for smoke in here.

"That's what I'm telling you — the daft old bat's left it to her cats."

At this moment, Dai, with his back to the pub door, is aware of someone pushing it open and stepping inside.

"Blinkin' 'eck," Denzil yelps, laying down a double six. It gives a satisfying click against the thickened varnish of the table top and kicks things off. "Talking of cats, you'll never guess what's been dragged in? Only Idris the Drain."

Dai twists around in his seat and is shocked afresh at the sheer extent of Idris Tudor. He'd forgotten those huge, bone-crushing hands and, seeing them swing aimless by Idris' sides, they make his stomach clench in fear.

"Remember him at school?" Denzil says. "Ooof, he stank. Teachers couldn't get no one to stand next to him in assembly — pity you being in his class, doubt they could get anyone to sit next to him neither."

"He was hardly ever there though, was he?" Dai is still coming to terms with the amount of space this man claims.

"Thank God."

Dai listens to Idris' baritone voice. The familiar wheeze, a sound identical to the father's. He is ordering the same beer Dai bought only minutes before. It was repulsive — this sordid swell of a man having the same taste as him.

"What the hell's wrong with you?" Denzil asks, watching Dai slide his unfinished beer across the table and seeing the snailtrail of condensation it leaves behind.

"Gone off it," he says limply.

"What — cos of that bastard?" Denzil, eyeing the beer, is measuring it out in his mind. Whether or not its contents can be transferred into his near-empty glass.

"Have it," Dai says, clocking his interest. "Honestly, I've lost the taste for it now." And he slots the first of his tiles alongside Denzil's.

"You're one daft sod, Dai Jones. You can't seriously tell me you've still got a problem with that idiot, after all these years? Come on man, get a —"

"Denzil," Dai interrupts, dispenses one of his sharp looks, a hangover from his courtroom days. "With all due respect, you haven't the foggiest idea of the history between me and that family of his. Sometimes things can't be forgiven — let's just say, you don't know the half of it, all right?"

"So tell me 'en." Denzil leans back, more interested in the juicy details of Dai's past than the game of dominoes or drink for now.

"It's too long a story." Dai waves him away.

"I'm goin' nowhere."

"Another time perhaps, not now." Dai, aware of Idris' bulk only yards behind him. "I'm not in the mood, okay?"

"Suit yourself." Denzil tips forward, places another tile down and sighs. "Anyway, talking of Idris, don't suppose you've seen that tasty-looking bird that's moved into his old cowshed? Got a look at her walking her dog the other day. *Phwoar* — we ain't seen the likes of 'er round these parts for many a long year."

"Her name is Rachel." Dai is firm, wanting to communicate he has absolutely no interest in playing along with Denzil's innuendo. "And yes, I have met her actually — she's very nice. From London. Had a rough time, I reckon. She's . . . I don't know," he pauses to think, kneading the end of his nose between thumb and forefinger, "sad."

Denzil coughs up a laugh, a croaky mocking laugh. "You soft sod, you always think people are sad. You want to stop listening to those dreary old records if you ask me. Mopin' around to the likes of that slop ain't gonna cheer no one up. And anyway, face it mate, we're all bloody sad — you'd have to be, to live in a dump like this, with the weather we have."

Dai returns his laugh and, appetite restored, picks up his pint and drinks deeply from it. "You're probably right," he says finally, looking at his line-up, and wiping his mouth with the back of his hand, he slaps down another tile on the open end Denzil has created.

"You heard from your Anthony?" Denzil, his words prompting thoughts of sunshine and warm sandy beaches, is reminded of Dai's boy living on the other side of the world. "You decided if you're flyin' out there yet?"

A sound of knuckles rapping the bar makes the men forget their conversation. Swivelling round in unison, they see Idris, big beneath his ripped jacket and muck-caked boots. "What d'you have to do to get served round here?" he bellows, waving a swiftly emptied pint jar in his giant paw. "Another of them." He points at the beer pump for Trevor to know. The landlord, himself not insubstantial in stature, is dwarfed by this plaque-toothed titan, who sprays his counter with his salivary request.

"He's got a nerve." Denzil, his skeleton creaking like rigging on a ship, stands up to swig down the last of his ale. "Another?" He gestures to Dai's glass, obviously wanting the excuse it will give him to go up to the bar.

"Go on then, I'll have a half. But you might want to wait until that one's sat down."

"Get off — I'm not afraid of him," Denzil says, indignant.

Dai watches him go. Hears him exchanging words with Trevor, giving no indication he has even noticed Idris who is still standing alongside. Idris sways under the weight of his body and, graceless as a seal out of water, moves away from the counter. His pint spilling over the toes of his boots as he drags his bulk into the furthest recesses of the pub.

Satisfied, Denzil leaves Trevor to pour the Double Dragons he's ordered and, on age-stiffened limbs, limps along the red-glossed corridor to the gents. Dai, meanwhile, turns back to the table, tries to forget about Idris and, looking for something to do, reaches into the rack of today's newspapers hanging beside the door. He pulls out the *Daily Express* and holds it aloft, reading the headlines. The faces of the now two murdered women stare back at him, diminished and lessened by the poor quality of the print. Issy Lake. Wendy Denny. Their names dispensed with, dumped, like their poor strangled bodies have been. Both blonde and strikingly pretty. He inhales sharply, mouths the blackened words of: POLICE INVESTIGATIONS NO FURTHER FORWARD. How vulnerable these young women are, he thinks again, his mind spinning to Beth as it has been doing with disturbing frequency since the barn was sold.

Deemed too insignificant even to be allowed to continue at school after the mother died. Too insignificant to be allowed a friend. Dai thinks of their secret meetings in the barn fifty years ago. A place of refuge for her, where the arm-achingly heavy atlas was riffled through and their chatter was thick with ideas: talk of adventure and escapade, a life beyond the one they had. She was hungry for everything. Dai remembers the maths books and science texts he would shove into his backpack along with the treats his mother made. The frantic pedal across the expanse of grazing, frightened of being seen, to share what he

171

learnt that day at school. When all he wanted was to stroke the soft skin on the inside of her arms and look into the deep pools of her eyes for the only answers he ever wanted.

Far cleverer, she caught on quickly, forcing Dai to work extra hard at school to stay ahead. He began concentrating closely, sitting upright at his desk within the grey-walled classrooms of Ysgol Dewi-Sant. He stopped looking out at the rain-drenched rugby fields, fretting about what was to come and focused on what teachers were telling him for the first time. To the pleasure of his parents, his marks improved and thanks to Beth's voracious appetite for knowledge, the headmaster — conceding Dai was never going to be a star on the pitch — encouraged him to spend his time more productively. So while his peers were thrashed by rain and teams from other schools, he was practising his trumpet or in the science lab, memorising the ivory bones of the life-size skeleton or the innards of rapidly defrosting frogs.

He became invisible, slipping beneath the radar of the bigger boys so they forgot about him and found others to pick on. Left alone, like a plant that isn't continuously ground into the mud, he began to sprout. He thinks of the notches that are still there on his kitchen doorframe, as he sips from his beer glass. His mother's voice, proud and making her only child stand still for long enough to measure him heel to scalp: "You're growing as tall as a beanstalk." With his fear of a beating diminishing day on day, his spots and complexion cleared and he grew more confident.

172

Confident enough to ask Beth to marry him on his sixteenth birthday. That was the day she kissed him. Not the usual peck on the lips but a lingering, loving kiss. One that led to them being as close as they ever could be, as close as they ever would be, because this was on the eve of what was to be their final trip to the fair at Porthcawl.

Snapping back to the present, Dai licks his fingers and turns the pages of the newspaper. His attention is grabbed four pages in by the photograph of a beautiful-looking young woman. A face he is sure he knows. Then he registers the name John Blundell tagged alongside it, and with it words like: parole board . . . served his time . . . to be released on licence. *Of course* . . . the connection dawning on him. The papers were full of this story around the same time Princess Diana died. He counts up the years that have come and gone since September 1997. *Really, that long ago?* He remembers it so clearly because Anthony had his face printed in the papers too. A poem he wrote won first prize in a national competition and, as proud parents, not wanting to miss any mention of their son's dazzling success, for an entire week, he and Elsie walked to the Esso garage and back. Bringing home armfuls of broadsheets and tabloids that they would trawl through for any mention of their brilliant boy. They couldn't fail to absorb details of these brutal crimes. How this farrier battered his wife to death because she turned up unexpectedly to find her husband holding a nineteen-year-old girl hostage in the holiday cottage he was renovating. Dai looks at the photograph of the young woman again. It makes sense to him now why her face would be familiar, but he still needs the prompt of the reporter for her name: Sarah D'Villez. Unusual, sort of French sounding. He is remembering more. *That's right, poor thing*. She managed to escape after being beaten and raped and held for more than a week. The trauma must have been unimaginable. Yes, she got away, but back to what? An experience like that — it's difficult to imagine you'd be able to have any life at all. And now they're letting him out — what's that going to be like for her?

"The fucker'd shuffled off by the time I got there." Denzil, hovering with two pints, is back at their table. Dai sees his request for a half has been ignored but says nothing, closing the paper. "You ever been there?" Denzil points to the headlines.

"Where? Ta for the beer, mate."

"Westburn-on-Sea." Denzil sits, pulls the paper towards him and stares hard into the faces of the two murdered girls. "One 'ell of a dive. Went for the day with me gran. One of them OAP coach trips, Chapel used to do 'em, they don't bother no more. I thought it was a good idea, sending the whingy old gits on away days like that. Especially them trips to manky seaside towns." He takes a gulp from his fresh pint, belches without apology. "Stopped their moaning when they got back 'ere — made 'em feel dead grateful about this place."

"I can't keep up with you." Dai rolls his eyes, something he does a lot of in Denzil's company and drains what remains of his previous pint.

174

"You never answered me question," Denzil prods, "*Westburn* — you been there?"

"No, I haven't."

"Not surprised," Denzil sniggers. "No way your folks'd let you go to a dump like that — too bloody posh by half, your lot."

"What are you on about now?" Dai is absent-mindedly making patterns out of the wet rings of condensation on the table top. It seems as though their game of dominoes has been abandoned before it properly got going.

"Aw, nothing." Denzil raises a hand then uses it to wave at the paper. "How many of them girls been killed now?"

"Two," Dai answers him.

"Any more and he'll have no one to shag."

"What you on about, Denzil?"

"Him. Idris. That's where he goes, innit — the West Country, on his haulage jobs?"

"Aye, I think he does." Dai nods, not really listening, still making patterns with the tip of his finger.

"D'you reckon he goes as far as Westburn?"

"Don't know, why don't you go and ask him?"

"Yeah, yeah. Very funny." Denzil slurps his beer. "Word is, he gets his end away nonstop when he's on the road."

"Don't talk rot, man — what woman's going to go for him?"

"One without a sense of smell and bad eyesight?" Denzil suggests, choking back a laugh, then pauses, clocking Dai's seriousness. "I'm only telling you what's

175

been doing the rounds — apparently he's got a few on the go in Somerset."

"Ha!" Dai throws his head to the ceiling. "You're even more bonkers than I thought if you believe that rubbish."

"You don't know? Them birds might be different in that neck of the woods." Denzil, grinning. "Might be an *afrodizic*, or whatever it is — him smelling like a cowshed. And don't forget," he sniffs, raises a finger, "he reckons he's a right fanny magnet in that truck he drives."

"More like a fridge magnet," Dai butts in, chuckling at his joke.

"*Fridge magnet* — ha, that's brilliant," Denzil, laughs, slaps the table. "Yeah, you're right." He slaps the table some more. "Git like him, whatever he might like to think of himself, there's no way a woman's gonna come willingly. He probably started them rumours himself."

"Sshhh. Keep it down, eh?" Dai wriggles about in his seat, concerned that Idris will hear what Denzil is saying. Denzil, who is becoming increasingly raucous with each pint he downs.

"So what if he can fuckin' hear, who fuckin' cares?"

Dai, wincing at Denzil's ripe choice of language looks sideways at him; at his slight frame, his prematurely crippled spine and swollen fingers. At himself. His big, soft body. "You don't know what he's capable of, that's all I'm saying — bad enough coming up against him when we were nippers, but now — I mean, look at us, he could crush us with one hand."

"You think?" Denzil, thrusting out his pigeon chest. The movement making him cough his old man's cough. "Yeah, well." He readjusts himself. "I was only saying, and anyway, I haven't finished saying what I was gonna say, as it happens —"

"Go on then, I'm all ears." Dai exhales through his words.

"You're not thinking about it, boy — *Idris*? Idris and Westburn? Got it?"

"Got what?"

"Keep up, will you? You're supposed to be the clever one round 'ere. It's him, innit — *him* doing them murders."

"Oh, Denzil — have you heard yourself? Somerset's a big county, you know. He probably doesn't go anywhere near Westburn."

"Course he bloody well does. Yeah, I bet it's him." Denzil, ignoring Dai, picks at the thread of his idea and pulls it taut. "Nothing to him them girls — look at 'em." Denzil prods the paper again, slowly, rhythmically, his arthritic finger bowing further under the force he puts behind it.

Dai would rather not, instinctively turning his head to the furthest corner of the bar, where Idris squats toad-like, malevolent, in the deepest of shadows, watching them.

"The cops are saying both them murders are down to the same person, got the DNA to prove it." Denzil is sounding pleased with himself.

"Yes, really clever that, isn't it — DNA?" Dai sarcastic as ever, squeezes the tip of his nose between finger and thumb. "Shame they haven't got anyone to match it to."

They sit in silence for a moment or two; Dai massaging his nose some more, Denzil shooting tentative looks in Idris' direction.

"Whatever. I still reckon he's got something to do with it," Denzil chimes in again. "Those girls wouldn't weigh as much as his arm; they wouldn't stand a chance. I'm telling you mate, I'm on to something here — I'm gonna do some asking around. Find out where he goes to, what he does — *exactly*. Then we'll have him, the bastard — for everything."

Course you will, Dai thinks, knowing his friend's bravado is just the booze talking.

"Oh yes, my friend," Denzil concludes, lifting his straight-sided glass high into the air, toasting Dai and slopping beer down his front. "Here's to nailing the fat fucker once and for all."

CHAPTER
THIRTY-SIX

Night drops suddenly. Tŷ Haf may have a south-facing garden and be bright when the sun shows itself, but it's as gloomy as a cave inside. A low-slung dwelling, the main source of light comes from the floor to ceiling glass doors, the rest lit by arrow slits, cut more than a century ago through the thick stone walls. These days, come half three, Rachel goes about switching on lamps. Avoiding the brightness of the ceiling bulbs, life in a nebulous fuzz suits her. Never one for stark, floodlit city living. Not like her mother. Or Spencer, come to that. A man who would go about turning all the lights on the moment he came home. Needing the clarity, she always thought, to negotiate his way through the choppiness of their relationship. Every aspect of his life demanding the same clinical exactness as his intricate laboratory studies, she could never make him understand how that kind of scrutiny didn't benefit their domestic set-up.

She visited Spencer at work once. In the months before her abduction. When their love, a nascent thing, was full of promise and hope. Given a square badge of laminated card at reception, the word VISITOR in red to fix to her lapel, she did as she was told and signed in,

179

before being directed up the stairs. The laboratories were over the easterly lecture block and so high, they grazed the amorphous Hatfield sky and looked down over the M1 flyover and ugly concrete sprawl of shopping centre, multiplex cinemas and multi-storey car park. The multi-storey often featured on the local news. A popular haunt with those Hatfield residents who, finding they could no longer stand life in this most dreary of settings, would throw themselves from the top with frightening regularity.

The laboratories, a series of elongated glassy rooms with wet sinks, reeked of blue paper towels and acrid chemicals that set her teeth on edge. The walls were cabinets filled with jars, rubber piping, metal clamps and test tubes. Interesting enough, until she saw the octopus. A vast tank, divided into five sections, that ran along the back, bubbling quietly and shot through with a Caribbean light. She remembers watching for some time, mesmerised by the slinky movements of these cephalopod molluscs. The unnerving stare from their two lidless eyes, summing her up, before showing off their moves and jetting headfirst through the water, their four pairs of arms trailing behind. They seemed to be in possession of an untapped, ancient intelligence and, feeling sorry for them, she stroked the glass asking: "Don't they miss the sea?" Only to be given a sharp warning by Spencer's only female colleague. A whale of a girl, whose fleshy ankles, she couldn't help noticing, spilled over her flat, brown lace-ups. "You mustn't provoke them; they're part of an on-going experiment." The girl, displaying a name badge Rachel didn't bother to read, rustled officiously under the crispness of her starched technician's coat. "The last thing we want is you bringing on one of their *deimatic* displays."

At this, Spencer intervened. Tipping himself sideways off his bench, he was by Rachel's side in an instant. Whispering, soft, as he was inclined to be in those early days, he tucked a strand of her hair tenderly away behind her ear and prised her fingers from the glass. "What's this one called?" she said pointing and playing the little girl she knew he liked. And selecting the one with the prettiest colours, was comfortable in the knowledge these were the only things of beauty she needed to compete with. That the imagined team of glamorous, bespectacled and brainy women she had been busily inventing for her new boyfriend's colleagues didn't exist. "Well, he's what you'd call our top banana," Spencer grinned, proud as a father. "Herby's our one and only Blue-Ringed Octopus." How obvious, she thought and, turning away, tried to conjure up something more original for the intriguing creature with fabulous turquoise rings and bright yellow bloom. "Incredible," was all she said out loud, enjoying Spencer's reaction. "I watched him change colour before my eyes — he was nothing a minute ago, you wouldn't have given him a second glance." The observation produced a grunt from whale-girl and made Spencer put an arm about his girlfriend's waist to steer her back to his work bench. "You don't want to go getting too friendly with him," he cautioned, wanting to keep it light. "Herby is what us teuthologists term as deadly to humans."

It was where she first heard this word. Strange and foreign sounding, she tried her best to remember it by rehearsing it over and over, securing it down within her mind. But however secure, it always escaped; the retention of words was never her strong point. When they were out socialising and it came to telling others what it was her boyfriend did, Spencer, feeling the need to butt in, would drop it into the conversation over her shoulder, making her feel stupid. Frustrated, she envisaged the word, as slippery as the tentacles of the invertebrate themselves and believed herself inferior by her inability to fish it from her memory in all the years they lived together. Funny then, for this camouflage of a word to slide so easily from her tongue nowadays. She wonders what Spencer would make of that.

Spencer's working environment was one that dried her eyes out and made her lips crack. It had a papery stillness, so bright it bleached out shadow. She can clearly see her nineteen-year-old self, sitting alongside him on that cold February day. Identifying the frisson that shivered the length of her spine whenever they touched in the first throes of their relationship, is more difficult. For this, she will have to trust her memory. A sensation that didn't last, she thinks, a little sad. Any more than the sweet way she pretended to listen, taking an interest in the intricacies and direction his research was taking him. How his talk took her on a journey to America's East Coast when they went for coffee in the staff canteen, the opportunities New England universities were offering young British marine biologists looking to specialise. A serious topic. One she was to take little notice of at the time. Too engrossed in his dark-lashed eyes, elbows glued to the sticky Formica-topped table, head in hands, lazily thinking she would follow him anywhere. The gravity of this conversation was to hit her later. Years later.

The thought is enough to make tears come. The dog knows it and is by her side in an instant. His eyes, along with hers, reflected back in the full-length glass of her French doors. He finds her hand, pushes his wet nose into it. This is how they communicate, in gestures and looks. It is all he has. All she wants. She opens up the left hand side of the door and watches him slink out. His unhurried shape hitting the mouth of the night, dark fur swallowed whole, he disappears up the gravel path. She waits a moment, ignoring the fingers of cold creeping up under her clothes. The stream at the bottom of the field is swollen by rain and its amplified rush, in the otherwise stillness, comes loud as a motorway. Strange it should remind her of that when there isn't a motorway for miles.

Rachel tips her head to a crescent moon. Gulps it down. Feels its sharpness cut out of the cloth of night. There are stars too. Millions of them. More than she has ever seen. Spooky policeman's buttons, they sparkle silver and look close enough to pluck free. It staggers her, this wide Welsh sky — this true blackness cities never know. Then comes the long tremulous hoot of a barn owl and, into the haunting echo, its mate answers the call. Their pairing makes her think of the company she will have tomorrow, the new friends she hopes to make at the coffee morning at Carole Deacon's. Rachel likes this feeling of being included and, since coming here, is feeling more part of things than ever before.

Cadno, appearing from nowhere, rushes back inside and she closes the door, lifting the handle to lock it.

A face at the glass.

There one second, gone the next. She screams. Breath glazes the window. Inside or out? She doesn't know. Frantic, she swivels round to check over her shoulder. Nothing. And in the dwindling seconds, unable to trust her senses, she can't be sure she saw anything at all.

The dog barks. Scrambles to be let out again. Panicked, her heart thumping loud in her ears, her fingers don't work. Too slow and Cadno is deprived of the opportunity to protect his property by seeing whatever it was off the premises.

Who the hell was that? There was definitely someone, but it's so dark out there, no streetlamps, no passing cars; no one would know if she was in trouble. She tries not to let these cold hard facts frighten her, convinced as she is that when Blundell is released he will come for her. That hiding away in the depths of Wales with a new name and different coloured hair isn't really enough to stop him, not when it was her evidence that got him put away. He'll do everything in his power to hunt her down, wanting revenge.

In danger of letting her imagination run away with itself, she tells herself to calm down, that none of this is possible. He isn't out yet, she'd know, she's been checking the internet every five minutes. And anyway, DS Blackwood promised he would be so closely supervised by the probation service that free movement would be impossible. So he can't be out there, prowling around, waiting for the right moment to finish what he regrets not finishing seventeen years ago. He can't. Can he?

CHAPTER
THIRTY-SEVEN

Carole Deacon's large detached house, set away from the heart of the village, is well-cared for and completely unexpected. Rachel is glad to be here, amidst people, their chatter forcing her to think past her fear that Blundell could be closing in on her. She didn't sleep well, shaken up by the face she thought she saw at the window; her mind's been working overtime.

She watches an enormous tortoiseshell cat tiptoe across lacquered wooden floors, the only live animal amongst hundreds of stuffed and preserved mammals, birds, insects and fish. The evidence of Carole's husband, Walford Deacon, is everywhere — down corridors, on the stairs, in the study where he works amongst the mahogany book shelves, sitting at his vast desk looking out through his window to the gently sloping lawn and the sharp jutting spine of the Brecon Beacons. Missing, only because he is a man who works away for much of the week. An eminent banker for Barclays, Tracy whispered, although she didn't have any specifics.

"Wally," Carole tells Rachel, leading her by the elbow, doing a room by room, "began collecting when he was nine and has been doing so ever since."

"Quite fascinating," she tells Carole. "I'd never've said they'd be my kind of thing, but your husband's dealt with them so sensitively."

"I'm glad you think so, they're not everyone's cup of tea."

Carole wrinkles up her delicate little features. "But if it makes him happy, then I'm happy — after all, I have my horses."

"Horses — you have horses? Here?" Rachel, curious.

"Yes," Carole seems surprised, cool — everyone has horses, don't they? "They're why we moved to Wales, well that and the need for a bigger house for Wally's collection, of course." She makes a clicking noise, returning her cup to its saucer.

"Have you much land?"

"Fifteen acres. Since the kids came along, I've downsized. I've only the two horses now: a Connemara and an Irish Hunter called Snapdragon."

"*Snapdragon*," Rachel repeats back the word. "How big is he?"

"Sixteen-three."

"I had an Irish Hunter — a while ago now, when I lived in Northamptonshire."

"Really? Lovely riding country."

"It was, not that I did it for long." Rachel laughs; tight, hard. "I had to sell my horse. Marriage breakdown." Carole nods sombrely as though this is something she understands. "Not ridden for ages — well, apart from a few weeks back, with Tracy, but that was a one-off."

"Doesn't have to be?"

"I don't think so," Rachel says, raising a hand. Images of her violent past crowding her mind again. "Reckon my riding days are over."

"Nonsense." Carole smiles a perfect lipstick smile. "You could ride Molly; she's as good as gold. Let me give you my number."

Rachel follows Carole along the hall, smelling her perfume, and on reaching the telephone table watches her write on a disc of sea-green paper fished from a decorative circular box. She spots a dark-leather bridle hanging from a hook by the front door, the glint of snaffle catching her eye. Without knowing why, she puts a hand out to touch it and finds it unexpectedly comforting.

"Oh, all right then, why not," she says, changing her mind. "Thanks, Carole."

Later, back at Tŷ Haf, Rachel thinks of the bridle she kept on a peg in the hall of Spencer's home, long after her big bay mare was sold. Part of her suspects she did it to wind him up, knowing how much he hated it hanging there — a souvenir of what had been, of what they then became because of it.

"What the hell d'you keep it for?" the first thing he'd say, pushing his key into the lock and striding in — regular as clockwork — unlike the hours he began to keep. A sour greeting delivered in the irritated voice he stopped bothering to hide once they were married. It deflected his need to find excuses for his incessant lateness, knowing full well she'd have been nowhere, seen no one. The question was enough to make her

188

turn away, hiding tears, giving the explanation to the wall: she kept the bridle to prove there were good times before everything was lost.

In the life to follow the nightmare that began that warm September afternoon, Rachel found it impossible to return to Pinkton Grange. That day when the world's focus was elsewhere, centred on the flag-draped royal coffin as it made its sombre way through London's streets. Leaving Westminster under the suffocating stench of rotting flowers, to travel up the M1 to Althorp. The black cortege passing only miles from the Great Billing housing estate where she and Spencer lived, turning off at junction 16 on the final leg of its journey.

Rachel watched the funeral on the telly. Wept along with everyone else at the brother's heartfelt speech, the revamped Elton John ballad. The tragedy of the little boy princes who, awkward inside their man-size suits, were drilled on how to hide the grief for their poor, dead mummy behind stiff upper lips. And later, because it was a Saturday, because it was a glorious afternoon and her florists, running out of flowers, closed early to show respect, she drove out to the stables, with the idea of taking Trinket for an early evening ride. The last time she was to make this journey, as things turned out. Rachel didn't have her ride — she didn't even get as far as lifting her newly cleaned, linseed-supple saddle from the back seat of her car.

A farrier, one she was to tell police she didn't recognise, was working on his own. The rear doors of his mucky-blue Ford Transit flung wide, filling the otherwise desolate yard with the scorched smells from his mobile furnace. She'd seen him on her way in, struggling to calm an iron-grey thoroughbred. There was nothing wrong with the horse, she told the detective who was to interview her eleven days later, he just didn't like being tied up and with there being no one else around, when the farrier beckoned her over, needing her help, she didn't think twice. Never stood a chance.

CHAPTER
THIRTY-EIGHT

Working in a sideways wind that comes in off the hill, Idris drags his bulk around his shit-slippery smallholding with the enthusiasm of a two-toed sloth. Kicking aside a flap of manky hens, he humps hay bales and sacks of feed up on to his back and carries them out to his last remaining ewes. Dumping them at intervals over his sagging barbed wire fences, wet-fleeced and nervy, they scatter to give him a wide berth and the curve of their eye, as his mind is busy unravelling the events of the previous evening. His unexpected visit to The Bear. A few pints of Double Dragon and making small-talk with Trevor, a man whose interest has only ever been in taking money, before settling down in the shadows for what remained of the evening.

The experience was every bit as bad as he remembered as a youngster, and proved to him how things in this backwater are as stagnant as they ever were. He doesn't know what possessed him to go. It was like stepping into a lion's den. Not that Idris has much to fear from the physical world, gossip is what frightens him. He feels it, a tangible thing, silting his veins, furring the walls of his heart. To Idris, Bryngwyn is like a maggot-ridden sheep carcass writhing with the ragged tongues of villagers: it's dead but it looks alive. Last night was no exception, his back to them, counting out his change, he was aware of their eyes. White and staring as the dots on the domino tiles Dai Jones and that wanker Whatshisname were playing with. Being unable to grasp the full contents of their clipped conversation frustrated him, almost to the point of barging over to their table and shaking it out of them. But he stopped short. Neither wanting to give them the satisfaction, nor play into their hands by living up to the image of him they bandy about. It was obvious what they were calling him behind their hands as they pretended to play their stupid game, picking apart his appearance, making judgements. He may not have had the schooling of that weasel Jones, but he isn't a complete idiot; this is how they've always treated him.

"Fuck 'em," he shouts into the slicing wind. Let them sneer. And his gaze settles for a moment on the only thing he cares about — apart from his Beretta — his gorgeous Scania haulage truck. Parked up on the special gravel-lined lay-by he made for it. The fat chrome bumpers shiny as the baubles on a Christmas tree. It is his absolute pride and joy. That cab he spends his nights away in is kitted out more comfortably than his living room, with its state-of-the-art telly, stereo system and DVD player. The means to boil water for his Pot Noodles. The mini fridge set in under the passenger side where he keeps his stash of petrol-station Melton Mowbrays cool in their crinkly wrappers. The once midnight-blue, now sun-bleached curtains with crescent moons he draws over himself for the privacy he craves in the lonely motorway service areas he will park up in overnight. Bliss. That's what he calls it. The freedom of the road. The power that driving such a gargantuan beast allows. He smiles, remembering the ashen face of a female motorist he nearly ran off the road. And again, days later on the A40 out of here, a horse and rider sent skittering into oncoming traffic. Great fun. Those twats slagging him off in the pub, they don't have the adventures he has; travelling the country incognito, copping off with women who expect nothing afterwards. His only regret is not starting his enterprise years ago.

After lifting and repositioning a giant steel door that has come off its hinges — a job that ordinarily would take two men — Idris slices open a bag of dry feed with the blade of his flick knife and scoops out what he thinks will last his dogs for the next three days into a pair of crusty metal bowls. The dogs, although salivating, stay well out of his way, cowering in the shadows, waiting for him to leave. He tests them to the limit, banging out the bristles of his broom against the far breeze-block wall. As he steps back, he treads on a chicken.

"Get out from under my bloody feet," he hollers into its squawking protest, making his dogs shrink further. "Go on, you feathery fucker." And he kicks its capon-weight, making it fly higher than its clipped wings will ever take it, across the pockmarked compound. The hen reminds him of the eggs that are his to claim, and he goes off in search of them — his dense black bulk with arms outstretched, as eager as a child on an Easter egg hunt. His dozen or so layers don't have coops; their plumy lives are left balancing in the mercy of Mr Fox who, with a family of his own to feed, will slink down from the velvety-smooth drops and dingles in the leaner months, gambling with the periodic firing Idris gives his over-under.

Familiar enough with their favoured haunts, he is quick to land on a clutch of eggs that are spattered, not unlike his skin, in fine russet freckles. Fossilised in filth, same as his fingers, he pops them, carefully as his clumsy movements allow, into the damp pockets of his oilskin and moves onwards in his hunt. He wants to take some to the girl in the barn before heading off later in the afternoon. Not that she seemed grateful the last time, crossing her arms and huffing. But he shakes any doubts from his mind about how she might not like him, putting her frosty reception down to the shock of seeing him there. Women are such curious creatures, making up for their vulnerability with that puffed-up bravado they do. Can't they see what a waste of energy it is and how much better off they'd be if they just gave in?

Dumb and motionless, the dogs wait on. Their red-rimmed sorrowful eyes trained on the metallic lips of their bowls. Until eventually, the slope of Idris' back disappears inside his hovel. The pitiful sight of his half-starved mutts, who inch forward nervously into what remains of the light to claim their meagre meal, is of no interest to him. Idris has more important things to focus on. Like how to ingratiate himself with that tasty bit of stuff down the lane. How to get her to invite him in.

CHAPTER
THIRTY-NINE

John Blundell is out. It's official. Rachel, doing her regular online scan, doesn't need to look far. His photographed face — the same one that haunts her sleeping hours — fills the screen. Further searches yield surprisingly little information; he doesn't seem to have spoken to anyone in the media. There is nothing about where he is going to be living or the conditions of his release, just more of the same regurgitated history of his crimes and although relieved to see no up-to-date pictures of herself, she finds some different ones of his dead wife.

Agitated, she scratches the scar on her wrist. A blurred starfish. The skin feeling puckered and thick under the softness of her fingertips. It's a bad habit and one that throws her back to the too-tight metal handcuffs he secured her down with in the dark that was as cold as Antarctica. The scar flares up from time to time, keeping step with her brain, because despite moving to Wales and living under a new name that even her mother doesn't know, she is still knotted up with fear.

Thinking of the way she defied her mother by leaving without a word makes her smile. Not that the smile lasts, slipping away as suddenly as it came, her expression darkening, remembering the scare she had at the Christmas market when she thought she saw her. She is safe here, isn't she — no one can find her? Surely the press would have come sniffing around by now if her new name and whereabouts had been leaked, there is nothing new about her on the internet. Clued up as she is to their *modus operandi*, she hasn't the stamina for them. Terrifying as a pack of slathering dogs, they wanted every gruesome morsel of what it was like to watch her abductor set about his wife with a hammer when she turned up unexpectedly to find him holding a younger, more attractive girl. Ordinarily, the papers would have tired of such a story; it's only the perceived list of unanswered questions keeping the embers burning. Churned up recently with this talk of his release, she worries it will whet appetites for up-to-date photographs and salacious gossip about what the gorgeous girl he took prisoner is doing with her life now.

"Going to have to go into town," she tells the dog, seeing how angry her scar's become. "Need to find a chemist."

Before she leaves, she remembers the washing she put out first thing, taking encouragement from the soft sunshine she woke to. Calling for Cadno and balancing her laundry basket on her hip in the way she would carry Laura, she strides off into the field and the makeshift line strung up between stable and woodshed. Taking hold of a nightshirt to test it, she finds it's almost dry, but she can't risk leaving it here, it might rain.

She gathers her clothes, folding them neatly into the basket placed at her feet. Jeans, socks, fleeces, cardigans, a couple of tops. Shoulder to shoulder, hem to hem. A thermal vest. Her filigree-trimmed bras. Hang on a minute. She sucks back her breath. *No — that can't be right?* A space in the line, two empty clothes pegs, some inches apart. A space where this morning her favourite pair of black, racy satin knickers had been. She feels cold. Frightened. Flings her head around, scanning the field, the drive, the lane, for the eyes she expects to see. Nothing. Nothing human. Just the merest hiss of a breeze scouring the branches of nearby trees. The cold caw of a crow; its black shape flung high against the vault of sky. She shivers under the creeping unease that crawls over her skin. To think someone's been here, taking her clothes — it leaves her feeling more exposed than she's done since she arrived.

CHAPTER
FORTY

Rachel's newly acquired Toyota Rav 4 takes the heaves and twists of the B4299 with ease. High enough off the tarmac for the torrents of water spilling from surrounding fields to be of little consequence, what forces her to brake is a slow-moving tractor. When finally it indicates left down a stone-filled track and the road ahead is all hers again, she puts her foot down. Leafless banks and hedges, bleached by weeks of rain, skim past at speed. The fleecy bums of last year's lambs thrust out into the road. Stained sage green and too fat to squeeze back into their fields, they roam the nibbling-strip of verge. The odd buzzard, perched high on telegraph poles, catches her eye at intervals and, dangerously distracting, the swoop of a kestrel against the humpbacked clouds.

Suddenly a juggernaut is coming right at her. The bulbous glare of fog lamps and alarm-red snout. Ugly with indifference to anything in its path, it roars up and over the withers in the road. But too wide, the tyres eat up more than what is fair and are way over on her side. She grips the wheel, unable to breathe. The punch of the horn makes her swerve into the hedge of barbed thorns, the screech of metal running the length of her car. The dangers of the water-logged verge bouncing beneath her wheels, she pulls her mouth wide in a scream. Was that Idris, or do all lorry drivers drive like that around here? Where the hell's a sodding police car when you want one? She's seen two pass in the last half hour.

Idris — he'll soon have something to answer for. "We'll certainly get an officer to check it out today," the girl at the RSPCA helpline had said, thanking her for alerting them. Rachel needing to hit out in some way at that filthy bastard who, she was sure, pilfered her knickers off the line. Reporting him for the inhuman way he keeps his poor dogs was a place to start — castrating him would be preferable, but all in good time, she thinks, squashing the image she has of the man's grimy face into a tight round ball.

Switching on the radio, which crackles into life along with her windscreen wipers, allows her to catch the last of the pips heralding the one o'clock news. She half expects there to be an update on Blundell but, following the headlines and a summary of the day's events, it is straight over to the BBC's local correspondent in Westburn-on-Sea. The mic amplifies the voice of Chief Superintendent Colin Bradley of the Avon and Somerset Constabulary. "We appreciate the public's concern," his bowling West Country burr sounds to Rachel as if he is wading through chest-high mud. "Especially in the wake of this second murder . . . and are urging women in the town to be vigilant . . ."

"What d'you say to the allegations you have a serial killer on the loose . . . that the police aren't taking this idea seriously enough?" The squeaky-voiced reporter drops his gambit.

"I can assure you we're making every effort to catch the perpetrator," the Chief Superintendent shoots him down. "Yes, DNA evidence suggests this is the work of one person, but I must stress —"

Rachel switches off the radio. Smacks the steering wheel. Bastard reporters, they're all the same. Making bad situations worse. Twisting things to suit their needs — a sensational story and sod the truth. She should know.

The B4299 drops away to sea level and the perpendicular symmetry of Llandafen Castle rises incongruous up ahead. The sky is clearing between the gaps in its ramparts and Rachel can see patches of blue. Changing down through the gears, she decides to take a left turn signed off the roundabout as CANOL Y DREF, which she knows is the Welsh for town centre. It is a change from her usual routine — normally she takes the exit for Tesco and the retail park on the edge of town, avoiding the centre altogether — but she feels like exploring now the rain has stopped and the sun is sliding into view. She could even find somewhere for a sandwich and a cup of tea.

Town is heaving, which is no surprise in the countdown to Christmas and, after waiting an age for the traffic lights over the bridge to turn green, she follows signs to park up by St David's church. Buying a ticket with shrapnel she keeps in the car, staggered at what the council charge for only a few hours, she slips herself into her dark wool coat, changing out of her driving shoes for the heels she thinks she needs and walks the length of Queen Street. Crowds of people laden down with shopping bags collide with her along the cobbles. Their faces, jolly and pink with cold, mimic the tawdry-looking snowmen and Santa Claus that have been used to decorate shop windows.

The sun is out and she stares up at the alien yellow orb as if it isn't something to be trusted. It hangs low in the winter sky and casts long shadows over the pedestrianised area. There isn't really anything she needs, apart from the oil she likes to rub into her scar, a box of hair dye, and something else to christen the house with perhaps, not that she has any idea what. It is enjoyable to walk around without the need to hunt for Christmas presents. Apart from Tracy, Hywel and the boys, possibly Dai, there is no one to buy for. Rachel doesn't have Mrs Pepper's home address and decided weeks ago she wasn't bothering with her mother. Busy with her horrible associates and whatever charity function the church has going on, she won't notice. And if she does, so what — isn't it about time they are honest and stopped pretending they care about each other?

Conscious of her grumbling stomach, Rachel finds herself a tea-room that is advertising its lunchtime snacks in a large bay window. Stepping inside, she immediately regrets it, but because she is shown rather forcefully to a small wooden table positioned up by the counter, she tells herself it's too late to change her mind. The heads of other customers turn, she isn't sure why and, slipping her arms out of her coat, works hard to focus her attention on the laminated menu thrust into her hand. After several minutes, the unsmiling waitress is back. Pad and pen ready, twitching impatiently for Rachel's order of smoked salmon on brown and Earl Grey tea. "No butter?" The woman stares in disbelief, jabbing the nib of her biro into the cushion of her hand-sized order book. She has blue ink on her fingers, a soup stain on her apron from the lunchtime rush, and Rachel hopes she isn't going to be the person to prepare her food.

The sandwich, when it arrives, is served with coleslaw and crisps but tastes of little. She goes through the motions, chewing and swallowing, inhaling the smell of burnt cheese and cloying perfume wafting over from an adjacent table that seats four well-made-up women of her mother's generation, speaking Welsh with a loud and confident flourish. She hadn't anticipated how self-conscious she'd feel in a room full of strangers and wishes she'd just bought a sandwich from Marks & Spencer. It's not as if there's any of the glamour of those Parisian-style coffee houses Alice used to take her to. Those were an adventure, an education. Towering club-sandwiches accompanied by the thinnest of fries. The toasted bread, secured down by little wooden pins wearing frilly caps, followed by scoops of tutti-frutti ice-cream. What would she make of this place? Rachel can't envisage her flame-haired aunt sitting in here, her silver thumb-ring glinting in the amplified hiss of the steamer working at full-throttle. Her earrings twirling like Christmas decorations through the over-blown conversations of others. And Rachel wonders again how Alice could be related to the mother who paces the darkened rooms of that house in Muswell Hill. A woman more interested in the souls of her dead babies than in the one daughter who survived.

The officious manner of the staff, delivering their endless streams of orders, only serve to make Rachel feel more in the way. As do the sounds of a crying baby. So with still more than half a pot of tea to finish, she goes to the counter to pay, dropping a fistful of coppers into the saucer of tips by the till. The girl who served her wishes her a Merry Christmas without emotion and within seconds she is back outside.

Wobbling along the cobbles in her heels, she stops intermittently to peer into the sparkly lit interiors of the bijoux-type outlets and delicatessens. Never moved enough by what she sees, she doesn't step inside. "Shops on a diet," her father called them, and he was right, they do have bugger-all to sell. It always puzzles her how businesses like this stay afloat, remembering what she had to do to meet the monthly rental, keep the delivery van on the road and pay the salaries of the few staff she employed at her florists. Shame she hadn't been able to carry on with it, a right little gold mine it was turning out to be. But John Blundell destroyed that too, didn't he? She lost everything because of him. They've got no right letting him out. Seventeen years inside? The bastard's not suffered nearly enough.

Then, up ahead, someone catches her eye. Tracy. Stepping out of the olive-fronted Dinefwr Arms Hotel.

Unmistakeable, despite the unexpectedly stylish cola-coloured wool-mix jacket belted tight around her waist, the knee-high leather boots and freshly-applied lipstick. But who is the elegant man she is with? Rachel doesn't know him. She tucks herself into a shop doorway to watch, taking care to keep out of sight. Sees the brief kiss they exchange. The light touch of fingertips as they separate off into the Christmas crowd. Intrigued, Rachel walks on towards the hotel and peers in through its bowed-casement windows at the white linen-clad tables, the fine damask napkins, silver cutlery, cruets and candlesticks. Quite a place, she thinks, opening one side of the large storm doors and poking her nose into the lavishly carpeted reception to breathe in the soft piped Mozart and warm smells of roast beef and red wine. Quite the place for a romantic rendezvous.

Leaving the cobbles behind, a hundred and one scenarios about what she has or hasn't seen whirling round her head, she stops to look at the prettily lit window display of an art gallery and, after a few seconds of deliberation, steps inside. The tinkling of a bell alerts a dark-haired man sitting behind a computer screen in the far corner.

"Hello," he calls out cheerily. "Nice the rain's stopped. Please feel free to have a look around." And he returns to whatever it is he is doing.

She smiles and, tugging her handbag higher on her shoulder, immediately sees there is much of the usual in here. Walls of large landscapes produced in oils that have been squeezed straight from the tube. Great jutting slabs supposedly depicting the grey Welsh slate, the country's sky and sea, that in spite of the dramatic subject matter, have little by way of distinguishable features or perspective. She wants to be wowed, in the way she had been as a child taken on trips to the National Gallery in London, but seldom is. She sighs inwardly at the plinths distributed around the gallery's floor space, displaying various sculptures in bronze and clay; they too are a disappointment. A shame, she could have been in the market for a horse's head or a wide-eyed hare, envisaging something of that ilk looking rather good on the shelves of her place. There is, of course, the usual array of eye-snarling abstracts, or pizza toppings, as she calls them. Garish canvasses in synthetic-looking colours that snagging at her memory, remind her of Laura's paintings. Those she tacked to the fridge door in Heron Way, that as her daughter grew, became overlapped by others. Infantile as they may have been, they still exhibited a greater sensitivity than some of these.

She sniffs, the theme of that children's TV programme *Take Hart* finding her out of nowhere as she digs a tissue from the pocket of her jeans. Then, looking up — she doesn't know how she missed it — there's an impressive sculpture of a fighter jet, suspended by silvery threads from a ceiling that has been painted to look like a summer sky: blue with fluffy white clouds. Except the plane isn't a plane. There are none of the usual sharp man-made angles, no hard metal casing or threatening propellers and undercarriage. Its shape has been made soft and benign by a padding of plump fleece, and its nose, body and wings look as gentle as a sheep itself.

"Wow," she says, the sound an involuntary one. And embarrassed, she makes a quick check of the man at the desk. Luckily, he hasn't heard, his gaze focused on his screen. She reads the blurb given by the artist, on the wall below the fleecy jet plane, thinks of the message contained within its woollen casing. Images come of the aborted calf she found drowned in its placenta halfway up the hillside. The upturned bulk of that dead ewe. *Fighter jets.* This montage is intriguing in its illustration of the untold damage these things cause, even here, amidst the soft Welsh hills they use as a playground. Forcing the viewer to question the wider reaching effects and what conditions might be like for those this war machine threatens for real.

"Clever, isn't it?" the man suggests, without moving his head, his right hand dragging and dropping, stays cupped over a tailless mouse. "The artist's a bit of an eco-warrior — anti-war, that kind of thing. It's not so much for sale — it's more of a statement really, a protest against the upset low-flying aircraft cause . . . there's a petition, if you're interested? It's through there." He gives the smallest gesture to indicate another room she hasn't seen yet. "We could do with all the names we can muster — but of course, there's no obligation."

Rachel thinks she sees him blush and gives him a shy little nod, before ducking beyond a low lintel and into another white-walled space. Immediately she is more comfortable, out of the imagined gaze of the good-looking proprietor. There are some intriguing pieces in here. Her attention is drawn to an especially beautiful watercolour hanging at chin height. A scene she recognises from her walks. The bracken, rust-coloured and bleeding into the feathery, leafless trees that look purple with cold. The weight of cloud jostling the horizon just as it does in this part of the world. Suggestions of cattle, the colours of pebbles, a scattering of sheep thrown like beads against the slope of hills. There too is what she believes is the familiar bow of the river Sawdde running alongside the chapel cemetery, cutting a cold, steel curve through the cleft of valley. Of course, she knows there must be dozens of scenes that look like this and many of them captured and exhibited in here. But something about this one grabs her and she decides to ask for further information.

"Excuse me," Rachel says to the man behind the desk. "The artist who painted the landscapes?"

He has deep blue eyes, almost violet. Encased in beautiful dark lashes that are as long as a girl's. She hadn't noticed them until now. Directed on her, they make her mouth go dry.

"Keith Hunter," he says in a way that suggests her choice pleases him. "A fine painter — one of my best. He's as popular in these parts as he is further afield and quite the collectable —" he says, stopping mid-flow to laugh. "Hark at me — forever the salesman."

"No." Rachel wants to reassure. "Not at all, I'm interested. I can see he's very talented. I was wondering . . ."

"Yes?" He gives her the ocean-blue depths of his eyes again.

Rachel takes a moment, thinks of the painting with its hills of auburn bracken, the smattering of yellow gorse. "Is he local?"

"Keith? Yes, I believe he is." Mr Blue Eyes swivels round in his leather chair and stands up. She notices his hands, the elegant length of fingers and manicured nails as he clicks out of whatever it was he was doing on the screen. He smells good too. Rachel, catching his aftershave as he moves towards her, sees the newly washed cotton of his indigo shirt that, open slightly at the collar, reveals a tight thatch of dark chest hair. Handsome, she thinks, wondering when she last had the opportunity to say this about a man.

They walk into the back gallery, him following inches behind and when they reach the painting, she turns and realises how tall he is. In his early forties, she guesses, taking in the rich gleam on his blue-black hair, greying at the temples. He has a five o'clock shadow like Spencer's, the unwanted connection sweeping her up like a wave and dropping her somewhere out of her depth.

"This is the one I like," she says firmly. "I'm sure it's the view I have on walks from my house."

"*Y Llwybr Briallu*," he reads the plaque on the wall, pronouncing the Welsh as fluidly as Dai had done.

Rachel, forgetting herself, claps her hands together excitedly. "I knew it — I recognised it instantly. That's The Primrose Path — it runs through my village."

"You know what it is in English." The man smiles, impressed. "Well aren't you the lucky one — living in such a pretty spot."

"Yes," she tells him feeling clumsy all over again. "It is lovely . . . really lovely."

"Bit out in the sticks for me," he says. "This is about as rural as I go."

"You live in town?"

"Above the gallery."

"So, this is your business then?"

"Yep, been going four years now."

"Where were you before here?"

"English borders — Monmouthshire."

"I didn't think you sounded like you were from round here." Rachel grins. "You sound too posh."

"Crikey, *posh* eh? Don't let my mother hear you say that. Good Valley's girl is my mother."

"This Keith Hunter." Rachel, her attention returning to the painting. "Does he always paint the countryside around here?"

"When he paints the great outdoors, which he doesn't very often." He steps back, his gaze drifting from one to another of the artist's work. "Landscapes aren't his usual bag, he tends to concentrate on still-life studies. These." His arm swings out in a generous arc to encompass five or so of the artist's landscapes. "Well, they're a bit of a diversion for him."

"I do like this one — but have you any others I can see?" Rachel asks.

"Not in the gallery, but I can show you more online."

She nods and the man turns on his heels and, ducking under the lintel, is back at his desk. She follows on, watches him sit and double click to open up the gallery's website. "Here we go — these are some he's sold, and these . . ." Rachel leans over, close enough to feel the heat off his skin, "are a selection I have in storage."

Rachel doesn't seem to hear. She steps back into the room with Keith Hunter's work, wanting to study the painting again. And not put off by the price tag, says, "I'd like to buy it." Clasping the bulky body of her bag tight to her chest. "It's just what I've been looking for."

"Okay — yeah? Great choice. As I said, he's very collectable, very popular — I'm sure it'll give you a lot of pleasure." The man pauses, looks down to study his hands as though he is about to ask her something completely unrelated. But he doesn't. Snapping back, his focus is returned to business. "Now, are you finished in town, or would you like me to wrap it for you to collect later?"

"No, I'll take it now, if that's all right — I was heading back to the car when I came in."

"Well," he says, looking at his wristwatch, "it's later than I thought — if you hang on a minute I think I might as well finish here for the day. Where are you parked?"

"Top of Queen Street, by the church."

"Great, I'm going that way myself — let me carry it for you." He pauses, sweeps a hand through his molasses-thick hair. "Actually, I'm on my way up to the Eagle Arms — early evening drink to wind down, you know . . . just an idea — and I hope you won't think me presumptuous — but . . . maybe you'd like to join me? Celebrate your purchase?" Eyebrows arching, he smiles expectantly, showing a perfect row of even white teeth.

Rachel scoots a sideways look at him, his invitation so unexpected. "Oh, erm . . . a drink . . . erm . . . I really don't think I can," she stammers, adjusting her face. Lovely as he is, this is way too sudden. "Another time, though?" she is quick to add, shaping her suggestion into a question when she sees his smile slide. "Thing is, I've been out ages already and I've a dog at home I need to see to."

Their chat is easy on the walk to her car. Dodging puddles one second, bumping up against each other the next. Making room for others to pass between them with their lumpy shopping bags, they exchange the bare bones of their lives. His voice is breathy, eager, telling her his name. Graham. Looking at him she decides it suits him, and listening, she hears how he was ten when his father died and his mother is frail, but in possession of all her marbles, and living in a care home in Monmouth. Asking whether he has any other family, Graham says he has a sister, Eleanor. He gives the name as if it is some kind of afterthought, which makes Rachel suspect the two of them aren't all that friendly. A single mother herself now, he tells how she and her husband split some years back, that Eleanor was left to bring up their two boisterous sons on her own. Yes, thinks Rachel, it usually is the mother who brings up the children when a marriage fails. But not her. When her role ended as a wife, it ended as a mother, too. The bond between Laura and her father was too strong. Daddy's girl — about the only thing Rachel and her own daughter had in common and, because of it, Laura will be forever lost to her.

Pushing her resentments away, she tells Graham about her recent move from the south east and that yes, she was married and ran her own business not all that long ago. That her father's death and finding herself at a crossroads in her life made her decide to come to Wales — a place of happy holidays as a child. No, they divorced ten years ago and, unable to use Spencer's name, she tells him how her ex now lives abroad, carefully avoiding all mention of her child.

She may feel comfortable in Graham's company, but never far away is the fear that stops her getting too carried away. Reminding her at intervals that she knows nothing about this man, of the terrible mistakes she has made in the past, judging it safe to trust, when really it wasn't. It nearly got her killed. After all — the voice of reason banging loud in her ears — this may seem like an innocent encounter, but she doesn't know what his intentions are. She cannot expect the feelings of trepidation that come whenever she is alone with a strange man, an anxiety that has dogged her for years, to evaporate like mist during a single conversation. This is something she will carry with her always, living with it so long, it shapes all she does. How could it not? Surviving something so traumatic, she's lucky it allows her any normality at all.

CHAPTER
FORTY-ONE

Quiet tonight. The weather, and it is awful, must be keeping the girls inside. But on the off-chance there might be someone mad enough to be out in it, I wait on, drawing triangles in the condensation on the window, listening to the rain hammer the roof. Got nothing much to listen to music-wise, I've given up on the radio. Beyond the news, and that's not for another hour, it's too late for much else.

I like the news, especially at the moment. It gives me a glow, hearing the name of the town that is on the map because of me. To think that people out there, in cars, living rooms, kitchens, are listening to the details of things I've done. It almost makes me want to go and hand myself in, give them my name. I'd be famous then. My face would be sent into orbit by every newspaper in the land.

Except I've not finished, I'm not quite ready to hang up my boots just yet. It's still way too exciting, the supremacy I feel when I've got a cute-looking girl in here with me. Especially when she thinks she's still in with a chance of getting away, when she's begging for her life. I hadn't realised what that would feel like — wielding that kind of power over somebody. And I have to say, if you haven't tried it out yourself, it has to be the biggest thrill going. So no, I don't think I'll be giving this game up just yet, not when there's still so much fun to be had.

CHAPTER
FORTY-TWO

Before turning out the light, Rachel, taking a last look at her newly acquired painting now hanging on the wall opposite her bed, is wondering what her mother might be doing. Was she filling her days any differently now that her husband was dead and her daughter gone? She paces through the house she keeps in her mind, finding nothing more inviting than a succession of closed doors that if she dared to open, would smell of wet autumn leaves and decay.

There are many who would say it's a shame Rachel lost touch with her friends. The only way she knew how to keep safe in the months following her abduction, and more so after her break with Spencer, was to cut herself off from the outside world. Maybe it is a shame, she thinks, counting the wasted years she spent in that house, but having no emotional ties made it easier to walk away from her London life and start afresh in Wales. She can't say she missed her friends. Like Aunty Alice, they didn't understand how surviving that terrible ordeal changed her and she could tell she frustrated them with her seeming inability to put it behind her. Rachel didn't need other people, she was always closest to her father, and he showed himself to be more loyal and understanding than anyone.

Throughout her childhood her father was permitted a room of his own. One so at odds with the rest of the house, the nastiness of school and the world going on outside its windows, that Rachel often sought sanctuary there. A beautiful room full of surprises. Padded albums of sepia photographs of his family in Canada, the grandfather and grandmother and uncles she would never meet. Sumptuous tassel-cornered cushions that would return to their original plumped up shapes when she pulled away from them. The crackly sounds of ancient records spinning on his turntable.

"Dance for me, my angel child." He would coo, swivelling in his toffee-coloured high-backed chair. His handsome face lit by the slanting rays of summer. And she did, wanting to please. Wanting to make herself worthy of the name he gave her. Spinning and twirling to the tear-jerking cello of Saint-Saens' "The Swan". Her toes sinking into the densely textured rugs that carpeted his room, giving her a sensation like walking on the sand on Westburn's beach. Pretending she was as glorious as Anna Pavlova, a woman so perfect she had a pudding named after her.

When she thinks of it, it is always summer in that room. The French windows flung wide for the birdsong and sunshine and the sweet smell of honeysuckle to spill in. And, perhaps because he had never been able to achieve it himself, her father would lay out his philosophy for life in this room. "Live for the moment — *carpe diem*," he would say, in a French-Canadian

216

accent he used until suffering the stroke that nearly cancelled it out. It is audible to her now, as her imaginary childhood hand touches again the bright gold flecks of his fleur-de-lis wallpaper that, set against a verdant backdrop, was also trapped within an eternal summer. A summer that existed for real in his garden — a setting singing with the hum of the honey bee and awash with colour.

Pushing her mind beyond this memory, she turns on to her side and closes her eyes . . . *Live for the moment*, she hears him. His remembered voice a whisper that rides Cadno's rhythm of sleep on the covers beside her. She is here, she has changed her name — the path for her future is laid and there is much to look forward to. The hack out with Carole tomorrow, for one, never mind Graham, the good-looking gallery owner, who rang earlier wanting to meet for coffee.

CHAPTER
FORTY-THREE

A fistful of hail is thrown against the bedroom window. Dai, waking from a sleep that barely began, listens to the volley of frozen rain as it moves over his house. Relatively snug beneath his duvet, he pictures it as something with fangs, gnashing and crushing everything in its path. Pulverising whatever is left of his vegetable beds, his treasured rose bushes, the first delicate shards of snowdrops. He turns over in bed for the umpteenth time. Apologises to his dead wife, momentarily forgetting she isn't there. His hand, vulnerable in its paper-thin skin, reaches out for her through the dark, wanting her warmth, the reassuring weight of her body.

A sheet of lilac-coloured lightning illuminates the room for a heartbeat and he counts in the way his mother taught him, reaching three, before a violent clap of thunder reverberates along his guttering. Another flash and he counts again, relieved to reach fifteen. His cat, Gabriel, jumps on to the bed and Dai smiles through the dark at the fluid weight of his paws, kneading and moulding the duvet, making a nest for himself. "Frightened, are you boy?" He extends a hand over the bedcovers, strokes the cat. "It's all right, it's moving over now. You *cwtch* up with me."

Still churned up from seeing that mass of a brute in The Bear the other night, Dai, now fully awake, is thinking of the effort it took to bat away Denzil's jibes. Squashing them down into the drink-sticky carpet, fearful Idris would hear. He still frightens Dai. And with good reason. That hiding he took from him and his brothers in the wake of the visit they had from the police all those years ago, would be enough to stick in anyone's memory. Accusing Dai of grassing them up about their sister, they nearly killed him. His injuries were so bad he needed the doctor out and a fortnight off school. His mother, jittery and nervous, bringing him soup and hot water bottles, badgered him for months for the names of the culprits he was too frightened to give. These things will never go away, he tried to explain to Denzil. Good company as he is, everything is so black and white in Denzil's world, he couldn't possibly understand the history between Idris and Dai. A history as engrained as the filth wedged between the furrows of flesh of that animal's jowls.

Denzil did make him laugh though, linking Idris to those two dead girls. Sure, he visits the Somerset area on a regular basis, and has both the opportunity and facility to entertain in that huge haulage truck of his. Positively boudoir-esque that cabin, from what he's seen, with its bedroom curtains and whatever else he's kitted it out with. It's where he sleeps when he's away; no doubt he's made it a right home from stinking home. But picking it apart with his lawyer's brain, this scenario is hardly likely, is it? Yes, the brute is more

219

than capable of violence, but it's a bit thin, nothing more than wishful thinking on his part. So what if he drives to Somerset . . . Westburn, even, it doesn't make him a killer. Dai doesn't believe for a second Idris gets his hands on any women, let alone these young good-lookers, how could he? They'd run a mile. No, to even contemplate this for a second is to breathe oxygen into Denzil's fantasy, or perhaps his own. Because let's face it, there's nothing he'd like more than the bastard to be guilty, to have him banged up for ever. For what he did to Beth, that's exactly where he should be.

Dai turns over again. Lets go a groan of desperation at not being able to drift off into oblivion. His mind, a carousel of twirling images, spins brightly lit scenarios and turns on a perpetual loop. *What goes around; comes around.* A favourite of his mother's, and the reason why she did all she could by baking angel cakes and giving Beth bars of scented soap — small things to try and make her life better. He doesn't blame his parents; they were good people, torn by the dilemma of knowing what they knew but not where to take it. Reporting suspected child abuse wasn't something you did in the sixties, you kept your nose firmly out of other people's business, even when it came to the life of a child.

Out of the darkness and quiet, now the rain has eased, Dai is conscious of a rasping sound. Abrasive, like sandpaper rubbed over a block of wood. He realises it is him and that he is crying. No wonder he can't bring himself to step back inside that barn, whatever amazing transformation it has undergone. He would still be able to sense her — the ghost of his childhood sweetheart.

CHAPTER
FORTY-FOUR

Carole Deacon, trim and chic in tweed hacking jacket and riding breeches, is waiting for Rachel to arrive on her front doorstep. All smiles under an ash-grey sky.

"Reckon the rain will hold off, don't you?" she calls out, swinging her legs into a pair of expensive-looking riding boots.

Rachel — not entirely sure this is a good idea after the episode with Tracy — is embarrassed about her ancient gear: the hastily mended coat sleeve and her outmoded hat. She is at least pleased with the way her jodhpur boots look after the polishing she gave them. Following Carole along the paved path cutting between lawn and house, she smiles as they pass an assortment of squat stone gargoyles, liking how there are people just as quirky as her. The paddocks are well drained and green despite the time of year, and are encased within neat post-and-rail fences. The small square of yard, when they reach it, is girdled by a selection of outbuildings that mimic the gabled design of the house.

"This is lovely — did you have these built specially?" Rachel asks Carole, who is busy unlocking the first timber door on her right.

"Wally designed it."

"Really smart."

"This is the stable block and that is Wally's taxidermy room." Carole points.

"Oh, yes. Of course, he would need a special space to do all that, wouldn't he?"

"Yes," Carole giggles, "no way I was having the entrails of dead animals in the house."

"No, I don't suppose you would." Rachel adopts a suitable face.

Carole has already brought the horses in, brushed them down and tacked them up. But it isn't until they are walked out into daylight that Rachel sees just how immaculate they are. Well shod, too, she can't help but notice, liking the way Carole has brushed over the same shiny hoof oil she used to put on Trinket. The liquorice smell takes her right back to Pinkton Grange, but only dispenses happy memories.

"We've just a small section of the A40 to do before we can ride on to the hill," Carole informs when they are both in the saddle. "They're good with traffic but take care to keep Molly well on the verge, they can come at a fair old lick along that stretch."

A pleasant day now the wind has dropped and, looking out from beneath her riding hat, Rachel sees some encouraging wisps of blue above. She leans forward in the saddle to stroke Molly's soft dark coat and watching the mare's ears flicking back and forth, doesn't see the dark blue juggernaut thundering towards them at breakneck speed. A bellowing horn, the hiss of air as brakes are applied, and the mare is bolting out of control. Happening in a flash, it catches Rachel unawares and, within seconds her feet are dangling free of the stirrups, the hard metal rings banging against the tender bone of her ankles. Molly, continuing to career into oncoming traffic, is making the world a blur on Rachel's panicked periphery and, groping around for the non-existent reins, she is unable to keep hold, until finally she is hurled free of the saddle and on to the road.

Unable to move, she lies on her side, the sounds of metal hooves and traffic terrifyingly close to her ear. Dazed, she watches the slow turn of the sky through the fingers of bare trees. Then she hears shouts. Picks out her name. But still she can't move. Won't move. Fearful it will hurt.

"Rachel . . . Rachel . . ." Carole, through sounds of hurtling traffic, is kneeling beside her, one hand holding a collection of leather reins. Looking sideways, Rachel can see her smart cream breeches are covered in mud. "Are you all right? Why the hell doesn't somebody stop?" And she waves her hands around in frantic helplessness.

"I don't know." One answer to both questions; mindful of the pain in her leg and arm. "I don't know." And she starts to cry. Cry at the shame of it. For what promised to be a wonderful afternoon out in the pretty Welsh countryside on a lovely horse with her new friend. "It's me he wants . . ." she mumbles. "Me he wants to kill . . ."

"What, what d'you say, sweetheart?"

224

". . . after me . . . bad man to involve you . . . should never have let him out . . . he's dangerous . . . stop at nothing . . ."

"What man, Rachel — what are you talking about?"

Rachel, her expression blank, looks stunned. "He didn't hurt you did he? Did you fall off?" she rambles, barely audible, her teeth chattering.

"No, darling, I managed to cling on. Just slipped running after Molly." Carole strokes Rachel's ashen cheek: motherly, affectionate.

"Is Molly all right?" she sobs.

"She's fine — don't worry about her, it's you we need to see to."

Finally, a car slows to a stop on the opposite side. What luck. It's Tracy, in her Defender, wearing her beautiful cherryred coat.

"Carole?" she shrieks through an open window, her face yanked wide at the unfolding drama. "My God, what happened? Is that Rachel — is she all right?" And leaping from the car, agile in spite of her heels, she races towards them.

"I'm okay," Rachel, manages to sit. "I don't think I've broken anything — can you help me up?"

Carole and Tracy swap looks then lift her to her feet.

"That was one hell of a fall, you poor bugger," Carole looks at Rachel, tears in her eyes. "Bloody idiots, the way they speed along here . . . could have killed us . . ." Tracy isn't listening; she's concentrating on Rachel who, prodding and inspecting the scuffed knees of her jodhpurs, is looking for signs of serious injury.

"Come on *cariad*, let's get you home." Tracy is close enough for Rachel to smell her hairspray and wonders if she's been off with that man again. "You going to be all right taking those horses back on your own?" she says to Carole. "D'you want me to call Hywel?"

"Crikey, no. I'll be fine," Carole assures, smoothing Snap-dragon's nose with a gloved finger. "I can ride Molly and lead him, it'll be fine. I've done it before."

"If you're sure?"

"I'm sure. You get Rachel home; she's had one hell of a scare."

"You both have." Tracy gives Carole a quick hug. "All right, look, I'll give you a ring later, make sure you're okay."

How badly designed humans are. Rachel, examining her wrist in the bath hours later, traces with a finger the crests of its starfish scar that has served as a permanent reminder of a past she would far rather dump. She examines too, the network of veins, blue-green tributaries running along the tender insides of her arms. We are nothing really, so fragile and weak. A flash of the hammer, the blood, that woman's screams as she fought for her life. She drops it — she can't keep going there, and exchanges the horror for an image of Laura instead. Laura at bath time, happy and playful amidst bubbles and toys. How Rachel would marvel at her perfect little body, counting up the ridges of her spine, her fingers, her toes. A painful memory, for different reasons — her child, now so far away. It scares her how long it's been and she worries whether she could pick her out in a crowd now.

Lathering her sponge, she washes under her arms, between her toes. Her body is bruised from her fall, but the water is soothing. Strange, but today's drama has invigorated her. Obviously, she could have done without falling off, but decides — as no real harm's been done; the driver was probably only Idris and her whereabouts are still a mystery — it is good to really *feel* something for a change. As a child she felt dislocated from the world, it made her want to punch the wall or hurl her school books — do a real physical thing to prove she made a difference. Not that the violent outbursts were part of her make-up then, those came later. Trapped inside Spencer's pristine house, when rabid and frothing at the mouth, she would take out on him the frustrations that had built up inside her on Grand Avenue. No wonder she frightened him, frightened Laura. Because these outbursts morphed into something far worse in the years after their daughter was born. So much so she couldn't trust herself, often slamming out of the house when Spencer was at work, Laura's baby demands too much for her when she felt so underdeveloped herself.

Is she over that now — have passing years and experiences cured her of such volatility? She can't be sure. And catching her reflection in the steamed-up bathroom mirror, she thinks how there hasn't been anything to test her in quite the same way since. So it will just have to be something she hopes — hopes she isn't that person any more.

CHAPTER
FORTY-FIVE

Jennifer watches from the doorway of her sitting room as Mrs Pepper bumps the vacuum up the stairs before venturing into the hall to drag a forefinger along the picture rail, nodding, satisfied, when she brings it back dust free. Moving along the passageway, checking other things that may have been missed, she is blocked by her reflection hanging shoulder-height in the ornate oval mirror. Old, she judges. Always harsh. And using the palms of her hands, pulls back the sides of her face and says, "This is how I used to look." Later, at church, kneeling in the cold, she will seek absolution for this, along with the other failings in her body. Imperfections and malfunctions that failed to deliver during her reproductive years; that in turn destroyed her marriage and the relationship with her only child. Whatever kind of a person Jennifer is, she does know herself, she is aware of her shortcomings. In many ways she is her own worst enemy.

Heading back into her spotless kitchen, she opens the odds and sods cupboard, hunting for stamps. Jennifer had forgotten she'd kept this. The scrapbook. Its purple pages feel coarse under the pads of her fingers and on rubbing it, like the genie out of a bottle, up pop images of her daughter. She should pass this on to Derek Barnes, it might be useful. It's not as if she can let him have what she found in Donald's room. Things she keeps shoved at the back of a drawer in her mother's old writing desk that make her insides go all cold when she thinks about them. No, she decides, she must wait for him to find Sarah first, talk to her before doing anything with those. She owes her that much.

Testing the weight of the scrapbook, she realises it's too heavy to post and would be easier if she trotted it round to his Highgate offices instead. She looks sideways at the card she's written to Sarah and left on top of the bread bin. A little of her news jotted on the blank left-hand side. But with still no address to send it to, in spite of the private investigator's continued efforts to track her down, the envelope flap stays open, quivering each time she breezes past it into the kitchen.

Using her Cuisinart Coffeemaker, the Arabica beans ground by her favourite barista in Highgate Village and her whitest china — a matching mug and saucer — she takes her coffee into the sumptuously dressed sitting room, settles down and lights up a menthol cigarette before opening the scrapbook on her knees. Grainy images of Pinkton Grange garnered from newspapers seventeen years ago. Their zigzag borders defined by her pinking shears. A pretty photograph of Sarah when she first left school. Ones taken of her some years later, cavorting in thick eye make-up and a low-cut top. Another holding a pint of lager and laughing. Beautiful Sarah. Dazzling Sarah. What those in the media term as *camera-ready*. No wonder they couldn't leave her alone, this face sold papers. As did the photographs of Blundell. All framed by the saw-tooth blades of her dressmaker scissors and pasted in here as if the whole sorry episode was something to be proud of. The mad farrier whose colouring reminds Jennifer of a sandy beach after the tide's gone out. A man whose job allowed him to prey on young women, these articles say. Not that there were any young women who came forward to substantiate this claim, she thinks, exhaling cigarette smoke. This was a label the red tops plucked from thin air and stapled to his already dodgy reputation. The same journalists who liked to inform their readers that Blundell had a penchant for spoilt little rich girls who looked good in jodhpurs with long blonde hair. A man who didn't even like horses, who was known, on occasion, to be cruel to them, rough with them, anonymous sources said. The same anonymous sources who were quick to brand him a loner, someone who liked working in isolated stable yards, where the girl and her horse were often the only ones around.

Jennifer, her eyebrows furrowing much as they would have done when reading this material for the first time, looks at her coffee and decides without trying that it is still too hot to drink. These statements didn't stand up to scrutiny at the time and they certainly don't now. Blow on them and they all fall down. But it's only the sensational that sells papers, what does the truth matter? Apparently little, there being no one, other than his dead wife, Linda — a woman he battered to death with a hammer — and the testimony of a then-teenage girl, to corroborate these sketchy details. Her awareness of this makes the editorials she has in her lap more unsettling. Especially when she is the mother of the girl who, dumped at the end of the road, disorientated and scared, unwittingly brought fragments of Mrs Blundell's skull imbedded in her hair and what remained of her clothes, into her home.

She recoils in disgust at the images she has kept of this man. The thought of his filthy working-class hands all over her beautiful daughter is almost too much. She reads on, hears her Sarah's voice echoing the printed words that are quoted to come from her: *I fought back* . . . Jennifer thinks again of those deep and ragged cuts Sarah had in the flesh of her upper arms, buttocks and thighs, that ugly five-pronged scar she still has on the inside of her wrist — *but he was too strong . . . said he'd kill me if I tried to escape . . . knife to my throat . . . middle of nowhere . . . blindfold . . . handcuffs . . . couldn't move, totally helpless . . . he raped me . . . and then his wife turned up . . . he went mad . . . couldn't help her . . . terrible . . . terrible . . .*

Jennifer snaps shut the scrapbook and stubs out her cigarette. So quiet in this room, she can hear the ticking of Donald's carriage clock — just one of many gifts he received on his retirement. Shame it was only ever Sarah he took on his trips to Somerset. Those overnights in B&Bs in quaint little seaside towns. It would have been fun, romantic even, because home alone she was left to imagine all sorts. But fearing their looks if she dare suggest she tag along with them, she didn't ask. She picks up her mug and drinks slowly. The sufficiently cooled coffee from the bridal-white porcelain tastes good. She notices the lipstick mark she leaves behind. Blood red and startling. It sparks memories of the rubbish those vultures went on to write about Sarah falling in love with her captor. How they splashed it over their trashy newspapers and tried to substantiate their claims by using psychiatric reports to prove it wasn't such an uncommon phenomenon. Jennifer feels her anger rise afresh. A helpless, voiceless anger, identical to the one she had then. How dare they. She slams the delicate china mug down into its matching saucer, making the occasional table wobble against the arm of her chair. As if anyone could seriously imagine a girl of Sarah's calibre falling for a murdering savage like that. The suggestion was monstrous.

Standing up, she goes to the patio doors to stare out at the garden. Mr Antonelli, snouting around in the frozen remains, is in the process of raking up the leaves and garden mulch that litter her dead husband's flower beds.

"Bloody fool," she sneers through the frost-patterned glass. "They'll be back an hour after you've gone."

"You all right, Mrs D'Villez?" asks Mrs Pepper, her housecoat bulging with keys, a spare can of furniture polish and other things she may need as she busies herself around Jennifer's home.

"Nothing the matter with me." Irritated by the sound of the cleaner's rubber-soled slippers fighting against the plush pile of her silk-mix Axminster, she swings around to face her, brusque as ever. "You still here? I thought you'd left ages ago." Her eyes follow Mrs Pepper as she expertly manoeuvres about the room; dusting the mantelpiece, the window sills, emptying the wastepaper basket.

"Just this last stretch now, Mrs D'Villez." Unperturbed as always by her employer's rudeness, Mrs Pepper looks away, resumes the job she is paid for. "I'll be out of your hair in a second."

"Have you done what I asked in Sarah's room?"

"What, sorry — Sarah's room?" Mrs Pepper stops dusting, her expression clouding behind her thickened lenses.

"Take down the curtains, clear her stuff out, lay dustsheets? I did say." Silence. Jennifer throws her arms above her head in an overly dramatic response. "I've the decorators coming first thing Wednesday."

"So you're going ahead with it then, I didn't think you were serious." Lifting ornaments, her chirpy yellow duster wiping beneath them, the domestic help continues to circle the sitting room with well-practised hands.

"*Didn't think I was serious?*" Jennifer echoes back. "I don't employ you to decide what I mean or don't mean — I gave you a simple instruction —"

Mrs Pepper doesn't speak. Her back to Jennifer, the air between them hangs with the artificial spray of polish, small sounds of clunking as objects are returned to their places. If they are to speak again today it is Jennifer who will need to fill the gap.

"If you've time now, can you sort it?" Jennifer's voice softens. "I'll give you a hand if you like?"

"No, it's okay, Mrs D'Villez, I've got time, I'll do it before I go."

Jennifer listens to Mrs Pepper shuffle off, the sounds of things being tidied into the cleaning cupboard, the flex of the vacuum wound away. Then her weight, as she climbs the stairs, moves along the landing and opens the door to Sarah's old room. Leaving Jennifer at the bottom of the stairs, fingers crossed and praying she did a thorough enough job of checking it. That her cleaning lady isn't about to uncover any more nasties like the ones she unearthed in Donald's room.

CHAPTER
FORTY-SIX

Christmas Eve, and Rachel has never seen such rain. It doesn't seem to come from the sky but twists down on the wind, and this is new to her. Never so exposed to the weather before moving here, she is learning the way of it now. On her walks to the village with Cadno tugging on his leash, she sees women carrying fir trees and sprigs of bright-berried holly into their houses. Balancing in slippered feet on stepladders to pin multicoloured lights under the moss-slippery weatherboards. She envisages their children, sitting up at high kitchen tables, writing letters starting with *Dear Santa*. It makes her think of Laura, and how flat this time of year feels without her, and she counts up the Christmases they have spent apart.

She walks to Garn Goch in an attempt to cheer herself. The weather certainly helps take her mind off things — it is wild, with the tumbling sky gobbling down the land by the fistful. By the time she comes home she is soaked through to her underwear. Nearly dark, but there isn't a light at Cwm Glas. The power is out all along the valley, so Rachel tries to rejuvenate the fire with the new delivery of logs that aren't really dry. They smoke miserably in the grate, smouldering down to blackened charcoal lumps without giving any proper heat. She goes about lighting candles, liking the way the smell of burning wax fills her rooms and, sitting under a duvet, the dog curled and dreaming beside her, she watches the fizz and spit of the feeble flames.

Then, before bed, feeling the need for it, she drinks down two schooners of the sherry she bought in case of visitors, and afterwards goes to stand outside to stare at the stars that poke through the ragged shift of cloud. She thinks of the miles of stone walls, crumbling under the weight of moss and darkness up on the hill. The skinny-hipped cows, with their new-born calves steaming into the cold night air, standing in the unforgiving quagmire and reeds. And how, come morning — what will be Christmas morning — the skies will again be filled with fluctuating clouds and whatever light is to be gleaned from the day.

CHAPTER
FORTY-SEVEN

"You want to show Dai what they've done with your place." Tracy, livelier in lipstick and mascara and looking different to the way she usually does when she's at home, passes Rachel a thimble of sherry and points to the bowl of crisps set out for her guests. Then turning to Dai, "Honestly, you wouldn't recognise it."

Rachel isn't listening. She is busy watching Tracy's sons, Llew and Tom, who are sitting on the floor and opening the presents she bought them. The way they hold them up to the lights under the Christmas tree and sneer. She drinks her sherry in one gulp. Feels embarrassed.

"*Oh*, now then," Tracy, sensing their twinned mockery, their silent looks that communicate only one thing: the ineptness of grown-ups. She tries to compensate. "Aren't they *lovely*. You make sure you thank Rachel properly for those, please, boys." And they do. Chiming their lie in unison. Making her feel twice as useless, so it is she who flaps their well-brought-up platitudes away. She hadn't appreciated how advanced they are. They have never looked much, the glimpses of hip to knee she has had of them as their father drives them to the school bus stop. But they are young men, with the taste and knowhow for all the latest gismos youngsters have nowadays. It makes her feel old. Out of the loop. Which of course she is. It being what she wanted.

Rachel leans back into the squashy sofa and absentmindedly brushes dog hairs from her black trousers as she holds out her dainty glass for the refill Tracy is pressing on her. Smells of gravy and sprouts follow her hostess in from the kitchen and, watching her return to her pit of steam waving away their offers of help, Rachel gives herself a few seconds to take in the room. Crammed with outmoded furniture and over-warm. The blazing orange of the woodburner crackles beyond its glass door and the room is far too bright. The fierceness, dispensed by a hundred-watt bulb above their heads, extinguishes any sense of cosiness. She stands and moves forward to inspect the tree, stares at her reflection in a huge silver bauble and yawns. The distorted image, an over-fat chin, distended mouth — it reminds her of the hall of mirrors along Westburn's seafront. She must have made an involuntary sound, as the boys, sitting cross-legged amidst a sea of redundant wrapping paper, nudge each other and giggle. She grins at them, wanting to show she is one of the good guys, but suspects the act of pulling her lips back only makes her appear more freakish. She leaves them to it and sits down again, tugging at the throat of her polo neck. It's so hot, she is regretting her choice of outfit, her thermal underwear. What was she thinking? She knows from the oven-hot interior of Tracy's car that she likes the warmth. But her decision was made on waking to the results of a spectacularly clear night sky, with the view beyond her rime-glazed windows shining blue with cold. Her mind wandering, she dips in and out of the chatter going on between Dai, Hywel and Hywel's mother without feeling the need to join in. The noise of the television — the melodrama of some Spaghetti Western — makes the effort it would take to join in feel too much like hard work. Instead, she watches the brotherly banter stirring between the twins who, teasing and pinching just under the radar of their father, are pulled back into line when they step over it.

When they are finally called through to the kitchen to eat, Rachel sees a table laid with a Christmas-red cloth, lit candles and expensive-looking serviettes ruched into long-stemmed glasses. She lets go a gasp of appreciation, sees Tracy smile, proud. A cracker has been positioned at a diagonal over each placemat. The kinds of placemats found in pubs, showing sepia scenes of long-ago lives. Young women in crisp white blouses and ankle-length skirts, leaning against gate posts and upturned ploughs, smiling coyly for the gentleman photographer. Was country living ever like this? She doubts it, looking at Hywel uncorking wine with hands raw from his toil on the farm. This man never stops, not seen, before today, out of gumboots and overalls. "Red all right for you?" he asks, smiling through his weathered cheeks. And she nods, thanking him.

Tracy unpacks the oven. Distributes hot plates with the hem of her dress and a warning, "Not to touch." The boys snigger, nudge one another in the ribs, entertained by some secret something. Rachel does her best not to think they are laughing at her and watches Hywel open his mouth, about to speak, to tell them to pull themselves together perhaps. He is stopped by a look Tracy gives him that Rachel isn't equipped to read. The language of the married, she gulps down a mouthful of merlot. Warm and soft, it coats her tongue, her throat. She remembers that look. It has something of her parents in it. Something of her and Spencer. Poor examples, she knows, as neither participant in these couplings spoke the same dialect, whatever illusion she may have been under at the time. Not like these two do, anyway. These two seem really special, and to think Tracy could be cheating on him with that man she saw her with in town, makes her sad. Rachel looks at them smiling across at each other — Hywel Morgan, handsome in his new Christmas jersey, Tracy, pretty in her woollen dress and suede plum court shoes. Her necklace swinging. "A present from Hywel," she said when Rachel asked, touching the moonstone, blushing.

She wouldn't mind something of what this couple have found. It's a dangerous game Tracy's playing if she's risking jeopardising this. Rachel wouldn't, if ever she were lucky enough to connect with another person this way. She allows herself to consider the merits of Graham for a second or two. To wonder what kind of Christmas he might be having at his sister's in Monmouth. Driving there and back in a day, he said, when they met for coffee for the first time last week. Too soon for her to be invited, of course, but maybe next year. Telling herself off for inventing such fantasies, she hears Hywel's mother asking her to pass the Brussels.

"Give yourself a heap on the way, dear," she croaks, her voice mechanical, like one of those old biddies off *The Archers*. "Tracy's done a sackful as usual, and knowing this lot, they'll only go to waste."

After the rigmarole of crisscrossing vegetable dishes, the pulling of crackers and the customary clamping of cheap tissue-paper hats on heads, Rachel feels her face becoming warm again. She is relaxing. Enjoying her delicious meal. Her numerous glasses of wine. These are lovely people, so generous. She thinks this as she looks around the table, studying each of their faces in turn. They have really helped to make her feel part of things in a way she has never experienced before. Watching Tracy. The way she speaks through silent gestures to her boys. This picture of family bliss is one she is determined to buy into, and so for the time being she banishes the image of Tracy in town with that man.

A cheer goes up as Hywel empties what must be half a bottle of brandy over the vast steaming pudding he proudly announces is his mother's doing. They raise their glasses to the ceiling and even the rosy-cheeked boys, managing to forget themselves for a second, squeeze out a smile. Tracy, on her feet again, dims the lights at the strike of a match, and after a whoosh, they watch in awe as the fabulous display of blue-yellow flames lick and curl against the dome of current-pitted skin. The Christmas pudding is delicious, so packed with fruit and booze that the room goes quiet, disturbed only by the sounds of appreciation between mouthfuls and the scraping clean of bowls.

"I thought I recognised you." Rachel turns to Hywel's mother during a break in the conversation. "We've met before — you had a stall at the Christmas market."

"Something about you was familiar to me too." Bridget Morgan beams. "Don't tell me . . . don't tell me . . ." Rachel watches her ferret through her memory. "You had a lovely blue jumper on and you bought something . . . took ages to choose."

"Crikey, you're on the ball." Rachel is impressed. "I did — I bought a little plum pudding — delicious too, I had it the other evening."

"Glad you enjoyed it, *bach*."

"Hywel," Rachel calls out across the table. "Your mum's amazing, can you believe she remembers seeing me? I can only have said two words."

"Everyone notices you Rachel." A smiling Tracy is the one to reply. "You've caused quite a stir in the village."

"Have I? Oh dear, I'm not sure I like that."

"Enjoy it, *bach*," Bridget pipes up again. "Lovely girl like you, hope you've a nice fella on the go?"

Rachel is suddenly shy and looks out from under her long dark lashes. "I might have met someone, yes." She feels herself blush, presses her fingers to it. "Of course, it's only early days, but we met for coffee in town last week."

"Wow, you dark horse — you never said." Tracy, standing up to offer up more of the pudding, waves a serving spoon over the table. "Who is he, where d'you meet him?"

"Is he handsome?" Bridget whispers, eager for news and grinning by her elbow.

"His name's Graham, he owns the art gallery in town."

"What — that posh place in Llandafen?" Hywel sounds impressed. "Nice work."

"Yes, but please, no one should get too carried away." Rachel, keen to quash their interest, is unsure how she ended up saying anything about Graham at all. "Honestly, we can't have spent longer than two hours together."

"Ah, but that's how all great love affairs start." Bridget Morgan sounds confident. "Trust me, sweetheart, no bloke with the sense he was born with is going to let a smashing-looking girl like you slip free."

The words, although meant as a compliment, make Rachel's blood chill in her veins.

"Tell me about the little girl who used to play in my barn," Rachel asks Dai on their walk home under a hood of steely stars.

"*Beth*, you mean?" Dai is momentarily thrown off guard. "Good gosh — however did you hear about her?"

"Tracy — when I asked about the origins of the place. She told me to ask you."

"Right . . . well, where to start? Beth — erm, well, she had a little dog. A Jack Russell called Tiny," he says eventually, and she hears the bones in his neck cracking as he tips his head to the sky.

"Did she play the trumpet?" Rachel, not wanting to slip on the icy lane, spreads out her arms to balance.

"The trumpet?" Dai, surprised. "Crikey, however d'you know about that? No, that was me — long ago mind, I doubt I could get a note out of one now."

"I found some sheet music in my shed. An atlas too." She doesn't mention the photographs, fearing he might want them back.

"You found my atlas." Dai is thrilled. "I thought I'd lost it." He takes a moment to breathe, to wrap the scarf the twins bought him, tighter round his neck. "Can I see it?" He asks in a way that suggests she might have thrown it away.

"Course you can, I'll drop it over. It's covered in cobwebs and the damp's got to it, but it's still readable."

Dai sighs, remembering. "Me and Beth, we loved looking through it — mapping out all the places we'd go when we grew up."

"And did you?" Rachel again. "Did you go?"

Dai laughs. This time a sad, hollow sound that is snatched up by the frosty fingers of night. "No. No. There wasn't the chance to go anywhere. Well, not together, anyway — nowhere further than the funfair in Porthcawl."

"That's a shame." Rachel, genuinely sorry. "Beth is Idris' sister, isn't she?"

"*Sister?*" Dai is miles away. "Idris' sister — yes, that's right, she was."

244

"Was?" Rachel asks.

"Is? Was?" Dai, quick to correct himself. "I don't know, we lost touch — years ago."

"I'm sorry," Rachel, aware Dai's voice is breaking under whatever the strain of the memory is. "Were the two of you sweethearts?"

"I loved her, if that's what you mean," Dai says simply, his candour surprising.

"I found some carvings in the beams upstairs. Are you D?" Rachel is careful; she can't see his face and is glad for it.

"Are they still there? Gosh, well, who'd have thought it?"

"Little heart shapes filled with B and D. Very sweet. It never dawned on me they could be you two."

"Why would it?" His voice is gentle. "Beth and me — we were from before you were born."

"You should come in and see." Rachel feels able to say, comfortable with this kind, slightly faded man who asks nothing of her. "I know Tracy said you wouldn't know the place, but I think you would — I'm sure it wouldn't feel all that different to you."

"No. No, I don't think so." Dai cuts her off.

A beat. "Because of your wife?" Rachel tentatively pushes her question through the dark. "Is it too soon?"

"You're a strange one," Dai says, and she can feel rather than see his smile. "You look too young to know anything of such things, and yet you do, don't you?"

Rachel, silent, listens to their footfalls bouncing against the crust of night — a blackness so velvety rich, she could poke her fingers into it. She waits for him to speak again.

"I've never been able to forget her, you see. I felt guilty about it when Elsie was alive, and now she's dead . . . the betrayal . . . it's worse. It may sound daft to you, but I feel I short-changed her." She listens to Dai breathing, steadying himself. "So yes, I suppose I do feel it's disloyal to her memory, giving in to my curiosity and coming to see where Beth and me were."

"It must have been innocent though, wasn't it? I can't believe, from what you've told me of Elsie, that she would have minded. We've all got a past, she probably had one of her own." Rachel takes a second to think of the small square photographs she found in her outbuilding. "I mean, you were only children."

"Innocent? Yes, we were." Dai doesn't sound entirely sure. "Whatever *innocent* means? There was this deep connection between us, right from when we were small. I used to think it was because of the kinds of kids we were — both bullied and Beth had the most terrible time at home. But as teenagers," he dispenses a small dry laugh, "I know this is difficult for you to imagine from an old fogey like me, but we had our moments — we spent a lot of time together, cosy in that barn of yours."

Rachel, staggered at his frankness, wants to know more. What did he mean when he said Beth had a terrible time at home, what happened to her — where is the sweet little girl in those photographs now? A distended image of Idris elbows its way into her thoughts and again it occurs to her, the damage that

246

Neanderthal of a man, with paws for hands, might be capable of. Dai meanwhile is deep in thought, and while she may have questions burning in her mouth, she won't push things, talking instead of her embarrassing funny turn the other day at the trekking centre. Keen to give her side of the story in case Tracy has mentioned her peculiar behaviour to him.

Within minutes they reach the turn into Tŷ Haf and Dai, placing a hand on her arm, tells her she mustn't feel pressurised into confiding things for the two of them to be friends.

"We're allowed secrets," he says, and, thinking he can read her mind, she blushes. The slither of moonlight catching the ridge of his nose, the noble crest of forehead. "Skeletons in cupboards, it's what comes from living. For me —" he chuckles, tapping his chest"— from living too long."

"*You?*" She echoes his laugh. "You're not old." She gives him a peck on his smooth-shaved cheek and smells her father: shaving foam, mothballs; his room with the fleur-de-lis wallpaper. "Happy Christmas," she says, cheered by how well the two of them understand each other. And, fishing out her door key, she heads inside to a waiting, wagging Cadno.

CHAPTER
FORTY-EIGHT

I've been looking for Beth Tudor most of my life, but there was a time when she lived no more than two fields away and we'd meet up in your old barn . . .

Days later Dai, sitting in his favourite chair, a mug of tea at his elbow, is thinking about what he should have said in reply to Rachel's question, walking home Christmas night. Instead of being vague, talking of inconsequential things like her Jack Russell and what big pals the three of them were. Sipping his tea, his thoughts spin to his earliest memories of Beth, a time before they became friends . . . a time spent watching her little hen-brown head bobbing around on the sloping concrete yard of Bryngwyn's Primary School through gaps in the fence. Spy holes made from knots of wood that fingers of previous generations had pushed through. Beth had a funny way of focusing on you and he couldn't work out why, until he saw that her left eye was slightly askew. It felt as if she was turning you inside out, that earnest, unwavering stare she had.

"Born with amblyopia," she informed him, as if he'd asked for a weather report. Always frank and to the point, she made him repeat back the word until he got it right — "Am-blee-OH-pee-uh." Not interested in

248

telling him how she knew of such a term any more than she was interested in sympathy. She had a funny eye, so what? He learnt quickly that Beth lived on a far higher plain, never one to weasel with words — it was what he liked most about her.

They first struck up conversation the day she got stuck in the fence. Straining to see over to the boys' side, the woollen sleeve of her too-big cardigan snagging on a broken slat, she called to him for help. Which he gave, without flinching, in spite of the jeers and taunts he got for talking to a girl.

"What did you want to see?" he asked, when the struggle of tugging free her buttons was over.

"Wanted a look at you lot, didn't I?" She grinned.

They met regularly at the bottom of the playground after that. The fence was lower there and meant, if they stood on tiptoes, they could look at each other. It also meant he was out of sight of the others, hidden by wild raspberry and loganberry canes and a bushy bank of laurel, its rich canopy of year-round green shielding him from the taunts of bigger boys.

"You're lucky you were born a boy," she said one afternoon, looking at the huge *Atlas of the World* he'd liberated from his father's bookshelves. "For a start, you don't have to wear your mother's cast-offs." And she laughed, showing him her little teeth and all the places she was going to travel to when she grew up, while he conjured up images closer to home. Images of the Tudors' farm. Deciding it was the opposite of his home: a happy place, smelling of his mother's baking, where you were guaranteed a cuddle. He would come to understand just how happy it was when he experienced what Beth lived amidst. And once equipped with the full horror, thinking about it, about her, in the safety of his trundle bed, his stomach would knot up, giving him bellyache like when he'd eaten too many of his da's gooseberries.

Cwm Glas farm was nothing better than a hole in the ground and this was the reason why, in the years before her mother died, Beth visited Dai's family all the time. Slopping down the lane in man-size boots that however old she got would have always been too big. Too shy to step into the garden, she kept an eye from the wall. Watching him straddle the rows of beetroot, radish and carrot tops in his gumboots, learning the mysteries of the earth from his father, father and son chatting like the good friends they were. This alone must have been strange to her. That as a child your place within a family could be something of worth. That you could be shown you were born out of love and were not just a skivvy or something to be used as a punch bag.

Their mothers were different too. Dai's would smile and ruffle his hair. A demonstration of love, if ever shown to Beth, made her cower under her hand, her eyes misting with tears for the beating she was always poised for. It took time for her to trust his parents, months before she moved beyond the gate, never mind into the embracing arms of his mother's kitchen for a golden-topped rock bun straight from the oven. Nerys Tudor, in comparison, was a fierce-tongued sloven who sat around in slippers and a filthy apron. Her kitchen, a cold and hostile place, had a muddy floor and food-splashed stove. Dai didn't once see her wipe a cloth over anything, in the same way he never saw her give her daughter any love. On the occasions he was allowed in the house, she'd shout for Beth through the floorboards, ordering her to scrub a sink-full of potatoes, or a sack of carrots. Once she was summoned to stand on a step-stool to stir a huge vat of the marmalade-like preserve Nerys Tudor insisted on metering out around the village at Christmas. Inedible stuff, not that Dai ever told Beth that, she was ashamed enough of where she came from. The bus for school used to stop outside Dai's house, and one day sticks out in his memory. A summer morning, perched on his front step, the year before she was stopped from coming to school, he looked up and saw her standing over him. The sun was blinding and he couldn't see her face, so put his arm up to shield his eyes. They stayed like this for a minute or two, staring at one another. They often did this, their thoughts forking off in different directions.

"You ever wonder where we come from?" he asked eventually, to break the silence.

"I've seen the bull with the cows," she said in her usual matter-of-fact way. "My mother makes me watch — says humans are just the same."

Such informed statements from someone so small, she always had the facility to surprise. That shy smile, always upbeat and grateful for the little she had; it made him think before moaning about trivia. If

251

someone like her could be cheerful, someone who had nothing, then so could he.

"These are for you." He would deliver his mother's message in the years to come. A message to accompany the blocks of lilac-scented soap, wrapped in pretty pink tissue, he'd push into her reluctant hands. Hands that belonged to a much older woman, way too big and raw for the delicate being she was. Flapping nervous as birds from beneath the frayed cuffs of her dead mother's knitwear, they lifted the sweet smelling cubes to her nose and it sent her fluttering off with the butterflies. Or so she said.

Watching Beth always made him feel sad. He knew these blocks of soap were her only snatch at luxury. But even he couldn't have guessed just how treasured they were. Not until afterwards, returning to the barn to look for messages she might have left, finding them hidden between the musty hay bales and mouldy bags of animal feed on the upper floor. A private place where along with the accumulating soaps in their petal-like paper, she hid a black plastic comb still thick with her mother's red hair, a silver thimble and a slim volume of R. S. Thomas' poems kept from school. Allowed so very little, even the clothes on her back didn't begin as hers and they were so engrained with the stench of the farm that however hard she scrubbed, it could not be eradicated. Only once did she have a dress and shoes bought new. A present from his parents. There's a photograph of her somewhere, looking pretty in the white cotton dress and flat brown sandals she wore on an outing with them to Porthcawl.

The annual trip to the funfair at Porthcawl was the only day Beth was allowed to leave the farm. Always the same week as Dai's birthday, the middle of the summer. He can see the two of them now, buoyed along by other happy day-trippers, on what turned out to be their last time. Beth loved the merry-go-round, asking for a second and third go, before finally agreeing to try the ghost train, the bumper cars and maybe the Crazy House. They decided the Crazy House was to be their final ride, as this would leave just enough money to buy candyfloss for the journey home and, holding the right change in their eager little palms, they watched the fairground man wipe black grease off his huge, rough hands on to the front of a waistcoat as brown and leathery as his bare skin beneath it.

"Hop on then," he said, his dirty eyes squeezed into two thin slits. "You're gonna enjoy this." And Dai read the names tattooed in scrolls down the length of his brawny sun-tanned arms: girls' names, punctured by bluebirds and roses; it was as if he'd been collecting them over the years. Collecting people, as he took his fairground ride from town to town. They reminded Dai of the memorial wall in Llandafen. The one that commemorated the two world wars by listing the names of the dead.

They didn't enjoy it. The Crazy House, throwing them high into the air, left them feeling like beaten sheets of metal, and when it came to a violent stop, Dai saw the same huge hands that took their money, reach inside to pull them free of the safety bar and let them go. They found a patch of ground and slumped to the grass where they sat shivering in the hot afternoon until they were calm again, and Dai reached into the pocket of his shorts for their change and Beth checked his wristwatch. "Got just enough there," she smiled, counting the coins quickly. "And then we'd better find your mam and dad."

Attracted to the nearest stall by its striped red canopy fluttering in the breeze, they stood in line to watch spinning sugar made into cotton wool by a woman sporting hair to match and a heavy rubber apron. Still trembling, when he was handed the first huge pink candyfloss, it felt too heavy in his hand, so he turned to pass it to Beth . . .

But she had gone.

CHAPTER
FORTY-NINE

Not him *again*. Rachel stops cleaning the slats of her blinds to watch Idris Tudor, lumbering huge as an ox, down her gravel drive to knock, knuckle-loud, on her stout wooden door. The dog barks, scrabbles to be let out. Answer it? Pretend she's out? No choice, he will have seen her car and won't give up; she has tried ignoring him before.

Making an exaggerated show of the inconvenience, she gives an amplified sigh, keeping her dog inside, as she peels back her front door and peers round, feeling the terracotta tiles in her porch clattering-loose under her slippers. She sees how his tobacco-coloured hair, while greasy, has been newly combed and for once he is wearing a clean shirt. The effort is wasted, what she can see of his skin still looks grimy and he stinks to high heaven, making her nose wrinkle on impact.

"More eggs — *how exciting?*" Rachel, spiky with sarcasm.

"I was thinking she must have run out by now." A hefty hand passes her the carton.

Rachel bristles at the "she" and a terrible thought jumps into her mind — that these fat, grime-ridden fingers may well have fondled the black slinkiness of her missing knickers. She wants to tell him to shove off. That "she" hates eggs. Hates him. How "she" wouldn't eat anything from that rancid dump of his. "Thank you," is all she says, wishing she could be mighty and curt and behave, just this once, in a way her mother would.

"Doing all right here on your own then, are you?" Rat eyes scuttle over her face, down the neck of her top, before gnawing deep between the cleft of her breasts.

"Yes, fine thanks." Repulsed by the slyness lurking behind his gaze, the inflection applied to *on your own*, she stretches her spine to make herself as tall as she can.

"Lonely spot for a woman like you though — innit?" He continues to stare.

"Hardly lonely," she squeezes out a laugh to disguise how annoyed she is with people pointing out the bloody obvious all the time. "I see Tracy and Hywel, and there's Dai at the bottom of the lane." She watches with interest the way Idris' putty-like pallor flushes. His birthmark turning a bright turkey-wattle red.

"Yeah?" Idris, angry and rattled, turns in the direction of his puke-yellow Toyota pickup parked on her bank. "Well . . . well . . ." he stammers, wheezing through his words. "You wanna watch yourself with 'im, d'you hear . . . yeah . . . he's not half as nice as he makes out . . . I should know . . . and you don't wanna go believing nothing he says, neither."

And he's gone. Swifter than she could believe possible. His bulk jammed back in behind the wheel. A scream of rubber. Then the blackness he left behind

256

clears, making room for the high strands of watery blue she can see in the sky.

Back inside, her skin crawling, Rachel swears never to answer the door to him again. She will stand firm next time, he can't harm her if she stays out of his way. The alternative only leaves her vulnerable, and she does feel acutely vulnerable whenever he comes sniffing around.

It occurs to her again how it isn't only Idris Tudor she needs to worry about. Even before Tracy's comment around the lunch table on Christmas day, she's thought she must be the topic of discussion with those living in the village. The gossip mongers amongst them coming up with stories to fill the gaps in her life they know nothing about. Saying things, like her family are all dead, that she won the lottery and bought the barn with that. Others swearing she's wealthy in her own right, that her philandering husband ran off with another woman and broke her heart. And when it grew late, down The Bear, it was common knowledge how the new girl on the block was on the hunt for a new man. Wanting to have a child of her own while there was still time. She could hear it as clearly as if she stood up at the mean strip of bar herself, how they all took bets over their games of dominoes, lifting their beer glasses to their mouths, imagining which of them would be the one to sire it, or worse, trying to guess the truth as to why she is here and who it is she is hiding from.

CHAPTER
FIFTY

Idris can still hear his mother. Capricious, wilful: his dreams fish her sounds from the unconscious depths of his mind to leave them floundering on the mud-coloured banks of his slippery eiderdown. Effervescent and gleaming like the silver-backed salmon he would watch leaping from the Towy as a boy, he imagines them slimy to the touch and biting into his knuckles, so he doesn't dare let them take hold.

His mother's cough — a sound that was to become her signature tune in the dying months of her life — would wake him as a youngster, much as it does now. Making his stomach clench, his body stiffen. Wide awake in a dark that has always coated him like a second skin; he pulls his great paws in under the blankets to press them to his sides, heavy as stones. Like a sick ewe, Idris thought at the time. Sick and staring, taken by the strangulating fluke his father was too mean to worm against. It claimed so many lives on the farm, and he knew when he heard it, his mother was done for.

There it is again. Curling, vaporous-grey, like the slow, creeping fog that visits in autumn. Engulfing, suffocating: claiming everything in its path. But he won't listen, telling himself the noise comes from somewhere outside. That it's one of his flock in the rain-sodden field beyond the lane. He shuts his eyes to block it out. Not that his mind will allow that. Bullying him, blind and blinking, out of his bed, barefoot along the corridor and down the stairs of his imagination. Wanting him to see her as she once was. Proud and apron-bound. Hair a cloud of cayenne pepper, bouncing about her shoulders. Smiling down as she had done, the fire in her soul refusing to be dampened, burning in her eyes. A sentinel at her post. Fiercely protective of her domain and the Belfast sink he will stand at, come morning, to fill his kettle. Except she never lived here. The ghost of her following on behind when Cwm Glas was sold off. Trapped within the pleats of her apron that now hangs behind the kitchen door of what was only ever his father's house. Before it was Wynn's. Before it was his. Picturing the apron from behind closed lids that are sticky with unfinished sleep, he sees its flowers. Pretty as a summer garden. After his mother was buried, Beth was tied into it until that August day fifty years ago when their lives were turned inside out.

How glad he is that his mam wasn't around for that. To see the fuss that girl caused, the ungrateful wretch. The Dyfed-Powys *Heddlu* turning up in the dead of night with their questions and accusations. Idris and his brothers made to stand shivering and bewildered in their makeshift nightclothes, rubbing sleep from their eyes, as the boys in blue busied themselves in the rain-slick yard, the hayloft, the cowsheds. A search warrant — that's what they had, snarling, disgusted, as they went about ransacking their home. From cutlery drawers to mattresses, they left nothing unturned. Him, his father and brothers were separated, taken in for questioning, for intimidating. "Just helping us with our enquiries," they said in tongues the same as his. What did they think they were going to find, what did they think had gone on here? The rumours, fuelled by publicised police reports, rumbled on for years. Spinning to the surface each anniversary. "Ask that bastard Dai Jones what he's done with her — she was with him, not us," his father, red-faced and panting, bellowed at whatever detective was coxswaining him, head down, into an awaiting Black Maria. A detective, no doubt armed with the gossip of the local bigmouths.

His da was right to fear the village grapevine. There were plenty who would have happily bared false witness if it meant Ronald Tudor receiving a hefty stretch behind bars. Culpable for Beth's disappearance — who cared? The poor girl was missing, that was all that mattered. Of course there had been foul play, everyone knew something of what her life had been under his brutal regime. Throw the book at him, the man was a savage, no better than the beasts that grazed his fields. A liability and loathed by those with the sensitivity to see what he was capable of, even if they hadn't been on the receiving end of his violence themselves. But Idris, much as he hated his father and would have loved for him to be locked away, knew the truth — the truth of how each of them were to blame. Mam, Da, Emyr, Rhys, Wynn and him. They all played their part. Even if it was only to force her into running away. Not that Idris believes this is what happened, any more than the local constabulary did. He remembers the disruption as clearly as if it were yesterday. Him, an indignant teenager, scowling from an upstairs window of the house the Morgans now own, as officers of the law set to work with dogs the colour of badgers, carving the boggy paddocks and gorse-packed hillside of his precious inheritance into grave-sized holes. All for that thing. All to try and find her remains. He could have told them, if they'd bothered to ask, how they were wasting their time. They wouldn't find her like that.

Coming back to the present, Idris thinks of the tasty bit of stuff living in the barn. Now there's someone with secrets. With her soft-skinned arms and perfectly round breasts that move braless and free beneath the flimsy T-shirt material he swears she wears for his benefit. That one definitely has a past. Why else would she choose to live in this godforsaken dump? Alone. Under the eternal battering of wind and hail. It wasn't as if she was fated to be born here, as he had been; surely she came from something better than this. Yeah, he sniffs. The vinegary smell of his unwashed feet coating his nostrils along with the inky black of night. That one's definitely on the run from something. Or someone. He'd stake his lorry on it.

Idris shifts a little to get comfy. Feels his flesh ripple on long after his body has stopped moving. He lifts what he keeps of the girl's face in his mind to chin level and stares at it in the way he sometimes stares at the moon. All she needed was another excuse to come calling like she did when her stupid dog ran off, and he felt sure he'd let her in. And if he let her in once, she would be in again and again, and then — he mulls over what little he knows of the order of such things — there would be trouble. One would be wanting a cup of sugar, the other the lend of a shovel. One would want help breaking ice in the water troughs and the other would want help mending a fence.

With such fractured scenarios forming like waves and breaking on the shores of his daydream, Idris feels a swell within the confines of his father's long-johns. What is fast becoming his favourite pastime is taking shape and nudging free, and he presses a clenched fist to it and holds it there, letting the sensation tingle the length of his brawny, freckle-speckled arm. But a woman would be such an encumbrance. He blushes under the burn of her erroneous attentions. She would smell his socks and make him take regular baths. Make him wash his hands before sitting up at the table to eat. Make him leave his boots tidy in the porch. She would whine on about how little attention he shows her, citing his ewes as the competition she has no hope of toppling. She would force him into driving her to the seaside whenever the sun dared to show itself. Packing them picnics of chicken and tomato sandwiches, rosy-skinned apples and home-made fairy cakes in those crinkly-sided paper cups. Or worse. Make him spend his money on cartons of chips. On lollipops to stain her lips when she'd tired of pinning him down to kiss her lipstick away. She would ask him questions: wanting to know where he had gone to, when he had gone nowhere more interesting than down the Spar for a pack of bacon. His life would cease to be his own. She would demand to come with him on his haulage trips, inspect his collars for traces of other women's make-up and sniff his underwear and accuse him of wearing aftershave. Is that what he wants? Because if he becomes involved with her, this is exactly what will happen. No, he thinks, why should he have to sacrifice anything of himself? Relationships aren't his thing. He knows exactly what he wants from a woman and when he gets the chance, he takes it.

CHAPTER
FIFTY-ONE

Gone midnight, and I've parked up in the long black shadows of the closed-up Sainsbury's, sharing my viewpoint with wheelie bins that spill their stinking innards on to the street. I sometimes come up here; it's a route home for many on weekday nights, with the clubs shut and the pubs along the seafront kicking them out before midnight.

Engine off. Lights out.

I don't have to wait long and pass the time by singing along to whatever's on the radio.

Here they come. And a right hotchpotch of stragglers tonight. It makes me smile the way they peck around each other, establishing the hierarchy. Their cheap heels clippety-clapping against the rain-slippery pavement. They remind me of chickens, their movements jerky and impulsive, and this lot are a right irregular jumble of skimpy clothes and naked flesh, with hair all colours of the rainbow. Up and down the curb they go, using the paving slabs as some perverse catwalk. It's as if they know I am out here, watching, and they want to show off.

But they can't see me. Like sitting behind a two-way mirror, hiding like this in the dark, I get to see all sorts. At the moment I'm looking at one squatting down to pee behind an upturned bin. So off her face she probably wouldn't care if she knew I could see her. I mean, look at her, wriggling out of her knickers, her bare arse lit by the slither of moon. Shameful, really it is; the way they get into such a state, night after night. I can hear this one, she's crying out for her friends to wait, but she is taking too long, can't summon the coordinates necessary to stuff herself back into her underwear. What do they care about themselves? It's obvious they've next to no self-respect. This is what sickens me most of all, the more and more I watch them. It's not that I'm a prude, but they haven't a shred of decency.

The way they behave in groups has always fascinated me. All that their pathetic little lives revolve around is getting the attention and approval of men. Men no better than that letch of a father of mine.

Just the last few now, I'll wait, there's no rush. I might get lucky; there could be one floating around on her own that I can have. It's not like I'm expected back anywhere, it's hardly like I've got anyone at home asking where I've been.

CHAPTER
FIFTY-TWO

Love.

What it means to Rachel blows like a ball of dead leaves across the horizon of her mind. Spencer was the one to free it years before and, like the song thrush that has taken to hurling itself at the glass of her French doors, it left its feathery smears on her heart. It's not something that has beaten its wings for some time but she can feel it perching nearby. On the sleeve of the coat she wore when Graham brushed against her as they walked past the rows of jewellers and little boutiques, cooing over their pretty tinsel-clad window displays. On her cheek when he kissed her goodbye the last time they met in Llandafen. On her car roof where his hands helped tie down the rocking-chair she bought for thirty pounds in a charity shop. That, fastened with a length of blue nylon rope, found in the storeroom of his gallery, reminded her of the swing her father put up for her in the garden when she was small and her hair was as long as a mermaid's.

Rachel never believed there would come a point when the word *love* would fly back to her. Flutter its wings in her face to make her notice it again. And it has, forcing her to say his name over and over: *Graham,*

Graham, Graham. She likes it. It makes her stomach flip like it did when she was a teenager. She can't sleep. Can't eat. Moons about the house, counting hours and longing for the next time she will see him.

They meet in town. In antique-laden tea shops with fussy tablecloths. In low-slung, black-beamed bars in the cobbled parts of Llandafen. Before he takes her by the hand and leads her up the stairs to his flat above the gallery to make love to her in the afternoons between his freshly laundered sheets. It has become a regular thing, since buying the landscape painting. The landscape she likes to think is the one she sees out on her walks with Cadno. They talk on the phone. Quiet in the gallery this time of year, he is free for hours. When there's a customer needing his attention, he will whisper his profuse apologies, ending the call, only to ring back half an hour later. She finds herself hovering by the phone, doubly cross with cold callers or the accidental wrong number. She will snap, hear her mother's voice coming out and hate herself.

So it is, all these years later, a different woman emerging in the mirror she looks into. Applying face-cream, smoothing out the beginnings of those creases she can see forming, just like her mother's, on her forehead. Brought in on the wind like a New Year gift, love is something she is happy to accept. For January brings the wind. Days and days of it. And like this new found love, it bites into the tender-most parts of her. The exposed section of wrist, where anorak ends and gloves begin. The rims of her ears sting from it, as she listens to it hissing through the bare brown branches of trees. The wind, competing with Graham's voice, the one she carries in her head as she pushes herself up the hill or down the lane to chat to Dai working in his garden. She wears tights under her jeans in this weather. A thermal vest, owned since school, which she amazes herself by still being able to fit into. And still the wind goes on. Battering her windows, lifting slates on her roof. A night-time visitor that, lying awake in the dark thinking of Graham, makes her body brace itself. Fearful it will, at any minute, blow her house down around her. Expose her to the elements like the big bad wolf in *The Three Little Pigs* story her Aunty Alice would read when she came to stay, doing all the different voices before lights out.

January isn't something Rachel is minding as much as she might ordinarily do. Her senses sharpened, her spirit enveloped in such overwhelming joy, she's become untouchable. She doesn't mind that horrible bloke from up the lane so much, either. Coming to stand on her doorstep to fiddle with himself through the pockets of his trousers. So upbeat, she even went so far as to thank him for bringing yet another tray of lousy eggs. Listening patiently to his tales of woe and livestock worries. The frequency with which he thunders past her house in his gargantuan truck is bothering her less too. The way its planet-sized tyres carve into the banks either side of the lane, tearing at the clusters of what will be primroses and daffodils. The minutia of which, she has taken to zooming in on, noticing as she does these days, the finest and most fragile of things.

It is to look at the world through a magnifying glass since Graham. Pausing on her walks to cup the delicate green-white heads of the yet to open snowdrops. Under her scrutiny, the buds mimic the ears of the first crop of New Year's lambs that, born bleating into the cold, their mothers wedge against the prickly blackthorn for shelter. Places where the tawny tails of catkins dangle amidst the bald briars and bright-red rosehips. Trapped in winter, they reflect back the wildness to her in a tear of rain.

Like Rachel, nature is holding its breath for spring. In spite of the harshness still to be wrung from winter, there's an optimism in the air, an optimism — as the weeks roll on and she continues to be safe — she thinks she can start to buy in to. It is held in the rain-encrusted cobwebs she sees strung out like diamond necklaces in more protected parts. Glistening and bright, these messages of the year's unfolding — as yet, too friable to touch — show the promise of all that is to come. As with Graham's tentative offerings of love, the spring waits in the wings for its turn to shine.

CHAPTER
FIFTY-THREE

The eggs obviously aren't working. She still hasn't invited him in. Pretending she wasn't home the other day, she didn't answer the door. But she was there, busying herself like women do. Gardening, he thinks these townies call it. Bloody joke, if you ask him, just because she's bought a pair of workman's gloves and a spade from Gwynfelin Farm Stores she thinks she's Charlie bloody Dimmock all of a sudden. What's a girl like that going to know about working the land? Sod all, from what he could see between the gaps in her hedge when he parked in the lane to watch her.

Idris thinks about the hedge. Remembers how dense it gets in spring and summer. He won't be able to stand there in the dark watching her moving around inside her house much beyond April. What's he going to do with his evenings then, when he isn't away in his lorry? Life will return to the way it was before she came, he thinks, groaning under the weight of the emptiness threatening to engulf him. He's going to have to come up with something to sustain a legitimate reason for calling round. Taking her those ewes was a good idea, but it only permitted the one visit — how he wheedles himself inside her home is the tricky thing. He could try taking feed over, just half a bag a time, tell her he needs to come back and check on them. She understands bugger all about sheep and with no one around to ask apart from that idiot Hywel Morgan, she'll be none the wiser.

It might work, but what he really needs to do is take her presents. Not frivolous things, like those blocks of stinky soap Dai used to bring his sister that he found in the barn after she disappeared — he should take practical things, things she can eat, treats to enjoy. She doesn't seem to like eggs and the sheep are hardly gratifying. It might be different if they were tame, from what he's seen of her, she loves fondling animals. Always fiddling with that bloody mutt of hers anyway. *Hang on a minute*, Idris, his brain turning like the wheel of the barrow he bounces around his pot-holed yard. What about those traps he laid the other day, down the bottom meadow — bet there'll be a brace of bunnies he can give her. *Brilliant idea*. Idris, thinking he's cracked it, gives himself a metaphorical pat on the back and, abandoning whatever it is he's doing, starts off over there.

Unpicking then retying the gate in the lane, the rain-eaten twine disintegrating under his fingers, he feels the ground transform under his boots, suddenly waterlogged. He sloshes his way over what has become, with the unending deluge of rain, an expanse of drenched, sky-reflecting land. He can't imagine it ever being dry enough to put livestock on again: if this weather keeps up then he is done for. No good to even rent out. He stands, legs splayed, his weight sinking into the sodden earth. He can kiss goodbye to a fair whack of his income, he sighs as the moisture seeps through the fraying seams of his father's boots, wetting his socks by the time he reaches the spot close to the engorged stretch of Towy tributary where he set the traps.

Idris is rewarded with more than he bargained for. Locating the deadly metal snares, their exacting snapping mechanisms. Yes, there are rabbits. Three of them. Their twisted shapes wet with blood, caught where they were sprung, make him rub his hands together with glee as they stare, dead-eyed, at an apathetic sky. But there is a cat too. Big and black, trapped by its one, soft white paw. Idris sees it twitch, open its mouth to give a mute mewl of pain, the steel-green of its eye oozing yellow from the effort to thrash itself free.

He doesn't blink. With a stone found from beneath a nearby thicket of bramble, he stoops forward and stoves its head in. Cat brain and bone spray the sleeve of his donkey jacket and settle into the cracks of his already filthy hands.

CHAPTER
FIFTY-FOUR

Rachel, looking exquisite in a new silk blouse and skin-tight jeans, pulls on her jacket and takes a look out of her bedroom window at the rain. Does it ever stop? She doesn't think it's let up for weeks, and yet it must have done, to make the improvements she has in her garden since December went and January well and truly blew in.

She might be cold, she assesses her reflection again; never sure of her choice of outfit, these aren't the warmest things she has in her wardrobe. But the sexiest, she decides, admiring herself, she can put up with being chilly just for the look on Graham's face. And he does a lot of looking. She feels the weight of his gaze travelling the length of her and likes it. She likes looking at him too. At the perfect arc of his eyebrows, the delicate cut of his cheekbones. The way his ears are just the right size and fit close to his head so that his dark hair curls, baby-like, round them. Statuesque, is what she would call Graham, if anyone asked her to describe him. Elegant and poised, she is proud to be out in his company; even if it does make her feel uncomfortable seeing the lustful appreciation he receives from other women. He is a good-looking guy, she is just going to have to deal with it; no way she's going to let her insecurities run away with her this time.

What a find he was, that dreary day, wandering Llandafen's streets, dogged by thoughts of her mother and pre-Christmas blues. And to think she nearly hadn't turned off for the town centre. She often thinks this, and the two of them have talked about it. Picking apart the fate that was to be their meeting is a favourite pastime. But Rachel supposes the real chance wasn't her driving into Llandafen and stepping into his gallery, she would have come around to that eventually, it was how she came to leave London and move here at all. Something that never felt quite right until recently. Of course, without her father's money, the considerable savings he left entirely to her when he died, she wouldn't have been able to do anything. Forever trapped within her mother's house, living under her rules with the mask of her pious-veiled disapproval slipping day on day.

Rachel has held on to that auspicious scrap of paper Mrs Pepper cut out of the Sunday supplement. She keeps it in her knickers drawer, where she will pull it out to scrutinise now and again. She wishes she could write and tell her how providential her thoughtfulness turned out to be. If she had the woman's address, she would.

Kissing the dog's head before moving into the porch to swap her slippers for driving shoes. A quick squirt of Coco Chanel on to wrists, under her hair, down into the neck of her blouse. She nearly forgets, in a separate

274

carrier bag, the boots she intends to wear when she is out with Graham.

The smell seizes her.

Death.

A tellurian tang that hurls her straight back to the dark, dank cottage where she spent eleven days with Blundell.

She swings open her front door. It feels heavier and, the shock of the raw streak of blood smeared across the gloss-white paint at head-height, makes her grab at her throat. A pair of dull grey-furred rabbits resembling the still-life paintings of Chardin she once saw in a book of French artists. Wet and streaked in slaughter, their death-stiffened bellies combed through by the wind coming in off the hill, they swing upside down from a nail she tacked to her door for the beautiful hooped wreath of holly she bought on that happy day wandering around the Christmas market. It wasn't meant for this. *What is this?* she gasps, appalled — some pagan offering?

Visibly shaken, she unhooks the poor fluffy creatures, which feel surprisingly heavy at the end of her wrist, and carries them, arm's length, out into the lane. At a loss to know what else to do with them, she tucks their rigid bodies, without touching, as far under the twist of blackthorn and bare bank of beech as she can. Then later, journeying to Graham, remembering them at intervals, hoping they will be gone by the time she gets home, she sniffs her fingers, imagining she smells the ghosts of them lingering there. Adding them to the ghosts she already cohabits with, the ones that, however

275

much progress she thinks she's making, will always be waiting to welcome her home, climbing into bed and holding her hand whenever she closes her eyes to sleep.

CHAPTER
FIFTY-FIVE

Dai switches on the radio. Melvyn Bragg's *In Our Time* spills into the room. Somehow Thursday has crept up on him without him realising. He stops polishing and, squashing the duster into a tight yellow ball, gathers up the months since Elsie died. The swift passing of time shocks him. Without his wife to act as chronometer, measuring out the days of his retirement in bite-sized tasks, his lack of discipline means he is in danger of misplacing time all together.

He listens to the programme for a second or two, unknown voices talking as if Aristotle had lived two doors down and they'd been the best of buddies. Dai laughs. Flicks the radio off. He'll put a record on, one of Elsie's. Something light. A Doris Day. He shuffles through the stack, which is still in strict alphabetical order from his wife's organising. Their covers, immaculate and dust-free, tell him his fingers are tacky from the Mr Muscle spray he had been using only seconds before. He pauses to wipe them off on the knees of his salmon-coloured corduroys and chooses the LP "Bright and Shiny" — he's doing the cleaning, after all.

Skipping the title track, he drops the stylus one groove on. "I Want to be Happy", one of Elsie's favourites, clicks in, and so does he. His singing building to a shattering crescendo ... *Life's really worth living ... why can't I give some to you ...* he plugs in the vacuum, switches it on and swings its eager sucking nozzle over the swirling pattern of his living room carpet. The job, because it's one he does every day, is finished before it has properly begun. Then he stops, the sweetness of Doris' voice making him bunch his lips and smile. With eyes moist with tears, the room spins and he sees Elsie and himself as they were. Barefoot, on honeymoon. Dancing on the buttery spread of Pembrokeshire beach at Saundersfoot. Elsie providing the accompanying tune in a fine mezzo-soprano that had been strong enough to earn her a place in the Llandafen town choir. This tune. It unfurls images of their shoes, sitting side by side, neat on the sand, their socks tucked inside as they would have done as children. Dai fussing, taking longer than necessary to ensure they were far enough away from the hungry lick of the tide. Elsie grabbing for his hand, telling him they were all right, squealing in eagerness to be racing with him into the waves.

It had been the summer those twin boys were swept out to sea. Rough water. NO SWIMMING signs. People out in droves, searching the inlets, the coves, rocks and cliffs. The coastguard, risking their lives out on waves churning like a washing machine. In the sky, looking down, the police helicopter, hunting with its white beam of light, late into the night. Him and Elsie

278

watching doe-eyed and inadequate, as the drama unravelled beneath the windows of their honeymoon suite at the pebble-dashed B&B on St Brides Head.

He knew they would never find them, in the same way they never found Beth. Although he took care to keep this to himself, with Elsie insisting they walk to the church before dinner each evening, to pray for the boys' safe return. Keeping vigil through that slow in-between time, before their little bloated bodies were at last fished from the water four miles out at sea. He can see the plain little church with its sandy aisles. Its pansies for sale and pots of lavender, lined up in a porch plastered with notices promoting the services of various tradesmen of the parish. How he went along with it, slotting into his new role of husband in a way that suggested he might well have read up on it beforehand in a manual that gave a step-by-step guide of what was required. Sitting with Elsie, feeling the length of her thigh pushed up against his, she was the only comfort in the otherwise whitewashed cheerlessness of the church's interior. Staring at the only thing of interest, its one stained-glass window, so smothered in ivy it obscured any light still to be wrung from the day. They took it in turns to light candles, tipping the tails of wick into ones already alight. He lit one for Beth, silently, letting Elsie think they were in it together. Kneeling, as she did, on a tapestried hassock, hands pressed together in prayer, he mumbled how he hoped Beth was safe and happy, willing her to get in touch if she could, it didn't matter he was married. He hated himself for lying to his brand-new, beautiful

279

bride, still fresh from her packaging and raven-haired beside him. The dark flash of her eyes wanting to believe that his offerings were, like hers, devoid of motive or self-interest, and only for the safe return of the twins neither had met. That they weren't for the ghost of a love she knew all about. That vast white sail she had seen flapping around behind her husband's eyes, that she hoped she could tie down to her mast, but was beginning to suspect, even in those early blissful months, how it might be something her married years would be forever pulled along by.

Dai remembers the lone fisherman who found the boys. Alerted, he told a local reporter, by the bump, bump against the hull of his boat. He thought it was a whale until he leant over the side. The worst catch of his life, the *Evening Star*'s commentary quoted, as they made sure he looked suitably sad for the flash of the camera lens and his flimsy hook at fame, although Dai doubts there would have been anyone to congratulate him on it.

He winds in the flex, sighing as he leans low under the beam to put the vacuum away and retrieves the duster from a coffee table that is now as buffed as the polished wood of his wife's coffin. This is how he preserves her. Maintaining their home to the standard she would have done, he is paying homage to the wife he can no longer make it up to in other ways. It is why he flosses his teeth before bed. Why he shaves each morning, pulling on a freshly ironed shirt over which he will choose a matching V-neck jumper. He won't let things slip; this is the only way he knows to thank her.

CHAPTER
FIFTY-SIX

Rachel tries not to stare at the phone, willing it to ring. When Graham calls just before noon, she can barely contain herself. A whole four days since their last meeting, made more memorable by finding those poor dead rabbits hooked to her door. The rendezvous that day was at a quaint little coffee house in the shadow of the castle, that along with the usual selection of hot and cold beverages, sandwiches and cupcakes, sold crusty organic loaves, cold cuts of clove-baked ham, tubs of fresh olives and other delicatessen-type fare, so fancy, even her London-based mother would have been impressed. Rachel, swayed into buying a slab of local cheese on Graham's say so, also succumbed to a box of handmade garlic crackers and a bottle of ridiculously expensive elderberry cordial. Her purchases, wrapped in brown paper, sat with them as they held hands over the table and talked again of the coincidences of life and the chances that needed to occur for the two of them to meet. Totally engrossed, their coffees forgotten, they were oblivious to the army of staff wanting to close for the day. Only appreciating the lateness when they were tipped outside under the yellowing spread of dusk and streetlamps bouncing into life.

Taking an age to shower and style her hair, Rachel applies her make-up and chooses what to wear. The light is fading when she locks up the house, and even before reaching the A40, she finds she needs her full beam. At least the rain has eased and, pushing the wipers into intermittent mode, their squeaking irritating, she thinks how she must remember to take her umbrella. Get her newly re-dyed hair wet out in that, with the amount of gel she sprayed on to keep it in place, and it will turn to jam.

The car park in Queen Street is virtually empty. There are none of the usual problems finding a space and with it being after five-thirty, parking is free. She changes out of her driving shoes and zips herself into a pair of knee-high black wedge boots. Nice with her skinny-jeans, she thinks, catching her full-length reflection in a Specsavers window. She takes small steps; she can't risk going any faster. Lethal underfoot, her boots have little in the way of grip and Llandafen's pavements, wet and lit by the coppery glow of streetlamps, are slippery as ice. She spots Graham's shape up ahead. The outline she is learning to recognise, locking the door of his gallery. Rachel heaves out a sigh in an effort to steady herself and presses a hand to her fluttering heart, which doing somersaults has landed in her mouth, leaving her speechless.

Unable to call out and forced to watch him walk away, she sees him almost collide with a gaggle of giggling girls. Out on the razzle, they are as sparkly and shimmery as the Christmas lights that, until a week or so ago, were still strung out along this stretch. The half a dozen or more twenty-somethings, having a great time and dressed to kill in next to nothing, are obviously a little worse for wear, judging by the way they swing along the pavement, but she can tell they are harmless enough. Conscious of cat-calls and shouting, Rachel is too far away to hear exactly what is said, but it's evident there is some exchange and that Graham fires off a response to thwart their exuberance. Whatever it is sobers them up in an instant. The delight and hilarity throttled in their throats. She can tell from their dazed expressions as they pass close to her, just how deflated they are. Affronted enough for one of the group to step out into the road, jab her middle finger through the air and shout after Graham, "Fuck you. No need to be so nasty, only havin' a bloody joke — we could report you, threatening us like that." The retort bounces off the sheen on his dark hair and he doesn't once turn round. Crikey, she thinks, troubled by what she's just witnessed. They were only having a laugh, most blokes would have played along with that, been flattered by it. Spencer certainly would have. She had no idea Graham was such a prude.

Rachel, continuing to follow mutely on behind, is familiar enough with the whereabouts of the wine bar he suggested they meet, so even when she loses sight of him, she doesn't panic. If she just heads in the general direction of the centre, beyond the cobbled parts and castle, she'll find it. Recognising the name on its façade, she stops just shy of the smoked-glass entrance, but is swept up and in with a gang of noisy office types keen to have their weekends underway. Dumped inside, she feels awkward and, shifting from foot to foot, sifting through faces, looks for his. At last. Graham sees her as she sees him. A quick peck on the cheek and she looks down, tucks a strand of her hair back behind an ear.

"What are you drinking?" he asks. "I know you're driving, but you can have one."

"Have they got Budweiser in here?" Rachel simultaneously scans the bar.

"A pint?" He smiles, her choice obviously meeting with his approval.

"Go on then, as you've twisted my arm."

"A pint it is," he confirms. "You go and find us a table — the sofas over there are cosy. Be back in a sec."

She watches him move to the bar, liking the elegant slenderness of him in dark blue jeans, dark shirt and jacket. So tall, she can wear these boots of hers and not drown him in the way she would have done Spencer. Spencer, who would no more have let her drink pints than let her wear heels.

The wine bar is packed with Friday night revellers and, observing the dynamism of them for a moment or two, her brain begins breaking them down into more manageable parts. They fascinate her in a way they might fascinate a visitor from a faraway planet, their moving mouths, lipstick, teeth, the hard pink patina of gum. All shown in slow motion, alien and strange — it's a world she isn't quite part of, one she has stepped into without warning, where even the music, piped overhead, sounds unfamiliar.

Hunkering down in a corner on a big striped sofa the colour of a mint humbug, she leans back to scan the walls, sees a series of monochrome photographs of jet-set couples on their wedding day. She recognises Elizabeth Taylor and Richard Burton, cutting their cake and giggling. Another of Marilyn Monroe and Arthur Miller clasping hands and wearing expressions that suggest they might be about to dive off the deep end of a swimming pool. Prince Charles and Lady Diana Spencer, smiling, awkward, not touching. Others she recognises but can't remember the names of. Some posed and traditional, seized on the steps of churches showered in confetti. Others waving from the seats of chrome-shiny convertibles decorated with Just Married signs.

"This place used to be a bank." Graham, back from the bar, sets their drinks down on the table. "Nicer like this — d'you like it?"

"Love it, got a great atmosphere." She feels the seat shift a little as he sits beside her.

"I knew you would."

"Ta for the drink — you got the same as me?"

"I have — nothing beats Bud on draft, does it?"

She takes a sip from her glass, thinks again how much they have in common. Cold and fizzy in her mouth, the lager makes her giggle. "Mmm," she says gulping it down and grinning. "Now that's the business."

"I agree," he says, smiling too.

"Graham?" she says, her fingers tiptoeing over the table top towards him. "I was walking behind you from the gallery." She gestures to her boots. "I tried to catch up, but with these on . . ." She smiles sidelong at him. "What happened, with those girls?"

"What girls?" Taking a sip from his pint.

"The ones who shouted at you, a group of them."

"Those slappers?" he sniffs, flicks his head to the ceiling. "Just told them they should have more self-respect. Carrying on like that — it's a bloody disgrace."

"They were all right; they were only having a laugh, weren't they? Can't blame young girls for coming on to a handsome hunk like you."

"You wouldn't think that if you'd heard what they said to me." Smacking his glass rather forcefully down on the table. "Filthy slags — like bitches on heat, the lot of them."

"Okay — that bad, was it?" Rachel says, raising her eyebrows.

"I can't tell you how much they disgust me, girls like that."

Rachel decides to drop it, reluctant to plough that furrow any longer and risk spoiling their evening, she tells herself that whatever those girls said must have warranted his reaction. After a moment's silence, their conversation turns to other things, and before they know it, an hour has gone.

"You can stay over if you like," Graham says later, draining what remains of his second pint. "We could grab a bite to eat, bottle of wine?"

"Stay over? I suppose I could." Rachel surprises herself with her reply.

He leans forward and kisses her without warning. His lips pushing hers apart, his tongue finding hers. It makes her gasp when at last he pulls away.

"You're gorgeous, d'you know that?" he says, stroking hair off her face. The gesture both tender and loving. Then, "Want me to fetch you another?" And standing, he is gesturing to her glass.

"Go on then, I will. Thanks. I'll give Tracy a bell — see if she can let Cadno out in the morning."

"Great." Graham looks thrilled. "I'll leave you to it — back in a jiffy."

Rachel wakes in the night to the warm smells of their bodies. She listens to Graham breathing, the sounds of stragglers heading home in the street below his bedroom window. Then pulling the duvet cover higher over her bare shoulders, she turns on her side and buries herself into his back.

"Thought you were asleep," he whispers as she runs the tip of her tongue along the creamy smooth flesh between his shoulder blades.

"With you lying next to me?" Her voice syrupy, vies with the rustling of sheets as she pulls him towards her, rolling him on to his back and positioning herself astride him.

"You're insatiable, you are."

"You don't know the half of it," she says softly.

CHAPTER
FIFTY-SEVEN

With the January streets around Muswell Hill still in the fist-hold of frost, it's curious how Jennifer has walked to and from Barnes and Lee Investigations in Highgate wearing little more than a pair of Armani jeans and a cashmere sweater. It frustrated her to find the suited presence of Derek Barnes absent, anxious for news on her daughter's whereabouts; she'd been hoping for some answers today. "Out investigating," his plump-faced assistant informed her in an equally plumped-up voice, and handing over the scrapbook, Jennifer made sure to convey its importance.

Opening the door of number seventy-seven she is hit by the smell of fresh paint and, climbing the stairs to poke the tip of her nose, shiny with cold, around the door of Sarah's old room, she still can't believe it. Transformed. With nothing of her daughter it is just another guest room to add to the two she already has. She sits on the bed that Mrs Pepper has made up with the platinum-grey covers bought in John Lewis' sale. She congratulates herself on how well they match the silver wallpaper and frost-glittery drapes that happen to mimic the hoary sky still governing the city. Subtle in its neutrality, unclaimed and personality-less, the room reflects her mood exactly. Mrs Pepper did a good job disposing of Sarah's clobber, her stash of paperbacks, the wall coverings of postcards with photos of Wales. She hated seeing them, the constant reminder. The toy fox Donald bought her has gone too.

Breathing in, she finds she doesn't mind the paint smell now she sits within it. Better than the scent of her child, the one she could always identify if ever she set foot in here before. It was why she took such care to keep the door closed. Not wanting to catch the faintest whiff of the faded remains of her deodorant, the woody scent of body lotion. *Or had you, by keeping the door tight shut, wanted to preserve her?* Another, louder voice inside her head bites back. *And are you regretting it now?* The same voice pushes. *Regretting the way you've eradicated everything in this joyless house of yours?*

Because there should have been joy in this house, the place should have been stuffed to the rafters with it. Following the safe delivery, finally, one snowy February night, of a healthy baby girl. The long-awaited golden child, born out of so much failure and grief. Grief not even Donald could fully understand, when each time a little more of Jennifer would ice over. She remembers those visits from her sisters in the years before and after Sarah's birth, resenting their milky, big-breasted presence. How could they understand when they had their own bouncing babies to go home to?

Only Alice — with their mother's complexion: pale, with fine creases like the skin on a cooling milk pudding — offered encouragement for the future, telling her she shouldn't destroy her life by striving for the impossible. Jennifer stopped telling the others, whether in the first flush of a new pregnancy and buoyant with expectation, or afterwards, when the inflatable ring of hope burst and there was no baby. "It isn't meant to be, Jen." Sympathetic Alice, pragmatic Alice. Her earrings: silver songbirds in her ears, flickering like tiny flares in the bruised lighting of her sitting room. "Whatever it is, it's telling you to focus on the family you have."

Jennifer did try not to let it bother her that she would never have the little girl she dreamt of. One that let her dress her up in pretty things and played with dolls, powdering their bottoms with talc and checking under their skirts for clean, white knickers as she had seen the daughters of friends do. If Donald was happy, then she was happy. Happy to watch his overt adoration for a child who sat cross-legged on the lawn, poking her fingers into the earth he felt such affinity with. She did try not to mind losing her husband to the only child she would ever have. Was it really her fault that in the end she just couldn't see past her jealousy?

Was she all that different to Sarah, as a child — was this the problem? Jennifer asked Alice. "No, you weren't," she smiled. "You say how like Donald she is, but all I see is you — you when you were that age."

Jennifer, wanting evidence of this, began rifling through the family photo albums. Memories padded in expensive-looking leather that her father chose to bequeath to her, amongst other things, in his will. She would carry them down from the loft when Donald was

290

away selling sweets on the coast and it always staggered her, turning the stiffened pages and slippery transparent divides, to see how happy they looked. But as Donald said, "Who takes pictures of unhappy things?" And he'd been right. Jennifer's father, widowed at forty-five, would only have recorded the things he wanted to remember. So there was nothing of that lost and lonely little girl she knew she had been in the years following her mother's death. That child who, in spite of her many sisters, invariably found herself alone with no one to play with, pattering off to her room, for the comfort she hid in there. Something that was to become her most favourite of things — the mole found drowned in the garden with its rotting fruit smell she kept in a shoe box under her bed. A box she kept her heart in. At night, lifting the lid to stroke the hard nugget of soft black fur until her fingertips went fuzzy. Making silent promises in exchange for ones that meant she could have her mummy back. Alice might have been right. Perhaps Sarah does have something of Jennifer after all.

Enough of the past, she sighs, listening to the house that is silent save for the rustle of her clothes, the thumping of pipes as the boiler kicks in. Then, the thought fizzing through her like a firework — supposing Sarah's with Alice and Pete in New York? Now there's an idea. She'll call them, find out. Giving her firm thighs a satisfying slap, she springs into action and pitches from the room. It makes her jump, the sound of the telephone on her way down the stairs, and picking it up on its third ring, she presses it to her ear.

"Hello, yes?" Jennifer says, a little too stern, she holds her breath for the caller.

"Mrs D'Villez." The smooth tones of her private investigator. "Derek Barnes here, I thought you'd like to know, I've some news — an interesting lead as to your daughter's whereabouts."

CHAPTER
FIFTY-EIGHT

Hang on a minute. I lean on the steering wheel and stop singing. Yes, look, there she is, waiting at the bus stop. Nice-looking, too — quite a set of legs in that belt of a skirt. No one about, so I slow to a stop along the pavement beside her, lower the passenger window and lean across:

"Filthy night, love," I croon, watching her expression stiffen in the winter wind bucking in off the sea. "D'you want a lift anywhere?"

The girl, all hoity-toity, flicks her long hair off her face with elegant fingers and leans forward. "No thanks." Chewing her scorn. "I'm waiting for the bus."

Talk about stating the bloody obvious I think, trying again. "I can see that, sweetheart," I say, giving her my best smile. "But you look so cold, I thought you could do with coming in the warm."

"I'm waiting for the bus."

And I see the way she wraps her flimsy cardigan over her equally flimsy top and read its message.

I'll get nowhere with her, it's not worth the risk. She can't be as pissed as I thought she was and I can hardly get out and grab her. What I do doesn't work unless they open the door themselves and climb inside willingly, to start with, at least.

"Okay," I say, sliding the window up. "Suit yourself."

CHAPTER
FIFTY-NINE

January slides into February and an almost unrecognisable Rachel is working outside under a torn blue sky. Flushed pink by the cold, her figure made indistinct by the layers of clothes to keep out the fingers of wind, she looks happy. With a spade by her side and hands caked in soil, the dog watches her, head on paws as she moves about, cutting lengths of string and matching them to the planks of wood delivered by a local builder's merchants.

She is marking where her vegetable plot will go and refers intermittently to a detailed pencil drawing she pulls, then returns, to a muddy-mouthed pocket of an old riding coat. The drawing, agonised over through the darkest winter evenings that are now behind her, is paying dividends. Keen to make a start, a providential break in the weather is letting her plan where best to divide, what will eventually go where. It won't be long before she can begin planting, heartened by the shoots of unknown things already pushing up through the soil. Daffodils perhaps, tulips too, she will have to wait and see. The prospect, exciting her, is fortified by a pair of gambolling red kites circling high above. Recognising their lengthy wings and deep-forked tails, that flash of white near the tips and the *tee-tee-teeaar* of their call. She stares in wonder as the majestic raptors ring a pitted disc of moon that has been thrown up between a gap in the cloud. Filling her lungs at the sight of them, she draws down the essence of spring, letting her spirits soar around with them. She thinks of Graham. How she wishes she could persuade him to leave the gallery now and again and come home with her to Tŷ Haf. Lie with him in bed under the dark oak "A" beam. To trace with a finger, the line of hair from his navel, as they listen to the beating rain on her roof. Even though she knows she wouldn't be able to sleep. That her quivering heart would bang in her ears like it did whenever they touched.

Then there were times she was glad he wasn't here. Plastering her face and neck in night cream that made her glow in the dark. Waking in the small hours to monitor the phases of the moon, check on the woodburner. Wandering around in her nightclothes, her father's old fishing socks. Watering her rubber plants with the tepid black tea she always lets go cold in the bottom of her over-sized mug. Dusting with the pulled-down sleeve of her dressing gown or a pair of knickers before pushing them into the laundry bin. Those mornings she barely bothers to wash or pull a comb through the tangles in her hair. When she will dress quickly, slip her feet into boots to take the dog out into the wild Welsh weather, without brushing her teeth.

The birds move over the brow of the hill and, focusing back on the job in hand, Rachel frowns in concentration as she consults her drawing before making a concerted effort with the first of her raised beds. Slicing into the cloying earth, a booted-foot pushing down, she hits stone, moves along and tries again. Here the ground gives easily, yielding beneath the slice of metal and releasing a series of satisfying sucks as she repeatedly lifts the spade free to thrust it in again. Then she stops. Something turned over in the earth. Lighter than a stone, she bends to pick it up, bangs it out against the handle of her spade and reveals a child's shoe. The leather upper, although quite eaten away, is unmistakable. She thinks she recognises it, her fingernail lifting the length of strap that forms a T-shape bar. That photograph. The one she found of the little girl in a white cotton dress, holding a small dog. The little girl she believes is Beth.

What a strange find, Rachel frowns, studying the shoe that just about fits into her hand. It unnerves her and she thinks again of what Dai did and didn't tell her. Didn't Dai say something about her having a terrible home life? Poor little thing — was she abused, is that what he meant? Not difficult to imagine, having met the brother. Crikey, she hopes she isn't going to uncover more of her the further she excavates. The saying "someone walking over your grave" comes to mind and, wanting to resume with her digging and push the uneasiness of this discovery away, Rachel sets the little shoe down on the path.

Working outside, in the earth-filled air, her mind hurtles on with thoughts of her father. The ghost of him caught in the tail of her eye. How he used to look straddling his vegetable plot, trowel in hand, combing the lines of green-spiked scallion with the thoroughness of a nit-nurse. The memory pushes her into working harder and within half an hour, what will be the first of her raised beds is taking shape.

Too engrossed, Rachel doesn't hear the slowing of tyres on gravel. The heavy thud of a slammed vehicle door. The crunch of gumboots on the carpet of last year's leaves that fringes her property.

"*Hello.*"

She jolts at the sound. The dog jumps up, barks. Telling him to *shhhh*, a finger pressed to her lips, he stops and they listen together. Rachel's hand, trailing backwards and forwards through Cadno's silky-soft fur.

"*Hello.*"

She recognises the voice this time, its slight wheeze. Her mood takes a dive. What the hell does he want *now?* The man's a bloody nuisance.

Thinking quickly, she ducks out of sight. Safe, she can't be seen from the front, but she wouldn't put it past him to come snooping along the lane. She pictures him: determined, grim, seeing her car, he won't give up; he won't care that she doesn't want to be found. She can't understand his dogged persistence, she hardly encourages him. She looks up, senses eyes through the interlocking branches of blackthorn and spindly briar, and squats lower, using her hands to balance. This is ridiculous — mindful, now stationary, of just how cold it is out here. Bloody hell, having to hide in your own home, it isn't fair. Things were supposed to be different here. She left all that creeping around and staying out of sight nonsense in London.

"What d'you want?" As assertive as she can make herself, she straightens up, brushes earth from her knees.

"Got feed for the sheep." His flaccid face, the texture of raw pastry, wobbles at her through the holes in the shrubbery.

"Well, leave it round the front, can't you? I'm busy here — I can give it to them later."

"I could . . ."

Rachel, aware of her heartbeat, is deeply troubled by this man.

"But I need to show you what to do."

"You need to show me?" Her irritation shown through thinning lips, she throws the spade and ball of string aside. "It's hardly rocket science."

"I can come back?" the wheezing concertina of a voice offers.

"Oh, no you won't." This is said fiercely, just out of earshot.

Rachel slides across her muddy garden and, with the dog following, heads for the side gate leading into her field. Idris is already there, a large plastic sack of sheep nuts rattling on his back. The dog barks as he lowers the feed to the ground as if it's nothing more than a bag of sugar.

"Got somewhere you can keep this?" his only greeting and she watches him wipe his nose on the cuff of his moth-eaten pullover.

"Follow me." Grimacing, she leads the way into her outbuilding. Dark inside, she reaches for the switch she knows is there. A fluorescent tube bounces into life and spinning round she finds him blocking her way. So close, she can smell the dank odour of his clothes. "You can put it there," she points, stepping away. "In that wheelbarrow."

"That's no good." His accent is strong, his breathing ragged. "You'll need something with a lid. Got to keep the rats out, see — I'm not paying to feed bloody rats. I'll drop something over tomorrow."

"Er, no. Sorry . . ." Rachel, struggling to think, doesn't want to give him the excuse he's looking for to call round again. "I'll find something. There's loads of stuff in here — I'm sure I've a dustbin floating around."

Idris grunts, shifts his weight from one trunk to the other. "You got something you can feed 'em from, then — like buckets?" His eyes work her from forehead to toe as the shadow of a smile edges across his face, pleased to have landed on another way to ensure a further visit.

"*Buckets? Buckets?*" Her mind racing, wanting him gone. "I've an old roasting tray and a big saucepan. So, when do I feed them?"

Idris sniffs as he yanks a sizeable flick knife from the depths of his trousers and, with a well-practised thumb, presses the button to galvanise the spring-loaded blade. "Handy this — don't go nowhere without it." He slashes open the top of the bag, flourishing the knife for longer than necessary. The cold flash of steel reflecting the glare of strip-light, hurls Rachel back to the time with Blundell, making her snap back her neck in panic. "Never know when I might need it, see." His leer both lingering and licentious.

"How much d'they need?" Rachel feels her pulse thumping beneath her scar, but refuses to buckle under the surge of fear that threatens to paralyse her. *Get rid of him, get rid of him.* Her galloping heart gushes its warning as he leans down and she sees the violent potential displayed in the beefy broadness of his torso.

"'Bout this much — no more." He scoops up a moderate amount in his giant's hands, demonstrating. "Don't want 'em *scarging*."

"*Scarging?*" Shaking her head, she doesn't understand.

"Shitting themselves — cos they will," he grins, enjoying her reaction. "Inside out."

Rachel can see his ewes from where she stands. She thinks of how she has taken to watching them from the rocking chair positioned by her landing window. How fond she's grown of seeing their big woolly shapes, placid and soft as cotton-wool clouds. Fancying she sees differences in their personalities, the way they interact, butting, nuzzling, seemingly the best of friends. They are surely having a better life with her; she doesn't want to have to ask him to take them away. Even without his sheep there would be other excuses he'd find to call round.

"Right, well, if that's all," she says, squaring up to him best she can. "I've things I need to get on with."

"Have you now?" Idris looks doubtful, bobs out into the bright daylight, waiting for her to lean back inside to turn off the lights. "I was wondering . . ." he says,

300

stepping forward, close enough for her to catch a whiff of his haddock-breath. Rachel does her best to hold her ground. "Fancy coming out for a drink? Down The Bear, quiz night?"

"Erm, no, I don't think so," she cuts him off, hoping he can't see her shaking beneath her layers. "I'm kind of seeing someone."

"Seeing someone, eh?" he echoes back. "Who's that then?"

You nosy git, Rachel thinks, facing her front door. "Someone from Llandafen."

"Llandafen? Oh, aye."

She watches him move towards his Toyota pickup, then stops, twisting round to face her. "Well, just so you know — my door's always open, if you're in trouble or anything."

In trouble . . . what are you going on about man? "I won't be, thanks," she says, bursting for him to go.

"Sure about that are you?"

She flinches under the implied menace. *I don't like this — I don't like this at all.* Tracy may think she's overreacting about this man, but he doesn't threaten her; he wouldn't dare with Hywel around.

"Can you just go, *please*?" Rachel, in her panic, slips on the steep rise of stone steps to her door, whacking her thigh against the large muscled arms of her squatting gargoyle. It was supposed to ward off evil spirits, the fifty pound sales-tag had claimed. *Not doing your bloody job are you.* She takes a sideways glance at it and steadies herself. Within seconds she scrambles out of her boots leaving her socks behind, the cold tiles of her porch sting her feet and make her gasp. Not that she stops to retrieve them. Swinging her door shut and locking Idris Tudor out is far more urgent.

In these frantic seconds, it occurs to her to call the police. To dial 999 and tell them how vulnerable she feels. That she is a woman living on her own in a remote spot and a male neighbour is stalking her. She thinks about it. *Stalking . . . really?* He's a pest, yes, but is he anything more than that? It isn't a crime to be uncouth and ugly, or even to say weird things. What has he actually done? A voice asks her. The voice of the imagined police officer. The one who will come to take her statement on whatever allegation she is making. A reasonable, rational voice that will tell her she cannot have someone arrested simply because they give her a bad feeling or she suspects they've been nicking underwear from her washing line. Anyway, she doesn't think she wants to go drawing attention to herself with the Dyfed-Powys Police. They might recognise her, put two and two together and then it would only be a matter of time before word got out and reporters came looking for a scoop.

Safely inside, she watches through the blinds of her living room as Idris drives away. Satisfied he's gone, she tugs down her jeans to inspect her leg. A bruise. Large. Showing itself already. Mussel-shaped, it hints at a blinding yellow like the unopened buds covering the banks of gorse out on the hill. She presses it, winces. Going to be a whopper, and she makes a point of monitoring its bloom in the week that follows. Funny, when she thinks of it later, that Graham didn't ask how she acquired it. Had he noticed, she might have told him. Filled him in on the bloke who lives up the lane. Not to say he was weird or anything, just as a way to let him know she has others interested in her. It wouldn't do any harm.

CHAPTER
SIXTY

Spying a break in the weather, Dai doesn't hang around. His breakfast of tea and toast done with, he flicks off the radio — cutting off the BBC broadcaster dispensing details of the continued search for the killer of two women in Westburn — and is out under the mottled sky with his corduroys tucked into his wellingtons. Trapped briefly within the darkened interior of his shed and unable to locate his own, he pulls on Elsie's gardening gloves. Age-stiffened, the seams are beginning to split, but feeling the smooth troughs where her fingers had been, he moulds them into his, wanting to claim them for his own.

"Hello."

Dai looks up as he steps back out into the comparative brightness and sees Rachel standing by the gate. She is in her usual walking gear, her dog by her side, but something about her is different. Happier?

"Hello." Pleased to see her. An easy one to like, he felt her sensitivity the first time they met. Nothing like the villagers he lives amidst, she isn't interested in petty tittle-tattle. "How's things at Tŷ Haf?"

"Great, thanks." She continues to smile and Dai, seeing her cheeks flushed pink with the cold, thinks she looks even prettier than usual. "What about you?"

"Doing fine. Enjoying the sunshine?"

"Lovely, isn't it — I've been able to work outside too," Rachel bubbles, more confident than usual. "Been pretty dire though, hasn't it — does it always rain this much?"

"'Fraid so," Dai chuckles. "Although I think we're the lucky ones, living up this end. Dilys was saying . . . you met Dilys?" Rachel shakes her head. "You will." He laughs again. "Well, anyway, down the village, the river's so high they've been putting out sandbags. You fancy a coffee?" he offers, changing the subject. "Come on," seeing her dithering, "you can interrupt your walk to spend a minute with me."

"I'm interrupting *you*, more like." Rachel, smiling, unclips the gate and steps into his garden.

"Nonsense," he tells her. "I've got all day. Could do with something hot — bit parky out here." He claps his hands together. "Fancy a slice of cake? Dilys made it."

"Makes you cakes does she, this Dilys?" Rachel, teasing, follows him to his front door, stopping short of the step. "Something you're not telling me, Mr Jones?"

"As we've established," Dai gives a playful little snort, "you haven't met the delightful Dilys Roberts, have you?"

Cold water splashes up his arm in his race to fill the kettle. Then setting it to boil, he prepares the tray with his usual care. Looking up, his hands busy unwrapping

305

Dilys' fruit cake, he sees Rachel walking the perimeters of his garden. Stopping to look at his raised seed beds and peer inside the steamy windows of his glasshouse. She calls to the dog who is cocking his leg up against Dai's shed. The way she darts a look to the window, unable to see him through the reflection on the glass, looking sheepish, it makes him smile.

"Where's your lovely cat — Gabriel?" Rachel asks when he appears in the doorway.

"Don't know — not seen him for weeks."

"That's odd."

"I'm trying not to worry — I know it's what cats do, but it's unusual for him. Apart from the odd night out, he's always with me."

"Anyone in Bryngwyn seen him? I'll ask around if you like, I'm walking that way in a bit."

"Would you?"

"No problem. He's probably wooing some gorgeous tabby as we speak — be home before you know it, you'll see." Rachel takes the plate Dai passes her. "Mmm, that's delicious." She nods vigorously through a mouthful of cake. "Really . . . rich." She strokes Cadno's head, which he has dropped into her lap, ever hopeful for crumbs.

"Oh, she's a good cook is our Dilys." Dai taking a bite and grinning.

"She married?"

"Dilys?" Dai blinks into the mental image he carries of her face. "No, never married."

"Someone missed out," Rachel says, licking her fingers.

He makes a small noise. "Think the old marriage lark takes a bit more than a talent for baking, don't you?"

"I s'ppose." Rachel pinches a corner of crumbs, drops them on her knee for the dog. "My ex used to like my cooking and he still buggered off." She gives a tight wheeze of a laugh.

"I didn't know you were married." Dai dips a toe in the water.

"Long gone." She flicks out her hand. "I won't pretend it wasn't difficult at the time, but hey, it hardly matters any more."

"Shame though," Dai says, awkward.

"I suppose, but you know," she shrugs, "life moves on."

"Me and Elsie, we hit a rocky patch — living in Cardiff, Anthony was small. She hated the city, was always trying to coax me back here . . . but I didn't want to."

"No?" Rachel sounds surprised. "Are you mad? This is such a peaceful spot. And the view . . ." Dai hears her exhale and follows her gaze across the dramatic curve of valley and the unknown pastures of blue and distant Wales.

"Elsie used to say we were the luckiest people alive, waking to this each morning."

"I think I'd have liked your Elsie," she says.

Dai squeezes the end of his nose. "And I'm sure she'd have liked you, too." He sips from his mug, takes a sideways look at Rachel. Something's happened to her, he thinks, something good.

"I've met someone." She beams, showing him her beautiful white teeth.

"Yes." Dai swallows the last of his cake. "I remember you saying something at Christmas — the chap who owns the art gallery — Graham ... Graham ... *Parnell?*"

"You know him?" Rachel, eyes keen.

"We've met ..." He nods, enigmatic. "It's a lovely gallery." He kneads the tip of his nose between finger and thumb again. A mannerism of his Rachel recognises. "The two of you been seeing a lot of each other then?"

"Since New Year, yes. And well, you know ..." Hiding under her eyelashes, blushing. "Things are moving along."

"You really like him, don't you?" How sweet she is, Dai thinks.

"Can you tell?" Bashful, she looks down at her rapidly cooling mug.

"I could tell something was different," he breathes his coffee breath into the crisp February air. "You've a real glow about you."

"A glow?" A hand flies to her cheek. "How embarrassing."

"Why embarrassing? It's what makes the world go round. You don't want to be on your own — lovely lass like you." He taps her arm affectionately. "I'm thrilled for you — Graham Parnell's a lucky boy."

"It's me who's lucky." Rachel strokes her dog's eyebrows. "Just hope I don't go screwing it up this time — I've a habit of spoiling things."

"I'm sure that's not the case. Honestly, it's luck — if you've had things go wrong in the past, it's only because he wasn't the right person."

"Thanks, Dai." She leans in, kisses his freshly shaven cheek. "I'll let you know how it goes." He watches her push her hair free of her face, in that way she does. "Thank you for the coffee and cake, we'll leave you to it." She calls to her dog, looks up at the sky, testing it. "You never know when it might start raining again — got to make the most of it."

"Rachel?" Dai calls, impeding her egress. "You and Graham . . ."

"Yes?" Arching her perfect eyebrows.

"Just enjoy it, try not to question things. You've met each other for a reason — he'll be good for you, I can tell."

"Thanks, Dai. It means a lot you saying that."

"See you soon."

"Let me know if Gabriel turns up?"

"I will."

And she's gone. The creak of the gate closing behind her, he waits a moment enjoying the news she has just given him. Good for you girl, he thinks, heading back to his pruning. Good for you.

CHAPTER
SIXTY-ONE

The interior of Idris' cab reeks of catnaps and stale farts. The girl he has brought back, a little bottle-blonde going by the name of Pauline, curls her studded-lip in disgust. He smells it too, but unlike her, the stuck-up bitch, he likes it.

"Fuck, it stinks in 'ere."

He wants to tell her to watch her mouth, to show some respect. This is where he lives when he's on the road, so what if it smells? It's the only place he has to store himself, to vent his frustrations. Anyway, she's one to talk. Ripe as a trawler-load of cod, in her ripped tights and chewed-down fingernails. Not even the quality of his usual sort, with their plumpness and skin as silky soft as his mother's dresses. Apart from the yellow hair, she isn't nearly pretty enough for his taste. And those ear, nose and lip piercings — he catches a flash of the metal stud through her tongue — are enough to turn his stomach.

"You wanna get on wiv it, or what?" Her accent is different too. Shrill. He thinks fleetingly of the sharp-eyed vixen he shoots on the hill back home. She wants to watch it — the others he's had back here, with

310

their soft Somerset drawl, didn't speak to him like this. "Cos I've a long night ahead of me."

"Well . . ." he wheezes, because although he's been here many times, he's still unsure how to kick-off proceedings. "Get 'em off then." Ungainly, he looks away, drags the curtains across his windscreen. Swapping the not quite black of a cloud-filled night by the sea for the imagined blue of midnight, speckled with hundreds of tiny crescent moons, trapping them further.

"You must be fuckin' joking. No way, matey — I don't do stripping for no one. I gave you me pricelist, I told ya what I do — if you're gonna start wanting extras —" She shoves a fist to her mouth, gnaws at the stubs she has for fingernails.

"D'you have to do that?" A giant paw of his own, flicking out at hers. "It's making me sick."

"That's nice innit, coming from you." She stops biting her nails, puts her hands in her lap. Contrite and reduced to the little girl so much of her still is. "We agreed — I just sit on you, right? It's what you said you wanted. Thirty quid's worth."

"Right." Idris rotates the bulk of his body. His huge knees rammed up against the dashboard, his frame too big for the space he has confined them to. He starts to undo the belt of his trousers.

"Lemme," she says, swivelling the slightness of her skeleton effortlessly towards him. In seconds, slipping her feet free of her white plastic stilettoes, she is up on her knees on the seat beside him. The exposed flesh of her scrawny cleavage pressed against Idris' jowls. He lets go a moan. A low, mournful, trough of a sound. A beast of the field, he gives into it, juddering with pleasure as a hand, not his own for a change, undoes his button, unzips his fly. She doesn't flinch. This girl is good, he thinks, watching himself grow in her working hand. *Worth the money?* He'll have to wait and see.

"Got a condom?" she exhales; her bubble-gum breath, close to his ear. Then, following the direction of his hand, the stub of dirty finger pointing to the glove compartment, the girl reaches behind her. Her pelvis, supple, allows her to lean right back without needing to remove her hand. He groans again, a noise coming from somewhere deep inside him. Stiff and hard, it pleases him the way he responds to her.

He watches her use her teeth — a neat little row of white and an equal amount of pink gum — to rip open the square of foil. Briefly, bringing a hand away from the job she is doing, careful to keep the other one at it, slips the sheath expertly over the purple-headed thing she can hardly bear to look at.

"Hop on then." Idris, the whites of his eyes reflected in the lights strung up along Westburn's deserted promenade, which find him from beneath the hem of curtain. To his surprise she does. These druggy bitches will do anything for money. He flings his head back into the upholstered seat, closes his eyes. The minutes pass. The girl, with a frame as narrow as Beth's, doing its stuff.

"This is no fuckin' good," he yelps, thinking he heard a faint sigh of, *come on, hurry up,* escape her lips. "Get

312

off me, you slag. Get off me." And he throws the girl to the side, wishing he hadn't thought of Beth.

A squeak of seats, a rustle of clothes. The girl, rearranging herself, asks, "Hell's wrong with you — we were going great there?"

"You're what's fuckin' wrong." There is violence in his voice. It makes her flinch before shoving her fist to her mouth again, teeth scraping against nails.

"Weren't my fault — you can't go blaming me cos you can't keep it up."

"Shut your gob."

"You better pay me," she whines, leaning into his space, claiming what she thinks she has a right to. "We had a deal — thirty quid, you said."

The girl doesn't make a sound when Idris' fist smashes into the side of her face. A trickle of blood from the silver stud of her pink-frosted lip runs down over her chin, into the bony cleft between her breasts. She just stares at him, in those dangling seconds before trying to make her getaway, not quite believing the terror that is taking shape behind her eyes.

CHAPTER
SIXTY-TWO

Dai is wiping down his kitchen surfaces in his usual methodical way. His dish cloth, like his mind, takes care to avoid the cliff-high Victoria sponge Dilys Roberts popped round with earlier. Sweating beneath its sheath of clingfilm in her outstretched hand, he took it without properly thanking or inviting her in as he might ordinarily do.

It wasn't kind, it wasn't polite, and now he is berating himself, but at the time, he hadn't been in the mood. Wanting to be alone with his thoughts, the woman brings too much disruption. He could tell he offended her and knows she will be out there making the most of it around the village. Slating him to the other women who will call him ungrateful as they buff and shine her thoughtfulness, impressing on her how the likes of David Jones aren't worth the trouble.

Making a mug of tea, he carries it into his living room. He won't cut a wedge of Dilys' sponge; he will show some self-restraint by sitting down and immersing himself in his Penguin Classic paperback instead. The Graham Greene he is halfway through. *Brighton Rock*, the last book Elsie was to read. Although he doesn't think she finished it, flicking through to find the scrap of paper with her handwriting she used as a bookmark, which he keeps buried inside the pages.

He read this story in his youth but, revisiting it aged sixty-six, he finds he understands more of its complexities. More of Pinkie's calculated evil and how the seemingly simple idea of him being a Catholic and so believing his retribution for the wrongs he commits do not lie in human hands, is a clever twist. One that leaves him wide open to the ambivalent and moral world of Ida Arnold. What he wouldn't give for an avenging angel such as Ida Arnold. Whose allegiance is with life, the here and now, a person who would, if she were real, take up the challenge of bringing the infernal Idris Tudor to an earthly kind of justice. He wishes he had the strength and courage to do it himself, but he can no more do this than step on a plane, fly to Brisbane and see his new-born grandchild.

In his armchair with the light dwindling beyond his windows is when he misses the company of his cat most of all. Usually about now, Gabriel would be indoors, warming himself in his lap or pushing up inside his fleecy-lined cat house that, empty for three weeks, still sits against the radiator. He loved his home comforts and Dai can't imagine what he's feeding himself on, or how he's keeping warm. The only thing he can hope is that someone has taken him in and given him a home.

Closing his paperback, he turns it over in his lap. He doesn't want to dwell on the whereabouts of Gabriel and can't seem to concentrate on his book, so he thinks of the story he has in him instead. Of a girl he once knew who, despite all he did and the promises they made, vanished into thin air like a cold puff of breath on a winter morning. Powder-skinned and dumb with bruises on her arms, he has no way of visualising her as a grown woman, with full breasts and hips and thighs. Striding along unknown streets, arm and arm with her husband, a family somewhere close by. He knows it is this that snares him into the past. This fluttering nebulous trick of the light, letting him think he sees her one minute, then gone the next. It surpasses cruelty.

He gets up, goes into his kitchen and, trying to push from his mind his disbelief that Beth could vanish voluntarily when they had such plans, opens the back door to call for Gabriel. Brandishing the box of Go Cat in the way he has always done to tempt him home.

CHAPTER
SIXTY-THREE

So young this one, I feel I should be asking what she's doing out on a school night, make her tell me where she got the alcohol from because no pub should be serving underage teens. It's obvious, from the state of her, she's had a skinful. But I don't ask, it's not my problem, and anyway, she's here now, climbed into the passenger seat like she was expecting me.

Only one there, pulling up alongside the deserted park railings, past the Sandpiper. A pretty little straggler, all her friends gone home — just what I was waiting for. The plastic sheet I've been putting down to protect my precious leather upholstery, crackles underneath us. The girl doesn't move. Sitting in a skirt that has risen up to her knickers, the skin of her legs washed-out by the cold vein of moonlight.

"... *with your long blonde hair and your eyes of blu . . . oo . . .*"

I don't know why, but I've had that song in my head all day, so I sing a bit of it to her, twisting round in my seat to give her a smile. But she doesn't return it, the little bottle-blonde; she isn't interested in making friends. Nervy, she chews her nails. A sound that goes right through me, so I smack her hand away, but in seconds she shoves them up to her mouth again, gnawing away like a hamster.

317

Now she's alongside me, I can see her mascara's run and her cheeks are red and blotchy. She looks as if she's been crying and there's blood on her top. *I'll give her something to snivel about if she starts that with me*, my thoughts echoing what my father used to say, before beating the crap out of me as a kid. I know it's down to him, the way I am, it's like I need to prove I'm worthy; more worthy than these pretty girls he liked more than me. And by forcing them to do what I want, it makes me the powerful one for a change.

I drive her out to the very end of the esplanade, thinking she might like to watch the waves shimmying under a moonlit sky. But she doesn't seem to notice, her eyes glazing over, still and silent, chewing her nails. Then she must see something shift in my face because she stops, sits on her hands.

It makes her look even younger.

It makes me feel bad. But not too bad.

There's something different about this one — up close, she's not half as brazen as others I've entertained in here. Yes, she's got a faceful of make-up, and there's her long yellow hair, but she's shabby, her clothes look cheap and her knees are dirty. Not things I could see when I was trailing her in the dark.

She doesn't smell all that great either. Not that I say anything, not about that. "Why've you got blood on your top?" is what I say instead. "Wanna tell me what happened?" But she won't answer; she just gives a little shrug and starts on her nails again.

So we sit, the girl and me, staring out over the oil-black water moving yards from the end of the bonnet, reflecting patches of silver-edged clouds as they drift over a sluggish moon.

318

CHAPTER
SIXTY-FOUR

Graham drives Rachel out to a winter sea. Llansteffan.
With its sharp-eyed castle standing sentinel above,
watching for trouble on the whale-grey horizon and
wide flat sands in the same way it has done for
centuries. The NO DOGS sign says nothing about the
months between October and May, so they let Cadno
go, and free, he gallops, gangly like the puppy he still is,
through shallows he has never seen before.

Laughing into the spray, they walk hand in hand
beneath a cloud-filled sky. The fine oblique slant of
drizzle sparkly on their hair. To the random passer-by,
they look cheerful, lifting a hand to wave a greeting over
the rippled sand the receding tide leaves behind. A
regular married couple, out walking their dog. She sees
what they project to the world and likes it, gripping
Graham's hand tighter in its woollen sheath of glove.

They buy fish and chips from the mobile van in
the car park and eat them standing up with fingers, the
vinegary smells suspended in the air. They drink from
tepid cola cans, the bubbles fizzing wildly in their
mouths, making them burp discretely into cupped
hands, facing seaward. Graham smudges ketchup on
his nose and she lets him keep it for when he goes back

for the polystyrene cups of weak black tea. Tells him afterwards. She gives a shy little dance before leaning in to scoop it off. This place of salty winds and gull-filled skies blows her back in time to Westburn and makes her smile a secret smile. Makes him ask: "What are you smiling about?"

"Memories," she tells him. "Memories of my dad taking me with him on his work trips to the coast when I was little."

"Lucky you," he breathes into her hair, giving her goose bumps that travel up and under the sleeves of her waterproof.

"What, for going to the seaside?"

"Daft," he says, pulling her to him and slipping an arm about her waist. "For having memories about your dad like that. I haven't got happy memories of mine." And he kisses her, wanting to lighten things, wanting to make her smile again. Seeing that what he says has made her sad, for a moment or two, until the wind snatches at her hair again, prompting her to grab his hand. And running, they laugh like children, over the spiny-backed dunes, across the sand and into the creamy foam at the lip of the sea.

When it starts to rain for real, they seek refuge in Graham's big black 4×4. They sit bunched up on the wide leather seats behind a steamed-up windscreen. Their bulky waterproofs rasping through the weight of wet-dog smells in the noticeably valeted interior. She likes the way he takes care of things in the same way she does, likes the methodical tidiness of him, and

320

smiles at there not being so much as a discarded sweet wrapper or tissue in sight. It comforts her to think how alike the two of them are, how much common ground they share.

Leaning back into the plush upholstery, they listen to the weather thrash the roof. Too loud to talk, although she can hear him singing under his breath as they watch the hooded-shapes of walkers, androgynous and indistinct. They see an upturned fishing boat. Its bleached-white belly, vulnerable as Cadno's when he rolls over to give them his tummy to stroke. A wall of creel pots, their limbs rusting beyond the trussing of nylon rope that, frayed at the ends, snaps back and forth in the wind. She thinks again of the blue nylon rope of her childhood. Of the swing in the garden that is the furthest away it has ever been.

"I love you," he says. His voice, finding her above the deluge of rain, levels her. Fishes her free from her past and hooks her into the present. Just like that. A statement so bald and pure she can't look at him. Only at his hand, his fingers, and how they look entwined in hers.

I could be happy with you, she thinks without sharing. Liking him for not asking about the scar on her wrist he has noticed and strokes with the pad of his thumb. *Can't risk telling him*. He wouldn't want her with all her baggage. *Can't risk losing him*. Not when he is the loveliest man she has ever known. Her father's face swims out to her. She thinks he is smiling, although she can't be sure, coming as the image does from deep beneath the waves.

"You would have liked my dad," she says finally. "I wish you could have met him." This is the best she can manage for now.

"Me too," he says, as if this was the answer he wanted and is satisfied. Gripping her hand, he leans over to kiss her, disregarding the gear stick and handbrake that threatens to separate their bodies. "Me too," he whispers as she tastes salt.

CHAPTER
SIXTY-FIVE

Left to her own devices in Derek Barnes' one-windowed office, the warm smells of fresh pastries from the bakery below seeping through the bare floorboards, Jennifer notices several framed photographs on an over-stuffed bookshelf behind the desk. She gets up for a closer look, keen for some insight into the man's background after she has given him so much of her own. One photograph in particular takes her interest and she picks it up. In it Derek is holding hands with a woman, and standing just off to the right is a man in a red serge tunic and wide-brimmed hat, holding the reins of a large bay horse.

"You've spent time in Canada?" she says, hearing Mr Barnes open the door to his office and step in behind her.

"Sorry?" he says, shuffling papers.

"The photo." She shows him what she's looking at. "That's the RMCP uniform . . . Mounties, isn't it?"

"Ah, yes." Derek Barnes nods, sliding the flat of his hand over his shiny bald pate and sitting down. "That's Gus, my wife's brother; that's my wife there." He points, taking the photograph she passes him.

"My late husband was Canadian. From Quebec."

"Oh, that explains the name." Barnes beams. "My wife's from Montreal."

"And that explains," Jennifer returns his smile, "why you pronounced my name so well."

"A fabulous country, isn't it?" he sighs, a little wistful. "Francine is desperate to go back; we're trying to work out a way to retire there."

"Strange as it may sound," she tells him, "I've never actually been. I don't know why, but my husband didn't want to go back." She shrugs, thinking of how she used to badger Donald, keen for news of his origins, of the name she had taken and signed as her own.

The telephone on the desk rings between them. She sees Barnes look at it, weighing up whether or not to answer.

"D'you mind?" he says eventually and she shakes her head, watching him take the call.

Disengaging from the conversation her private investigator is having, her mind drifts and she thinks how Canada, even before Donald came along, was a part of the world that fascinated her. A country so diverse and picturesque it was on her list to visit. But he flatly refused, reasonably and without raising his voice. Unlike Sarah, Jennifer never knew how to play him. Not in their early years and certainly not in the dwindling ones when his health was deteriorating. She remembers the effort required to cajole him into eating. Sitting him in his big swivel armchair in his fancy-wallpapered room, a jolly-coloured napkin tied about his neck, patiently spooning whatever succulents

324

Mrs Pepper had prepared into his mouth. But even in this most basic of tasks she succeeded in rubbing him up the wrong way. Watching his slow burn of impatience, he would redden like the bars on an electric fire. Silent and obstinate, Donald communicated his discontent more powerfully after his second attack and he lost his ability to speak, than when he was vocal. The inability to move or formulate words hadn't affected his brain; he knew what he was doing. How behaving this way forced his wife into calling for Sarah. He would eat for Sarah. She was someone worth staying alive and keeping secrets for. His blue-eyed girl, killing him with kindness, sitting with him for hours, stroking his hand and scraping the bowl for the tiniest morsel. Not Jennifer. It hadn't been Jennifer for a long time.

She must have made a noise, involuntary, enough for Derek Barnes to turn his head to her and then end his telephone conversation.

"Right," he says, tidying his notes and re-joining her. "Awfully sorry about that. Now, where were we?" He rubs his plump palms together. "Ah, yes . . . Canada . . . your surname, *D'Villez*. Yes." He looks directly at her. "Unsurprisingly the name has drawn a blank; Sarah's obviously not using it. Can you think of another she might be going under?"

"I suppose she could be using her married name, Moran. Sorry, I should've given you that," Jennifer apologises, watching him write it down.

"Good, good." Mr Barnes looks up. "Well, as you know, I've been focusing my initial investigations in mid-Wales, the tourist areas you felt Sarah had a fondness for, and what I've got so far is a handful of properties that've been sold or rented out to single women about the time your daughter left London — and there aren't many. So," he breathes into the doughy smells that fill his tiny office. "This is a significant lead. The most positive so far — if indeed she's gone to Wales." He gives a measured smile that doesn't quite reach his eyes. "The next thing is for me to visit these places," he says, twirling a chewed biro between his fingers. "But they're pretty spread out, so it'll take time," he pauses before adding, "and of course money. So, Mrs D'Villez, the question is, do you want me to carry on? Bearing in mind these leads may come to nothing. That she could have gone anywhere, abroad . . . to Canada even," he says in a way that makes Jennifer think the thought has just occurred to him. "I remember you saying how close she was to her father, and with the family connection . . . it is possible."

Jennifer nods. "I did wonder about her leaving the country, I haven't been able to find her passport. I went so far as calling my sister — she and her husband live in New York. Did I say?" She watches Barnes shake his head. "Well, it was worth a try, in case she'd gone there, but she hadn't. I never thought of Canada, probably because we're not in touch with any of my husband's relations — but yes, it's possible."

"This is what I'm saying." Derek Barnes twiddling his pen again. "Supposing this hunch of yours is wrong and she isn't in Wales at all? It's an expensive way to

326

find out." He pauses, chuckles; the sound rumbling deep inside him. "I know I'm probably doing myself out of business here, but maybe there are other avenues I should try first? Ones that mean I don't have to leave my desk."

"Very good of you to be so honest." Jennifer blinks through the dust motes that float in the strips of light. "But I really would like you to try Wales as well. It's imperative I find her and I'm pretty sure that's where she's gone, her father loved the area so much, you see."

"I understand." The private investigator's expression is earnest. "Okay, but let me share another idea — there is somewhere else I've thought of."

"Oh yes." Jennifer raises her eyes to his.

"The reason why you think it could be Wales is because you think she's chasing memories — happy childhood memories of her father?"

"That's right."

"Well, could she have chased them to Wesburn-on-Sea instead? You mentioned it was a regular haunt of theirs, didn't you?"

On her walk back to Grand Avenue, Jennifer mulls over the idea that Sarah might have gone to Westburn. Clever of him to think of it, she'd completely forgotten the connection. Suppose she is there? The idea is more alarming than she first thought when she remembers there's a killer on the loose. Someone targeting pretty blondes, according to the news reports. Oh, dear God, she presses a calfskin-gloved hand to her forehead, as if

327

she doesn't have enough to stress about. Please don't have done that, Sarah, she pleads silently; your looks have got you in enough trouble in the past.

CHAPTER
SIXTY-SIX

The weather keeps Rachel awake. It hasn't let up all day. The car park at the top of Queen Street was flooded when Graham dropped her off and meant a mad dash from car to car, transferring the dog, trying to avoid a soaking. Driving away from Llansteffan, over the thump, thump of windscreen wipers, Graham talked of his mother. Told Rachel about putting her in a home, laying down his guilt like a blanket the two of them could lie on. He talked candidly of the bleak episode leading to this decision. The horror of finding her, frothy-mouthed and blue-lipped, on the lino of her kitchen floor.

"Since then though, I've fallen out with Eleanor."

A vague recollection of the name, Rachel assumed Eleanor was the sister. It was the most he'd given of his family so she hadn't wanted to ask for clarification, she wanted him to talk.

"We just get Mum settled and she wants to move her again."

His voice, louder than usual, needing to compete with the lashing rain, but there was frustration in it too. "She can be so bloody selfish."

Rachel tried to comfort him, but sensing his rising agitation, the two of them fell into an awkward hush.

"What you singing that for?" he asked, suddenly snatching at the silence.

"Singing? No, I wasn't." And she'd been sure of this.

"Yeah, you were," he smiled, then gave her a snippet, "*With your long blonde hair and eyes of blu-oo . . .*"

"I hadn't realised, sorry." She laughed. "It was you, I got it from you — you were singing it earlier."

"Was I?"

"Yes. You're always singing, didn't you know?"

"I have been told." He reached out, clasped her hand then let it go again. "Although let's agree not to sing that one any more — I hate it."

Fearful she could kick the tune off again, she put the radio on, only to find little relief there. The pips were followed by a news bulletin and the impartial-voiced broadcaster saturating their already damp mood . . . *the body of a young woman from Westburn-on-Sea, believed to be that of the missing eighteen-year-old Pauline Keene, was found on waste ground earlier . . . Pauline's sister reported her missing when she failed to come home . . .*

It was his hand that reached out to switch it off, beating her to it. In perfect harmony with each other, Rachel remembers smiling at how alike they were. She hadn't wanted to think about murder on their drive home either, not after the lovely time they'd shared on Llansteffan beach. So she has no idea why she remained on the subject, long after the radio was silenced.

"That's the third one," she said as she gazed into Graham's profile. Tracing it with her mind so she could imagine it later. "Horrible, isn't it? Their poor families."

Graham said nothing, his frowning concentration firmly set on the centre road markings, the only thing visible through the sheets of rain.

"You ever been to Westburn?" she asked, pleased at landing on something — although still connected to those grisly killings — that might lead to more pleasant things.

"No, I haven't," he said mildly, blinking through the condensation that refused to clear on his extensive sweep of windscreen. "Why d'you ask?"

"No reason — just I went there with my dad a few times, that's all. On his work trips. I thought I said."

"You said about his work trips, but you didn't say you went to Westburn."

"Didn't I? I meant to. When we were in Llansteffan, it reminded me of it."

"*Llansteffan?*" His tone, scornful, made her feel stupid. "You are joking? It's nothing like Westburn." He let go a false little laugh.

What she wanted to say was: *how the hell would you know if you've never been there?* But she didn't. Not in the market for defending the place or her reasoning behind the comparison, she said simply, "No, you're right, it isn't. To be honest, I thought Westburn was a bit of a dump when I was a kid, I dread to think what it's like now. It was just the beach, I suppose." And it had been her turn to dredge up a laugh.

With the dog occupying more than his share, she thinks it's probably a good job Graham didn't take up her offer of coming back here to share her bed, there wouldn't be the room. Feeling Cadno shift, coiling down into the shell-shaped swirl into which he makes himself comfortable, she turns over, sees the blueness of dawn through her curtainless windows. The rain must ease enough for her to fall asleep, her thoughts of Graham converting to dreams, until a thunderous boom shakes the foundations of her barn and wakes her. A crashing, rolling sound. One that makes the dog spring into action, leaping to the floor and barking wildly.

No real mystery — it's that creep from up the lane. Setting off at first light in his articulated truck. Carving up the banks, terrorising the wildlife, going hell for leather. God help you if you meet him coming the other way along that stretch. She remembers her ride out with Carole. She thinks too of that time with Dai, when they were nearly run down, and swears she saw Idris smiling up there in his cab behind its grubby-blue curtains. What a loser. Except he's the one with the power — he's got her cage well and truly rattled.

When Rachel re-awakens, it's morning and, in the moments before pushing herself out of bed, she revisits the account Graham gave the previous day of finding his mother collapsed on her kitchen floor. It makes her think of the second close shave her father suffered. The summer Spencer kicked her out and she moved back in with her parents. She woke in the dead of night to a strange sound curling along the landing. A faint, animal sound, like something injured. She isn't sure how she heard it, but when she did, she understood it immediately and knew what to do. Witnessing a girl suffer a seizure at school, the memory had stayed with her. Rachel acted quickly, shoving her mother's ineptitude away by shouting at her to *get a grip and call a bloody ambulance.* She doesn't remember speaking to her mother this way before, or since — the panic of the moment, the excuse to order her about had been exhilarating.

"Dad. Dad," she said, wanting him to stay conscious. Remembering what Miss Fenton had done with Jane Hames at school. Jane, who looked awake, but with only the whites of her eyes showing, wasn't really there. The saliva, frothing white, from the corners of her mouth. Blood on her chin, down the front of her school blouse. Blood like her dad. So she did what her teacher had done, shoved something between his teeth to stop him biting his tongue. In the shiny-walled corridor of Sacred Heart High it had been a text book, this time the edge of an eiderdown. She waited, stroked her father's hair and cooed, motherly, as his body jerked against her own. Her own mother, helpless, useless, flapping around like a wet blanket with the telephone receiver in her hand and her back to the wall.

It was over before the ambulance arrived. The turgidity of her father's body lessening until it stopped its involuntary writhing and dropped down to the mattress. The paramedics congratulated Rachel on her quick reaction and her knowledge of first aid. Saying what she did would no doubt help her father's recovery. She thinks of her mother's face, rereads its hateful, silent look: *You caused this, the trouble you've brought to this house — if he dies, I'll blame you. YOU, with your dazzling looks and honey hair.*

He was gone three whole weeks while they monitored his heart rate and edged him through scanners taking pictures that let them peer into his brain. Rachel would take herself off to sit in his room, smell his fatherly smells. Play his old records, swivelling round and round in his big leather chair, praying he would live. And alone in here, she chose to squirrel away some of her most private and precious things, things she didn't want her snoop of a mother to find. Hiding them deep in the back of a cabinet, a place she knew her father would never go. So how could she have been so stupid to have left them behind? She can only blame it on her urgency to get out of London. Perhaps it would have been better to have destroyed them, now there is a danger they could be found. But she knows she could never have done that, her vanity wouldn't have let her; it was something she needed to have when she was older, to remind herself of what she once was, and what she could do. Now that they are not where she can get them, there is a fear that sometimes wakes her in a cold sweat.

When her father returned, he couldn't speak. She feared the seizure had damaged him more than first thought. But by the end of his first week home, he confided in her, propped up in his rotating armchair, a tartan rug over his knees. Overcome perhaps, being

334

back with his fleur-de-lis wallpaper, surrounded by his books, his gramophone records and coffee smells. "I bit my tongue, I bit right through it." And he cried. Pressing his eyes to her shoulder and sobbing. "But you're not to tell your mother," he said recovering himself a little, "I don't want her knowing I can speak."

CHAPTER
SIXTY-SEVEN

"Things going well for you and your new bloke, then?" Tracy, dressed for working around the farm for a change, brakes alongside Rachel, who is on her way back from a walk. Her window, sliding down on the Defender's interior, pumps over-warm air into the wet lane. "Me and Hywel," she chuckles, chewing. "Not that we're being nosy or nothing, well, we wondered, what with seeing his SUV parked up outside your place all the time."

"*SUV?*" Rachel blinks at her from under the rim of her woolly hat. Unsure of the term or if she even heard Tracy correctly. With the dog barking and tugging impatient on his lead, desperate to chase off that idiot from up the road who has just hurtled past them in his lorry.

"Yeah, that big black, spanking Mitsubishi Shogun — it is him, isn't it? We thought it must be — far too smart for anyone round here. What's his name again?"

"Graham," she tells her quietly. Her mind racing. *Is that what he's got — a Mitsubishi?* She doesn't think she knows what one of those looks like and hadn't taken much notice of what he was driving when they went to Llansteffan. Too engrossed in him she supposes, although she's always been hopeless with the makes and models of cars. Whatever it was it was black and large enough to be called one of those SUV things, she supposes. Certainly bigger than her RAV anyway.

"Graham. That's it." Tracy breathes out her toffee-rich breath. "He owns that smart art gallery in town, doesn't he? Right up your street I bet, all that."

"When was it you saw it?" Rachel sniffs, picks through her anorak pockets for a tissue.

"Well, it was here last night. Yeah, for sure. On our way back from Llanybydder, we were. Later on, it was dark, about six or so."

"You sure it was him?"

"Well, who else is it gonna be? No one round here got one of them, trust me. Tasty bit of kit that. And cos we've been seeing it parked up on your bank — I don't know . . ." she bunches up her shoulders, "we just assumed."

"No, Tracy — you must've got it wrong." Rachel, eyes wide, expectant.

"Got what wrong?"

"Graham's never been here — I have asked him, but he's reluctant to leave the gallery. Security — you know, what with all those paintings." She lifts her arms then drops them by her sides. "Anyway, he prefers to be in the hub of things . . . think it's a bit too sleepy around here for him. It's why I ask you to look after Cadno — I stay with him in his flat above the shop."

"*Right.*" Tracy's cheeriness sliding free. "So who the bloody hell's been parking up outside here then?"

A beat.

"I don't know, could be anyone." The idea unsettles her more than she lets on, remembering the face she thought she saw at her back door that night and the time she swears she saw her mother at the fair. Maybe that's it. Maybe her mother's hired someone to find her. Although, that kind of thing would take imagination and because Rachel doesn't credit her mother with having any, she strikes the thought off as too fanciful. Then she looks at Tracy, remembers the elegant man she saw her holding hands with in town. Perhaps whoever it is comes to see you, parking up here so you can meet away from the farm, she thinks, but doesn't say, twisting her face into the wind. The same person you sneak off with when you're all dressed up. "Whoever it is, it's got bugger-all to do with me," she says eventually, her expression resolute.

CHAPTER
SIXTY-EIGHT

From downstairs comes the snapping of the letter box, the crunch of gravel and squeak of garden gate. Dai moves to the window, looks down on Evans the Post's bare dome of a head. Its skin, shiny as the glaze on an upturned soup bowl. "Fine head for *cawl*." Elsie's remembered giggle resonates through the dust motes. He'd forgotten how much he missed it.

Evans was the one who brought Elsie her wig. Hovering on the doorstep that blustery January morning, wanting to know what it was. Had the franked logo on the box given it away or was it Elsie, bald as Evans himself, coming to the door in the days she was still able to walk? Reading his curiosity and lifting it out of his hands — Elsie who liked to shake the tree now and again — saying: "Ooo, has my hair arrived?" The man hadn't known where to put himself.

Dai resumes his dusting. Lifting and spraying, the yellow cloth now quite wet in his hand. He stops when he reaches the dressing table. The crop of framed photographs taken in the years before Elsie lost her hair. Too proud, in the latter months of her life, to have the way she looked recorded. "Wait until it grows back." She would cup a hand over the eye of the camera should he direct it at her, on those rare days out, when she was feeling just about well enough. Dai driving them to Carreg Cennen with a picnic in the boot she didn't have the stomach for. Or out to Mumbles, where she would pretend to enjoy a restaurant lunch by pushing it around her plate with a fork. "Honestly, love, no one can tell it's a wig, you know," Dai doing his best to convince her, seeing her dismay should she catch sight of her reflection, hating her alien curls. "Thank you, sweetheart." She would give him a dry little kiss and squeeze his hand to reassure in return. "I know I'm being silly, it's only hair — I don't know why it's so important."

He thinks of how her only concern was for him. How he was coping, how things would be for him when she had gone. "Don't talk like that." He had been determined, as if his will alone would save her. But she knew, as in touch with her body as the nature she moved within. She knew from the moment she was given the test results in a busy ward. A crowd of student doctors round her bed, their hands clasping clipboards, poised to document her reaction. Hearing of it later, Dai had it out with the baby-faced consultant. Plastering him to the wall with a dictionary's worth of medical terms and facts that, to this day, he has no idea of the origins of. Keeping on until Mr Complacent backed away, raised his surgeon scrubbed-pink palms and conceded defeat by apologising for his behaviour.

Elsie endured six months of chemotherapy, followed by eight sessions of intense radiotherapy. Bloated and fat from the steroids that were prescribed, she grew

340

unrecognisable in the final weeks and incapable of stepping beyond the living room. Not that she complained; trapped inside by her failing body, watching him move about the garden she loved as ardently as him. Much of Dai believes she only endured the aggressive treatment with its debilitating side-effects to give him the hope she thought he needed.

A crack. He looks down at the glaze of the photograph, the one he had forgotten he was holding. His grip so fierce, he's snapped it clean in two. The shards of glass puncture his memories as well as his thumb, and pulling his hand away he sees the blood. Watches it, drip, drip on to the plush cream carpet of his bedroom floor.

CHAPTER
SIXTY-NINE

Rachel studies Graham. A towel wrapped around his waist, rubbing his hair with another. He doesn't stand still for a minute. Wandering room to room, barefoot in his *pied-a-terre*, as she has come to call it, making him laugh. She likes his laugh. The way his blue eyes crease at the corners, making her think of a Mediterranean sky and happy holidays. She likes the look of him wet, too. His skin slippery under the row of halogen lights in his little kitchen before ducking out again, back to the bedroom and the whooshing sounds of the hair dryer.

Needing the bathroom, she steps into his expended steam, his smells of aftershave and shaving foam. Wiping condensation from the mirror with her sleeve, she peers into her reflection to check her make-up.

"We've run out of bread," she hears him call out, closing the fridge door. He must have dressed in seconds. "No trouble, look, Co-op's open, it's only round the corner. Be there and back in a jiffy. Will you be all right — want me to fetch you anything?"

"No, thanks," she says, stepping into his living room to smile at him. "I'll have a look through the papers, keep me out of mischief."

Sounds of feet being pushed into shoes, the fastening of a zip, she watches the door close behind him. This is the first time she has been alone in his flat, it feels different, filled with shadows. Moving through the artificial Sunday silence, she picks up one of the mugs of tea he poured before realising he needed to go out. She sips it, pleased again with how alike they are. The black tea. Jam not marmalade. Wholemeal toast without butter. Even keeping the bread in the fridge.

She wanders over to the big bay window where the sofas are. Vast white marshmallowy things, no wonder he doesn't want her dog in here. Rotating the slats of the blinds, she looks down on the street. Llandafen's wet pavements, the darkened interiors of shops and red brick passageways dropping away into blackness. It feels strange waking up to this view. She feels a pang for hers. For her dog who has spent the night with Hywel's in the lambing shed at Cwm Glas. She'll say she needs to be heading back after breakfast. Wanting only what she knows of Graham as company on her walk up the hill: his habit of inventing songs and singing without realising, how he looks when he stares intently at her, making her forget to breathe. Alone, she has the space she needs to play out their time together, to wallow in the intense misery that comes from missing him.

Wanting a top-up of tea, she stands up at the counter, waiting for the water to re-boil and unfolds his *Mail on Sunday*, making room for it amidst the tea bags, the jars of jam and crumbs from the empty bread bag. More information about the three murdered girls in Westburn. She doesn't read it, wants to bypass the

343

inevitable despair that comes from looking into their melancholy faces. Choosing instead to turn the pages choked with the sparkly lives of the rich and famous, the perfectly whittled-down existences and perfect white-toothed smiles of the Duke and Duchess of Cambridge, the entourage of clingers on. All glorious, all meaningless. Until something stops her dead. A face from her past. One that, although never far away, always comes as a shock.

John Blundell.

Sucking back her breath, she braces herself for some unforeseen revelation, the bone of her hip pressed hard against the counter. Snatching at words: *Probation board satisfied . . . released on licence . . . reintegration into the community . . . served his time . . .* she realises there is nothing new here and relaxes a little.

The phone rings and she drops the article to look at it. Her face, hot under her hands as she checks the door. *Better answer it.* And taking the few strides necessary, lifts the handset to her ear.

"Hello?" she says. Her voice, a noise she hadn't expected, sounds far away.

"Oh, hello. Sorry to bother you on a Sunday — is Graham Parnell there, please?" A woman. Older. Well-spoken.

"I'm sorry," she tells the caller, "he's just popped out. Can I get him to ring you back?"

"If you wouldn't mind . . . it's Valerie Lamb — he'll know who I am, but I'll be out of the office for the rest of the day, so he'll need my mobile."

"Just let me find a pen. Sorry . . . bear with me," Rachel cuts in, her nails scrabbling over the cluttered surfaces within reach. Then, seeing the handle to a compartment in the cabinet the telephone lives on, yanks it open with an urgent outstretched palm. "Here you go," she exhales her relief, her hand landing on a spiral bound pad and, burrowing deeper, a lidless felt-tip pen. "Okay. Valerie?" Rachel repeats back the name, making the V before the pen runs out.

"Yes, that's right, Valerie Lamb, from The Pines — it's regarding his mother."

"His *mother?* Oh dear." Rachel presses the dried-out nib to her tongue to liven it up.

"No, no, there's nothing to worry about," the woman assures. "Just ask him to give me a ring when he's got a moment." And she gives her number to Rachel.

"No problem, I'll pass your message on soon as he comes back."

"Thank you, dear."

"Goodbye."

Rachel returns the handset to its charger and, ripping the sheet off the spiral spine, sends confetti-like pieces spinning to the floor. She shoves the pad and pen back inside the mouth of the drawer, but before closing it sees, partially buried beneath bank statements, rubber bands, boxes of paracetamol — a substantial glossy brochure, its cover a photograph of a synthetic blue sky and wide yellow beach. She pulls it free, registers: The Pines Residential Care Home. Thinks: This is the place the woman she just spoke to was ringing from — where his mother is. Reads: Knightstone Road, Westburn-on-Sea, North Somerset.

Westburn-on-Sea. *Westburn-on-Sea?* Rachel goes cold. Graham said he'd never been to Westburn, but surely if his mother's there, he must have. This is her first thought as she shoves the brochure away. Why lie about something like that, it makes no sense — what else has he lied about? With an uneasy feeling clawing deep in her stomach, Rachel hurls these questions around as she gathers her belongings together. Hurriedly checking nothing has been left in his bathroom, his bedroom, stopping only briefly, to pen him a line with the dodgy felt-tip. Citing her dog, her words beginning their lives as bold and direct but fading to nothing by the withered nib, wobble through her tears. Barely legible, she doesn't care, ripping it out and placing it beside the message from Valerie Lamb. Rachel just wants to get out of there, she doesn't want to see him, doesn't want to listen to any more of his lies. Needing to be on her own to think about what all this means, she hurries down the stairs and is out on the street, sprinting for her car in seconds.

CHAPTER
SEVENTY

Mrs Pepper's secret comes from a time long before her husband Stan. A time when she was only a child herself. She named him in the few minutes she was permitted to hold him. Knowing, before they ripped him from her arms, the insurmountable grief she was feeling would never leave her. Even now, her hand swimming out to her tummy from time to time as she sits and drinks her coffee, she is imagining him, thinking of him — it is as if the umbilical cord was never severed.

At first sight Mrs Pepper looks to be the cheeriest person. Those who drift in and out of the café she likes to stop in at on her way home think so. Nodding their hellos as she sits contentedly in a corner, a cup of frothy coffee at her elbow, a copy of the *Evening Standard* spread out in her lap. Just an ordinary woman. Stout, in her duffle coat, sensible shoes and raspberry felt hat. Except if anyone was to take the time to examine her more closely, there is something in the bulk of that grey coat, those plain lace-up brogues and little hat — far too jolly in colour — that give her the air of a woman who has made her mind up to run away. That at any moment she could stand up, collect a small case waiting at her ankles and walk out into the darkening evening, never to be seen again. And, as if this wasn't enough, there is the way she blushes whenever the waiter comes near. As if he is privy to her dreadful secret, the one she cannot forgive herself for.

The two big windows at the front of the café in Muswell Hill's Grand Avenue Park, face the lake. Customers, who sip their way through the variety of hot and cold beverages, sampling fresh cream cakes from the refrigerated counter, can watch the swans and moorhens and, in summertime, the occasional boat, floating up and down past the fringe of island planted with trees. The side windows look across another part of the park and down below to a flower stall. The top of the striped awning is visible from here, the frills of bright blooms spilling out of their buckets, where along with the regular abundance of fresh flowers they sell plants in boxes, clusters of wet gleaming rubber plants, miniature conifers and perky green palms in jars. The old men who flog them scuttle about like crabs, wrapping and calling, bending and arranging, in old-fashioned aprons that scrape the ground like the crinoline of Edwardian ladies. Really, Mrs Pepper often thought, there was no need to go anywhere else; it was all happening around her. Even down to the velvet curtain, with its dark tasselled fringe hanging over the counter in the café, giving the feeling everything had been arranged on purpose to form a pattern. The teapots with their misshapen lids, the bowls of sugar with crystallised clumps formed by the wet spoons of others, the little milk-jugs, the well-thumbed newspapers

348

in their wooden stand, the crinkly paper lampshades on the tables. Mrs Pepper was someone who noticed everything, and fancied all she surveyed was part of some grand still-life she was bound to draw. So different from the home she kept like a new pin, with everything in its place, it was good for her to come here; here was somewhere that made room for the living.

Every day is much the same for Mrs Pepper. She rises before it is light, makes Stan his breakfast of porridge and tea and sees him off to work with a packed-lunch wrapped in clingfilm. Prior to leaving the house herself, she will tidy its rooms and put the washing on. Then, slipping her arms into her coat, she will head off to one of her many cleaning jobs. It was in the evenings, on her way to the tube, finished up at Mrs D'Villez's along Grand Avenue, that she usually called in at the café. Nothing particularly odd about that. Except those in the business of noticing will see how there are things that aren't quite right about this particular evening. That something about her is different. For a start, she has chosen a window seat close to the front of the shop. Secondly, she has styled her hair, made-up her eyes and is wearing her best garnet-coloured court shoes. Thirdly, it is odd the way her hand repeatedly pats the pocket of her duffle coat, wanting the reassurance that whatever is in there is still safe.

CHAPTER
SEVENTY-ONE

There's a terrible moment when I think they may be on to me.

I'm parked just down from the Lamb and Flag, watching the stragglers in my driving mirror. I've not been along this stretch for a while, deliberately staying away from my usual haunts, what with the fuss after the last one I did.

Well, anyway, there's this tap at my window and turning, I see the face of a copper in Day-Glo close to mine on the other side of the glass. So close I see the web of capillaries across his eyeballs. It makes me jump out of my skin. He taps again and I drop the window down.

"Anything the matter, officer?" I'm clever, I make sure I'm the first to speak. "Only I just pulled over to make a phone call." And I hold up my mobile to demonstrate, watch his expression shift from: "Got you" to "yeah, okay, that sounds plausible".

"Well, if you could move along as soon as you're done," he says. "There's no parking along here tonight, we're keeping the roads clear."

"Of course, officer." I nod my agreement. "No problem."

CHAPTER
SEVENTY-TWO

Returning home from a walk, Rachel has an urge to pick up the phone and ring her mother. It's the same feeling she had when she moved to Northampton to live with Spencer. Those first nights away from home aged nineteen. But in the same way she did then, she resists now, recognising it to be nothing more than a tapering moment, girdled in gold like a sun-lit cloud that threatens to slide her back inside the rooms of coffee smells, menthol cigarettes and the summer sounds of cricket commentary on the television. What would happen if she took her mother into her confidence — shared her fears about Graham, the truth about how she lost Spencer? How he came home from work to find a hand-sized bruise on Laura's face that she put there.

Remembering this makes her think it was a mistake to go back to Muswell Hill. Maybe not the first time, immediately after her abduction — that was only ever going to be temporary — but certainly the second, seven years later when Spencer threw her out. What she should have done is spread her wings, moved right away, because once back there, with her father so ill, she found she didn't have the spirit to leave. It was

Spencer's fault. His plan to rent out his Northampton home while taking a sabbatical at the university in Maine. Coming out of the blue, as he said it did, it gave her no time to find an alternative. Rachel often thinks about the unfairness of it, how she should never have allowed him to treat her that way. But at the time, as with so much else, she didn't have the strength to fight. What they had, she's able to admit to herself, regardless of Laura, hadn't been worth battling for. "Don't worry, I'm going," she told him, before heading upstairs to sling her belongings into a single suitcase. "I know where I'm not wanted."

Frightening to think where she would have ended up if her parents hadn't taken her in. If Mrs Pepper hadn't been around to confide in she could easily have been carted off to some psychiatric hospital. Spent what remained of her days rotting away, for all Spencer cared. She doesn't remember him showing the least interest in where she ended up, just informed her coldly of his intention to stow the stuff he wasn't able to take to America in storage and that if she happened to pull herself together and found her own place to live, then she was welcome to it. Otherwise, he stayed silent. Carrying her case to the car, on the drive to the station — it made her feel like a naughty child. The last time she felt him touch her was when he leant across to open the passenger door. No doubt she had been taking too long. Tooted at by the car behind for parking in a no-wait zone, he virtually pushed her out on to the pavement. She saw his pale, oval face, unreadable as always, through the rain-spattered windscreen as he

352

drove away. It was the last time she saw him, Spencer making it a condition of their divorce that she didn't contact him. Although Rachel suspects he keeps in touch with her mother. That he sends photographs of Laura. And if her father had been in any fit state, he'd have told her of any such correspondence, but by the time she returned to number seventy-seven the second time, he could barely sit up or feed himself.

She doesn't know if her mother was ever given the full story. If Spencer filled her in on his wife's Moment of Madness, as he liked to term it. He promised he wouldn't, in the same way he promised to keep it out of his divorce petition if she held up her side of the bargain by not kicking up a storm and allowing him full custody of Laura. "After all," he told her in that cool, scientific way he delivered bad news. "You really don't want your private life raked through again, do you? You know how much you hated it the last time." Cruel of him to say so, but he was right; the threat had been enough to keep her mouth shut, to accept Laura was to go with him. To accept that she was probably never going to see her child again. And when it all got too much, when she felt herself buckling under the grief, she took care to remind herself of what she had so stupidly armed him with. Whenever her brain would cloud over with fantastical thoughts of mounting a legal protest, she would stop. Remind herself how easily he could go to the police with what she did, press charges, even now.

"Laura'll have a far better life with her father. I mean, look at me." Back in London, the bald statement had stopped her mother fussing around her state-of-the-art kitchen and made her focus on Rachel properly. "I'm a mess, Mum. How can I give her what she needs?" Her mother sat across the pine rectangular table. Silent, staring, stunned. Smoking her way through a packet of cigarettes and sliding a series of jolly-glazed mugs of strong black coffee into her daughter's shaking hands.

Rachel would have far rather had a cuddle. Her need to be pressed close, to feel the warmth of another human being made her ache. She would have been able to cry then, and crying would have released so much. But her mother didn't do touching. Demonstrative love, when she digs through what made up her childhood, didn't feature any more than the exhibiting of raw emotion. Coffee and expended cigarette smoke was all there was, so it needed to be enough. Puzzling to Rachel though, the lack of questions, because along with the habitual smacks dished out in that house, there were always questions. Strange then, following the frankness of her statement, how there was no further discussion. Not even about her reasons to move back home for an indefinite time. Her mother barely blinked when she turned up on the doorstep in a state not unlike the one she had found her in seven years before. She silently directed Rachel up to her old room, giving measured instructions to air the bed and bleed the radiator. Rachel's only conclusion was that her mother had prior warning; that she was in cahoots with Spencer all along.

So no, she concludes, let's not kid ourselves. She and her mother were never friends; and there's nothing Rachel can do to change that now. So instead of telephoning, she washes every part of her house. Kneels on the flagstone floor, cold through the legs of her jeans, scrubbing until her hands are red and sore. She dusts and cleans the window sills, the windows. Clears her dark hair from the plughole. Polishes the taps. Puts bleach down the toilet, swills it around with the brush. Thinks: I should have seen this coming. And sees Graham as she has come to know him over these past few weeks, standing in the open doorway of his gallery, a watery sun reflecting off his shiny black hair. Ending his telephone calls with, "Good to hear from you; speak again soon." Tugging out his bottom lip whenever he concentrates, and singing all the time.

No, she hadn't believed him, not quite. Chatting to her like that the first time in the gallery, talking of love when he hardly knew her. But why lie — about something so small? People only lie when they have something to hide, she should know. None of it made sense.

Sparked by updated information on the radio regarding Pauline Keene, the third woman to be killed, Rachel decides to drive to Westburn the following morning and calls Tracy, asking her to come and see to the dog.

She can almost see it — The Pines Care Home . . . the length of promenade . . . the sapphire sash of sea. The town won't have changed much, it shouldn't be

355

difficult to find, she thinks, pressing a hand to the sick feeling she has in her stomach about Graham.

Later that evening, needing milk from her freezer and thinking about the journey to Somerset tomorrow, Rachel rushes outside into the dark, down her slippery stone steps and headlong into a body.

Idris blocks her way. The spooky whites of his eyes caught in the flash of her torchlight.

She screams, girdling his circumference, nearly falling. "What the hell are you doing skulking around, scaring me half to death?"

"See that jeep's here again," he wheezes.

"What?" her voice puncturing a hole through the tyre-black night that hangs between them, thick as rubber. "What are you on about?"

"That black jeep." Idris thrusts a heavy arm out through the darkness to indicate the lane. "It's always parked there."

Rachel is as startled by Idris as she is by the unknown threat from elsewhere. Although she hasn't seen the vehicle for herself it doesn't make it any less troubling. "Look, I don't know what the hell you're on about," she shouts.

"Not from round here though, is it? Way too posh. What is it, some Japanese thing? Dead expensive them are. Must be loaded, your admirer."

"*My admirer?*" Rachel shouts. "Look, will you please just clear off my property." She doesn't care what she sounds like — screeching banshee, madwoman: descriptions Spencer often used — this man frightens her. His size, his potential, it strikes her again how he could snuff her out, easily as a candle, if he chose.

"Sorry missus," Idris, unmoved, pumping puffs of white breath into the cold air. "Was only looking out for you — thought you'd like to know you've got some bloke hanging about."

"What? There's someone inside it?" Rachel shrieks.

"Oh, yeah — sitting in it now, he is." Idris pushes a grin to her through the dark.

"How d'you know it's got anything to do with me? They could be here to meet anyone." Her mind galloping: *get inside, get inside. Ring Tracy.* "Anyway, whoever it is, it's got bugger-all to do with you." She doesn't wait for Idris to leave. Milk for tomorrow's breakfast abandoned, she dives up her deep stone steps, throws herself inside and bolts the door.

"What, it's there again? Look, don't worry, I'll send Hywel over." No one in at Cwm Glas, Tracy, up to her elbows in the lambing shed, answers her mobile. Calm and measured through the loud, distressed bleating of birthing ewes. "Hang tight now; don't go out."

By the time Hywel arrives the vehicle has gone and Rachel feels silly for bothering them.

"I suppose it could be Graham," she concedes when all other logical likelihoods have been negated. Sounding unsure, she knows she needs to give Hywel something, keen as he is to return to his flock. "Bit weird though, isn't it? I mean, I can't imagine him driving all the way out here just to sit in his car; he'd come and see me, surely?"

"Perhaps you've got another admirer." Hywel's mind is back with his lambs.

A pause. Rachel staring down at her thumbs; looks perturbed. "What if it wasn't anything to do with me," she says quietly. "What if whoever it is comes to see someone else?"

"Someone else?" He gives a hoot of a laugh, wiping his hands down his overalls. "Like who then?"

"I don't know?" Rachel, still unwilling to make eye contact. "Maybe it's a friend of Tracy's?"

"Friend of Tracy's . . . *friend of Tracy's* — what friend of Tracy's?"

"Look," she says stepping away from him. "I've probably said too much already."

"Said too much? You haven't *said* anything." Hywel, his face furrowed in uneasy suspicion, gawps at her. "What are you trying to say?"

"Oh, I don't know," she shows him the flat of her palm. "Look, like I said — I've said too much already. You should be talking to your wife about this — really, it's nothing to do with me."

She lifts her eyes to Hywel's, sees his expression etched in distrust: a distrust that is directed squarely at her. It makes her feel uncomfortable; it makes her wish she hadn't bothered trying to help him see what a fool his wife is making of him.

CHAPTER
SEVENTY-THREE

With his breakfast of marmalade on toast going rubbery on a plate Dai stares at his television, absorbed by the images of Westburn's rundown seafront and depressed town centre. "The police have released further information regarding the latest victim, Pauline Keene ... an eighteen-year-old hairdresser from London ..." A chilly-looking BBC reporter, buttoned to the chin, is needing to shout over the crowd of protestors who have gathered in front of the police station demanding retribution with placards.

What a place. Those poor girls. Their three dead faces hogging the screen. The red-nosed reporter is eventually joined by Chief Superintendent Colin Bradley of Avon and Somerset Constabulary. A dark-eyed, prematurely greying man, donning full dress uniform. Not unlike that actor George Clooney, Dai thinks, except this poor bugger sports a nasty-looking set of hammocks under his eyes and doesn't look like he's slept in weeks.

"We're appealing again," the Chief Superintendent's West Country burr, forceful above the jeering catcalls of demonstrators, "for the driver of a dark blue haulage truck, seen in the area the night Pauline Keene went missing, to come forward immediately in order to help police with their enquiries. Information we've received suggests the number plate may contain the letters E and J. It is really important we trace the driver. If anyone is able to give any assistance on this matter it would help us . . ."

"What? What? Dark blue?" Dai, jumping to his feet, his untouched breakfast flying to the carpet. "E and J? E and J? I don't bloody believe this — that's Idris' number, that is." Idris Tudor, travelling off in his low-loader, bragging up his haulage trips; the string of women he's got on the go down Somerset way. "Don't tell me Denzil was right all along . . . oh, crikey, I should have gone to the police . . . if this is you — you'll bloody pay for it this time. And for what you did to Beth and me — you bastard."

Snatching up his anorak and car keys, Dai doesn't turn off his television or rescue his meagre meal that lies face down on his living room floor. Stopping only fleetingly to lock his door, push his arms into the sleeves of his coat, he is fired up and behind the wheel of his silver Fiat Uno in seconds. His foot pressed to the floor, wishing he'd listened to Elsie and upgraded to a newer, more powerful motor when he had the chance.

CHAPTER
SEVENTY-FOUR

On her two-hour drive to Westburn Rachel thinks of Laura. How anxieties over cot death and asphyxiation dwindled with her emergence from infanthood to toddler and were replaced by other troubles. Troubles that came when Laura began asserting herself, recognising her facility for independent thought and that life offered choices. Her choice being her father. Wailing and shoving her mother away with her toddler fists, rebuffing her attentions, her cuddles, preferring her father's love over her mother's every time. It was a blossoming belligerence Rachel found she was ill-equipped to deal with. Powerless to rationalise the rejection, believing it to be unreasonable and asking what Spencer had done to deserve such favouritism. He wasn't the one who carried her for nine months, endured the pain of labour and turned his life inside out. What had she done that was so wrong? Why hadn't she been enough for Laura? Other people's children didn't behave like this.

It wasn't long before Rachel's overriding need to be loved curdled into a clotted resentment. Never good at dealing with rejection, it gnawed at her insides, clouding the more reasonable suggestions made by the experienced mums at the Bonding with Baby sessions down at the community centre. How it was nothing more than a phase her daughter was going through and, given time, something Laura would grow out of. It was "what children did," they chimed, sensing her distress, her need for reassurance. "They do it to test you."

Then a day, confined by the weather, with Rachel trying to coax Laura to the lunch table. Her favourite meal of fish fingers and peas cooling on a Peter Rabbit plate. "I want Daddy." That was how it started. The request, especially perverse, as it was a weekday and *Daddy* was in his laboratory. Laura's distress magnified with the rapidity of a bush fire and within minutes mutated into a full-blown screaming fit. Rachel, fearing neighbours, was at a loss to know what to do. With clenched jaw, she shadowed her tottering child from room to room. "I hate you. I hate you. You're not my mummy. I hate you."

Laura's eyes were as big as saucers in the seconds after Rachel's hand swung out. Striking her hard across the cheek and making her topple over. A piteous sight, replaying it pricks at her eyes. Not that Laura cried, she was strangely silent. So silent in fact, Rachel could have imagined she hadn't struck her at all. Except for that burgeoning mark. The falcate loop cut just under her eye, where her engagement ring collided with Laura's flushed little face.

Rachel isn't sure why she's thinking about this today. Her eyes travelling the grey tusk of unmarked road, twisting and turning and flanked by sodden verges, where the only colour in the dreary winter undergrowth comes from the spread of the leather-leafed ivy. She slides down her window for a second or two and tries to dump the memory in the way she would an expended apple core, wanting to concentrate her mind on the day ahead, the questions she wants clarifying. Then, registering the sky, brightening and thinning the further south then west she travels, it in turn begins to lift her mood.

Her journey, leaving before it was properly light, has been straightforward enough to Newport, but since the Severn Bridge and hitting the M5, there's been snarl up after snarl up. She doesn't recognise the approach into Westburn with so much of the surrounding countryside developed, she only realises she's arrived by reading the sign. With the fields of new red-bricked housing estates, the out-of-town shopping centres, a sprawling drive-thru McDonald's, there isn't a blade of grass in sight. To Rachel, the place has become just another depressing glut of concrete. Indistinguishable from so many of the towns she's driven through today. Until she sees the sea. And gasps her amazement. The tide is in and its belt of blue twinkles under a dazzling February sun — the glare through her windscreen temporarily blinding her. The promenade is devoid of the jolly candy-stripe of deckchairs she remembers from trips with her father, the bucket and spade brigade and the assortment of vans dispensing Mr Whippy cornets or capricious configurations of burgers. Instead it is busy

363

with walkers. Dog walkers. Striding out through the wind with gritted teeth.

Royal Parade, the map in her mind tells her, becomes Knightstone Road and means The Pines Residential Care Home should be up on the right. And it is. Seeing its weather-bleached sign, she slows to indicate, pulling down into a sloping black square of tarmac, divided up into stark yellow boxes. Bay fronted, The Pines' stucco-clad façade is a flaking hyacinth-blue and stands out a mile from the concrete Sixties apartment blocks it sits within. High-sided buildings, more akin to the tenement blocks of East London than a seaside resort. Except that, devoid of graffiti, each with a plant-filled balcony overlooking the Bristol Channel, they don't look half bad. All The Pines seems to offer its residents by way of a room with a view is an immense Victorian-looking conservatory, perspiring like a greenhouse beyond its great glass casements.

She carries this feeling of heat with her as she steps into the spacious foyer. Beyond the sucking sound of the automatic doors the atmosphere is as humid as an indoor swimming pool. Rachel immediately peels herself out of her coat and, waiting for the receptionist to finish her telephone call, fiddles with the collar of her blouse, the belt of her trousers, acutely uncomfortable beneath the synthetic fabric of her clothes.

A clunk as the telephone receiver is replaced and the receptionist looks up, smiling.

"Can I help at all?"

"I was wondering," Rachel begins, "if it would be possible to see Mrs Parnell? I'm sorry, I haven't made

364

an appointment or anything — I just happened to be in the —"

"April?" the chubby youngster asks. "April Parnell, room fifteen?"

A question or fact? This accent is hard to interpret.

No request for ID, no reason needed to validate her visit. Rachel, shown where to sign her name in the visitor's book, is doing so as a fat arm shoots out with instructions to take a left into the corridor, and April Parnell is just before the Day Room.

Self-conscious in clipping heels, Rachel walks away. Unpicking the name as she goes, rootling it out for clues on Graham. *April*. She turns it over, checking for booby traps or explosives hidden down between the letters. *April*. A time of quickening skies and sudden showers, she imagines half-blown daffodils in sharp yellow sunshine bobbing along the verges of her mind. Deciding anyone given such a name will be harmless enough.

She reaches the door marked fifteen in seconds, but hearing voices in an adjacent room prompts her to lean around its doorframe to investigate. Quickly wishing she hadn't. What she finds is a depressingly barren and uncomfortable-looking space, as harshly lit as an operating theatre. Linoleum-floored, its bare walls are lined with high-backed chairs that have been packed tightly together and positioned around its perimeter. Beyond it, the glass roof and walls of the sweating conservatory she saw from outside. *Uch*, she judders, inhaling school-dinner smells that, churned through with the fierce acridity of urine, make her clamp a hand over her mouth.

Rachel, alerted by the voice of a care worker, sees the big, broad back of a woman who, singing along to some tune carried in her head, barges authoritatively around her charges. The face is hard, a make-up-laden mask, pale as the moon. Outmoded in Union Jack Doc Martens, her PVC-shiny black bondage trousers, decorated over with D-rings and zips, straps and pockets, are incongruous not only with her white nylon tunic but with the dreary setting she moves within. Getting a bit long in the tooth to be going about looking like that, aren't you? Rachel thinks. Siouxsie Sioux on steroids, she stifles a laugh with her fist as she clocks the nose ring along with the head full of backcombed, jet-black spiky hair — must be knocking on fifty at least. Intrigued by this ghoulishly comic character, she watches her squat down beside a clutch of residents. Still singing — what, she can't quite hear — Rachel sees the carer grab an elderly shin and with impatient hands forces a foot into its Velcro-fastened slipper. Mute and toothless, too weak to protest, the inmates sit open mouthed, the joints of their over-large fingers, knobbly branches of trees, cupping the dribble-sticky arms of chairs as if each were journeying the rollercoaster rides of their youth.

Stepping away to knock on number fifteen, Rachel feels the flimsy plywood shift under her knuckles, its sharp slice of metal for a handle. *Please don't let me end up in a place like this.* A small noise from inside and Rachel opens the door.

Hot. The darkened interior comes as a shock. Her face flushing, she presses the back of her hand to her cheek and breathes in the chemical odour of hospitals along with something else, from nature, like lavender.

"Be a poppet," says a voice from the gloom as she makes her mind up about the smell. "Open the curtains for me, let the sun in."

Rachel steps across carpet, her legs brushing the turned-back covers on a single bed. She pulls the curtains aside, but it doesn't make much difference. Despite the clear bright day going on outside, there isn't much light to be had. Any sun is obscured. A courtyard crammed with unkempt laurel and frowzy trees, their leafless branches strung out with Tesco bags and crisp wrappers. Her eyes follow a lattice of drain pipes and guttering that show cracks that look deep enough to sink her fingers into. There is no view. Unless a jumbled graveyard of wheelie bins and haphazard diagonals of roof tiles is your thing.

"That's better," the voice again. "I can see you now."

Can you? Rachel thinks, looking at April Parnell who is immaculate in pleated skirt, cream blouse and navy cardigan. A mother-of-pearl brooch is pinned at her neck and sheepskin slippers neat against the footrest of the wheelchair.

"Mrs Parnell." Rachel tests the name against the muted lighting. "My name's Rachel, I'm —" and before she can say more, the woman interrupts her.

"Rachel . . . oh, my dear, dear girl." April's black eyes, shiny and round, remind her of the toy fox her father gave her when she was small. "Have you come to see me for my birthday?"

Rachel takes a breath, presses a hand to her mouth. "Oh, sorry — no ... I didn't realise it was your birthday. If I had, I'd have brought you something. Oh, I feel bad now."

"Don't be silly," April assures her, "it's just lovely to meet you at last — that's enough of a present for me. Graham's told me so much about you — sit, please." An arthritic bow of a finger wags at the only chair. "Sit down, sweetheart, tell me about yourself."

Rachel looks at her, at what is left of her startling white hair. An angelic face, surprisingly young-looking in comparison to the frailty of her body.

"I'd like to offer you a tea, if they'd let me have a kettle in here — shall I call for one? The girls, they're pretty good."

"Please, don't worry on my account," Rachel says, turning her head to the woman's singsong lilt, warming herself in it as she twists her hands in her lap, finding and worrying the ridges of her starfish scar. "It's just nice to ... finally meet you."

"Well, thank you, dear. It's nice to meet you too — and what a pretty girl you are, I can see why my Graham's so taken with you."

Rachel can't think of anything to say. She isn't entirely sure why she's here. What did she hope to find, travelling all this way like she has, on a whim? Ridiculous, expecting this poor old biddy to reassure her about a man she thinks she loves, but now feels she hardly knows. She doubts the two of them are close, why shove her in here, in a town so far away from where he is? A town he lied about having any knowledge of.

"How was your journey, dear?" Mrs Parnell, the diaphanous skin of her hands chafing in the paper-dry atmosphere.

Rachel tells her. About her drive through the countryside, how she's never known such rain. Of her move from London, why she chose to live in Wales, how happy she is in her lovely new home. About Cadno.

"Cadno ..." April Parnell, her mind turning the word over. "Don't tell me ... don't tell me — that means fox."

"Yes," Rachel, surprised. "You speak Welsh?"

"Only a little now, as a child I was bilingual, like so many little ones are — but if you don't use it, you lose it." She giggles, her mouth bunching up in an O. "Lovely name for a dog, what sort is he?"

"Border Collie."

"The best." Mrs Parnell claps her hands, an animated seated-figure in the gloom. "Brilliant with sheep. My father had them, before he sold the farm." And she stares off into the distance, her memories leading her elsewhere.

Rachel smiles, keeping the joke to herself and doesn't fill Mrs Parnell in on Cadno's shortcomings so far as his sheep-herding skills go. Leaving her host for a moment, she lets her eyes travel the room. Notices how, aside from the bedside table with its small crop of framed photographs, there is only a bed, a small wardrobe, a hand basin with mirror and a couple of empty shelves. No pictures, no books. Dismal really, the woman has hardly any belongings and she must be well into her seventies. Is this all she has to show for her life?

"Tell me how you and Graham met," the woman, whose hair is like a half-blown dandelion, asks.

Rachel leaves her answer to hover in the over-warm room, focuses on how it was, that first time in the gallery. "I bought a painting from him. A landscape of where I live." The image it gives makes her smile, forgetting for a moment the trouble clouding her horizon. The lie he told that has brought her here.

"Oh, lovely, the countryside," Mrs Parnell says. "Although I was surprised Graham was happy to settle so far in-land. He always loved the sea. Said the sound of it was soothing, companionable."

"He took me to the seaside recently; he did seem to love it," Rachel tells her.

"So, you met at the gallery then," April Parnell clarifies. "A good head for business, my boy. The spit of his father, he gets none of his talent from me. His father was a musician you know, did Graham say? Graham's the same. Lovely voice — have you heard him sing? He's always singing. Anyway, his father was ever so talented. And handsome — * oooof*, was he handsome." She gives the words slowly, sucking back her breath, and Rachel imagines she is thinking of her long-dead husband. "Yes, like two peas in a pod, him and Graham — it broke our hearts when he left us, but it was Graham who suffered the most. If I'm honest, I don't think he's ever recovered from the shock."

370

"Terrible." Rachel shakes her head, pushing sympathy into the old woman's eyes. "And for you to be widowed so young."

"*Widowed?*" April jolts upright in her wheelchair, choking on a laugh. "Whoever told you that? Oh no, no, dear, he didn't *die* — he abandoned us. Graham ten. Eleanor eight. Cleared out one night, not so much as a goodbye — left us good as destitute."

"Crikey, that's awful." Rachel leans forward; she doesn't want to miss a thing.

"We had a chippie along the front here, in Westburn. Oooh, years ago now. Early eighties. Right little gold mine it was. My father's business, he had real nous my Da — bought it as a going concern when he and Mam sold the farm. We took it over when they retired . . . me and . . . my husband . . . *funny*," Mrs Parnell, fetches up another strangled laugh, "even after all these years, I still can't bring myself to say his name. Well, anyway, he was nicking from the till. Sucking the life out of the shop, there was nothing left by the time he cleared off. Pocket money, he called it, for his nights out playing the clubs. And I turned a blind eye, you know, what with us having a family, a lovely home. But I was a fool. A stupid, stupid fool."

"Was there someone else?" Rachel, at a loss what to say, her mind picking over what Graham did and didn't tell her. *The spit of his father.* April's words spin like a merry-go-round, the sensation making Rachel feel queasy. Graham has duped her, just like his father did his mother.

371

"*Someone else?* Oh, yes, there was someone else all right — and the way he was getting through money, bleeding us dry, I should have guessed." Rachel's expression is one of bewilderment as she watches April Parnell rummage around in her history, looking for how best to express what she seems so desperate to share. "A different one every night of the week," she says at last. "Working his way round the clubs, sleeping with girls half his age. Probably lock you up for it now." Rachel, astonished at the woman's candour, her vehemence, sees her judder and pull a face from her wheelchair parked up in the shadows. "And what it did to Graham, I can't tell you." Mrs Parnell makes a whooshing sound as she draws down air. "The way he reacted, it frightened me; he was so eaten up, still is, by the shame of it. Honestly, dear, I swear, if he'd been just that little bit older, he'd have killed him."

Back in the ice-bright sunshine, under a swirl of squabbling seagulls, Rachel descends the steps of the care home and makes for her car. Her distress clearly visible, she walks head down, her hands, rapid and agitated, repeatedly pushing away non-existent strands of hair from her eyes. Alarmed by what is unravelling in her head, she is at a loss to know what to do with it all. Should she go to the police — tell them about Graham's disproportionate reaction when he saw those girls in Llandafen and his lie about knowing Westburn? Could what his mother's just revealed about his father be some perverse motive? She needs to do something. Supposing it is him parked up on her verge at night and he suspects she is on to him — he could come after her next.

Rachel doesn't see the big black SUV parked up and facing the automatic doors of The Pine's glass entrance. The man in the driving seat staring out at her, his face inscrutable. The skin stretched taut across the contours of his knuckles, choking the life out of his steering wheel.

CHAPTER
SEVENTY-FIVE

The things Jennifer found in Donald's room before Christmas have vanished. She is adamant, scrabbling around in a blind panic, that she put the thirty or so Polaroids in a drawer of her desk, tucked in behind Spencer's letters for safekeeping.

Something else that seems to have vanished is her cleaner. She hasn't seen Mrs Pepper for days. She's been ringing the only number she has for her, but with no answer. It doesn't take a genius to work out what's happened, and putting two and two together somehow makes Jennifer feel strangely calm. Perhaps it is better to be betrayed by the hired help, someone claiming to be a family friend. But why — for money? Because it is doubtful the woman has gone to the police with what has come to light. Selling her discovery to the newspapers would ensure immediate impact and a fat reward.

But how awfully sordid and disappointing, Jennifer blinks at what she can see of her reflection in the glass of her study window. There she was, trundling along; crediting good old Mrs Pepper as someone of integrity. She certainly never had her down as a snoop. So why now, if this was her game all along? The woman could have sold out to reporters years ago. The vultures have been skulking in the wings for ages and would have happily paid a pretty penny for any tit-bit on the day-to-day goings on in the D'Villez household. Unfortunately, the interest in her family has never gone cold, those in the business of selling newspapers have been worrying away at this old carcass of a story for years. Still as much of a mystery now as it ever was, why John Blundell — wife-killer and rapist — didn't dispose of Sarah when he had the chance. Why he let her live to testify against him. It wouldn't take much to rekindle. The great British public would pay good money to read details of Blundell's Blonde Beauty, as the tabloids called her — her messy divorce, the reason she lost custody of her only child. That scoop alone would have been enough to sell a few thousand extra rags. Never mind the weirdness of her subsequent domestic set up. Forced to live back home with her parents, single, friendless, incapable of holding down a job and too afraid to go out. They could have cooked up something really juicy with that, especially with the spicy details Mrs Pepper's been privy to.

Jennifer knows that whatever has happened to the Polaroids, there is little she can do about it. Sarah's stupid fault, she should have destroyed them when she had the chance. What the hell was she keeping them for? Some warped souvenir? But Jennifer knows that Sarah would never have got rid of them, the nature of those images would have been something to have satisfied her vanity and her filthy ways. All Jennifer can be sure of is she won't have long to wait for news, she'll no doubt be reading about it before the week is out. Her family's reputation dragged through the mire again. She sighs — nothing new there. After all, it was how she learnt about the alleged depravity her daughter had been subjected to during her captivity. Sarah being unwilling to tell her face to face. Jennifer supposes she should be grateful that at least her daughter thought enough of her not to do that. What is a wonder is how Mrs Pepper never landed on the prints before. But she supposes Donald barely set foot out of his room since retirement and certainly not during his years of illness, the woman would have needed to clean while he was in there. Sarah was the only one permitted unfettered access. Trusted, when his hands no longer worked, to take his prized records out of their paper sleeves, slip them on to the turntable and set them playing. To read to him when he could no longer focus on the printed word. Pour out his coffee and feed him ginger nuts she would soften in her black Earl Grey. It's painful to think her husband could have been helping their daughter secrete vital evidence, and although she can't quite believe he would do such a thing, it does explain his illness — the strain must have triggered his attacks. Not that Jennifer could have done anything, the goings on in that room had nothing to do with her. A fact Donald made perfectly clear, insisting his entitlement to a space of his own and, agreeing, she stayed away.

The discovery of these happy snaps may have answered many of Jennifer's unresolved questions, suspecting from the beginning that things were never as they seemed. But there is one question remaining —

who really killed John Blundell's wife? A vision of Sarah finds her and her body jolts. As shocking now as it was then, her daughter on that warm September day: hysterical, shrieking; the dark shadows of her hammering fists raining down on the stained-glass panel of the front door. How bloodied she was when Donald let her inside. Ragged swathes splashed over her scanty clothing and in the strands of her beautiful blonde hair, as she stood frozen and looking shocked on the hall rug they had to throw away afterwards.

Jennifer shudders. Reconsidering this image of Sarah she's been carrying around with her for years, she fears she may now have the answer.

CHAPTER
SEVENTY-SIX

They come for Idris just before dawn. Blue lights, along with the rain, pulse against the thick stone walls of his cottage. His first thoughts are of the cold and how strange the light is. Then he thinks of Beth. Sees her face, ghostly pale, floating feather-light at the bottom of his bed. As wispy and ethereal as she was the last time he saw her. They must have found whatever is left of her. That's what this is. After fifty years of searching they've found her body and come back for him. Wanting to enact justice on her last surviving relative.

The smallest of scuffles and Idris is out on the lane. Barely given time to dress, he hauls a pair of trousers over his long-johns along with his donkey jacket reeking of dead cat. They think it needs three of them to manoeuvre him into the police van. Stupid bastards. Can't they tell he hasn't the stomach for it? Not after all this time. He isn't a teenager any more. If they've found his sister then so be it, he'll answer their questions.

"Idris Geraint Tudor?"

He grunts confirmation.

"You are required to accompany us to the station, sir. A vehicle registration matching the description of your

... seen in Westburn-on-Sea ... in the vicinity of where Pauline Keene's body was found ... questions ... eliminate you from our enquiries ...."

Addled by sleep and snatching at only some of the words, he thinks they mean Beth. Who the fuck's Pauline? The fools have got it wrong. Only vaguely aware of a fist in his back, the radio of the young police officer crackling as he steers him towards the patrol vehicle. When Idris looks up into his face, he sees it's Neville Rees' boy — Neville who was always happy to share a dirty joke with him down the mart. Idris makes a noise, an indistinct, unintelligible sound. About to kick off? The other officers are quick to rally round, hands on truncheons, handcuffs, primed for trouble. Nothing. Idris' compliance and apathy comes as a disappointment. They'd been up for a fight, to slap an arrest warrant on him for assault, but there is none of the aggression the neighbour who put them on to him had promised.

Stripped of his personal effects, Idris is photographed and fingerprinted. DNA samples are taken from the insides of his mouth and a swab from the skin of his hands and arms. He is asked if he wants to telephone anyone, or if he has a solicitor he would like to call. He shakes his head to both of these and is told, in that case, a legal advisor will be found for him. Jostled from reception to a holding cell, he looks around him, remembering the place from when Beth went missing, when he and his brothers were brought in for questioning. The reception desk may look different, with its flat-screen computer, its bulletproof glass and the CCTV camera honed in on Llandafen Police Station's entrance. The grey and lemon linoleum floor tiles is an updated version of whatever was here fifty years ago, same goes for the seats, the posters, the vending machine. But it still smells the same. There's no mistaking it. That reek of fear, of perspiration and rubber, like his old school gym after PE sessions.

Idris has never been in a cell before. The door slams shut, a key turns and he's locked in. Things are strangely quiet. He expected the screams of other inmates like on the telly, but no one speaks and it's as if no one else is here. The smell of vomit, barely disguised by a floral disinfectant, stirs in his nostrils. He sees dried-on splashes of it up the metal legs of the single bed that, with its mattress no thicker than a slice of bread, groans under his weight like the wind does when it pushes against the stone walls of his cottage. He looks up at the only window, at the grey square of sky, too high to reach. No birds, no clouds, no movement. He looks down at his hands, pushes his sleeves up to his elbows for something to do. The light is so stark, the sprouting russet-colour of his arm hair looks alien, more pronounced and profuse than he ever realised. The grime-filled pores on the fleshiness of his palms become deep as craters the more he stares.

"Yeah, I know her." Idris, escorted hours later along the corridor and into a cream-walled interview room, pokes a grubby finger into the photographed face of Pauline Keene. It sounds as if he is bragging, indicating with relish, his familiarity with the third murdered girl. He ignores the faces of Issy Lake and Wendy Denny who are also spread out on the table. "So what?"

"Would you mind telling us how it was you knew her, Mr Tudor." Detective Inspector Nathan Watts. Easily a match for Idris. A man who keeps himself rugby-fit for his old club Felinfach RFC, should they find themselves a man down and in need of a prop forward for a Saturday game.

"She fancied it, I fancied it — it's not illegal." Idris leers at the attractive young Detective Sergeant Helen Monroe. Blonde and slim, his eyes amble over her, she is just his type.

"Having sex? No, you're right Mr Tudor, it isn't illegal." Detective Sergeant Monroe, sharp as a tack, top of her class, isn't about to let this creep crawl under her clothes. "But *murder* is."

"Murder?" The word of obvious interest, Idris tilts forward, slaps his fleshy arms down in front of him. He is as vast as her father's new John Deere baler, Monroe thinks; the suspect doing his best to disturb her with his smile. "And who am I supposed to have murdered then, *cariad?*" He jabs the three dead faces with such force, he makes the table shake. "I ain't murdered no one."

"So, what — you picked her up in your haulage lorry? Had sex with her in your cab, did you Mr Tudor?"

"If you say so."

"Oh, indeed, we do say so." Detective Inspector Watts shakes a three page print out supposedly issued by the pathology department under Idris' nose. "Care to explain how Pauline Keene's blood ended up on your seats, Mr Tudor?"

Idris shrugs. Drags his considerable hands back into his lap.

"For the tape, please, Mr Tudor?"

"Yeah, all right, she was in my cab."

"And?"

"And what?" Idris smirks through the creases of his face. "You want details, do you?" Directing his question to DS Monroe. "Get off on it, d'you, love?"

"Yes, please, Mr Tudor. Everything you remember, everything that was said."

"Well, we agreed on what she was gonna do for me, and then ... well ... she started going back on it, didn't she?"

"I don't know, Mr Tudor, did she?"

"Yeah, the bitch — stank like a fuckin' fish counter 'n all. Nah, she weren't even my type, to be honest."

Monroe and Watts take a second to look at each other. Working in close proximity for some months now, these two have teamed up on a fair amount of cases, but none quite as repugnant as this one. Normally, even the most depraved scumbags, when cornered, show some element of contrition. Even if it's only an act, in the hope it will lessen their sentence. But Idris Tudor — he doesn't show the tiniest smear of remorse. Frightening, the size of him, they've seen the pictures of these murdered girls, pictures that can't be printed in the papers or shown to their families. Nothing to him, their sparrow-thin bones, they'd snap easy as twigs in those hands. No more significant than garbage, their broken, bloodied bodies, dumped like rubbish. Beyond pitiful. These women were daughters, sisters, girlfriends.

"Why slice her up?" Detective Sergeant Monroe, glassy-eyed, slides a colour photograph Idris hasn't yet been shown, of Pauline Keene's mutilated body. Alarming, not that either of these well-seasoned police detectives show it, the way Idris doesn't flinch.

"I don't know nothing about that," he says, picking it up to look at more closely.

Detective Sergeant Helen Monroe watches him. The sicko is enjoying this.

"A neighbour of yours reckons you had a violent history with your sister," Detective Inspector Watts says, wanting to throw a spanner into the works. "That she disappeared when she was fourteen."

"Oh, let me guess." Idris, jerks back his neck, eyes wild, making the two police detectives recoil into their seats. "We're talking Dai fuckin' Jones here, are we? Am I right? Am I right?" Monroe and Watts say nothing, they are watching intently, willing their prime suspect to dig himself into an even bigger hole than the one he is already in. "I'm telling you, you don't wanna go taking notice of nothing that runt tells you — jealous, see. In love with her he was, the stupid bastard. But she was just like all the others, a silly little slag who couldn't keep her knickers on. Not my fault she preferred me and me brothers to him."

"Don't mind telling you, Guv." Out in the corridor, Detective Sergeant Monroe pulls a hand through her blonde hair, breathes in relief. "I'm glad to be out of there. What was all that about, with his sister? I'm telling you, I need a wash after listening to that."

"Aye, enough to make your skin crawl, isn't he? Going to have to fumigate the place 'n all." Detective Inspector Watts walks in the direction of the Control Room, long strides gobbling up the carpet, Monroe needs to jog along beside him to keep up. "Get Briggs to give that neighbour of his a ring, will you — what's his name again?"

"David Jones, Guv."

"Yeah, right, ask him to find out if he's any more to say about the sister, what he thinks might have happened to her. He says the police were involved when she went missing — a long time ago I know, but there'll still be files on it somewhere. I don't know ..." Detective Inspector Watts, reaching the door of his office, hesitates before opening it. "Just, the more we can throw at this bastard the better."

"Got him though, haven't we, Guv?" Monroe, hovering. "He's got no alibi, his lorry's crawling with Pauline Keene's DNA. It's pretty conclusive, isn't it? Got Forensics searching his house as we speak, with any luck they'll find the murder weapon, that knife he uses? Can't imagine he's washed it, or his clothes, going by the state of him. We can charge him then, surely?"

"Hang fire a bit, I want to let him sweat — we've had clearance, we can hold him for another twenty-four hours, and a further twelve if we need to. I want to do this properly, Helen, I want a signed, sealed, confession from the slippery bastard. Certainly something more tangible before I hand him over to Avon and Somerset."

"So you still don't think we should notify them — I thought we agreed we were getting them to send one of their guys over?"

"I do hope you're not suggesting I don't know how to do my job, *Sergeant*." Detective Inspector Watts takes care to stress her rank.

"No, course not, Guv, I just —"

"Look . . . I might be just flying a kite here." He softens towards her. "Just give it a few more hours, trust me. I think he's on the verge of it — I can smell it."

"Bad choice of words, Guv." Monroe pulls a face and Watts smiles into it. "But, yeah, I agree. Leave the fucker to stew."

"Your language, DS Monroe," Watts chuckles, everything back to normal. "It really is getting out of hand."

"Learnt it all from you, Guv," she laughs, heading off to the washrooms.

CHAPTER
SEVENTY-SEVEN

Out under a sharp shaft of sunlight with only a breath of wind for company, Dai, in thick pullover and wellingtons, is working his way along his vegetable beds. Preparing them for springtime planting, he pushes the rigid metal prongs of his gardening fork into the heavy water-logged soil and turns it out on to the surface. He is whistling. Some tune he can't remember the origins of, its words lost somewhere along the way, he stops to bask a little in the surprising warmth given by the late winter sun, wanting it to coat his back and lubricate his bones. A robin hops on to the rim of a nearby bucket, jittery on its needle-thin legs. It gives him the hard black bead of its eye and the shock of its plump red breast makes him smile.

"Hello, little fella," he says to it. "Been a long slog, hasn't it — but hang on in there, something better's just around the corner."

"*Coo-eee!*" Dilys Roberts. The robin flies off. Her high, singsong call, swinging through the evergreen ivy and the gaps in his hedge, jabs trowel-like between the furrows of his ribs. "You heard the news?"

Dai gives a lozenge of a sigh and turns to face her. "And what news might that be?"

386

"They've only gone and arrested Idris Tudor."

"Arrested? Who — the police?" Dai, seeing the way she rubs her hands together in glee, plays dumb. He's learnt from past experience that he'll harvest more from the village spokeswoman if he keeps his mouth shut.

"Aye," Dilys says, eyes glinting, enjoying the power this knowledge gives her. "Came for him first light, they did. Evans the Post told me; called it a *dawn raid.*"

"Crikey. What for?" Dai, raising eyebrows as he blows his nose on a tissue fished from his sleeve, is careful to keep up the act.

"Reckon he's something to do with them murders on the news."

"What — those women in Westburn?"

"Yeah, that's it. Someone saw his lorry parked up where one of them was dumped, apparently."

"And the police have linked him to it?"

"Got them *forensicks* up at his place now." Dilys nods vigorously. "Crawling with them it is, all in them white paper overalls, just like *CSI* off the telly."

"*What,* you've been up there to look?" Dai leans on the handle of his gardening fork, he can't help but smile.

"Soon as I heard — but they've got the place all thingied off, you know, with that tape stuff they use for crime scenes. You can't get near anything."

"Well, well, well." Dai stifles a laugh with the back of his hand, smelling the soil on his fingers. "D'you know how long they're planning to keep him in?"

"Suppose it depends on what they find, doesn't it? Mrs Jenkins was only telling me the other day that her Albert heard Idris bragging about how many women he had on the go down Somerset." Dilys sniffs, places her woollen-clad hands on the slats of his closed garden gate and squeezes. "What d'you think they're looking for up there then?" She swings a burly arm out in the direction of the lane that leads to Cwm Glas, Tŷ Haf and Idris' tip of a small holding.

"DNA of the dead women, I expect. A murder weapon too." Dai has been thinking about this all night. What it would need for them to actually charge him, ship him over to the Somerset Police Force.

"Ooo — it doesn't bear thinking about, a man like him, living so close to us, does it?" She gives him a theatrical judder. "I'm not just saying this, but he's always given me the heebie-jeebies."

"You fancy a cuppa?" Dai, still feeling guilty about not inviting the woman inside the other morning, blows on his hands to warm up. "I was just about to make myself one."

"No ta," she says, catching him off guard. "Got people to see — can't be standing around here all day."

"I've still got some of that delicious cake you made." What's he doing, *she said no, didn't she? You bloody fool*.

"No, honestly Dai, another time — hot news this, need to get it out there." And she's gone, as suddenly as she appeared, leaving Dai to grin his relief at the news of Idris' arrest into what remains of the morning.

CHAPTER
SEVENTY-EIGHT

Rachel is long gone. Driving away from The Pines, purposeful, determined, she knew exactly where she was heading and exactly what she was going to do, stopping to ask for directions to Westburn's police station from a couple walking two yellow Labradors. But now, parked up outside the building for twenty minutes, any surety she may have had in those initial moments is ebbing away with the ticking of time. Her brain, clear enough in the moments following April Parnell's startling revelation, is now a hive of buzzing scenarios, competing with each other for her attention.

What is she doing? She can't seriously think Graham had anything to do with the murders of these women. Surely the shame he feels for what his father did wouldn't be enough of a motivator, any more than his obvious hatred of drunken, skimpily dressed girls. She just can't picture it and, trawling back over the times she's spent with him, she can't feel it either. She knew him, trusted him. More than she had dared trust any man for years. He's too gentle, too kind. Why else was he so easy to fall in love with? Yet her mind won't let her forget how he lied; lied about knowing Westburn.

Why would he do that — it nags at her, refusing to be pushed away — unless he has something to hide?

She sits, squinting out at the sunshine and streets half-remembered from childhood. Undecided about Graham, she bounces her car keys up and down in her hand: dice she is about to cast.

Rachel is too far away from The Pines Residential Care Home to hear the laughter that is now coming from inside room fifteen. Too far away to see a delighted April Parnell — cheeks flushed, blowing out candles on a beautifully iced cake, a glass of bubbly in her hand.

"Happy Birthday, Mum." Graham, sitting on his mother's now made-up bed, raises his glass. "And may I say how smart you're looking — is that the brooch Ellie gave you?"

"It is — lovely, isn't it," April Parnell giggles, strokes the mother-of-pearl at her throat with crooked fingers. "You've spoilt me rotten, both of you."

"There's more to come yet." Graham smiles, his eyes shiny with emotion.

"You having some of this gorgeous cake your sister made?" His mother, knife poised, has three side plates waiting in her lap.

"Later, Mum, I'm saving myself for this grand lunch we're treating you to." Graham taps his midriff.

"Oo, you soft sod — thin as a racing snake — you can have a slither?" She cuts a piece for herself, slides it onto a plate and licks her fingers. "Do you a bit, shall I, Ellie?"

Ellie, *Eleanor*, is as dark haired and slender as her brother, but with her mother's face she is pretty and looks nowhere near her thirty-nine years. It is something that continues to astonish her mother — how that no-good waster her daughter married had the audacity to leave her. Bloody men, she sips from her glass. Might as well pin your life to the wind as depend on them.

A knock at the door and in bounds Beverley Crane in her Union Jack boots. All gusto and bluster and larger than life, she throws the room into jaw-dropping silence.

"*Are you lonesome tonight, do you miss me tonight?*" she warbles, forcing a vibrato and grinning from ear to ear while manipulating the crimson-tipped spikes of her coal-black hair. "Well, if it ain't the beautiful birthday girl," she chirrups, slipping an arm around April's shoulders. "*Drip, drip, drop, little April showers . . .*"

Ellie and Graham gawp at her, at their mother who is wearing an expression that would curdle milk.

"You guys 'aving a good time?" Beverley continues to treat them to her pantomime act. "There anythin' you need?" She gives them a second but there is no reply. "No? Okay then people, I'll leave you to it . . ." She hums "April Showers" again. "You have a great day now." But before she goes, unable to resist the little mirror above April's hand basin, she snatches a violent red lipstick from the top pocket of her tunic, a magician flourishing a bunch of flowers, and leans in to realign her ghoulish mouth and tease out yet more spikes over her forehead.

The door closes and the three listen to the strains of, "*Once had a love and it was a gas — la li la* . . . Hey, Gladys — you fancy swappin' that zimmer and doin' some pogoin' with me, you old darlin'?" as Beverley Crane retreats down the corridor and back to the Day Room.

Graham, Eleanor and April look at each other.

"Well, she's fun. Bet she livens things up around here for you." Ellie, obliged to break the silence.

"Oh yeah, a right performer that one — every room's a stage as far as she's concerned, and we're the bloody captive audience." April gives her sour appraisal.

"And did you see that nose ring?" Ellie, not really listening to her mother. "Crikey, I bet that hurt."

"Where I come from only bulls had them — needed it too, with the nastier beasts," April spits. "Hated them punks first time round."

"Aw, Mum. She seems nice enough."

"Huh, don't be fooled — she's as spiky as her hair that one." April, having none of it, mutters, "Bloody dyke — she gives me the sodding creeps."

Eleanor, cringing at the crassness of her mother's comment, continues to unpack the ornaments, books and photographs brought from the care home in Monmouth. "Have it looking like home in no time," she says, the shelves filling with things remembered from childhood.

"I've brought a couple of watercolours from the gallery," Graham pipes up. "I'll fetch them in when we come back. They'll look nice in here — could certainly do with cheering up. I was expecting Ellie to have

392

sorted you a better view than that." His voice bordering on critical as he flicks a slender-boned wrist at the window.

"I did try," Eleanor, quick to explain. "I asked for a sea view, but there's a waiting list, apparently."

"Hush now you two, everything's fine," April Parnell is quick to intervene. "I hardly spend any time in here — now, you having a piece of this cake or not, young man?"

"He'll be watching his figure, what with his new woman an' all." Ellie teases carefully, taking the plate her mother holds out for her.

"Want me to buy you another armchair, Mum?" Graham, his expression hard, determined to change the subject. "You could do with something else to sit on — you're going to be inundated when your old mates find out you're back in town."

"They're all in here," April Parnell chuckles. "We're forming a club — calling ourselves The Decrepits."

They laugh.

"You settling in all right?" Graham asks his sister stiffly. "Are the boys okay?"

"They love it. I was worried they'd miss Monmouth, but they haven't at all."

"And your new job?" her mother asks, finishing the last of her cake with a moistened finger.

"So far so good. Yeah, nice bunch. I like it."

"Shame you're so far away from me, Mum," Graham adopts a sad face. "I still don't see why Ellie had to move you all the way here."

"Get away." His mother, reaching again for her fizzy wine. "It's not so much further than Monmouth and with Ellie close, you don't have to be worrying — I should think you'll be wanting to spend your free time with Rachel. Did I say how lovely I thought she was — and fancy her coming all this way to see me. Such a dear girl, make sure you look after her. About time you settled down." She winks, making Ellie giggle again.

"Yes, Mum." Graham stares at the floor; his annoyance at Rachel's unexpected visit not something he wants to show. "And you're sure this place is okay for you?" he adds to divert attention from himself; perturbed at not being able to get to the bottom of why she left his flat without a word last Sunday, never mind her reasons for driving all the way here when she can't even be bothered to reply to a simple text message of his. Perhaps the lovely Rachel isn't the girl he thought she was. Perhaps she's more trouble than she's worth. "It's not half as grand as Grange House."

"Not half as expensive neither — no, honestly, please, it's nice to be back. *Really.*"

"No bad memories?" her son asks.

"No bad memories." April Parnell rolls forward on her wheels, clasps her son's hand in hers. "Same goes for you too, I hope. I know how much you hate this place."

"It isn't that," he says, squeezing her hand a little in return. "It's just the associations it has, you know, with Dad."

"I know, sweetheart. It makes me ashamed too."

394

"Come on you two, don't go all maudlin on me," Eleanor booms authoritatively, stepping between them. "We're not going there again, certainly not today. Today, we're celebrating; it's not every day your mum reaches the grand old age of seventy-five."

"Quite right, love," April laughs, tipping what remains in her glass to her lips. "It's certainly an achievement to be proud of at my age."

CHAPTER
SEVENTY-NINE

Idris can tell the Filth have been all through his house. It smells different, chemically, the way he imagines latex gloves and the all-in-one paper suits he's seen in crime dramas on the television smell. Except that on the television, aren't they supposed to leave the place as they find it? He looks around, sees that the contents of drawers and cupboards, shaken free, have not been put back properly. They obviously didn't think it mattered; the place being such a tip anyway. But that's not the point, is it? It incenses him, the idea of his mother's dresses being rifled through, her jewellery box tipped out on the bed, their stinking fingers rolling over the strings of fake pearls, her earrings, her bracelets, even the gold-plated chain him and his brothers clubbed together to buy her one Christmas.

Sitting down on the slippery eiderdown, his neck sunk deep into his chest, he pulls the jewellery box into his enormous lap and turns the little silver key in its back. Click, click, click. A sound that has always summoned memories of his mother. He opens the lid and watches the pirouetting plastic ballerina. Her arms held in a teardrop, high above her head. The once-white, double-layer netting of a tutu glued round her middle. He hums along with the flaky little tune.

They let me go, Mam. He tells Nerys Tudor. After two days and one whole night. *They didn't charge me, they've nothing on me — so everything's all right.* They gave him back his watch and keys, the small amount of loose change. Nothing was missing; he took care to count it out before signing for it. Allowed him to have his jacket back, too. The one they confiscated when he first arrived, refusing to let him have it with him in the cell. Thinking it preferable to provide him with a jumper stinking of cat piss from the box of lost property, three sizes too small. Jesus, it was cold in there. He thought he was used to the cold. This place, along with his childhood home of Cwm Glas, has been a lifetime's preparation of cold. But that police cell was something else. He could have done with that coat. Trapped inside a six by eight with something little better than a bucket to piss in, and a blanket stiffened by other bodies. They had no right keeping him locked in there. That spotty runt of a solicitor they assigned him was about as useful as a chocolate teapot. Well, they were hardly going to give the likes of him access to Perry fucking Mason, were they, the Pigs? Not when it was their game to fit him up. The pathetic little bastard hardly said a word and Idris hated him on sight, reminded of another spotty runt much closer to home.

He still isn't entirely sure why they let him go. The unlocking of his cell door came as a surprise. He thought he was in for another night, it hadn't gone well in the interview room, and Forensics poking around his home — the arsehole Watts said — had turned up that slag's blood on a shirt of his. Well, they would, wouldn't they? He could have told them that and saved them the trouble. If he thought it wouldn't incriminate him further, he'd have said how he smacked her one, that the grasping cow deserved it. Glad though, when they led him out. The thought of another tray of that shitty food he had tried to shovel down because he was starving, that paid him back by repeating on him all bloody night. He used to give his mutts better than that to eat — before the bloody 'thorities took them away. Bet that was down to that twat Dai Jones, too.

His dogs. He remembers them in the gathering gloom. Not out of any affection, just simply aware of their absence. By now, with empty bellies, they'd need feeding, there'd be their hungry whining, the sounds of chains clanking — but not any more. Shuffling downstairs, he pushes his arms into the stiffened sleeves of his jacket, pulls on boots and gawps at the empty space where his treasured Silver Pigeon should be. His eyes filling with angry tears, remembering its beautiful buffed walnut stock, its silver game-scene engraving. Seized just as he was, except he won't be having it back. *Illegal*, that stuck-up bitch, whatshername said. He isn't allowed to keep it because he doesn't have a licence. And not likely to have one now, is he? Not after all this. That bastard Dai Jones has got it coming.

Out in the lane in a slanting wind, Idris plods off in the direction of his liver-coloured lean-to. *Monroe*. That's right — her name finding him and making his eyes water. Silly cow. Didn't she know he could crack her like an egg? Empty out her innards in the way he deals with the rabbits — or cats — he snares in his traps by the stream. Not half as sexy as her curvy namesake, Marilyn. Although, taking a moment to visualise again the considerable attributes of the young police detective, Idris decides he would probably condescend to give her one if she asked nicely.

Dropping the image of Detective Sergeant Monroe's pretty face, he gazes over at his lorry. At the faded blue curtains hanging in his beloved cabin. They've been crawling all over that too. Snooping through his fridge, poking his pork pies, his plastic pints of milk. He'll have to refurbish it. Bad memories now, bad memories. The police slapping a caution on him, telling him not to leave the county.

Everything, *everything* spoiled because of that tosser Dai Jones. Pushing his hand deep into a sack of dried sheep feed, he pulls out his flick knife and extends the blade. He takes a minute to appreciate it before snapping it away again. Amsterdam. The pleasures contained within the city's red light district. It was his one and only time abroad and the memory is enough to make him smile. Bloody miracle the Pigs didn't find it; the thing was one hell of a buy. He turns the knife over in his hands thinking again what a lucky break it was, sneaking it back through UK customs. Especially as he was still half-cut behind the wheel of his transporter, stinking of his night with a cute-looking Russian bird with breasts like grapefruits.

"This'll do," he says, testing the sharpness of its razor-edge over the flat of his thumb. His fleshy lips peeled back on the clammy darkness, the snub of a wheeze bouncing back to him from the corrugated sides of his shed. "Yeah, this'll do nicely."

CHAPTER
EIGHTY

I have to admit, I really wanted this one. Was sure I'd seen her around and about before tonight. She stood out you see, tall and slender, classy like, with gorgeous waist-length hair. My absolute ideal, you could say. So I follow her.

Lights off, barely moving; inching along the abandoned seafront, then up behind the skeleton of Grey's Hotel.

"Go on, go on . . . you know you want to . . ." Breathing my encouragement from behind the wheel, the engine straining, under pressure in first gear. "Go down there — go on . . . it's nice and dark down there."

So pissed, she's no idea I'm shadowing her — hasn't once turned around. Stupid, aren't they, these girls? Out on their own in the dark, with all that's been going on — there's those that'd say they deserve it. That they've got it coming.

She had it coming, the vision, in her short dark velvet dress. Took her time to pick her way along the pot-holed and pitted tarmac. Gazelle-like in red stilettos, giving me the naked flesh of her long, slim thighs, bathed pale as petals in the meagre street light.

"You want a lift somewhere, darling?" Moving in close, barely able to contain myself; I lower the driver's side window to call to her. "Lonely out here — for a girl like you."

She stops, turns her beautiful almond-shaped gaze on mine and fixes me to the spot. Everything happens in the blink of an eye. Flashing blue on my periphery. Sirens squealing through the night-time drizzle.

A set-up. The honey-haired bitch led me down a cul-de-sac, and I was so absorbed with her I didn't notice. Behind me, in front of me — swarming with half the police force. I'm trapped.

CHAPTER
EIGHTY-ONE

Violent pummelling on his front door. Enough to shake Dai awake. His hand, through his confusion, reaches blind from under the duvet to flick on his bedside lamp. Disorientated and blinking in the unaccustomed light, he pushes his naked feet into slippers and gropes his way out of his bedroom and along the landing. Inching downstairs in candy-stripe pyjamas, no time to pull on a dressing gown, he calls out through the riotous thundering.

"All right. All right. For God's sake, hang on . . . I'm coming . . . all right." And fumbling with the lock he opens the door.

Idris Tudor.

Huge as his haulage lorry, he gobbles up the threshold and barges inside. Before Dai has the chance to draw breath, he has him pinned by the throat and flattened against the opposite wall.

"You've had it this time, runt boy." Idris' sour breath is hot on Dai's ear. "Should have sorted you the first time you grassed me up, you fucker. Remember — remember?"

Dai can hardly breathe, certain his neck will snap, Idris' Mastiff-sized paw shaking the life out of him.

Eyes popping and wild, the man is vacant beyond the purity of his rage in the way Beth would describe he was with her.

"Say something then, you bastard. Say something. Go on. You're the hot-shot fuckin' lawyer," he bellows, his strawberry mark close to Dai's face. "Got enough to say when it comes to blabbing to the police though, haven't you?" Idris squeezes tighter, lifting Dai's flaccid body higher off the floor. His legs dangling, his slippers dropping free. "Had me banged up they did — the bastards. Cos of what? Cos of you," he slobbers, showering Dai in froth. "And I swore sitting there, in that stinking shithole, once as I was out, I was gonna come and finish what me and me brothers should have done years ago."

The blade is long. A pointed slash of steel refracted in the small light from a single lamp in Bwthyn Dewen's front room.

It is the last thing Dai Jones sees.

CHAPTER
EIGHTY-TWO

Mrs Pepper's heart lurches when she pushes open the vast glass doors of the Dean Street Wine Bar. Rooted to the spot, she thinks there is no way she can move into the busy lounge area just yet. The pendant lighting, the chrome tables, the soft leather sofas — it would be marvellous if she had the courage. Her and Stan, when they were first courting, often went off to parties, shows, dances. Places like this where you sipped at something that tasted like fizzy peach juice but cost twenty bob a bottle. It took her breath away, not that Stan ever turned a hair. Only once she saw him tipsy, flushing pink as a rose and making her fall in love with him, his young cheeks whorled through with crimson like the image of that Al Jolson song the band was playing, "Angel Child". But by the time they walked back to her lodgings he was quite recovered, and they said goodnight to each other as though they'd done nothing more exciting than walk home from the fishmongers. She remembers the disappointment even now, flushing at the recollection of her younger self and the expectations she had.

Clipping noisily on unaccustomed heels, she paces around the foyer, looking confused. Would they be left, right, or through here? She decides to ask one of the sleek-looking girls on the desk and is directed through one of the entrances beyond the bar. The luxuriousness when she finds the Ladies' knocks her sideways. The button bulbs around the mirrors, more akin to some imagined West End dressing room than public conveniences, make her smile. The array of hair and beauty products, according to the little notice, were there for all to use, so she makes the most of it by lifting up a bottle moulded in the shape of a woman's torso and giving herself a squirt. It makes her wrist smell nice.

Back in the foyer, she takes out the letter she has been so careful to keep safe inside the pocket of her coat all day, and rereads it. You can tell from the intensity of her countenance how important whatever she waits for is. How agitated the ticking down of time makes her. Watching, she looks to be on the verge of something, it's written in the way she stands; in the way she has buttoned her coat to the throat. It seems she is ready to take the plunge and is done with the world of secrets she's been living in the shadow of for so long. Her husband will understand how natural it was for her son to want to find her all those years ago, how perfectly normal for him to want his mother's help when he was in the direst of trouble. Who else did the poor boy have — those no-hopers she handed him over to who brought him up? She doesn't think so.

Yes, she decides firmly, her expression clearing momentarily. When I've seen my boy right, I'll come clean with Stan — we can be a proper family, the three of us. But first there are things she must do, and waiting amidst the sea of indecipherable voices, her child seems as far away as ever. Thinking of it, her eyes prick with fretful tears, making the black and white tiles of the foyer swim, so Mrs Pepper doesn't see the woman — a professional-looking thirty-something, kitted out in expensively tailored suit and killer heels — push through the glass doors behind her.

"Excuse me?" A voice, assertive, suddenly at her elbow. "Excuse me, are you Mrs Pepper?"

"Yes. Yes, I am." She squints from behind her thick lenses, drinking in the woman's perfume.

"Felicity — Felicity Northcoat." And out comes a hand for her to shake. "Sorry I'm late, I do hope you've not been waiting long," she breathes, touching Mrs Pepper's upper arm and leaning forward: "Shall we go through to the bar, get ourselves a drink?" The suggestion a conspiratorial whisper. "You can show me what you've found then."

Mrs Pepper follows the well-groomed woman and feeling braver in company is quite able to step over the threshold into the plush carpeted space with its low-rise tables, its squashy-looking seats and opt for the far corner of the room.

"Shall we get down to business?" Ms Northcoat, returning from the spangle-lit bar. Something fizzy with ice and a chunk of lemon bobbing about in it for her, a large schooner of sweet sherry for Mrs Pepper who, pausing for the briefest of sips, unclips her handbag to pull out a small plastic folder holding thirty or so Polaroids and spreads them out like a deck of stiffened cards over the table between them. The Polaroids are in colour, smeared with fingerprints as if they have been well-handled, and faded with age to a strange sunset pink at their edges.

"Well, well, well." The woman from the *Daily Mail* shuffles forward in her seat to have a better look. "You were right, these are interesting. *Very* interesting." And reaching in, she picks one to look at more closely.

Mrs Pepper watches the journalist's face stiffen at the sight of a smiling nineteen-year-old Sarah D'Villez captured alongside an equally happy-faced thirty-three-year-old John Blundell. The man he was before being projected to the world as a psychotic wife-killer, rapist and kidnapper. A man recognisable, yet different. What Felicity Northcoat — a junior reporter involved in the press coverage at the time — sees is a softer, gentler-looking man: one she would go so far as to describe as handsome, under his sandy sweep of hair.

The print shows D'Villez and Blundell standing in a wide, green meadow. It is high summer and the dappling of strong sunlight shot through the trees lights up their hair. His tattooed arm is looped about her shoulders and the other is stretched out, holding the camera, so its lens is turned on the two of them. What would be called a selfie now. They look happy. They look in love. They look like any other couple. The journalist dives on the others, gathering them greedily to her in a bundle. More of the couple in thin summer clothes set against a rich tapestry of lush green countryside, John Blundell's hand entwined in Sarah's long blonde hair and her pressing as close as she can,

408

smiling adoringly up at him. Then, skipping through, the journalist finds herself staring into the face of a very different Sarah D'Villez. Brazen and confident, her features accentuated by heavy make-up, her hair deliberately dishevelled. In these Polaroids she is positioned on all fours and posing seductively, naked but for a skimpy G-string and four-inch stilettoes. Others show her spread across a tangle of sheets, her wrists handcuffed to the headboard with Blundell lying beside her, semi-naked himself. They are laughing as he cups the young Sarah's bare breasts in one hand and snaps these intimate shots with the other.

"Wow . . . now these tell us a very different story — very different indeed." Ms Northcoat nods, as tomorrow's front page takes shape in her mind. The wording: clipped, concise and shocking; a scoop that will give her the career boost she's been waiting for.

Mrs Pepper watches the woman from the *Mail* take her time, sees her carefully analyse each of the snapshots in turn. Her movements: methodical, rhythmic, are at odds with the indistinguishable thump of background music, the rising hum of conversation filling the bar around them. The raunchy images slide under the journalist's fingers, the lovers caught for eternity in a series of provocative poses. Some are of a smiling John Blundell, but the majority show them together, fondling one another on the same rumpled bed that features in the bulk of these photographs. Obviously wallowing in some kind of sadomasochistic sex game, Sarah is shown blindfold and roped down with Blundell sitting astride her; on the chair, on the bed, close-ups of the two of them fervently kissing and totally absorbed in one another.

"D'you happen to know where these were taken?" The reporter is the first to speak.

"Erm, well, most of them's at John's cottage, out Brampton way. Northamptonshire."

"What? The cottage Sarah D'Villez claimed he took her to after seizing her at knifepoint from those stables . . . what were they called again . . . Pinkton Grange?"

"Yes, that's right — John was in the middle of renovating the place."

"The hovel where Sarah said he raped and tortured her for days on end?"

"Yes."

"Hardly *torture*, is it?" the journalist snorts, her disdain plain. "Look at her, she's lapping it up — quite the little poser, isn't she?"

"John said she liked dressing up —"

"And dressing down," the journalist cuts in; then raises a hand to apologise.

"He said she liked him to be rough with her too, when they were having sex. That she wanted him to hurt her, tie her up, that sort of thing." Mrs Pepper looks into her lap, a sign of embarrassment to match her reddening cheeks. "But when things didn't go her way, when he told her he wasn't going to leave his wife, she turned all that against him — told the police she never knew him."

"Didn't she just. And with her blood and every other bodily fluid all over that cottage from what they were doing in these photos, it made it easy for her, didn't it?"

410

Ms Northcoat gives a pinched little smile. "Uch, it's so obvious now, I can't believe John's lawyers didn't see it."

"They saw it all right," Mrs Pepper tells her. "But they could also see what he was up against. How the evidence stacked against him, how credible she was as a victim. He pleaded his innocence in all the statements he gave the police, but in the end his barrister persuaded him it was too risky, that if he pleaded guilty to manslaughter and abduction then his sentence would be lesser than if a jury found him guilty of murder."

Felicity Northcoat picks through the shiny-faced prints again. Lets go a sharp little laugh. "Yes, this was quite the little love nest, wouldn't you say?"

"John called it his perfect rural idyll, right in the middle of nowhere it was. Him and Linda —"

"Linda, his wife?" the journalist wanting confirmation.

Mrs Pepper gives it. "They bought it for next to nothing, it was to be their holiday retreat when he'd finished fixing it up. Then in those months John and Sarah got together he used the place to cheat on her."

"You sound as if you disapprove?"

"Of course I disapprove — but John always said, not that anyone would listen, how obsessed Sarah was with him."

"Did John ever tell you how they got together; how it all started?" the journalist asks.

"Chatting about fishing, of all things," Mrs Pepper sniffs. "Apparently it was something she used to do with her father. John said she knew a lot about it. And when she found out the owners of Pinkton Grange allowed him to fish their stretch of the Nene, she started pestering him to take her, and when he wouldn't, she'd follow him on her horse . . . I suppose you could say she wore him down in the end. It isn't something he's proud of." She coughs, removes her glasses to clean them on her skirt. "But . . . I mean . . . what chance did he have? Look at her . . . gorgeous, young, from the top drawer. There aren't many blokes who'd be able to say no to that."

"Coupled with the fact she was offering it to him on a plate, that she liked kinky sex." The reporter curls her lip.

"And Linda, poor thing, nice as she was, was a bit of a plain Jane and the two of them had been married a while. But then Sarah went all weird — flying into rages, badgering him to run away, saying she was going to dump her boyfriend."

"The boyfriend . . . that would have been Spencer, was it?" The journalist pulls the name from her memory and scribbles something down on a notepad retrieved from her bag. "Didn't they marry a year or so after the trial?"

"That's right, had a daughter too." Mrs Pepper pauses, spectacles back in place, she fiddles with the material of her skirt some more. "She'd be . . . oooh . . . twelve, thirteen . . . yes, she'd be thirteen now."

"And where's she — where's the daughter?"

"With her father, in America."

"*What?* The ex has the child? Bit odd, isn't it — why's she not with her mother?" Pen hovering, expectant — nothing like an allegation of child abuse to give a story extra spice. Not that this one is going to need it.

"Something happened, something between Sarah and the child — Spencer had custody. It's all I know." A shrug.

"Sarah's mother'll know. I'll give her a call; see if she'll give me an interview." The reporter makes a note. "Although, from what I remember of her," Ms Northcoat squirms, "she's one hell of a slippery customer." Then her face brightening, looking directly at Mrs Pepper, "You could tell her if you like — tell her she's better off talking to me, that she'll have no chance when the big boys get wind of this."

"Er, no." Mrs Pepper shakes her head fiercely. "I'm not setting foot in that house again."

"No, I don't suppose you will. And you won't have to, not after this." The journalist gives a withering look. "As I've said — give me exclusive rights and it's a fat fee for you."

"I've not done this for the money, if that's what you're thinking . . . you can keep the money. It was John who insisted I take this to the press." Mrs Pepper, affronted, is quick to defend herself. "He said you'd know what to do with it. He doesn't trust the police, even with evidence as strong as this. Of course he knows you'll have to tell them eventually, but at least this way people will get the chance to hear his side . . ." She is about to say more when the journalist's mobile bleeps from somewhere deep in her bag. Mrs Pepper watches her pluck it free, flip open the leather-cased front and pull a face at whatever the text message communicates before putting it away again.

"Where exactly did you find these?" Ms Northcoat, back in business, waves her pen over the Polaroids.

"Well, as you know, I've been working for Jennifer D'Villez, Sarah's mother —"

"I was going to ask you about that," the journalist interjects. "How the hell did you stick it out all those years, knowing what Sarah'd done?"

"Oh, that wasn't difficult, believe me — I grew up needing to play a part just to stay alive." Mrs Pepper coughs up a dry laugh. "But that's another story. Suffice to say, I know all about acting, working for Mrs D'Villez was a doddle — and anyway, I was doing it for John. Thought if I was there, in the thick of it, I'd land on something eventually. He told me he'd taken pictures of them together — said if I could find them, they'd clear his name. I didn't think it'd take me seventeen years."

"How did you know Sarah hadn't destroyed them?"

"I didn't," she says; her expression blank. "But after John told me how fixated she'd been about him, I reckoned she was twisted enough to hold on to them — and I'd been right."

"And how did you — how did you find them in the end?"

"I just got lucky — saw Mrs D'Villez find them in her husband's old room, then where she put them, and when she was out . . ." Mrs Pepper shrugs for a second

414

time, takes a sip of her sherry and returns it with a small click to the varnished table top. "I overheard plenty over the years, I can tell you, but I'm no eaves-dropper — all I wanted was something to corroborate John's version of things. Something to prove his innocence."

"How come you know so much about John's side of things?" the journalist asks.

"Because he's my son," she replies with no hesitation.

"*Your son?*" Ms Northcoat, on the edge of her seat. "I didn't realise John Blundell was your son?"

Mrs Pepper stares at her hands, picks the skin around her thumb nail. "I was very young when I had him, years before I married — it was a terrible thing for me, to have to give him up. He said he'd been searching for me for years, I got his call just before all this went to trial."

The journalist reaches out, places a hand over Mrs Pepper's and gives it a little squeeze. "It makes so much more sense now," she says softly. "I'm sorry if I upset you by insinuating you'd done this for money."

The two women exchange smiles.

"I interrupted you," Felicity Northcoat says, leaning back into her seat. "You were saying how you overheard plenty in the D'Villez household over the years."

"I did." Mrs Pepper, adjusting herself. "It was a right weird set up, I can tell you, and that Sarah . . . crikey, she's some storyteller. She caused no end of trouble in that house, the things I'd witness her doing. It's why I never gave up looking for the Polaroids. The more I got to know her, the more convinced I was that she'd kept them — not just to have some sick keepsake of their time together, but because she was so wrapped up in herself and how she looked, and these pictures show all that and the power she had over my boy. Yes," Mrs Pepper exhales. "That girl, she's quite deluded you know, little wonder she had no friends."

"No friends?" the journalist echoes, scribbling it down. "Odd, isn't it?"

"Odd all right. She never went out neither. Day in, day out, cooped up for ten years in that house, she was — it isn't normal for a young woman." Mrs Pepper, back into her stride. "The few friends she did have when I first started working there, well, they soon got fed up with her bleating on. As sick of her as I was, they just stopped calling round. I blame her father; he spoilt her rotten. No wonder she convinced herself she'd done nothing wrong — it's what must come from growing up thinking you're perfect."

"D'you think her father knew about the Polaroids?" Ms Northcoat asks.

"I don't think so. I know he doted on her but he was a decent man — I can't imagine he'd have let an innocent man go to prison. No, Sarah must have hidden them in his room when he was in hospital that time, he was way too frail to do anything other than sit in his chair when he came home."

"Fooled him as well then." The journalist pulls a face. "I remember the way she behaved at the trial — all demure and meek. She had the jury eating out of her hand."

416

Mrs Pepper sucks air down into her lungs. "Didn't she just. Probably been playing it that way from the moment she arrived back at her parents' house covered in Linda's blood and John's DNA."

"I've been meaning to ask — how *did* Sarah get back to London afterwards?"

"She made John drop her off at the end of her parents' road."

"*John?*" Ms Northcoat looks stunned. "Bit stupid of him, wasn't it? Letting her out of his sight?"

"I suppose, but you have to remember," Mrs Pepper, focusing hard, mouth firm, "that girl had him wrapped around her little finger from the very beginning. And after what she'd just done, my poor boy was in a state of shock. She took control, well, didn't she always? The idea — *her idea* — was to get herself cleaned up, then the two of them could go to the police together. Tell them Linda's death was an accident."

"An *accident!*" Ms Northcoat splutters. "Come on, that'd be stretching it a bit, wouldn't it?"

"I know, it sounds bizarre to you and me sitting here; but imagine the state he was in. He wanted to stand by her, was going to say it was a crime of passion, something like that. Tell them how Linda turned up at the cottage and found them together — John thought she was in Cornwall, her sister'd just had a baby y'see, he wasn't expecting her back for a fortnight — and things got out of control . . . Linda got hysterical . . . and with those dangerous tools all over the place from the work John was doing there . . . that it was self-defence on Sarah's part."

"On Sarah's part? *Self-defence?*" the journalist shrieks. "She stoved the poor woman's head in with a hammer, for God's sake." Then seeing Mrs Pepper flinch, says, "Sorry."

"I know what you're saying — but it's what they agreed at the time, it never crossed his mind to doubt her."

"And then she went and changed her story?" The journalist stops her scribbling to look up.

"Well, yes — and the first John knew of it was when they arrested him."

"So, in the short time he let her out of his sight, she'd worked out a way for him to cop for the lot — convincing the police he snatched her, held her hostage, raped and tortured her and, when his wife turned up unexpectedly, that he was the one who killed her?"

"Yes, in a nutshell. But the wheels had already been put in motion, don't forget. Not that those two would have been aware — walled-up in that out-of-the-way cottage with no telly or radio, no newspapers — but Spencer had called the police when Sarah failed to come home, so from the outset everyone thought she'd been abducted. They were in the middle of a nationwide search by the time John drove her back to London." Mrs Pepper makes a quick guess at Felicity Northcoat's age. "You're probably too young to remember, aren't you?"

"No way, I remember it all right — I was a junior at the time and, well, she had one of those faces, didn't

418

she — and launching it sold papers, the fear she'd been kidnapped had public sympathy from the off."

Mrs Pepper nods. "Not that she'd have given a damn about the worry she caused her boyfriend or family by not letting them know where she was. That just about sums her up if you ask me. Selfish doesn't come anywhere near it."

"*What*, you're telling me she told no one she'd be going away?" Felicity Northcoat gasps.

"Well she can't have done, can she? Otherwise they wouldn't have been searching for her."

"So what was she intending to do when she came back? Announce to everyone she'd been staying with her lover? That she was dumping Spencer?"

"I've no idea what her long-term plans were, but John had no intention of leaving his wife. All this," Mrs Pepper flicks a hand in the direction of the Polaroids, "I don't think he had a clue what he was getting into really."

"No, I don't suppose he did. Fortunate though, for Sarah I mean — as things turned out," the journalist says, her mind massaging an idea. "You could almost think she planned it from the off . . . bump off the wife, have John to herself . . . although," she adds, muttering under her breath as she lifts her glass to her lips and drinks, "how the mad bitch thought she'd get away with it and hold on to him, I don't know."

"It is possible," Mrs Pepper only hears the first part of what Ms Northcoat said. "I wouldn't put anything past that one."

"Sarah knew there'd be no one apart from John to contradict her story. No one was aware of their relationship, not once his wife was dead." The journalist picks up her thread. "*And*, of course, let's not forget, Sarah would have been conveniently covered in cuts and bruises from their sadistic . . ." she checks Mrs Pepper's face while searching for a softer word, "*shenanigans*."

"You see now, how my boy never stood a chance?"

"I do. It's frightening, really. It was a set-up from start to finish." A frown breaks on the smooth shore of Ms Northcoat's forehead. "A thirty-something adoptive son of a pair of fairground workers versus a beautiful, well brought-up middle-class girl — I remember what was printed in the papers, I was part of it — it didn't take much to convince people he abducted her and did all the things she said he did."

The two women look at each other in the silence that drops between them, heavy as an anchor.

"But these . . ." the journalist pipes up again, pointing to the Polaroids. "These are all the exposure we need — you wait, they're going to blow this fantasy of hers wide open. We're going to clear your son's name and prove how he was wrongly imprisoned, of that I have no doubt." Ms Northcoat tilts forward. "Incidentally," she breathes, taking her time. "Where's Sarah living now, d'you know?"

Mrs Pepper pauses, pensive; a small smile curving her mouth. "Oh yes . . . I know where she is — I'm the one who sent her there."

"You sent her there?" Ms Northcoat, intrigued, leans in further. "However d'you mean?"

"I found the place for her. The barn she's in. Knew she'd love it the moment she saw it. Strange really, how things turned out, because it's where I used to live as a child."

"Where you used to live? How interesting — where was that, Mrs Pepper?"

"Oh, please, dear, please . . . call me Beth."

CHAPTER
EIGHTY-THREE

With the radio on for company, Jennifer is emptying the dishwasher. She sees from the food trapped between forks, the greasy smears of crockery and the coffee rings inside mugs, that she didn't load it properly. That she neglected to put in the correct amount of powder, or set it on the right cycle. She lets go a sigh as she bends forward, her face the picture of despondency, as she shoves back inside what she had started to take out.

The Byrds version of "Mr Tambourine Man" sparks a memory of Donald. The first time he moved in close to kiss her. The two of them parked up in his baby-blue Ford Capri listening to Bob Dylan on the radio. Him saying, "Listen to this, this is great." Her making a show of turning up the volume, straining interest, her unaccustomed tights chafing the already charged atmosphere whenever she moved. An eighteen-year-old Jennifer, coal-black eyes and a curtain of long black hair she liked to hide behind. Old enough to vote, to drink openly in public houses. To drink too much. A thing she had a tendency to do in the sweet new weeks when she was finding out about Donald D'Villez. When she would gasp at the sight of him, thinking he looked just like her handsome idol Billy Fury in the film

422

That'll Be the Day. When the shock of his white-blond hair still surprised and fascinated her, watching when he pulled his fingers through the thickness of it and it didn't seem to move.

Had she drunk too much that evening too? Sitting beside him with the windows wound down, looking up at a London night sky. Where instead of the ceiling of stars he described in a voice that belonged to a much older man — to the explorer in him — there were only the red and green blinking lights of jumbo jets. He talked to her, this new Jennifer — or this is how it felt, smelling like a fruit salad after squirting her hair with her sister's Charlie perfume before coming out — about the slip-stream of the planes he'd watch as a boy in the acres of sky above his father's farm. How he would yearn to be flying to Great Britain. For in his mind, working behind a horse and plough in the chest-high wheat fields, Britain was where these jumbo jets were heading. A country he was shown on a map of the world in his timber-clad schoolroom. A tiny jagged island, cut from a cloth of rich sea blue, where it was all happening.

Donald had loved her then. This emerging young woman. When only part of her had hardened over from the loss of her mother and the rest of her was still soft and up for grabs. No longer interested in doing things to please her father, her teachers, Jennifer had wanted to study him and learnt, from close observation, just where his frown buckled his forehead when he talked of his Canadian childhood. The faint lilt of his accent, that once studied, allowed her to differentiate it from the

American, to never mistake it as others did when Donald spoke. She learnt too how he would develop a bout of the hiccups when nervous, his lean frame jolting against hers, making her press him close to try and absorb the staccato shock of them and rewarded by the dazzle of his film-star smile.

She began staying out with him all night. Driving around in his car, parking up in Hampstead Heath to watch the horizon lighten together. The hour of scuttling birdsong and foxes sloping back to their holes, before the rest of the world woke up. Her teachers began pulling her aside after assembly to question whether she was well, what those violet half-moons were under her eyes, and was it true that Miss Phillips had caught her dozing in her French class? It was true. She had no interest in what an education could offer her any more. It was Donald and his car she wanted to know the inside of, not geometry books and pencil cases. Crawling back under her cold bedcovers, holding her breath for any sign in the house that she'd been heard, the teenage Jennifer would lie with the smell of him on her skin in the minutes before the alarm went off. Did she sleep at all in those heady days of 1973? If so, it was only in snatches. On the bus to school, at the back of classrooms, in the armchair at home before preparing herself to go out to meet him again.

"I expected better," was all her father said; the results of his youngest daughter's A Levels in his hand. And she was never sure whether he meant her final grades, or the news she gave him one Sunday over the lunch table, that she and Donald were to be married.

The news is kicking in somewhere in the background as she realises her cupboards are bare and, with nothing to drink coffee out of, is reduced to retrieving a white bone-china beaker from the top drawer of her state-of-the-art Smeg and washing it by hand. Something the Radio Two broadcaster is delivering over the sounds of gushing water makes her turn down the tap . . . *Avon and Somerset Constabulary have charged a forty-nine-year-old woman with the murders of Issy Lake, Wendy Denny and Pauline Keene* . . . Jennifer, squirts too much Fairy on to her cloth and the suds foam out of control . . . *Beverley Crane, from Westburn-on-Sea, a carer at The Pines Residential Home in the town* . . . *known locally as Bev the Punk* . . . *due to appear at Bristol Crown Court on Monday* . . . she doesn't rinse the washing-up liquid off thoroughly enough, her mind elsewhere . . . *We go over now to our local correspondent who has been following the case since October* . . . Her longed-for cup of Arabica medium roast, when she makes it, tastes of scented chemicals. *Uch,* she tips it down the sink, switches off the radio. Bring back Mrs Pepper, she sighs, looking at the detritus that makes up her kitchen. She can't cope; she isn't used to doing things for herself, not on the domestic front.

Sashaying along the hall, Jennifer sinks down into her telephone chair. Rereading the note that since its arrival has sat propped up on her telephone seat-table. It's Alice, telling her she's flying into Heathrow a week tomorrow. The visit is prompted by her call the other week to ask whether Sarah was with them, Jennifer could tell it worried her. *It's been way too long,* the flouncy handwriting says, *we've so much to catch up on*. And indeed they have. Jennifer failed to inform her sisters, not even her favourite, when Donald died. His refusal — in life and in death — to have nothing to do with the Catholic Church meant she sent cards with the news, weeks after his funeral. And although there were hardly any mourners at the crematorium and next to no wreaths or messages of condolence, sitting up front with Sarah in an otherwise empty row of hard wooden chairs, she'd been glad none of her family could see. The place provided no more reverence than a village hall, with its pine-clad walls and high glass ceiling. No effigies of Christ, none of the Virgin Mary — it went against everything she's built her life on. She blames the succession of dead babies — the stillborns and the miscarriages — on not having their marriage blessed by the Catholic Church. For agreeing to marry in a registry office, with no one to give her away. It took years before her father spoke to her again, blankly refusing to acknowledge Donald as his son-in-law, until he began staring his own mortality in the face. It was a close shave and Jennifer often thinks how she might have been cut out of the will and never known the likes of this beautiful house, its beautiful furniture. Even with Donald's substantial salary and subsequent pension from Rowntree's, the finances would never have stretched to providing her with such lavish surroundings. Incapable as she was to take up gainful employment herself, marrying at eighteen, she forfeited the chance to go to college. Yes, she tells the face in the mirror opposite, Donald's obstinacy could have cost her dearly.

The rasp of nylons as she crosses her legs under her clover-tweed skirt surges through the tepid atmosphere. Fingers flicking through her leather-bound address book. *Mrs Pepper. Mrs Pepper.* Where the hell are you? It is a number she has rung repeatedly over the past few days, and one she is sure she knows by heart. But still she wants to check, reading and speaking the numbers as she presses them into the corresponding pads on the receiver.

It rings. Six, seven, eight times. Nothing. She taps the red phone symbol, returns the handset to the charger. How little she knew her, Jennifer thinks again. How little the woman shared of her life, and Jennifer never thought to ask. All those years coming here, moving around her rooms, voiceless as a ghost. She thinks she catches sight of her now — that slight stoop, the shadow of her duster moving over the surfaces of her sitting room. The slop, slop of her slippers against the carpet. A sound that had the facility to drive her up the wall. A sound she was forced to remove herself from so many times. She wishes she could hear it now. The customary scrabbling around under the stairs, the whirr of the unwinding flex of the vacuum cleaner, the *shhh, shhh* spray of furniture polish. The way she would insist on finding Jennifer to say goodbye each time, the give-away smattering of biscuit crumbs on her ample chest. Had Jennifer really minded that much? If she hadn't been so mean, the woman might not have needed to sneak the odd one from the biscuit barrel. Fearing the suck of its rubber surround would betray her. All Jennifer's friends employed cleaners and they let them have the run of the house. Let them have whatever they fancied out of the fridge, said it made them work harder if their appetites were satiated. She had never offered Mrs Pepper so much as a sandwich, and sometimes the woman was here all day. *Perhaps, perhaps,* Jennifer has a life's worth of these. But perhaps, in this case she shouldn't have been so hard. If she had been kinder, who knows — Mrs Pepper might not have taken those Polaroids, the two of them might have been friends.

The phone rings. It might be Mrs Pepper. Jennifer snatches it, the diamond on her ring colliding with its shellac-hard casing.

"*Hello,*" she says, sharp, waiting for the caller to speak.

"Hello." The voice is chirpy, buoyant. Jennifer immediately bristles, taking it to be yet another marketing call about cavity insulation. "Am I speaking to Mrs Jennifer *Deevillers?*"

"D-Vil-lez," Jennifer snaps back the correct pronunciation of her name. "Yes, this is her speaking."

"Good morning," the voice continues, its original sheen intact. "This is Felicity Northcoat speaking."

"Yes," Jennifer, ignorant of the name, cuts in. "What do you want?"

"An interview, Mrs *Deevillers.*" The request coming clear and clean. "I work for the *Daily Mail.* We've new information regarding John Blundell and your daughter. Nothing that's been verified yet, but it would be in your

428

interest to talk to us before we hand it over to the police —"

Jennifer pulls the receiver away from her ear, snarls at it, before slamming it with considerable force back into its cradle.

The phone goes again. Answer it? Don't answer it?

"Look, I've said I don't give interviews — how many more times —"

"Mrs D'Villez," a man's voice interrupts her. "It's Derek Barnes here."

"Oh, sorry Derek, hello," she breathes, her expression brightening.

"I've some very good news, Mrs D'Villez. I've found her. I've found Sarah."

CHAPTER
EIGHTY-FOUR

Dilys Roberts is the one to find Dai. Calling round the following morning, a pink-patterned plate of sugared offerings perspiring beneath a wrapping of clingfilm. The effervescent bounce of spring resonating in her greeting.

"Dai?" she chirrups. Her call vying with the house sparrows that, although fluttering all year long within Bwthyn Dewen's bank of honeysuckle, over the past few days have sparked into jubilant song. They are responding, she fancies fleetingly, to the honeysuckle's bright shoots of green in the same way she is.

"Dai?"

No answer. Not that this is all that unusual, Dilys pushes wide the already open front door expecting to see him, mug of tea in one hand, his breakfast of wholemeal toast and marmalade balancing in the other.

The pyjamas throw her. So jolly, the candy-stripe. Like the coloured canvas of seaside deckchairs from remembered childhood holidays. What's he still doing in his nightclothes, with bare feet? It's freezing in here. Why is he lying face down on the carpet? Dilys, disbelieving, sees his splayed hands above his head and decides he must have fallen over when he was dancing.

It is possible. He and Elsie were always dancing. Dilys used to watch them through their windows, envious of their love, swirling about to their old 78s in this room. He must have tripped on the hem of his pyjamas, they look way too long, she thinks, trying to make sense of the unfolding scene. But why no music? Eyes darting to the record player. There has to be a mistake, look at him — so cold and still.

"Stop it, Dai, I know you like a joke, but you're scaring me now — come on, get up, stop buggering about." Inching closer, gingerly, she sees how ashen his face is. His usually quite rosy complexion has taken on a lilac hue. And there is blood, that when Dilys notices, she can't believe it hadn't been the first thing she saw.

It is splashed down the length of him, across the backs of his calves, over his upturned heels. Blackening, clotting. Filling the air with its metallic breath. His pyjamas are sodden and sticky with it. The sheer vulnerability of him strikes her and, in the dangling seconds, she becomes horribly conscious of the involuntary movements her own body is making. The rise and fall of her ribcage, her blinking eyelids, as she stands, unable to move, mouthing her shock through the horror as her arms hang limp and useless by her sides.

Dilys doesn't scream, not at first, the shock hits later. What she does is step calmly away from the slaughter. The soles of her shoes tacky from Dai's blood, tug at the fibres of the arabesque-swirl of his living room carpet. Reaching the telephone, she dials 999 and lifts the receiver to her lips. Her voice comes strangely calm, dislocated, asking the person on the other end to send paramedics.

"It's my friend," she says firmly, wanting the voice to listen, to understand. "He's been attacked. Can you hear me? Can you hear what I'm saying? My friend . . . my friend — he's been attacked . . . he's not breathing."

CHAPTER
EIGHTY-FIVE

In the days to follow, back at Tŷ Haf, Rachel is pleased she decided against talking to the police in Westburn. It had dawned on her, sitting outside the station with April Parnell's story of Graham's troubled childhood stinging her ears, that she should first clear her head. That what she needed was to find somewhere to park, stretch her legs, have a coffee, something to eat, and mull it over before settling on anything. Experience told her no good ever came of knee-jerk reactions, look at the way she jumped to conclusions about Tracy. She can kiss goodbye to any friendship with her after the insinuations she made to Hywel the other night. That man she saw Tracy with in Llandafen turned out to be her brother, visiting from Bristol. Why must she always think the worst of people? What was it Spencer used to say? We all judge others by our own standards. It is as if she wants people to be living spurious lives, for them to have secrets when there are none. Perhaps she does it to make herself feel better. Whatever her reasons, she was adamant, sitting inside her car that bright blue Monday morning, she wasn't going to repeat past mistakes.

The tide was out when she parked up along Westburn's promenade and it felt as good as those times as a child on the beach with her father: the wind tugging her hair, pulling her cheeks wide. Of course there was no way she could take her shoes off to paddle in the shallows at this time of year, but regardless, the experience was just as exhilarating as she remembered. Later, a bacon bap and a carton of not half bad coffee, bought from one of the spruced-up café's along the front, she sat on a bench and took the time to think, patiently, calmly, which, as it turned out, had been the right decision.

She has to admit, she hadn't been thinking straight earlier. Probably the fault of the journey, an empty stomach, or the over-stuffy interior of Mrs Parnell's room. Except she knows her quandary began days before driving there. It began with that phone message she took from the woman running The Pines Care Home. But sitting on the bench, under the banner of circling herring gulls, untangling his mother's revelations, the answers were so straightforward. Of course Graham would deny all knowledge of Westburn with the awful history of his father. The place would harbour terrible memories, ones he'd be desperate to dissociate himself from. He didn't lie, not really, he just didn't want to admit it — who would want to disclose a thing like that? Admitting might have meant the need to explain his upbringing, his father's shameful obsession with younger girls, it's obvious he's touchy, she thinks, recollecting the incident with those scantily clad youngsters in town.

No, she had nothing to go to the police with — poor Graham hadn't done anything. Being ashamed of

434

where he came from didn't make him a bad man. What she needed to do, she decided then — sitting looking at the far off horizon, the sparkling band of sea, sipping from her polystyrene carton — and again now, back in her lovely home, was to ring him, arrange to spend the evening together and forget about Westburn, it isn't worth jeopardising their future lives together. Because if there is anything Rachel is sure of, it is that she wants her future to be with him. With Graham she has all the passion and excitement she had with John — even more perhaps, but unlike John, Graham doesn't have a snivelling, needy wife in the background, making what they have illicit and wrong and tainting their love. Yes, at least this time there isn't a wife she will have to get rid of — a wife she will have to kill.

The dog barks. Rachel looks up and goes to her front windows to peer through the slats of the blinds. What she sees is a big black Mitsubishi Shogun parked up on her verge.

"Oh my God," she squeals in delight. "Oh my God — it's Graham. It's Graham." And she dives on a wagging Cadno to give him a spirited rub. "He's come to see us, boy — can you believe that? He's come all this way to see us."

She rushes to the mirror that hangs above her kettle, wanting to check her face and liven up her hair. Everything's going to be all right, she tells herself, giddy with excitement and rummaging through her handbag for the lipstick she knows is there. Maybe it was him parked out there all along, just too shy to come inside for whatever reason. What did any of that matter now? She knows she shouldn't have shut him off without a word the last few days, but she can explain, it will be all right. All she cares about is them being together, she grins at her reflection, happy with it.

Holding her breath for the expected knock, she rushes to it in eager anticipation. Opening the door, her welcoming smile is paralysed by what greets her. Instead of Graham she is confronted by two grim-faced men.

Rachel looks from one to the other, confused. "Yes — can I help you?"

Without answering, the taller of the two reaches into his jacket pocket and presenting his warrant card, asks —

"Sarah D'Villez?"

Shocked at hearing her real name, she is unable to find her voice.

"Are you Ms Sarah D'Villez?" The detective repeats his question and she nods her head. "We are here to arrest you for the murder of Linda Blundell. You do not have to say anything, but . . ."

Six Months Later

"This is where I used to come and hide when I was little."

Beth, with her son John on one side and husband Stan on the other, hovers in the lane looking down at the familiar stone walls of Tŷ Haf. How smart it looks with its new roof and large glass doors, she wonders who might live here next, how it would make a happy home for a family who knew nothing of its history. The post displaying a big bold, West Wales Properties FOR SALE sign, driven into the verdant verge, is set amidst towering foxgloves and a whispering mass of feathery willow herb.

An unwanted image of Sarah D'Villez's face finds her. A face that has been filling the papers since the story broke.

She blinks it away.

No need concern myself with you any more.

She relives the moment the news came of Sarah's confession: to Linda's murder, her consensual relationship with John, how she lied to the police from the very beginning; and allows a smile to curve her lips.

Watching her son move away, down into Tŷ Haf's gravel-lined drive, to peer in through the narrow,

arrow-slits of windows to the barn's interior, wanting a closer look, Beth bends forward at the waist. With bones creaking in the same way the rickety ladder to the hay loft in this very building had done as a child, she plucks a single stem of bright pink campion and pushes it into the button-hole of Stan's best jacket, then kisses him.

"Thank you for bringing me here," she murmurs, stroking his broad bronzed hand, and he can tell she is on the brink of tears. "Thank you for everything."

"D'you want to see if we can go in, have a look round? Could pretend we're in the market?" Stan smiles at her.

"No," Beth says, twisting away and pressing her back to the past. "I only wanted to see it from the outside."

She doesn't look in the direction of the narrowing lane either. Leading away to the stinking hovel that, until his recent arrest for what he did to Dai and now on remand awaiting trial, had been her brother Idris' domain. And she won't look over to the farm house, Cwm Glas, her childhood home, its horrors as fresh as they ever were and still a feature of her nightmares. She prefers instead to turn her face to the wide blue slopes and spread of fields, hoping for a glimpse of Dai. Dai as he was fifty or so summers ago, pedalling towards her on his bright red bicycle.

What must you have thought, me disappearing like that? I'm so sorry.

And a memory of the funfair, the whirl of sounds and smells on that blistering August day, finds her again. Dai, traipsing off to buy candyfloss, clutching what remained of their spending money in his hot little hand. Beth, reluctant to leave him, but wanting the toilets.

"You got a child inside you, girl."

That woman, that gypsy woman, with her urgent, thrusting finger. Her big, black shape and yellow teeth. Who, cutting a hole through the white, bright sunshine and casting her in shadow, stepped out of nowhere and grabbed her wrist. Making it hurt. Making her listen.

"You not safe, d'you 'ear me — you can't go home. It ain't safe for you to go home." Close enough to smell the sourness off her clothes, the sickly sweetness of gin coating her tongue. "Let people 'ere take care of you."

And that's just what Beth did. Believing the woman's fierceness and knowing what she said to be true, knowing her father would kill her if she went back to Cwm Glas with what she had growing inside her.

"Sure you don't want to go in?" Stan's voice, bringing her back to the present, wanting to confirm.

"No, really. It's fine," Beth tells him. "I've done with the past — it's only the future that's important now." Eyes swimming with emotion behind her spectacles, she tilts her head sideways and beams up at him. "Thank you for understanding . . . for forgiving me," she says carefully, putting an arm tight around him. "The way you've been so welcoming to John too . . . it's . . . it's . . ."

"Welcoming to John?" He beams. "Well, he's family, isn't he? He's like the son we never had."

"You're a darling man. Far more than I deserve." Beth, quite overcome by his sentiment. "I know I was wrong not to tell you sooner but I was so ashamed, you see . . . ashamed I gave him away . . . it's all so long ago, I don't think I can really explain. Just the longer it went on . . . everything such a mess . . . him in prison . . . it got too hard too . . ."

"Hush, pet." Stan cuddles her close, strokes her hair. "Hush now. Don't go upsetting yourself. Everything's okay now, everything's okay. The most important thing is John is where he should be — with us." And pressing his cheek to hers, they turn to see a smiling John sauntering back towards them.

Without speaking, the three walk in the direction they have come. Either side, the jam-packed hedgerows are loud with bees and other airborne insects, and they let the riotous sounds of summer fill the thoughtful gaps in their conversation. Each looks up in turn to see the swallows dip and dive. Fascinating, the way these winged fair-weather visitors skim the surface of the silver-skinned river, before spinning high into the extreme blue sky again. Pausing a moment, the trio watch their black scythe shapes darting against a spread of lush green meadows, dotted over with cotton-wool balls of plump and placid sheep.

"What a beautiful place this is." Her son, John, his skin browned by the sun that since his release he can't get enough of. "Must have been heaven growing up here."

"It is beautiful, yes." Beth looks into his profile, reads the pain between the premature lines that map his face. "But too far for you to see, the fluke and the foot-rot and the fat maggot." John looks at her, eyes quizzical.

"It's from a poem," she smiles, wanting to reassure. "Written by someone who knew the truth of life in these parts — I'll read it to you later; it'll explain things better than I can." And she slips an arm about his firm, slim waist, feels the warmth of him through his shirt. "I know I've told you before — but I'm so sorry I let them take you away from me all those years ago." Her face quivers, preparing itself to cry, so she turns her head away. "Thank you for finding me."

Her voice, small and reedy, is barely audible, but John hears, and taking her by the shoulders he rotates her towards him, his expression earnest.

"I found you when I needed you most and you didn't let me down. All you did for me when I was inside . . . you believed in me, you got them to clear my name. I can start again because of you." He cuddles Beth close, blinking back his own tears. "So it's for me to thank you, Mum."

The little family reach the bottom of the lane and are mindful of the lack of cars and lorries. All is intensely quiet, save for the intermittent birdsong and the rustle of the balmy August breeze pushing through the dense canopy of broadleaf trees and the buttons of their clothes. There is nothing here of London, or the constant clamour of life as it has been for John behind bars at HM Prison Full Sutton in Pocklington, East Yorkshire. In fact there are no manmade sounds at all. Bryngwyn seems almost otherworldly to their sensibilities and the experience unnerves them a little.

Beth inhales sharply at the sight of the long white house as they turn down towards the village. An image comes of Dai's mother. The warmth of her smile, the glassy sheen on her sleek dark hair. Her arms thrust wide in that way she would welcome her. Beth makes a small sound. It is enough to alert her son.

"You all right, Mum?" John asks, stepping up beside her.

"This is where Dai's parents lived; it was where he grew up. We used to catch the bus for school there . . ." She points at something, before breaking away to stride ahead, as if being pulled along by an invisible thread.

John and Stan know all about Dai, but say nothing as they follow on behind. Sensing Beth is more lost in private thought than she has been all day, they are happy to watch from a distance. Watch her reach the little timber five-bar gate and put a hand out to touch what is left of the flowering honeysuckle before walking the length of the pretty garden path. Watch the way the door of the house swings open and a tall, good-looking man with thick dark hair, ducks out into the sunshine to greet her.

There is a brief introduction neither can hear, as an attractive young woman, her head a mass of soft blonde curls and balancing a cherubic baby on her hip, steps out into the garden to join them, along with a sheepdog, bright-eyed with generous black and white coat, wagging-eager for attention.

"Come in . . . come in," the man with the hint of an Australian accent calls out to the men who hover, hesitant, at the gate. "Hi, I'm Anthony." He strides forward, arm extended. "You must be Stan." And they shake hands exuberantly. "This is my wife, Merrill, and this little one is my daughter, Seren. We've so much catching up to do. Honestly though, I have to say, since Beth's call last week and us telling Dad you were coming — he's been that excited, he's talked of little else."

John, unsure, needs further coaxing to step into the bird-filled garden. "Come in, please . . ." Anthony encourages. "Dad can't wait to meet you."

Joining him, John, still hesitant, pauses to rub the end of his nose between forefinger and thumb. A mannerism Anthony recognises as one of his own.

His own, and his father's.

Other titles published by Ulverscroft:

EUROPA BLUES

Arne Dahl

A Greek gangster arrives in Stockholm, only to be murdered in a macabre fashion at Skansen zoo, his body consumed by wolverines. As the Intercrime Unit — a team dedicated to solving international violent crime — investigates what brought him to Sweden, eight Eastern European women vanish from a refugee centre outside of the city; while an elderly science professor, the tattooed numbers on his arm hinting at his terrible past, is executed at the Jewish cemetery. Three cases, one team of detectives, and an investigation that will take them across Europe and back through history as they desperately search for answers, and the identities of the killers.

FREEDOM'S CHILD

Jax Miller

Most people know that Freedom Oliver works at the local bar and likes a drink or two. What they don't know is that Freedom is not her real name; that she has spent the last eighteen years living under Witness Protection, after being arrested for her husband's murder. They don't know that she put her two children up for adoption — a decision that haunts her every day. Then Freedom's daughter goes missing, and everything changes. Determined to find her, Freedom slips her handlers and heads to Kentucky, where her kids were raised. No longer protected by the government, she is tracked by her husband's sadistic family, who are thirsty for revenge. And as she gets closer to the truth, Freedom faces an even more dangerous threat. She just doesn't know it yet . . .